Heinz Meistermann

Whitecap
Travels and Adventures of Simon Brown

Volume 1

Heinz Meistermann

Whitecap

TRAVELS AND ADVENTURES OF SIMON BROWN

VOLUME 1

VERLAG 28 EICHEN

BARNSTORF

Editorial office: Dietlind Grüne, Mannheim

Translated from the German original by:
angusi expert translations (www.angusi.de)

Jason Green, Jannifer Hackney, Amalia Lebetzis, Kate McCane,
Aongus Murtagh, Catronia Shaw and Matthew Vollgraff

ISBN 978-3-940597-97-7
© by Verlag 28 Eichen, Barnstorf 2016.
Cover: „Ships at sea" (1867)
by Anton Melbye (detail) © by Olaf R. Spittel 2015.

CONTENT

BOOK 1

BOOK 2

BOOK 3

BOOK 1

1. A happy event on a foggy day

02.12.1804: Napoleon Bonaparte is crowned French Emperor in the Notre Dame Cathedral in Paris.
26.05.1805: Napoleon is crowned King of Italy in the Milan Cathedral.
02.12.1805: The battle of Austerlitz ends in glorious victory for Napoleon.
12.07.1806: In Germany, 16 states form the Rhine Confederation, leaving the federation of the Holy Roman Empire of the German Nation.
24.06.1812: With 675,000 soldiers, Napoleon's Grand Army, the largest in European history, crosses the River Memel.

A foggy day in May. Thick, heavy clouds are passing overhead. Everything is grey and drab. It's been raining for hours and the wind is blowing. It's the 27th May 1812. Balthasar Braun is standing across the road from his house on the waterfront and watching the slowly flowing Rhine. Every now and then, a low-lying barge floats by. Mighty draft horses tread out a path alongside the water, towing the barges behind them. But downstream, everything seems to glide along with the help of invisible hands.

Balthasar's mind is on his wife, Josephine-Christine, who is currently in labour upstairs. Dr. Anton Krone – a friend of the family – and the midwife are attending to Mrs. Braun and are at any moment expecting the birth of her third child. The Brauns already have two healthy children: a boy named Christoph and a girl named Josephine. The midwife is a small, slightly stocky woman who has already helped bring hundreds of children into the world. She has already told Balthasar not to worry, but he just couldn't stay in the house any longer and has gone outside to the banks of the Rhine instead. As he stands here now, the rain pelts down on him, but he doesn't take any notice.

The wine merchant, Balthasar Braun is quite a handsome man with a tall frame and a full head of dark hair. His father, who was a winemaker in a

7

large winery, passed on the love of wine to him. It was only natural, then that Balthasar would take up the same profession. Little by little, he has established his own wine business, in which he acquires German wines in bulk and then sells them abroad – chiefly to Britain. He met his wife, Josephine-Christine in England. The daughter of wine merchant Simon Hill from James Street, London is a picture-perfect, slim blonde, and Balthasar Braun fell in love with her at first sight. Josephine liked Balthasar's strong and attractive appearance. She was especially fascinated by his calm, reliable and determined manner. He also spoke decent English and was able to fit in just as confidently 'on the street' as in English high society. She finally fell head over heels for the young German. The pair married two years later and Josephine-Christine followed her husband to the Rhineland. Here in Mainz, the Brauns belong to the distinguished merchant class.

The pouring rain makes the river's surface look almost as if 'Father Rhine' has goose bumps. Balthasar prays and asks God for a healthy third child. If it's a boy, it will be named Simon-Balthasar. Simon for his grandfather in London and Balthasar after his father and grandfather from Mainz. If it's a girl, it will be named Marie, after grandmother Mary in England.

A woman's voice tears Balthasar away from his thoughts. "Mr. Braun, the baby has been born! It's a boy, Mr. Braun!" calls Rosi – the 'shining light' among the servants. Rosi is a diminutive, dark-haired woman of delicate appearance. She's in her mid fifties but has never been married. She has worked in the family household since Balthasar's father's time. She moved in at the age of seventeen, and the entire family has since grown very fond of her, thanks to her loving way of caring for everyone.

It's only now that Braun realises he's drenched through and through with rain. Nevertheless, his serious, worried expression softens into a smile. Quickly returning to his senses, he says, "Thank-you Rosi." Stepping through the granite doorway, Balthasar Braun climbs the broad marble staircase with quick, long strides, heading for his bedroom.

Auguste the midwife comes towards him, "Congratulations Mr. Braun! It's a boy."

"How is my wife?"

"Everything is fine. Your wife is well, and so is the little one. Fifty centimetres long and around eight pounds!"

A smile forms on the new father's face. "What a big boy!"

In the bedroom his wife lies exhausted on the couple's wide double bed with sweat on her brow. But, holding the newborn in her arms, she smiles at her husband. Dr. Krone stretches his right hand out while stroking his beard with the left, "Congratulations Braun. Unfortunately I must be off." He takes off his gown, slips into his dark green jacket and says goodbye.

Balthasar Braun kisses his wife on the forehead. "He makes a strong impression, Josephine," he says smiling.

"You're completely wet! What happened?" Josephine-Christine looks at him questioningly.

"I was outside. I couldn't stand the suspense any longer. It's pouring!"

"It's all over now. We made it through without any problems," answers Josephine-Christine.

I had now come into the world. At first I lay on my back; then I started to crawl and eventually I could walk. I can't remember the first few years of my life. No, the more I think about it, the more I'm certain of that. All that I think I know comes from stories others have told me.

2. The disrupted red wine cask

19.09.1814: Opening of the Vienna Congress; formation of the German Union.
18.06.1815: Napoleon Bonaparte is conclusively defeated at the battle of Waterloo.
20.11.1815: The 1815 Treaty of Paris between France, Prussia, Austria, Russia and Britain is signed.
05.05.1816: The Duchy of Saxe-Weimar-Eisenach obtains a constitution. This counts as the first constitutional monarchy on German soil.
04.03.1817: James Monroe replaces James Madison, becoming the fifth US president.

Christoph, Simon – stop it! Are you still beating each other up?" The young Brauns' tutor, Rudolf Vonecken stands in the doorway of their villa. Down in the yard, the boys are waving wooden swords at each other. "You can't get me!" calls Christoph, and he spins around so fast that he hits Simon on the seat of the pants with his 'sword'. "Ow! Just wait, you loser. Now it's my turn!" Before Simon has a chance to finish his sentence, Christoph shaves the side of his face with his sword. Blood streams out of the graze on his left cheek, but Simon grits his teeth and gallantly fights on. Rudolf Vonecken knows that, in their imaginations, the boys are lost in a world from the past. No matter what he says, they won't calm down. Stepping between them, he forces them apart by grabbing each boy from the back of the neck. With a calm, stern voice he announces,

9

"That's enough. You will both be seated at the living room table in five minutes. Simon, you go to Rosi in the kitchen, please and get your cheek attended to!"

Balthasar and Josephine-Christine place extraordinary value on raising and educating their children. All three – Christoph, Josephine and Simon-Balthasar, or Simon – have been receiving private tuition from early on. From the beginning, Josephine-Christine reached an agreement with Balthasar that English would be spoken in the Braun household. She did after all leave the Thames for a new life on the Rhine. The Belgian Rudolf Vonecken was chosen as a teacher because he spoke not only his native French, but also fluent Spanish and German. He travelled to most European countries at an early age, gaining a broad range of experiences, which he can now pass onto the children very descriptively. Thus the children take language, science and art lessons from Monday to Saturday, from morning until well into the afternoon.

Afterwards, Christoph and Simon usually disappear into the wine cellar, since there's always something to see and experience there. On the other hand, the blonde Josephine is frequently called into the parlour by her mother. She's afraid that it's no good for the girl to be overly influenced by the boys' rough behaviour. She'd rather let Josephine escape to the kitchen with Rosi. Josephine is all too eager to take a glance inside the great, big pots; and sometimes she's allowed to help with the cooking or baking. In such a large kitchen, that caters to more than twenty people, there's always something happening. At the Brauns', it's normal for all office employees and other workers to receive a warm meal during the day.

The Brauns' wine cellar buys white, rosé and red wines by the barrel from wine growers in the Mainz region. These are then either bottled or sold as they are to wine importers in England, Holland, Denmark and other countries. The most popular wines abroad are the tangy Rieslings.

The large, heavy, double-panelled, oak door opens just a crack, only to immediately close again mysteriously. In the large, rectangular room that lies behind the door, countless wine-filled oak barrels of all sizes rest in neat rows, stacked one on top of the other. It's cool and relatively dark here. The only available light comes from a few small window openings at ceiling-level. When one visits for the first time, the hall looks like a cathedral, almost scary. But Simon has had the habit of wandering around here for such a long time! In a single bound, he jumps as quietly as possible behind the first row of barrels piled up near the door. He remains crouched as his eyes slowly become accustomed to the darkness and then he begins to notice each individual row of barrels in the room.

10

Simon has searched for Christoph in every imaginable hiding place. This hall is the only place left to search. Staying low, the boy slowly slides through the rows. Each time he places a foot on the ground, the sound of grinding stones is heard, because the hall floor is covered in gravel. On the corner of each row of barrels, Simon stops to listen carefully for a few seconds. But everything remains absolutely silent. Slowly but surely, he places one foot in front of the other, heading ever deeper into the dark hall. Suddenly he hears a loud laugh that turns into a scream. Simon sees a shadow high up in the third tier of one of the barrel rows, and then the shadow is gone. Only the scream lasts a moment longer. Simon runs to the spot in the next row where he thinks his brother has fallen over. Then he sees Christoph stand up. In a daze, Christoph looks at Simon while shaking gravel out of his hair. A wooden creak is heard. Out of the corner of his right eye, Simon notices that a barrel on the topmost tier is moving. In a couple of seconds it will crash down and bury everything beneath it! Quick as a flash, Simon runs towards Christoph, literally flying over the last metres before leaping towards him and ramming his head into his brother's chest. Within seconds, his brother loses his balance, falling backwards almost two metres. There's a loud bang on the gravel floor, followed by a huge splash of red wine that gushes over the barely recovering boys.

With a short, loud squeak, the large, heavy hall door panels swing open. Conical sheaths of light flood into the room, and the two boys can be seen sitting in a bright spot next to what was until a few seconds ago, a full barrel of wine. In the blinding light, Christoph and Simon can make out the outlines of two figures hurrying toward them. One is tall and thin. "Simon, Christoph, what in heaven's name happened?!" Balthasar kneels down next to his sons with a worried expression on his face. Christoph holds his chest with his right hand.

"Are you hurt?"

"Yes, that was close! If Simon hadn't rammed into me with his head, the barrel would have fallen on my head."

"That was once a fine Portuguese red," notes the other person dryly. Winemaker Wilhelm – short, round and bald – turns over one of the barrel's staves in his raised right hand. "How did the barrel get from up there down here? They're all individually secured." Wilhelm attempts to climb up towards the row of barrels, but his big belly gets in the way. In a couple of well directed moves, Balthasar swings up to the top row and immediately realises that the safety wedges have slipped out of place. "Wilhelm, we really should consider fastening the ends of each tier more securely!"

"Yes, we should definitely look into it," agrees Wilhelm. "But first I'll fetch a wheelbarrow and clean up this mess," he adds, before heading off towards the exit.

"Right, you two are coming into the house with me now." Balthasar places his hands on his sons' shoulders.

"Father, are you angry at us?" asks Christoph. Then turning to his brother, he says, "Simon, that was truly at the last moment. Thanks. You rescued me!"

"We were all very lucky!" booms their father. "It's not your fault. It could have happened to anyone. You've detected a fundamental problem. Whenever you're in the cellar, keep your eyes open and your wits about you ..."

Balthasar puts his arms around his sons and leads them into the equipment hall. They pass by the wine presses, the fermentation barrels, the pumps and other equipment used in a wine cellar. Everything is spotless. As was the case for his father, Balthasar sees cleanliness and orderliness as an important maxim. "We work with grapes, in other words, with food. And cleanliness is the most important thing here," he keeps reiterating to Christoph and Simon.

Father and sons step through a wide, oak door into the large courtyard where horse-drawn carts can turn around without any trouble. All the buildings have been built around this courtyard. Behind the imposing looking forged iron gate, a well-manicured gravel path lined with gigantic old trees leads to the Brauns' villa.

Back then I was gripped to the bone with fear. And I must have thought about the situation for weeks afterwards. What did I learn from that experience? In some cases it's better to think long and hard about situations and problems in order to be able to assess them more closely. And at other times it's advantageous to undertake a task immediately. But when is each method appropriate?

3. Surprise, underestimate, appreciate

29.01.1819: Sir Thomas Stamford Raffles founds a harbour and settlement at the fishing vil-
lage of Singapore for the British East India Company.
22.02.1819: Spain sells Florida to the USA.
01.01.1820: Coup d'état in Spain. The country becomes a constitutional monarchy.
07.09.1822: Brazilian declaration of independence.
17.03.1824: The Treaty of London resolves disputes between Great Britain and the Netherlands in East India. Sumatra is allocated to the Dutch.

Darkness shrouds the night in silence. But not in the Braun family house, which is in uproar. It is almost 8 pm and Simon, the youngest child of the family, still isn't home.

"Balthasar, what if something has happened to him"

"Oh, I expect he has probably just forgotten the time again."

"But an eleven-year-old boy shouldn't be out on his own so late."

A short creaking of a door – Josephine gestures to her husband to keep quiet, pricks her ears, jumps up and moves swiftly to the door to open it as quietly as possible. On the marble stairs a gentle tip-tapping of a child's feet can be heard; and there he stands before them, completely petrified.

"Simon, where have you been?"

"I'm sorry, Mummy!" Eyes wide in surprise, Simon looks up at his mother.

"Are you insane? Do you have any idea how worried we have been? An eleven-year-old boy still out on the streets at this time of night!"

"But Mummy, I am nearly twelve!"

By now, Balthasar had also reached the door and said in a calm but firm voice, "Whether you are eleven or twelve years old is neither here nor there. Think about what you would do if your little boy didn't come home until so late. We will discuss this matter again tomorrow, by which time I will have thought of a suitable punishment for you!"

Grumbling to himself, Balthasar Braun retires to bed. He still has much to reflect on concerning his youngest child. Whilst Christoph is spending every spare minute he has in his father's wine cellar and enthusiastically tries his hand at every task, some time ago Simon began exploring the vine-yards and wine cellars of the surrounding area. He loves roaming through the vineyards with their different grape varieties, enjoying the view and talking to the people he encounters. He is also interested in everything sur-rounding the fruit of the vine and wants to learn even more – to hear what other people think – and what they do differently to his father. During his excursions in the area around Mainz, Simon has adopted the habit of looking in on various vintners and wine cellars. It has quickly became apparent to him that, because of his friendly character and courteous manner, he is always a welcome visitor. Since his father is a respected and well-known merchant, Simon's curiosity is always gladly catered for.

Balthasar rises very early the next day. Rosi has prepared his breakfast and serves it to him in the parlour. By 6:30 am Balthasar is sitting in his Landau carriage drawn by two Trakehner horses. His long-serving chauffeur, Joseph, drives him to town. He has a number of administrative matters to clear up at the town hall in Mainz.

At around midday, on the return journey, the Landau carriage practically 'floats' over the cobbled high roads with its leaf-spring suspension. Joseph, an experienced driver, has the energetic Trakehners firmly in his control so they make speedy progress. It has turned into a glorious, sunny day. Balthasar is now wearing a wide-brimmed hat as the sun is shining straight onto his brow. He leans forwards towards the coach box, "Joseph, please make a stop at the Gielings, it's practically on our way!"

"As you wish, Mr. Braun."

After a couple of miles, the Landau carriage takes a right-turn at an ancient wayside cross onto a paved road which climbs through the vineyards leading to a small vintner's house. Joseph halts the carriage, and the horses, snorting, come to a stop. He leaps down from the coach box, whilst holding the bridle with great care. He then, with what could almost be construed as tenderness, strokes the brows of "his" temperamental Trakehners.

Balthasar Braun crosses the courtyard in the direction of the front door. A farmhand is already coming towards them to approach Joseph, for the horses would need water.

"Good afternoon, Mr. Braun."

"Good afternoon, is Mr. Gieling at home?"

"Yes, he's in the kitchen, I believe you know the way."

"Thank you." Balthasar goes through the front door and enters a dark hallway with the kitchen immediately on the left. He knocks politely on the half-open door.

"Come in, Mr. Braun, I already saw you in the courtyard!"

"Good afternoon, August." With a slight creaking of the hinges the door opens and Balthasar enters the rather small, but cosy, kitchen. The vintner August Gieling is sitting next to his wife at the kitchen table, his right arm tightly bandaged from hand to upper arm. His wife looks up to their guest. "Please take a seat with us, Mr. Braun. May I offer you a cup of fresh coffee?"

"Yes, I would be glad to accept, the coffee smells delicious."

14

Balthasar sits next to Gieling. "August, I wanted to ask you if it would be possible to increase our contingent of Riesling wine – at the same price. Demand from England and Scandinavia is high. But what has happened to your right arm? It looks to have been recently splinted."

"Didn't Simon say anything to you at home?"

"I left home very early this morning, and last night he once again came home very late and had some trouble with Josephine and myself."

"Simon often drops by here when he is on his wanderings through the vineyards."

Balthasar raised his right eyebrow, "Oh really?"

"Simon asks many questions about the work here at the vineyard and also looks over my shoulder in the cellar. You have a son who is very interested in wine-making, Braun. How old is Simon?"

"As he emphasized yesterday: Almost twelve years old! What do you mean, he often drops by here?"

"I know from friends and neighbours that Simon wanders through the whole region; he's sure to become a world traveller when he's older."

August laughed and then carefully raised his broken arm. "This, by the way, happened yesterday. I wanted to tap some white wine and pump it into another barrel. I attached the pump and placed the other end of the hose in the empty barrel. Then I climbed up the ladder to the full barrel. It would appear that I hadn't really placed the ladder very firmly when it started to move and the next thing I remembered was waking up lying on the floor. I was quite dazed and had a dull pain in my arm. As I was unable to move the arm, I assumed that it was broken. Whilst considering how I might be able to stand up, your son poked his head round the corner. He grasped the situation immediately and helped me to pull myself up. Simon then fetched my wife, but my most pressing problem was the job I had started. I really couldn't leave it unfinished! Simon then offered to pump the wine for me. Indeed, we only have a small hand pump, but when my wife and I returned from the doctors a few hours later, the wine had been pumped into the other barrel and everything left spick and span. You have a wonderful son, Braun! Since evening was drawing in and Simon still had the long walk home, my wife persuaded him to stay for dinner. The journey home would be easier on a full stomach!"

Balthasar Braun had not said a word during the vintner's tale but had listened closely. He now sets the hot cup to his lips and takes a careful sip of the wonderful coffee. Mrs. Gieling looks on and adds, "Simon will make his way in the world. And it's not the first time that I have heard of him lending a hand when needed. Mrs. Dietzenberg from the Berghof Vineyard recently told me how young Braun helped her husband harvest the grapes when it started to rain heavily on a harvesting day. Simon covered the harvested grapes that were on the wagon with a sheet to help protect them from the rain and then drove the wagon with both horses into the vineyard. He's got a good hand with the horses, Dietzenberg said."

Balthasar is astonished: This is something he would never have presumed Simon was capable of. "It is easy to underestimate people, even one's own son!"

"Indeed, Braun, but back to business! You want to trade wine, more of my best Riesling than was originally agreed. Well good, I have another three cartload barrels available. However, I am sure you can imagine that I also have some other responsibilities."

"August, I'm sure we can make a deal! Tell me – each cartload barrel contains thirty ohms, correct?"

"Yes, thirty Frankfurter ohms!"

Balthasar quickly calculates in his head: Thirty times 1.43 hectolitres equals 42.90 equals 4,290 litres. "August, I'll give you an extra five on top of each hundred!"

"It's a deal, Braun, and you'll be sending someone to collect the three cartload barrels."

"Very well, consider it done."

Balthasar Braun offers his sincere thanks to August Gieling and his wife and then bids them farewell to take his place again in the Landau carriage. He puts on his hat and leans his head back so that the beaming sun shines directly onto his face. His thoughts are on Simon. "Joseph, is Simon often with you in the stable?"

"Yes, Mr. Braun."

"Does he go riding?"

"Yes, Mr. Braun. He does ride the odd horse now and again."

"Are you telling me that he rides around the area for hours alone on a horse?"

"Errr … yes, Mr. Braun."

About an hour later, the Landau carriage with Balthasar and Joseph drives through the avenue and approaches the Brauns' Villa. Rosi sees the carriage stop at the entrance and runs out to open the door for Balthasar.

"Thank you, Rosi."

"Good afternoon, Mr. Braun, I hope you had a pleasant journey."

"Wonderful weather, a great carriage and a good journey." He climbs out of the carriage and turns on the wide steps towards the front door. "Is my wife at home?"

"Yes Mr. Braun, in the sitting-room."

16

Balthasar steps through the dark, heavy, front door into the reception hall and climbs the broad marble stairs past the oil painting depicting scenes from the vineyards of the 'Red Slope' on the Rhine front. Josephine smiles at him and strokes his short-cut beard with her tender, well-manicured fingers. "How was it at the town hall?"

"Everything was conducted to our satisfaction. I let Joseph take me to visit the Gielings. I managed to acquire the amount of Riesling we need. You can rely on August Gieling."

"Darling, what shall we do about Simon? I'm really very worried. Rudolph Vonecken told me that the boy was, as always, very good in class today. Christoph is in the wine cellar with two of the neighbours' boys, Josephine with Leni Rückert. But it would seem that Simon is out and about again, even Rosi doesn't know where he is!"

"Josephine, to me, Simon appears to be like a puzzle, and we have to fit the pieces together. It is true that he is 'almost twelve', but if everything is true that I have heard today, then …"

Balthasar relates to Josephine everything that he had heard from August Gieling, Gieling's wife and the chauffeur. His wife sits with eyes wide and her mouth open. "And now? What are we to do?"

"Darling, on my way home, I had an idea. I do not think it is going to be possible to keep the boy at home for much longer. We should listen to his version of events and perhaps we can find a solution together …"

After dinner, Simon, Josephine and Balthasar sit quietly together in the sitting room. Simon is prepared for a serious telling-off. How could he explain the reason for his late homecoming? Of course, the matter with August Gieling is a good excuse, but it wasn't the only reason. What if the explanation sets off a chain reaction and brings much more to light than he really wishes to have to explain? No, better to keep his mouth shut and take his punishment!

Balthasar addresses his son, "Simon, your mother and I have talked this afternoon about you and what happened last night."

"Yes, Daddy, I'm sure you have thought of a suitable punishment for me. I will accept it!"

Simon's answer reveals to Balthasar that the boy is taking a gamble. He would only admit to what they could prove. Well, sonny, let's see, almost twelve and already a sly old dog!

"Simon, your mother and I don't have anything in principle against you helping Dietzenberg to cover his grapes when it rains, or driving his carriage to the vineyard. Also, we're not angry that you have at various times taken horses from the stable to ride around on. And Mummy and I are proud of you for helping August Gieling when he broke his arm and that you tapped his wine for him."

"How do you know all this?" Simon looks as if he has been seriously affronted. They know everything, he thinks to himself.

"However, Simon, your mother and I would be very pleased if in future you would tell us yourself what it is you intend to do, and not to tell us later what it is you have already done!"

"Mummy, Daddy …" The concept of gritting his teeth and waiting for his punishment being no longer an option, Simon explains to his parents everything that has happened. Josephine and Balthasar listen intently. "And what about if you are not at home?"

"Simon, when neither your father nor I are at home then you are to inform Mr. Vonecken, Rosi, Joseph or Wilhelm in the wine cellar what you are planning! If you can manage to do this for the next couple of months Daddy will be taking you with him to visit your grandparents in London, as he did last year with Josephine and Christoph."

"Oh yes! That would be great!" Simon leapt up and embraced his parents.

"So, now follow the others up to bed! I'll be looking in on you shortly," Josephine orders, smiling to him as he leaves the room.

I was very impressed by my parents' attitude: No shouting, no beating and no confinement. What they told me I understood, and what I have remembered is this: Always tell the truth, for you can never know for sure what the other person knows! London, England, was an exciting prospect for me. London – the "capital of the world", the capital of the great British Empire!

4. An unintentional experience on the post road

It is the 29th May 1824 and still early in the morning. Balthasar and Simon are sitting in the Landau carriage on the way to the stagecoach stop in Mainz along with all their luggage and a few sample bottles of wine. They want to board the stagecoach to Koblenz there.

On May 22nd, his birthday, Josephine had announced to her Simon at the breakfast table, that his father would take him along on his trip to England in two days' time. The boy was beside himself with joy the whole day – the afternoon coffee with relatives didn't particularly interest him – he could only think about England. The following day also went by awfully slowly. Only while packing his suitcases was Simon distracted for a short time.

Saying goodbye to his mother this morning was not easy for Simon though. He could not hold back the tears although London excites him so much. Josephine, too, had tears in her eyes – it is the first time that she has to get by without her youngest child for three or four weeks. As Joseph finally drove the Landau carriage out of the yard, the mother, Christoph, Josephine, Mr. Vonecken and Rosi stood before the front gate and waved at the two wayfarers.

With his mind on the farewell, the time in the coach flies by and they have already arrived at the coach station in Mainz. Joseph and Simon unload the luggage from the Landau carriage while Balthasar is in the coach station paying the fares for two places on the next coach to Koblenz. Eyes wide, Simon stands next to the luggage and watches the goings on at the stage-coach station. Many people are shuffling around in an apparently aimless manner; coaches arrive, are unloaded and then loaded before setting off again to an unknown destination. Simon takes in the images and situations while quiet and loud and sometimes strange sounds ring in his ears. Over-whelmed, he does not notice that his father is now standing next to him again and is speaking to him. Joseph places his left hand on Simon's shoulder and leans down towards him. "Goodbye Simon!"

"Oh, Joseph, sorry! I was lost in thought."

Balthasar smiles at Simon. "Indeed. I've just been telling you that we have to board the yellow coach over there, and that we will drive for about ten hours to Koblenz." Then turning to his coachman, he says, "Thank-you Joseph. Have a safe trip home."

"Yes Mr. Braun. I hope you have a pleasant trip, and good luck." Joseph climbs to the Landau carriage's driver's seat, releases the brake, and with a precise flick of the reins, the two Trakehner horses spring into action. Simon watches them leave and is only torn from his thoughts by the movement of the luggage cart. A man wearing a smock and a blue peaked cap has collected the luggage and taken it to the yellow stagecoach. Following his father, Simon looks on as a rider arrives at the stagecoach station at full gallop, jumps from his horse, and unfastens his saddlebags.

"Dad, look. The rider in front of the coach station, why is he in such a hurry?"

"That's a post rider, a so-called courier. He takes letters and documents from one station to the next and passes them onto another man with a new horse. That's how the mail gets quickly from the sender to the receiver."

Travellers stand in front of the shiny, yellow coach and wait for all the pieces of luggage to be strapped onto the roof racks. The Brauns' suitcases are also properly loaded and strapped down. Simon counts six other passengers aside from the coachmen. Two young men sit right at the back of the coach. Under the extended black folding roof, they are protected from strong sunlight and rain. Two couples board the front of the coach. Simon then follows and sits with his back to the front across from a slightly plump-looking fine lady. Finally, his father boards the coach and sits next to Simon while pulling the wagon door shut behind him.

"We are leaving now, ladies and gentlemen!" announces one of the coachmen through a small window above Simon's head. With a short jolt, the four-horse yellow stagecoach sets off. The wheels roll evenly over the cobbled road. In the coach, their rattling is heard only quietly.

Simon sinks back into the dark, worn leather-upholstered bench. The man sitting to his left converses animatedly with the lady sitting opposite. He has hung his suit jacket on a hook behind him, in the corner of the coach. The conversation is about fashion. The elegantly dressed lady looks at Simon for a moment, smiles at him, and then continues speaking about the empire style. Simon doesn't understand a word. The word 'empire' makes him think of the British Empire, which is his travel destination.

"Excuse me Mr. Braun, could you please hang my jacket on the hook with yours?" asks the other gentleman, holding out his suit jacket in front of Balthasar. The man makes a stern impression on Simon, and is of a slender build. Simon now looks out the window to the right and sees buildings, people and vehicles pass by. After a while there is more and more green to be seen: trees, bushes, grass and flowers. They leave Mainz behind them.

Simon closes his eyes, the even rolling of the wagon wheels helps him drift into daydreams. He thinks about London, the biggest city in the world, the capital of the empire.

"Are you travelling with your dad?" the woman sitting opposite interrupts his daydreams. Simon looks at her. "Yes, I am."

"What's your name, then?" asks the lady, smiling.

"Simon, Simon Braun from Mainz."

"My name is Amelie Konrath and this is my husband Theodor."

Nice smile, thinks Simon, and she's actually not at all chubby, she just appears to be. He has been comparing her with the lady sitting to her right, who is very thin. Aside from this, the woman opposite him is wearing one of the latest dresses, which, thanks to its little puffed sleeves on the upper arms, makes the neckline appear very broad.

"Do you have a long trip ahead of you, or are you only going to Koblenz, like us?" asks Mrs. Konrath.

"We're going to London to visit Grandpa and Grandma."

"Your grandparents live in England?"

"My grandparents are English. My mother, too. I mean, she was. Now she's German."

The coach brakes and Simon sees through the window that they've stopped in front of a building with the words POST STATION written on it in big letters. The little window above him opens. "Ladies and gentlemen, we will take a short break of twenty minutes here to change horses. You may drink coffee or make other purchases in the coach station."

Balthasar places a hand on Simon's shoulder. "Come on Simon, get out! We should stretch our legs."

Everyone leaves the coach. The coachmen have jumped down from their box and two men from the station bring four new horses over. Balthasar and Simon stand in front of the station with the two young men who have been sitting on the back of the coach and watch how nimbly and swiftly the changeover takes place.

A few minutes later they are all sitting in their places again and the coach starts moving once more. Balthasar turns to Simon. "Koblenz is a very old city. The area here has been settled since the Stone Age because the land is very fertile."

"Yes dad, and near Koblenz, the Moselle flows into the Rhine."

"Exactly. And at the moment there is a gigantic building site in Koblenz. Right now, the city's fortress Ehrenbreitstein is being renovated and extended by King Friedrich Wilhelm III. The building works began nine years ago, but when will they be finished?"

The gentleman sitting opposite Balthasar, Theodor Konrath, raises his right index finger. "Sorry for interfering, but I can offer more information on the subject. I am a civil servant and am in charge of finances in Koblenz. The order to refortify the city and the fortress Ehrenbreitstein was enacted on the 11th March 1815, and it should be completed by 1832. Of course it could take one or two years longer. It is not possible to accurately predict the duration of such a large building operation."

These dates do not really interest Simon. He looks out the left-hand window, and sees only trees. They are driving through a forest. Balthasar and the civil servant are now discussing taxes and duties. How boring, thinks Simon to himself.

"How old are you?" asks Amalie Konrath suddenly from opposite. Simon eyes her carefully. Something looks different about her, he thinks. Her amber coloured hair is still pinned up and her dress is the same … the sleeves! The sleeves have been pushed up and the broad neckline is now narrow and plunging. He's never seen such a thing!

"Twelve, I'm … twelve years old." Simon has to concentrate. He looks deliberately at Amalie Konrath's face. Just don't do anything wrong, he thinks. "The day before yesterday … I had my birthday the day before yesterday."

"The day before yesterday?!" Amalie Konrath places her right hand on his left knee, on his bare knee, since he's wearing short pants. "Happy birthday Simon," she says, as she rises from the bench, and bends down to kiss him on the left cheek. While she does this, Simon has a perfect view right into her cleavage, of two large, round breasts. After Amalie Konrath has taken her seat again, Simon realises that he is beginning to blush. For a couple of seconds, he had been able to see what his big brother Christoph already told him about a few weeks earlier. He had secretly watched Rosi getting changed, and had seen her bare breasts.

Amalie Konrath seems to be able to read Simon's thoughts exactly and smiles flirtatiously straight into his face. Simon doesn't know what to do. The situation is too embarrassing for him, so he looks back out the window.

Luckily, the civil servant now turns to him. "Simon," he says, "as we are about to ride into Koblenz, we will cross the Moselle. Then we will drive over the Balduin Bridge, which was built in the 14th century by Balduin of Luxembourg. It took 85 years to complete."

Some time later, the coach stops in front of the Koblenz coach station. All passengers alight and after the coachmen have unloaded the luggage from the roof, they say goodbye. Simon waits by the luggage as his father asks about the next coach from Koblenz to Cologne in the coach station. On returning, he says to Simon with a smile, "The coach to Cologne leaves from here tomorrow morning at half past seven. I've already bought tickets for us."

"Where will we sleep tonight?"

"At the inn called 'Zum vollen Fass' ('The Full Barrel') across the road over there."

The inn consists of a white, double-storey half-timbered house with a slate roof. The window frames are small and the windows are leaded. Already from outside, the buzzing of many voices can be heard coming from the parlour, and as they step into the public bar, Simon gets the feeling he is standing in a market place. A jumble of voices and laughter, as well as smoke, fumes and the odours of wine, beer, fried potatoes and pork chops suddenly affront him. Under a roof with dark wooden beams, small yellowish glowing lamps hang over the tables, shrouding the room in a warm, inviting light. Men and women sit and laugh or are engaged intensely in conversation at the tables. Following his father, Simon weaves between the rows of tables while heading toward the bar. A big, bearded man stands behind it and is in the middle of twisting a corkscrew into a bottle.

"Good evening," says Balthasar in a friendly voice. A stocky waitress squeezes past the two of them with a tray full of empty glasses on her way to the bar.

"My name is Braun, I …"

"Two natural Moselle Kabinett Rieslings, two Elblings and three beers," yells the waitress over the bar, grinning.

"Sure. I'll have the Moselle opened in a flash!"

"Oh I forgot, I also need two pork chops with potatoes!"

"Excuse me," says Balthasar in the hope of interrupting, "I'd like a double room for the night."

With obvious tension in his face, the bartender looks at Balthasar while strenuously pulling the corkscrew along with the cork out of the bottle. "Yes, I have one. Room Eleven." He turns around and yells through a hatch into the kitchen, "Two pork chops with potatoes and, Margarethe, please come out and show Mr. Braun and his son to Room Eleven!" A few seconds later, a sliding door behind the bar is opened and a dark-haired young lady comes out. "Good evening, Mr. Braun. Would you please step this way?" She shows the Brauns a side door that leads to a separate hallway.

"Our luggage is still waiting in front of the inn."

"No problem, the entrance to the inn is just here in front of us and your room is up the stairs there."

Room Eleven is a double room with separate beds. It is very small, but clean and quiet. Even the noise from the pub does not reach all the way up here.

After having eaten and drunk well in the parlour, Simon is so tired that he barely remembers how he made it to bed. "That was a long day," says Balthasar. But Simon does not answer him.

I can still remember that on this day, I fell asleep in no time, and immediately sunk into dreamland. I slept so soundly that my father had to vigorously shake me out of my slumber the next morning. You would like to know what I dreamt of? I don't know any more, but it was most likely something along the lines of 'hills and valleys' – if you catch my drift.

5. A helping hand on the North Sea

The next morning, Simon and Balthasar are sitting in the coach once more, this time on the way to Cologne. In the following days, they make their way from there through Aachen, Maastricht, Brussels, Gent and Bruges to the port town of Oostende in the province of West Flanders.

Simon stands by the quay in the port of Oostende, only a few metres away from the water, his gaze fixed on the hustle and bustle of this place. Large and small ships are docked here, with masts that soar high into the sky. People run around chaotically; they load and unload the ships. Among the chorus of sounds in the air the squawking of seagulls can be heard. Simon breathes in deeply. Astounded, he remarks, "The air is so fresh here. It smells like salt and iodine – just magnificent!" A hand rests on his shoulder, his father is standing next to him. "So, Simon, this is your first time by the sea!"

"Daddy … can you smell the air?"

"Exciting, isn't it? Listen, first I have to find a ship for the trip to London and some accommodation. Perhaps there is still something available at the 'van den Booms' in Kapucijnenstraat – I have already stayed there several times. Then we can visit a customer here in Oostende tomorrow, and the morning after that, we can head off to London."

Balthasar raises his left arm and points westwards. "If you follow the quay in that direction, you'll come to the beach by the open sea. If you want, we can meet there in half an hour or 45 minutes."

"That would be great!"

Barely has Simon answered, when he already sets off. Balthasar watches him. No running, no rush – an overwhelmed Simon turns to look every which way as he absorbs all that he sees.

The closer he gets to the sea, the stronger the wind is that blusters in Simon's face. Soon he is standing atop the dyke. Before him lies a long, sandy beach and the never-ending sea. He runs down the embankment to the water's edge and sits on the fine, white sand. The waves crash and foam up as they peter out on the beach. Seagulls are circling above Simon's head, and he can see people as small as ants working on the incoming and outgoing ships, high up in the sails. Again and again, Simon pushes his hand into the fine sand before letting it trickle through his open fingers.

"Hello Simon." Suddenly his father is standing next to him.

"Dad, look at the ships, they're swaying in the sea!"

"True, the swell should build up even more. On the pier, I heard that the sea is expected to get quite rough around here, so that maybe no more ships will cross the channel as of the day after tomorrow. We will therefore have to leave tomorrow morning."

"Hey, no pushing back there!" shouts a sailor on the gangway. "We'll take you all to London." Many people still want to cross the channel on the last ship. One after the other, the passengers board the ship via its narrow gang plank. On each side, a thick rope serves as a handrail. Balthasar lets Simon go first to keep an eye on him. The two-masted sailing ship is noticeably rising and falling; the rough sea has visibly swollen even more.

"Madam, go around and to the right! The passenger cabins are at the back of the ship," yells a sailor with tousled hair.

"Which cabin number do we have?" Simon looks at his father questioningly.

"Number six."

A sailor holds the door to the lower deck cabins open, so that the passengers can easily go downstairs with their hand luggage. He smiles straight at Simon as he shouts a hearty "Good morning."

The cabin numbered 'six' is quickly found. It contains two separate beds, a small cupboard, a small desk and a little, round porthole. The interior is painted white and the beds look like two boxes.

"Why did they put a board in front of the bed?" asks Simon wonderingly.

"So that we don't fall out of bed when the sea is rough. In case you feel unwell, you should go out and get some fresh air."

"I'm fine at the moment, I don't need anything."

"That could change very quickly once we're at sea. If you need to throw up, then it's best to do it over the railing – but not against the wind direction, do you understand? And if you happen to see others on board who feel sick, bite your lip and don't laugh at them."

"All right, all right."

"Please be careful when you're running around on board the ship! The deck could be slippery. To be on the safe side, always keep one hand on something that's fixed down."

"Have you ever sailed in such conditions?"

"Yes, about four or five years ago," remembers Balthasar.

"Back then, the storm emerged very suddenly. We had just covered little more than half the distance of the English Channel when the ship was battered and shaken so much by the waves, that many passengers were afraid for their lives."

"Actually, what kind of ship is this?"

"A mail ship. I cannot tell you any more."

"May I go on deck now?"

"Go on!"

A short while later, Simon is sitting on a heavy, securely moored wooden box in the middle of the ship and watching the sailors work. Some of them stand on the deck, grappling with mighty ropes while others nimbly climb the rigging up high into the sails.

"So, my boy, who are you then?" Simon suddenly hears a coarse, deep voice ask. He turns around. Standing next to him is a bearded man in a dark blue uniform with a cap over his white hair and a thick pipe between his lips.

"My name is Simon Braun. I'm travelling with my father."

"I see. My name is George Thomson and I'm the captain here."

"The captain! Then you could definitely tell me what kind of ship we are on. My father didn't know."

"Is this your first time at sea?"

"Yes. We come from Mainz on the Rhine and have a wine cellar at home."

"I don't know all that much about wine, but in case you would like to drink an excellent beer later on, remember Smithwick's Ale. It comes from a brewery in Kilkenny, Ireland. By the way, you speak very good English!"

"That's not surprising: my mother comes from England."

"Oh, then you're most likely visiting relatives. But now to your question: the ship was christened 'The Repatriate' – which means something along the lines of 'the one that returns'. It is called that because it always runs the same route back and forth between London and Oostende. As for its type, it's a brig, and she has two masts with square-rigged sails and a gaff-rigged sail on the aft-most mast. You see up there – the square-rigged sails are suspended crossways to the ship. The gaff-rigged sail goes in the same direction as the ship's bow and is hoisted up in between the gaff at the top and the boom at its foot."

The ship is now slowly moving out of the relatively calm waters in the bay towards the open sea. It starts to sway more and more. Relaxed, Captain Thomson draws on his pipe while the first mate faces his back to the wind and shouts short commands over the deck.

Simon points up at the main mast. "Am I allowed to climb up there, too?"

Captain Thomson reflects for a moment before answering, "First you can watch the goings on from down here, and we'll see about that later." He touches his cap in salute. At the same moment, Balthasar Braun comes over from the quarterdeck.

"Daddy, we're sailing on a brig."

"Brig – I've heard that name before. Incidentally, Simon, we are now in the English Channel. How are you?"

"Good, everything is fine!"

"I'm only asking because a few of the passengers on quarterdeck are already looking a little off-colour."

Simon looks up at the masts. The sails swell in the wind; the ship leans slightly toward the right as it plunges through the rough sea.

"Dad I'll be right back – I just want to go to the front."

"Be careful! Always hold on!"

A moment later, Simon is standing at the 'Repatriate's' bow, enjoying the view of the waves. In front of him, the never-ending sea. With every surge the ship seems to rise up to the sky, only to keep dropping back down again. To Simon, it appears as if the ship is about to plunge straight into the North Sea, and in the last moment raise its nose back up to ride the next wave. He becomes carried away by the spectacle that promises him freedom, excitement and adventure.

Back on the quarterdeck once more, Simon joins his father and a few other courageous passengers. Two gentlemen and a lady lean over the railing with their heads down. Their faces are as pale as ghosts.

Balthasar turns to Captain Thomson. "How long will we need to get to London in this weather?"

"With an average westerly wind it should take twelve hours from Oostende to Southend-on-Sea at the mouth of the Thames and then another six hours until we arrive in the London Docks. With this south-westerly I would estimate nine hours to Southend-on-Sea, and then roughly one hour longer on the Thames, making it seven hours."

The captain interrupts himself. Among the constant noise of wind and sea, a piercing scream is heard. "Help, help, heeeeeelp …" A sailor hangs high above in the rigging of the main mast. Only a few moments ago, the first mate had arranged the sails' reefing. The sailor, who is hanging helplessly in the rigging, must have slipped from the part of the mast that runs beneath the yard. He can only hold on with one hand – but for how much longer? The man's body is swinging in the wind, over thirty metres high.

All eyes on deck are pointed upwards. The passengers hold their breaths. "That's Frank!" yells Captain Thomson, and heads toward the first mate.

Balthasar Braun looks to Simon – but he is gone! Having judged the situation in the blink of an eye, the boy seizes the opportunity to climb up into the sails. In just a few seconds he is back next to the moored wooden box he had been sitting on earlier. He knows that a coiled rope lies there and throws it over his head and shoulders. Without hesitation he climbs the rope ladder up to the main mast. "Stay calm, concentrate and always hold on with one hand!" he says to himself.

Just before reaching the first platform, Simon's right foot slips off the rope ladder. He holds on with all his might and regains his balance a moment later. All the time he has spent balancing on the rafters up above the high piles of barrels in the wine cellar with his brother, Christoph now pays off. Fear of heights and dizziness are both unknown to him. Purposefully, he also climbs the shorter rope ladder above the platform up to the highest yardarm. Carefully, so as to avoid swinging too much, he steps onto the uppermost rope, which the screaming sailor is holding onto with his right hand. Simon leans down over the yard, lifting the coiled rope from his neck, and makes a loop in one end. Then he slowly leans toward the sailor below and tightens the loop around his wrist. As short as possible, he ties the other end securely to the yard. That way, the danger that the sailor might slip from the rope into the sea or fall onto the deck is avoided.

Another sailor now joins them. "Hey, well done lad! Now stand on the other side of Frank so that I can approach him too. Then we will pull him up together."

All eyes of the large group gathered below on the quarterdeck stare at the tip of the main mast and watch as the sailor, Frank is freed from his seemingly hopeless situation.

"Son of a gun!", cries Captain Thomson skywards. "Braun, what a son you have – not a trace of fear and he climbs the rigging like an old hat!"

Up on the mast, these words of praise cannot be heard. Simon and the two sailors climb back down the rigging. Once on the main mast's platform, Simon looks down for the first time and sees that the deck is teeming with people. Big clusters of passengers stand on the quarterdeck, staring up at them. Simon looks at the water all around and deeply breathes in the fresh, salty sea air.

As they happily reach the deck, the sailors attend to Frank, who is exhausted and shocked to the core. He grips Simon's hand and a shaky "Thank-you" escapes his lips. Simon smiles at him. In the same moment a sailor approaches them. "To the captain, Joseph! You're to report to the captain immediately!"

"Aye, aye," answers Joseph and grabs Simon by the sleeve, dragging him toward the quarterdeck. As they climb the steps up there, the crew and passengers applaud. Joseph reports to the captain and pulls Simon to his side.

"Ladies and gentlemen, I am very relieved that Able Seaman Frank is once again fit and standing on deck. That could have been fatal. As captain of this ship, I would like to sincerely thank the two rescuers. I am most amazed by the conduct of our young passenger, Simon Braun. I can see in all your eyes that you share my sense of amazement. Even before only one of us was able to think of what to do, Simon had already assessed the possibilities for Frank's rescue, and as nimbly as a fox, he was up in the 'Repatriate's' rigging, showing us his lion's courage."

The captain shakes the hands of both rescuers before turning to Balthasar Braun. "Mr. Braun, I admire your son. He promises to make his own way in the world."

"He already is!" smiles the father. And lo and behold, as he turns to face Simon, the boy is no longer where he was standing only a few seconds ago. He is already back at the bow of the ship, enjoying the head wind.

What an experience that was for me! Today I wonder a little about the courage I managed to muster up. The fact is, when a young person pushes himself to his limits, or a little beyond them, it is easier later in life to recognise precisely where those limits lie. After all, back then, my father always said, "I cannot means I don't want to." But where there is a will, one learns that more often than not there is also a way.

6. In the deep cellar under London

Simon, Simon Braun!" There's a knock at the cabin door numbered 'six'. Balthasar Braun opens the door and sees a sailor standing before him, cap in hand. "Mr. Braun, the captain would like to see Simon on deck. He's allowed to climb up into the sails."

"Thank you! Dad, I'll be on the deck!" Already, Simon is squeezing past his father and the sailor. Next, he runs up the stairs and presents himself to Captain Thomson. "Here I am, Captain."

"Simon, you are now under the command of the first mate." A few minutes later, the boy is climbing with the other sailors, lifting himself high into the sails …

At about 3:20 pm, the 'Repatriate' sails into the mouth of the Thames at Southend-on-Sea. She passes Canvey Island, Gravesend, Grays and Greenwich. The closer they get to London, the more ships they encounter on the Thames. There are also more and more buildings lining the riverbanks. Simon stands next to his father on quarterdeck and observes everything carefully. Captain Thomson displays outstanding control of the 'Repatriate'. He ably sails close to the wind, navigating around all the ships, barges and boats lying in his path.

At 10:30 pm, the brig lands at the London Surrey Docks quay. Dozens of people, coaches and carriages are waiting at the quay for the arriving passengers.

"Simon, look over there – it's your grandpa! In front of the red coach – do you see him?"

Simon has only seen his grandfather twice before – two times that he can remember. But straight away he remembers the white-haired, patient man with the friendly face and broad nose. The grandfather has also found Balthasar and Simon in the crowd and is waving at them.

One after the other, the passengers leave the ship via its gangway. Captain Thomson is drawing on his pipe with pleasure as he stands at the railing and watches the goings on. When he sees Simon and Balthasar, he steps toward them and offers Balthasar his hand. "I hope you enjoy your stay in London, Mr. Braun."

"Thank you, Captain Thomson. That was certainly an exciting trip over."

"Not least because of your son. Simon, thank you once again for your service! You should stay exactly as you are! Should you decide to travel back to Oostende on my ship, my crew and I would warmly welcome you back on board, and would gladly see you back in the sails, Simon!"

"Thank you Captain. I hope we travel with your ship again!" says Simon. He then turns to the gangway, runs straight up to his Grandfather Simon and throws himself into his arms.

"Hello grandpa, how are you?"

"Gosh, haven't you grown, Simon? How was the journey?"

"A bit windy, but otherwise fine. Now I'm in London for the first time!" Simon's eyes are beaming.

A moment later, Balthasar is also standing next to his father-in-law, Simon Hill. "Hello Simon, how are you?"

"Well. Balthasar, let me give you a proper hug for a change. It's been a long time! It's so wonderful that you're both here."

"Yes, luckily – after such a trip!"

"Did something extraordinary happen? Simon says that everything was fine."

"That depends on how you look at it. But let's just go home first. We are really tired. It was an exhausting day."

Once the luggage and samples are loaded and everyone has taken his place, the red coach sets off on its way. It drives over Waterloo Bridge, through Lancaster Place, and then down The Strand and Southampton Street before going around Covent Garden and into James Street.

The massive, multi-storeyed red-brick building that Simon's grandparents live in stands on the corner of James and Floral Streets. Simon especially likes the small tower from which he can look down into James Street and over at Covent Garden.

The next morning, Simon is woken by his father Balthasar, with whom he is sharing a room. A short while later they are sitting and eating a huge breakfast with Grandpa Simon, Grandma Mary, Uncle Charles, Aunt Betty and cousins Elisabeth and Janet at the big table in the room at the bottom of the tower.

His grandpa looks over at him and says, "Simon, you really showed a lot of courage when you rescued the sailor – you must have truly had your head screwed on right!"

Aunt Betty reckons, "Well, I never would have known exactly what to do in such a situation. What were you thinking, Simon?"

Balthasar can already guess what will come next: Simon will simply switch to a different topic. That's what he did when he courageously leapt to save his brother, Christoph from being crushed under a falling wine barrel; and he did the same thing after having helped August Gieling to transfer his wine from one barrel to another.

"Aunt Betty, the tea is wonderful. What kind of tea is it?"

"That's 'King George Tea' from Fortnum & Mason in Piccadilly. Your grandfather can tell you more about it. But tell us more about the sailor!"

Humming and hawing, Simon looks to his grandfather, who jumps to the boy's assistance, saying, "King George is one of the finest of black teas, and consists mostly of the best Darjeeling blends with small amounts of sweet Assam and flavoursome Yunnan from China."

"You always send my mum English Breakfast or the English tea blend 'Victoria's finest'. Are they also from Fortnum & Mason?"

"Yes, Simon. All the teas we drink here are from Fortnum & Mason. I know the family that owns the shop and some of their management staff. If you are interested in tea, we can pay them a visit and you can get to know all the teas first-hand."

"I would find that fascinating. Tea seems to have as many different kinds of flavours as wine."

"Good. And when your father is busy visiting his customers, I will show you our wine cellar and our wines."

Simon jumps up and steps towards the tower window to take a look down at Covent Garden. "Grandpa, those market stalls down there, are they always there?"

"Yes. Covent Garden is a market place. Its name comes from the words 'convent garden', which was an expression that used to describe the fruit and vegetable garden belonging to the abbey or convent of Saint Peter's in Westminster. Today, Covent Garden is probably the most important market in England. Exotic spices, teas and many other things from faraway lands are on sale there. There is even talk of covering the market, with plans for permanent market halls so that it's less dependent on the weather."

"That's exciting! Can we also go there, Grandpa?"

"That's enough now!" interrupts Grandma Mary. "Simon, sit back down and finish your breakfast!"

Once Balthasar sets off to visit the first customer of the day, Simon accompanies his granddad to the Hill family wine and spirit shop. The boy is overwhelmed. He knows the wines from the Rhenish Hesse region of Rhineland Palatinate, but what he sees here is simply unbelievable. The shelves are stocked with reds, rosés and whites from the French wine-growing regions Bordeaux, Burgundy, Alsace, Languedoc and the Loire Valley. There are Italian wines from Piedmont, Chianti and Emilia-Romagna, and wines from the German wine-growing regions Moselle, Saar, Rheingau, Rhenish Hesse and the Palatinate. There are even wines from Spain, Portugal, South Africa and California there.

"Grandpa, I had no idea that wine is produced in all of these countries. Is it made from the same grapes we are familiar with in Germany?"

"No, Simon. There are several thousand different varieties of grapes in the world. Different kinds are planted depending on the earth, climate and history of the place. Now let's go down into the cellar."

With a great deal of effort, Grandpa Simon opens a heavy oak door. Armed with two wine glasses and a jug, Simon follows his grandfather down the long, wide, stone steps into the deep cellar.

"Grandpa, how many rooms are there down here?"

"Lots. On one side, the cellar reaches far beneath James Street, and on the other it goes under the cellar of the building next door. We buy some wines and spirits in bottles and some in barrels. We then bottle the drinks that we've bought by the barrel here on our premises. Last night I spoke with your father and we agreed that I would show you the various drinks and let you taste them. But you have to promise me not to swallow any of it. Rather, you will have to spit it all out again. That's why you're carrying the jug."

"And where do we start, Granddad?"

"I think Bordeaux is best. You know, we have a special relationship with Bordeaux here in England. That's why Bordeaux wine is the best-selling wine in this country."

"Why? Do they produce a particularly good wine? More red or more white wines?"

"Through the marriage of Henry Plantagenet, who later became King Henry II of England, and Eleonore, the Duchess of Aquitaine, a large part of western France – including Bordeaux – came under British rule. Bordeaux's citizens negotiated privileges with the English king, which meant that over the years they were guaranteed a kind of monopoly on the wine trade with England. In 1300, the Bordeaux wine fleet was made up of almost 900 ships, and about four million litres of wine were exported to England. When in 1453, after the Hundred Years War, Aquitaine became French again, the French king officially certified the Bordeaux citizens' privileges. And to answer your second question, a lot more red wines are produced there as compared with white wines. Red grape varieties such as Cabernet Sauvignon, Cabernet Franc, Merlot, Petit Verdot and Malbec grow in Bordeaux."

"How can anyone remember so many wines?"

"You know how the wines from Rhenish Hesse smell and taste and why they each have their own qualities. But if you, like us English, weren't able to produce much wine in your own country, and had to judge the wines you imported from the whole world, then it would be more difficult. You would do best to then fall back on the standards you have acquired. These standards should be universal so that you can exchange views with many different wine traders and connoisseurs. Such general standards based on appearance, fragrance and flavour, typicity, consistence and quality are our great advantage in the international wine and spirit business."

Hours and days pass as Simon spends time in the Hills' wine cellar, tasting and discussing the 'wines of the world' with his grandfather. In so doing, Simon looks very carefully at each of the wines by candlelight. He uses his nose to try and distinguish between the many different aromas, finding descriptions for them and remembering as many as possible. He then takes a small sip, draws a bit of air in over his tongue and swishes the wine to and fro, before spitting it back out into a wine jug.

He speaks with his grandfather about typical German and Alsatian Rieslings, Pinot Noir from Burgundy and South Tyrol, or the qualities of Bordeaux's top red wine cuvée as contrasted with 'the aroma red wine bomb' from Australia. They speak about various soil structures, a vineyard's optimal alignment with the sun, and the varying wine storage techniques in different countries.

Grandpa Simon, this calm, well-travelled man with his wide-ranging knowledge and his interesting stories, puts Simon under such a spell, that the boy is literally hanging on his every word.

I can still remember very well: The days I spent with my Grandfather Simon in the wine cellar were an unbelievable experience for me. The large assortment of impressions I gathered – of colours, fragrances, aromas and taste sensations – have had an impact on me to this very day. Never before in my life had I learnt so much in such a short space of time.

7. A Gentleman and a pickpocket in Piccadilly

Simon, have you finished your breakfast? We have to get moving!"
"Yes Grandpa, I'm coming."
Simon jumps up from the breakfast table, plants a soft kiss on Grandma Mary's cheek and runs down the elegant marble staircase. "Are we driving to Fortnum & Mason in the coach?" he asks excitedly.

"No, we're walking. It's only a short distance to Piccadilly if we go down Oxford and Regent Streets and then cross over the Circus."

What Simon sees as he enters the brazen double doors at Fortnum & Mason at his grandfather's side leaves him gasp. The shop is elegant and noble, and there are wondrous aromas in the air. Simon discovers rare spices and specialities from the wide world on display, along with a few wines and spirits and a huge selection of teas from many different countries.

A tall, lean, middle-aged man approaches the pair with a smile on his face. His dark suit and black bow tie lead Simon to the conclusion that he knows a thing or two about this shop.

"Good morning Simon, how do you do?"

"Good morning Richard – splendid! May I introduce you to my grand-son, Simon? As you already know, he's Josephine-Christine's youngest."

"Hello Simon. Is this your first time in London?"

"Yes, it's my first time!"

Grandpa Simon turns to his grandson and says, "Richard Morrison is one of Fortnum & Mason's managers and a friend of the family."

"Good morning Mr. Morrison," says Simon, smiling.

"I apologise for just ambushing you like this, Richard. But it would please me very much if Simon can learn some more about tea and the tea trade first-hand."

"That suits me fine, since I don't have any special duties to carry out today. Would you be so kind as to follow me to the storeroom?"

Walking down long, sporadically-lit corridors, separated from one another by heavy, oak doors, both Simon the older and the younger follow Richard Morrison's quick strides into the large warehouses. Simon gets the impression that this Mr. Morrison is a true gentleman: he is wearing a per-fectly fitted suit complemented by the bow tie and highly polished shoes; he is tall and slender and keeps perfectly upright while walking – as though he has swallowed a broomstick. Simon studies him carefully. His bony fingers, in which each joint is clearly visible, suggest that Mr. Morrison has never spent a day doing hard, physical labour.

Simon is torn from his thoughts when he hears Richard Morrison say-ing, "We must work absolutely dryly here. I mean to say that moisture damages the tea stored here, as does too much light. Simon, there are many tonnes of various teas stored here, that come from every tea-grow-ing country on Earth. The bulk of it, however, comes from China and India."

"Are there different kinds of teas like the grape varieties used in wine-making?"

"There is an original tea plant species called the Camellia thea sinensis. And there is also Camellia thea assamica, which was found in Assam, India last year. According to legend, the history of tea begins with the Chinese emperor Shên Nung, who ruled from the Honan Province – south of the Yellow River in 2737 BC. He used to have his water boiled for hygienic purposes, and one day some tea leaves floating in the wind drifted into his hot water. The water then turned golden. The emperor tried it and felt refreshed."

"Do you mean to say that this happened 2737 years before Christ was born? It's now 1824 – that means it happened 4,561 years ago!" says Simon, astonished.

The three wander around the tea stores for hours on end. They speak about the growing conditions and maintenance of tea plants, and about the different processing methods to turn the plants into black, green and oolong tea. As they do so, they keep stopping in front of piles of tea boxes to smell their contents and to examine the tea leaves carefully.

"Mr. Morrison, how did the tea actually come to England?" asks Simon once they are finished with their tour.

"In the mid-seventeenth century, tea became more and more popular in Europe, and therefore became more available. Those responsible for this were the East India Companies, which were commissioned by their governments to engage in trade with India and East Asia – and especially with China and Japan. The company responsible for England was – and still is – the British East India Company. In 1800 there were already five-and-a-half million pounds of tea imported into England each year. And you can count on the same amount again being smuggled in without paying duty tax."

Simon hears a light squeaking sound, then a thud, as though a door has just been opened and shut. Next comes the sound of heels clicking on a hard floor, and suddenly a young, blonde lady is standing next to Simon and is smiling at the group.

"Yes, Ann?" asks Mr. Morrison.

"Mr. Morrison, the tea sampling is now ready."

"Thank you Ann, we'll come with you right away," says the manager, turning to his guests. "Well, you two: I've arranged a tea tasting session so that Simon can get a sense of the essential tea varieties."

"That's great, Mr. Morrison – thank you!" blurts out an impressed Simon.

He follows Ann to the tasting room with his grandfather and Richard Morrison. It's a very sterile looking, lightly furnished room in which everything is white. There are two things that strike Simon as positive: the light flooding through the great big windows and the wonderful aroma of tea emanating from the white teacups.

The day goes past so quickly there and before he knows it, Simon and his grandfather are saying goodbye to Richard Morrison.

"Richard, you have to let me know if I owe you anything for this tour. I have a crate of Château Palmer red wine from Bordeaux and it's reserved for you."

"But Simon, it was a pleasure!" objects Richard Morrison, holding up his right hand in protest.

"Goodbye Mr. Morrison," says Simon, and a moment later he is standing with his grandfather on the footpath.

"Grandpa, that was great!" says Simon to his grandfather as they walk down Piccadilly.

"So my promises weren't exaggerated?"

"No, that was very exciting – all those fragrances and different flavours!"

There is a lot of hustle and bustle in Piccadilly. Coaches and carriages jostle for space on the road, while crowds of people rush pell-mell along the footpaths.

Grandpa Simon bumps into someone with his right shoulder and turns around in shock. He sees a man with a long coat looking back at him angrily as he hurries away and shouts,

"Watch out, why don't you! Next time look where you are going!"

Simon Hill apologises, reflects for a moment and then, as a reflex, he grips the spot where he keeps his pocket watch. "Gone … Police, police! It's gone! Someone stole my pocket watch! The man in the long coat … Police, police!"

Simon quickly catches a glimpse of the man in the long coat. "Police? What's the point of that? How can they get here so fast?" he thinks to himself before running off in pursuit of the man. Zigzagging, he dodges the many people on the footpath. Concentrating and without a sound, he sprints behind his target. In time, he gets closer to the man in the long coat, who keeps turning from one street into the next. The man either feels safer the further he gets from the crime scene, or he is running out of stamina.

Simon wonders how he should get his grandfather's gold watch back from the man. Asking politely wouldn't work – after all, he is maybe four or five times older than Simon. He then has an idea that could work. In one short spurt, he sprints directly up to the man from behind and with lightning speed jumps feet first between the thief's legs to trip him over. Still in full sprint, the man cannot move his right leg forward and falls with all his weight on his left knee before ending up sprawled out on the cobblestones.

He lets out a scream and a wail as Simon jumps straight back to his feet. But how to get to the watch that the thief is clutching in his right fist? He kicks the man in the face with full force. The man cries out once more, opening his hands and drawing them up to cover his face. In doing so, he leaves the pocket watch on the ground. Simon picks it up and says politely, "Thank you for my grandfather's watch!"

"Ow, you bastard! Some day I'll get my hands on you and then …"

Simon doesn't hear the rest. He has already turned around and is heading back toward his grandfather.

A fairly large crowd of people have gathered around the spot where he left his grandfather in Piccadilly. In the centre, Simon can see his grandfather and a policeman, who is taking notes. He pushes his way through. "Grandpa, excuse me, here is your pocket watch." Simon puts the watch into his grandfather's left hand.

"Simon, how did you get it back?"

"Who is that, Mr. Hill?" interjects the policeman.

"This is my grandson, Simon. He ran after the thief … and he managed to get the pocket watch back. But how Simon?"

"There isn't much to tell. Can we go home now?"

"Mr. Hill, what should I do with the report? You now have your watch back and we're not likely to readily catch the thief."

"Thank you sir. I think we can let the matter rest after all."

Late in the afternoon, at tea time, Simon Hill tells his wife, Mary about the events at Fortnum & Mason and the adventure involving the pickpocket. How Simon managed to get the watch back is a mystery to his grandfather. But now that he has had a few days to get to know the boy, the old man knows it will remain a mystery. Simon is back in the shop once again, studying the labels of different wines, whiskies, cognacs and other delicacies.

8. A painful encounter and a joyful encounter

I t's dark and quiet," thinks Simon to himself, "damned quiet. I wonder what time it is – five in the morning?" He draws back the warm blanket, gets out of bed and begins to dress – not quickly but quietly … very quietly. Still very cautious, he opens his bedroom door, goes downstairs, and before he knows it, he is standing on the street and facing Covent Garden, the object of his curiosity. Sitting on the steps in front of his grandfather's house, he quickly slips into his shoes and ties his laces.

A few minutes later, Simon is pushing his way through the crowd among the Covent Garden market stalls. Noisy people bustling around, exotic fragrances that he has never smelt before and sounds he has never heard before – all this casts a spell over him. Simon looks at all the people. There are fine gentlemen in coats and hats who are carrying canes, as well as people in only shirts and pants – some of whom have no shoes and are walking around barefoot. Some people have very pale faces; while others are tanned or even almost black. Simon hears languages he doesn't know, despite the fact that he can speak German, English, French and Spanish. Intrigued, he goes from one stall to the next, gazing at the displays and looking over all the goods on offer. He skilfully manages to skirt the people standing directly in front of the stalls, popping up only to soon disappear once more.

"Cardamom, my boy, that's cardamom," answers the dark-skinned, exotic looking merchant after Simon asks the same question twice.

"Cardamom – what's that?"

"Cardamom belongs to the ginger family. Malabar cardamom comes from southern India and Ceylon cardamom comes from the island of Ceylon, south-east of India."

"Excuse me, I have one more question." Simon points with his right hand at something at the other end of the stall. "That over there, the really expensive stuff – what exactly is it?"

The merchant turns his head, following the direction of Simon's hand with his gaze. "That's saffron. Saffron comes from Persia and is one of the most expensive spices in the world. It blossoms for only two weeks in autumn and a picker harvests two to three ounces a day at most."

Simon quickly thanks the man and wanders off to another oriental stall, where he can open his eyes, ears and nose to its wonders. There are such finds here as pepper from the Indian Malabar Coast, and the finest vanilla from the islands of Madagascar and Réunion; there is aromatic Ceylon cinnamon, as well as Cassia cinnamon from China.

At a large market stall, Simon reads names on a seemingly endless array of wooden crates. Some of the names are ones he has already seen at Fortnum & Mason, such as Yunnan, Huo Shan Huang Ya, Luan Gua Pian, Sencha, Bancha … A friendly and smiling older gentleman speaks to Simon in articulate English, but with an accent that makes it clear he doesn't come from England. His pitch-black hair and sun-tanned skin also indicate that he must come from a country somewhere in the south.

"Good morning, sir. You're up early!"

"Yes," replies Simon with a smile.

"What brings you here, then? This is not really the place for a boy of your age, and also not the right time, is it?"

Simon shrugs as he replies, "Pure curiosity. All the different people and the things that are sold here interest me greatly. Do you sell tea? I recognise some of the names on the crates. Huo Shan Huang Ya, for example, is a typical, traditional Chinese black tea. It's roasted in a pan and is slightly sweet to the taste."

"Tell me, young man, you're not from England, are you? Your English is perfect, but I somehow get the impression …"

"I come from Germany but my mother is English. May I ask where you come from?"

"I come from the British crown colony of India but have been working for an Indian tea merchant here in England for many, many years."

Simon asks more and more questions, some of which go into fine details, which seems to amuse his conversation partner. Whenever someone steps up to the market stall, Simon politely steps aside so as not to disrupt the vendor's conversations with his customers.

"What's your name?" asks the salesman in between customers.

"Simon Balthasar Braun."

"I'm known as Abhay, which means 'fearless'."

"You may certainly call me Simon. After all, you're an adult and much older than me."

The time flies by and Simon finally says goodbye to Abhay in order to visit the rest of the market stalls. He suddenly realises that he's already walked halfway down Southampton Street.

A thought jumps into his mind, "It's not far to the Thames from here." Minutes later, Simon is sitting on a big log and his eyes are running over the first row of Southwark riverside houses on the other side of the Thames. Lost in thought, he watches the large and small sailing ships passing by.

Suddenly someone shouts, "Hey you!" behind Simon. Torn from his daydreams, he turns around. Standing a few yards behind him are six young boys. Their clothing is dirty and tattered. Simon sees no trace of friendliness in their faces. No, it looks like trouble.

Simon rises from the log, the panic inside rising with him. "Yes?"

"Give us your money and valuables or else you'll cop it!"

"I have three shillings and ten pence, but nothing valuable. Here, take it." Simon holds out the coins he has just pulled out of his pocket and offers them to a boy with blond hair, who in turn grabs the money quickly with his left hand while gripping Simon by the collar of his jumper with his right. Dragging him downward, he knees Simon in the stomach. Stifling a cry, Simon falls to the ground. The blond boy starts to kick him and, gaining strength, the other boys join in. Simon curls up like a hedgehog, covering his face with his arms and clenching his teeth. He can't completely suppress his cries because it's painful. He hears shouts and then … nothing – nothing at all.

"Hello Simon! Simon, wake up!"

He slowly opens his eyes. His head is spinning, he's in pain and he can feel every bone in his body. The blurry silhouette of a man shimmers before his eyes. It is Abhay, the Indian.

"Hello Ab …" – Simon has lost consciousness once more. When he comes to again, he can feel his back, his arms and his legs. Everything is there – but oh the pain! After a few minutes, Simon begins to survey his surroundings. He is lying on a mattress with a woman and young girl sitting next to him. The woman is wiping his face with a cool cloth.

"You're safe. I am Abhay's wife, Harsha, and this is our daughter, Marala."

"Hello Simon," whispers Marala with a smile.

"You're probably in a lot of pain, but it's not really so bad. Tomorrow you'll be able to walk again. You have a lot of bruises but you haven't broken anything," says Harsha in a gentle voice.

"Home – I have to get home. They don't know where I am!"

"Simon, it's dark outside. You can't go home now."

"But my family will be worried!"

"Marala will take you home tomorrow. Can you sit up far enough to drink a cup of tea?"

Harsha sees that Simon is in pain as she helps him to sit upright, but the boy doesn't make a sound. He slowly tastes the revitalising tea. He sizes up Harsha, Marala and the entire room with his eyes. It's modest, clean, tidy and decorated in much brighter colours he is accustomed to.

"Where is Abhay?"

"He'll be back soon. He's bringing more water because you need to drink a lot," says Harsha.

"What do your names mean?" Simon wants to know.

"Marala means 'beautiful swan' and the meaning of Harsha is 'the happy one'. You're an inquisitive one!" With these words, Harsha strokes Simon's right cheek.

Simon looks at Marala. "She must be about my age," he thinks to himself.

Harsha holds the teacup in front of his mouth and Simon sips the hot tea. Then he hears a door open and shut. A moment later, Abhay is kneeling next to him. "How are you, Simon?"

"All right so far."

"What happened?"

While Simon tells of what happened to him, Harsha serves him a small meal that she calls 'thali'. It consists of chapatti – a flat, unleavened Indian bread – spicy, hot rice, chickpeas, onions, peppers …

"Where is Simon? Has anybody seen Simon today?" asks Grandma Mary at the dinner table. But neither Grandpa Simon, nor Uncle Charles, Aunt Betty or their daughters, Elisabeth and Janet, have anything to say. Betty jumps up from her seat, dashes out of the dining room and is back within a couple of minutes. "I just had a look in his room and I think he's been gone since the morning. And none of the servants have seen him all day."

"I hope nothing's happened to him!" Mary Hill gives her husband a worried look.

"Mary, what do you want me to say? It's already past seven o'clock. All we can do now is wait. If he's not back by midday tomorrow, I'll visit the police station."

"Can't we do anything? And how are we supposed to reach Simon's father? He should be in York on his business trip by now!"

"No Mary. Your husband is right," says Charles, agreeing with his father-in-law. "Where do you want to search for Simon? And how do you suppose you can contact his father? You know what Simon is like, so let's just wait until tomorrow."

When Simon opens his eyes the next morning he once again has a brand new perspective on the world. He has regained his courage, curiosity and optimism. While it's true that he can still feel every movement he makes, it's bearable. As he sits up he notices Marala sitting in a corner watching him.

"Good morning, Marala!" – his smile is back, too.

"Shubh prata, Simon. How are you?"

"Better, much better."

"Amma has made breakfast. You may eat with us if you like. Appa is already at Covent Garden."

"Yes, please. I'm really hungry."

"Shall I help you out of bed?"

"No, no, it's fine."

In the dining room, Marala and Harsha sit on rugs at a small table teeming with dishes.

"Shubh prata, Simon," says Harsha, smiling.

"Shubh prata – what does that mean?"

"It means good morning. Please take a seat here." Harsha pours Simon a cup of tea.

"I would sincerely like to thank you for looking after me like this. I feel very comfortable here!"

"You are very welcome, Simon! You're a very polite boy and Abhay and I appreciate that."

Marala smiles at Simon. "So do I!"

42

"Abhay told me you come from Germany. Where are you living in London, then?"

"At my grandparents' house in James Street. At Hill's – the wine and spirit shop."

"Oh, that's right near Covent Garden."

"Yes, I can walk home."

"Marala will come with you – just to be on the safe side."

"Let's stop for a moment here on the bridge, Marala. Look at all the ships coming into London on the Thames! I wonder where they all come from and what kind of cargo they have? Exciting, isn't it?"

"Some could come from where my mum and dad come from – from India. That's pretty far south on the globe and is very far away."

"Were you born in India?"

"No, here in London. My father works for an Indian tea merchant and has had a good job here for many years. Appa and amma were married in London and then I was born. We're doing very well here."

"By the way, how old are you?"

"Twelve."

"So am I!"

"Come on, let's go! Your grandparents are most probably very worried."

At Covent Garden, Simon and Marala visit Abhay's stall. He smiles when he sees them. Marala leaps into her father's embrace. "Hello appa! I'm taking Simon home."

"Shubh prata, Simon."

"Shubh prata, Abhay. Thank you for taking me home yesterday. Thank you for your help." Simon offers Abhay his hand. Abhay lets go of Marala and accepts Simon's gratitude with a smile.

A few minutes later, the two children are making their way between the Covent Garden market stalls, continuing toward Simon's grandparents' house. They barely make it through the heavy front door and into the hallway before news of Simon's return spreads like a wildfire throughout the house. And in no time at all, Simon's whole family and the servants alike have surrounded the pair.

"Where were you, Simon? Where did you come from? What have you been doing? Are you all right? Did something happen to you? What are those bruises on your face and grazes on your hands? What stopped you from coming home?"

"Everyone keep calm," Grandpa Simon's incisive voice cuts through all the fuss. "Let's go and sit in the drawing room, where Simon can slowly tell us the whole story."

"James, please take the little girl to the kitchen where she can have a cup of tea and something to eat," says Aunt Betty to the butler.

"No, no," interjects Simon, "that's Marala and she's coming to the drawing room."

"Don't be silly! She's an Indian – they're backward!" retorts Aunt Betty.

Grandpa Simon silences Aunt Betty, "That may be well and good, but Simon doesn't understand you and you shan't dissuade him. So let's just retire to the drawing room."

Betty holds him by the sleeve and whispers, "But father, it's just not possible!" Grandpa Simon leans over and replies into her ear, "If we want to find out what happened to Simon, we will have to take the girl into the drawing room. She appears to be able to behave herself. Otherwise you won't be able to get a word out of the boy. I'm sure of that."

Right up until lunchtime Simon keeps the family fascinated by his tales of adventure. He tells how he left the house early in the morning, careful not to wake anyone, about his experiences in Covent Garden, by the Thames, and at Marala's house. He tells of how warmly he was received and how sympathetically he was looked after there.

For weeks I thought about the affair with the six boys by the Thames. Why did it escalate so? And is there something I could have done to avoid it? I was in the wrong place at the wrong time and they used that to their advantage. Next time I will have to react faster, search for the strongest or the weakest of the lot and actively attack them.

My Grandma Mary and my Aunt Betty tried a couple of times to explain what the difference between 'privileged society' and the 'underclass' is. I wanted to hear as little about it back then as I do today. For me, a person's character is what's important, not his appearance. Over the decades I have met so many 'noble' but stupid idiots, that I would rather spend my time with people who know what they are talking about and who do as they say.

9. Farewell and oddly thoughts

Wonderfully tender lamb. How lucky we are today!" Simon Hill chatters to everyone present. "Balthasar is back in London, the whole family is eating dinner together and we have such a great roast on the table."

"Grandpa, could you please pass me the bowl of vegetables once more?" asks Janet.

"Here you go, Janet, which I can also give you!" Simon passes the steaming dish over to her.

"Balthasar, it's good to hear that your wine sales went so well," continues Grandpa Simon.

"Yes, the trip was really worth it. German Riesling is in great demand here in England. Our customers were very happy to see me and I was welcomed with open arms everywhere I went."

"It just goes to show once again, that quality prevails. A well-made Riesling is plainly one of the best white wines in the world. It has such a fresh, invigorating character and unmistakably clear aroma. And then there's the light, tangy impression in leaves on the palate … simply unbeatable!" gushes Simon Hill.

"Father, you really should sell my Riesling all over England and not just here in London!"

There are smiles and smirks all round. "That's all I need – old Simon Hill traipsing around the entire island …," grumbles Grandma Mary.

"Daddy – Grandpa and I spent a few days in his cellar tasting all sorts of wines – and whisky, cognac and rum, too. It was all very exciting!" relates Simon, glowing with enthusiasm.

"Did the alcohol go to your head?"

"Oh no! I think I must be a champion spitter by now. We always spat everything out again … at least I always did and Grandpa did so most of the time!" Simon grins at his grandfather.

"Simon, never reveal any secrets!" Everyone has to laugh as Simon Hill is found out.

"And then there was the day spent with Mr. Morrison at Fortnum & Mason in Piccadilly," continues Simon impatiently. "The whole day revolved around tea."

Grandpa Simon nods. "Balthasar, I think Simon will also become a tea connoisseur. But the day only began getting exciting once my watch was stolen …"

"And how did you finally get it back, Simon?" Balthasar asks his son.

"Well …" Simon yawns ostensibly with his hand in front of his mouth. "I'm suddenly very tired!" He gets up to say goodnight. "Dad, I really must introduce you to Marala and her parents tomorrow!" Simon exits the dining room with astounding speed.

"I knew that would make him leave," says Grandpa Simon. "I get the impression that in the past few days, this city has become 'Simons London' more and more."

"Well, I can tell you, Balthasar, we were so worried when Simon didn't come home one night! The suspense of not knowing what could have happened to him!" Betty is beside herself at the memory of it. From beginning to end, she retells what Simon and Marala, the little Indian girl, told them and adds that Simon couldn't be dissuaded from allowing Marala to join him in the drawing room – an affront in Betty's view.

"I can very well imagine that", answers Balthasar without a hint of reproach in his voice. "If Simon weren't involved, I would tell you the story is unbelievable."

Grandpa Simon nods. "Over the days I spent with Simon, one thing has become clear: the boy is incredibly strong-willed and has boundless energy."

"True. Josephine and I have always puzzled over how we should treat him. He doesn't seem to know the meaning of the word 'fear'. On the other hand, we also couldn't say that he blindly acts without thinking. We get the feeling that he thinks long and hard about what he does."

"In any case, you can't keep the boy at home forever," offers Grandpa Simon. "He wants to take over the world!"

"You're right about that, Father! Now I'll just have to wait and see what Simon has to show me tomorrow!"

Two days later, the 'Lone Star' leaves its berth at London's Surrey Docks. The ship that will make the first leg of Simon and his father's journey home is older than the 'Repatriate', which was under Captain Thomson's command. The two of them stand at the stern, waving at Grandpa Simon, Grandma Mary and cousins Elisabeth and Janet. Gradually, their figures become smaller and smaller. Tears are already pouring down Simon's cheeks and his father puts an arm around his shoulders. "Saying goodbye is always difficult, and will stay that way for the rest of your life! If you want to travel a lot, you will often have to say farewell. But you'll get used to it."

"Yesterday we met Marala on the bridge over the Thames. Do you remember, Daddy …?"

"Hello Marala, how are you?"

"Hey, Simon!" The girl embraces Simon warmly, pressing him against her.

"This is my father."

Balthasar looks at Marala and smiles. He is struck by her big, dark-brown eyes, which give her tender face a decidedly friendly character. He stretches his right hand out toward Marala. "Good morning, Marala."

A little cautiously, Marala shakes his hand. "Good morning Mr. Braun."

"Yesterday, Simon told me quite a lot about what the two of you have done and discovered together. It sounds very fascinating."

"Yes, we've really been through a lot," beams Marala. But her face turns sad as she asks, "Do you have to return home now?"

Simon looks at Marala wistfully. "Yes. Tomorrow. On the one hand, I'm looking forward to seeing my family – my mum, Christoph, Josephine and all the others, but on the other, I would love to stay here in London." He turns to his father. "Strange, isn't it, Dad?"

"That's completely normal, Simon. At home, everything is familiar, and here you get to see something new and unknown. It's typical of you, Simon Balthasar Braun, that you love both!"

All three of them break into laughter – but in Marala's case there are also a couple of tears rolling down her cheeks.

"You know, Dad, I already miss Marala. I have a very strange feeling in my stomach. When Marala hugged me as we were standing in front of their house with Harsha, I could have cried!"

"I understand," answers Balthasar. "But yesterday evening was nice, wasn't it?"

"Yes, it was great that so many friends and associates were there to say goodbye to us."

Nothing worth mentioning happens during the passage to Oostende. To be honest it's downright boring. But that makes no difference to Simon. Although its bright and sunny, he spends a large part of his days at sea sitting on a teak chest on deck, watching the goings-on while contemplating his experiences in London and thinking about Marala and his feelings. His longing for home but also his desire to go out into the big, wide world. But also, the apprehension of having to say goodbye to someone you feel like you know very well, even though you only met her a few days ago …

Then on Sunday 18th July, 1824, it's lately over: They stop in front of the Mainz coach station. And Simon is just happy to finally be able to see everyone again. Christoph will be happy to finally have a brother to tease and squabble with once more …

That was my first long journey and I solemnly promised myself that it wouldn't be the last. At the time, I didn't have the slightest notion of all the things that were yet to happen to me. When I look back, I'm amazed at everything I was given the chance to learn and experience. And at the adventurous situations I was able to handle.

That strange feeling in my stomach mixed with the muddle in my head, which I first experienced when I farewelled Marala, is something I have since come to understand better. I now know that it had less to do with travelling and much more to do with the opposite sex ...

10. The mysterious Dutchman

10.04.1825: The first hotel opens on Hawaii.
06.08.1825: Bolivia gains independence.
27.09.1825: Maiden voyage of the world's first public railway service, the Stockton & Darlington Railway.
13.10.1827: Russian troops capture Erevan, Armenia's capital.

On a sunny Saturday in July 1827, as Simon is clambering down one of the narrow, rough and steep paths that lead down the vineyard's slope, he pauses to catch his breath for a moment and realises that he's in 'the Dutchman's' vineyard. It looks different to the locals' vineyards because the owner uses a different system of vine training. Simon takes a look around. Yes, he can see 'the Dutchman's' estate, although it's a little obscured by the vineyards. He can hear his mother's voice ringing in his ears, "Simon, don't hang around there. That man is supposed to be a little peculiar. Promise me that!"

Simon's father has told him that the man everyone calls 'the Dutchman', is a former seafaring man who settled near Nierstein a few years ago. People say that he makes outstanding wine. But because he only sells it in the Netherlands and leads a very reclusive and private life, hardly anyone has any contact with him. According to the rumour mill from Nierstein to Mainz, 'no one knows what he does up there'. Simon has already heard some scary stories about 'the Dutchman'.

Driven by curiosity, Simon continues further down the bumpy path, through the vineyard and towards the estate. The path gets narrower and steeper, and suddenly a stone gives way under Simon's foot, sending him off balance. Before he knows it, he has slipped a few metres down the hill, falling between the grapevines. Green vine leaves flash quickly before his eyes, then the Rhine, the ground, the sky, the Rhine – and then a pain shoots into his knee before he sees the sky – and then nothing else.

As he regains consciousness and opens his eyes, the sun is shining blindingly in his face. Simon presses his eyes shut again and everything is spinning behind his eyelids. Only now does he realise what has happened. His knee hurts and he can hear someone saying something.

"Are you hurt, boy?" murmurs a calm voice. Simon squints with eyes that are slowly becoming accustomed to the brightness and makes out a figure standing before him. "What happened?" he asks.

"Well you must have fallen from up there."

Simon examines the white-haired old man and his wrinkled face – a face wrought by sun and sea. "Are you the one everyone calls 'the Dutchman'?"

"Are you the snotty-nosed brat called 'the German'?" comes the sharp reply.

"I'm sorry. I haven't fully regained my senses yet. My knee!" moans Simon. "The pain is piercing."

The old man bends down and peers at Simon's knee with a scrutinising eye. "There's nothing to worry about. It's bleeding, but it looks like it's only skin-deep … We just have to clean it. Do you have any other pains, or do you think you can walk?"

"No, I think I can manage." Simon bravely tries to get up with the old man's support.

A short while later, he finds himself recovering in the estate's sun-drenched courtyard. 'The Dutchman' is sitting beside him on the teak bench.

"Just take it easy, boy. I'll be right back." The old man stands up and disappears into the house. As Simon watches him go, he notices that he feels strangely safe and secure here.

A few minutes later 'the Dutchman' returns with a bandage and a clean, carefully folded white towel in one hand and a wine bottle without a label in the other. Sitting down next to Simon on the bench, he dabs a colourless liquid onto the towel before saying, in a steady tone, "You're a right strong lad! This will sting a little, but I have to disinfect the wound with alcohol." And without hesitating another second, he presses the towel against the boy's bleeding knee. Simon's face seems to take on the old man's wrinkled features. A cry escapes his lips, but he instantly bites down to suppress it, so as not to show any weakness.

"Very courageous, my boy."

"It's not the first time you've done that, is it?" asks Simon.

'The Dutchman' chuckles. "During my long life I have seen, experienced and done so much."

At this point, Simon remembers his manners. "Thank you very much for your help," says he. "Braun, Simon Braun is my name."

"Braun … hmm … Balthasar Braun's son?"

"Yes, that's my father."

"I've heard a lot about him. He must be a decent, upstanding man. My name is Jan ter Bruggen."

He rises and with hurried footsteps, disappears into the house once more, taking the bandage, towel and bottle with him. Simon notices the man's broad shoulders and large stature. A few minutes later, he is sitting beside him again. Now standing between them on the bench are two glasses, a bottle and a plate of bread and sausage. The old man raises the bottle. "Grape juice."

He cuts several slices of bread and puts sausage on them. He then fills the two glasses with juice.

"You have to build up your strength now. That will do you good. As you already correctly mentioned, I come from the Netherlands – from Dordrecht on the Oude Maas. For almost three decades I sailed around the world for the Dutch East India Company, the VOC. I spent most of my time in South Africa and Asia. A couple of years ago, I came here to retire. And now I spend my time watching the grapes grow and producing wine."

"Where did you learn to make wine?" wonders Simon aloud. "It's really not easy."

"For a few years, I was stationed by the VOC as a merchant at the Cape of Good Hope in South Africa. And it was there that I met a few winemakers. You know that in 1652, the Dutch set up a resupply outpost at Table Bay for the company's trading ships to use en route to India and China. Even its founder, Jan van Riebeeck, had grapes in tow from Europe. But many of the Germans – and especially the French Huguenot immigrants – brought a lot of 'wine knowledge' into the country."

"What are the Dutch doing in India and China, then?"

"Those of us in the company started trading with the Indians and the Chinese. Porcelain, tea and above all, spices, all come from those countries. We then sell the products in Europe. But that's a long story."

"I would love to keep listening, but I have to go home now. Otherwise it will get too late. By the way, I know an Indian, too. I met her when I was in London with my father. She's a girl named Marala and she's as pretty as a picture."

50

"Marala, hmm, that means 'beautiful swan'. Do you think you can walk?"

"Yes, I'll be fine Mr. ... ter Bruggen."

"Why don't you call me Jan? Just say Jan. You're welcome to come by again."

"Thank you, I will. Perhaps as soon as tomorrow!"

So that was my first encounter with the mysterious Jan ter Bruggen. I had to come up with a story about where I injured my knee and who bandaged it up for me. There was no way I could mention 'the Dutchman' to my mother ... I knew I would think of something. Jan really seemed like a very friendly person. He gave me the impression that he was confident and worldly.

Over the next few months I spent a lot of time with Jan ter Bruggen. His way of explaining the really important things in life really fascinated me. He gave such good advice as, "People will judge you by your deeds – not your words"; "Don't rush through life chasing unattainable goals, because if you spend all your time looking up at the stars, you will no longer know which path you are on"; and "Never give up or lose sight of your aims, because success is often a long way off in the distance."

For Jan, each individual grape from which a wine is produced was paramount. He would say, "Pay attention to nature. You should develop a good sense of each specific occurrence. Only healthy, perfectly ripened grapes can produce a good wine. In the vineyard, that means a lot of care and smaller yields, because less is more. In the wine cellar, you should interfere as little as possible, only doing what is absolutely necessary so that the individual elements fall into place to produce a truly great wine."

Over the following two years I helped Jan a great deal with whatever work came up in his vineyards. And he in turn, showed me all his tricks and strategies. His almost loving handling of the grapes really captivated me.

I believe my parents knew with whom I was spending my free time, but they very nobly stopped short of mentioning anything to me.

BOOK 2

1. Bad surprise and final decision

22.01.1828: Arthur Wellesley, Duke of Wellington, becomes Prime Minister of the United Kingdom.
01.07.1828: The machinist, John Cree becomes the first railway accident victim in history when the Locomotion No. 1, that he is driving along the Stockton–Darlington line explodes.
04.07.1828: The foundation stone for the USA's first railway line is laid by "Baltimore & Ohio Railroad".
03.12.1828: Andrew Jackson is elected seventh President of the United States of America.
04.03.1829: Andrew Jackson enters office as the seventh President of the USA.
14.09.1829: The Peace Treaty of Adrianople ends the war between Russia and the Ottoman Empire.

H ello Simon. Why the long face?"
Simon stomps into 'the Dutchman's' kitchen looking dejected and serious.

"Just take a seat." Jan ter Bruggen points at the bench in the corner.

The tall and wiry-looking young man sets himself down mechanically, runs his fingers through his short, pitch-black hair and places both arms on the solid oak table. He is holding a piece of paper in his left hand. Without a word, Jan takes two glasses out of the kitchen cupboard and reaches for a tall, brown bottle on the sideboard. He then sits at the table opposite Simon and pours from the bottle into the glasses. "Here, drink a little Riesling first, and then shoot. What's troubling you?"

"I'm seventeen years old – it's been five years since I was in London – we've been writing to each other the entire time, and now this!"

"What? What are you talking about?"

"Five years ago I was given the chance to see the big, wide world. Since then I have been busy learning and working, and I've always been a good son and the nice boy next door. I have only tolerated the situation because I met you and was able to learn so much from you – about another way to make wines, about the facts of life, and about new countries and continents."

"Simon, what are you talking about?"

Simon stretches the piece of paper out toward Jan. "Read it, please!"

A letter, thinks Jan, very neatly written and in English.

"For five years, we've been writing letters to each other, sharing our secrets. She knows more about me than any other person in this world. And I thought it went both ways."

Jan reads the first few words: My dear Simon … He skims over the first few lines, then stops and begins to read it word for word. I am to marry on the 7th June this year … You don't know him, it's the tea merchant that my father works for … We are greatly indebted to him … My hand has been promised to him.

They sit there in silence. Jan doesn't know what to say. Of course Simon had carried on about Marala, the little Indian girl in London, but Jan had dismissed it as nothing more than calf-love and had never taken it particularly seriously. He never would have thought that the two had corresponded the entire time.

"He's probably as old as Marala's father, at least fifty years old. Marala is seventeen – how is that supposed to work? I mean … in the long run." Simon stares gloomily into space.

"Simon, in India and in many other countries, it is quite normal for young girls to be betrothed to adult men. It has to do with gratitude and honour."

"Then I don't give a damn about gratitude and honour – that's not fair at all! When Marala is thirty, he'll already be approaching seventy. Jan, that can't be possible!?"

"Just calm down again. If what she writes is true, what can you do to change it? If Marala has accepted her parents' decision, then you won't be able to change anything."

"I have to think about that."

"Yes, you do that. Take your time to think about it. And now come with me to the wine cellar. There's something I want to show you."

Jan grabs Simon by the arm and pulls him to his feet.

The thick, heavy oak door opens slowly and the two men, the old one and the young one, go down the long, stone staircase leading to the wine cellar. On the way down, Jan lights candles on each side of the steps, so as to light the way into the deep, dark pit before them. When they get to the bottom, they light the lanterns they have brought with them and then walk purposefully through the labyrinthine passageways. Simon gets goosebumps – not because of the darkness – but rather from the cold temperature down here. Up in the vineyard on Jan's estate, it should be a good eighteen degrees on this Spring day. But here in the cellar it's barely five degrees. Simon follows Jan deeper and deeper into the cellar. 'The Dutchman' lights a few more candles and takes two glasses and a pipette from a shelf on the wall.

This remote part of the wine cellar houses smaller wooden barrels, known as 'barriques'. Simon knows that, as opposed to the usual German barrels, they only hold 225 litres.

"Here in these barrique barrels, made from French oak, a few interesting reds from the year before last are maturing", Jan ter Bruggen now explains. "That means they have already been ageing for thirteen to fourteen months."

"We do the same thing, except that it takes less time and our barrels are much bigger."

"The first contrast between my red wines and yours is that I wait longer, allowing the crushed red grapes to stand – you know, the phase during which the grape juice is in contact with the grape skins before fermentation, so that the colour and tannins from the skins end up in the must. Aside from that, all these wines have undergone malolactic fermentation."

"You mean the lactic acid fermentation during which the harsher malic acid is converted to softer-tasting lactic acid, so that the red wine later tastes smoother?"

"Exactly Simon. Well observed! After that phase, I store these stronger reds in the barrique barrels."

"Aren't all barrels the same?"

"No, Simon. You make your big barrels 'neutral', meaning that the oak is not meant to influence the taste of the wine that comes out of it. The smaller barrique barrels, however, are supposed to impart red wines with a slight to strong flavour of oak, as well as toasty or smoky aromas and flavours. That's how a red wine ends up full-bodied. Metaphorically speaking, it should develop broader shoulders."

"I think I understand."

Jan has removed the sealing plug from the nearest barrel and is dipping the pipette in so that he and Simon can try a quarter-glass each.

They each hold their wine glasses up to the light of their lanterns and swivel the wine around evenly so that it can absorb oxygen.

"It's really dark, your red wine," remarks Simon.

"That's because of the maceration time. By letting it stand longer, the wine has simply had more time to absorb the colour pigmentation from the grape skins. But now, stick your nose in the glass ... Can you smell the smokiness?"

"Yes – the wine is defined by ripe fruit, it reminds me of strawberries and cherries. And in the background, the smoky aromas are clearly distinguishable. Now I really understand what you mean."

"Try it," says Jan, as he rolls his eyes and slurps loudly through his teeth.

Simon also expertly takes the wine on the tongue before swishing it to the left and to the right, the way his grandfather taught him to do in London. "You're right," he then says, amazed. "It's much firmer on the tongue than our late Pinot Noirs …"

"Congratulations! You immediately recognised it as a Pinot noir. Most Germans who I've offered a taste of this wine have not recognised the grape variety. Perhaps that's because small barrels are not used in Germany. What do you think of it?"

"Great, Jan, truly an excellent wine!"

"Come, I'll show you a couple more …"

"Simon, take a seat. We're eating dinner!"

"Good evening," Simon sits at the table where his whole family is gathered. "I've already eaten at Jan ter Bruggen's house." While speaking, he places a large bottle of Burgundy on the table in front of his father. "From Jan, for you all to try." Simon removes the cork from the bottle.

"Now I must say I'm curious," says Balthasar Braun, rinsing out his crystal glass with a mouthful of water. He then pours a little into Christoph's glass and a little into his own. They pick up their glasses, swivel them, place their noses deep into their glasses and finally take a decent amount on the tongue before slurping it and ultimately swallowing the wine. One would be forgiven for thinking they were taking part in a synchronisation competition. And then they both blurt out in unison, "Now that's a good wine!"

Balthasar looks at Simon. "I've tasted such a wine a few times at your grandfather's in London. That's what a Pinot noir from Burgundy smells and tastes like. I must say: Jan ter Bruggen knows how to make it properly!"

All day, Simon has distracted himself with wine. But lying in bed in the evening, he can't distract himself any longer. There's a candle lit on the bedside table beside him, so that he can read and re-read Marala's letter.

Then it comes to him, "I have to go there". "I have to go to London and find out from her personally whether she really wants to marry that old man!"

The next afternoon, Simon is sitting next to Jan on the teak bench where their friendship began, with a glass of grape juice in one hand and a piece of spelt bread and butter in the other.

56

"Jan, I'm going to London. I have to make sure for myself that the wedding is not happening against Marala's will."

"My boy, we both know that this marriage is not ideal for Marala, otherwise she wouldn't have written you all those letters. But you should respect her decision!"

"What do you mean by that?"

"It may not be her wish to marry this man. But if she has agreed to it out of feelings of honour and gratitude toward her parents, then you have to accept that. You won't be able to change her mind – trust me. I was in Asia long enough."

"You mean I should let her do something that I'm absolutely convinced is wrong?"

"What is right and what is wrong? Is the marriage wrong for Marala or for you, because then you won't get to marry her? Are you thinking about her or more about yourself, Simon? Don't humiliate her by telling her that her decision is wrong. Accept that decision. That's size! So do you really want to go to London?"

"Yes, I'm travelling to London and then I'm going to America. I've been reading a lot about America in the newspaper lately. People can really get things established there. I'm the third child in my family: Christoph will take over the wine cellar and Josephine will marry and leave home. If I were to stay, I'd only ever be the uncle."

"Emigrate? Are you sure?"

"Yes, I'm sure … I've always wanted to see the world. You've also explored it. And now you're here and have consciously chosen to live in Rhenish Hesse."

"But I was older than you when I went out into the world."

"The earlier I start, the earlier I can finish," replies Simon with a grin.

They both burst out laughing and then Jan places his arm around Simon's shoulders. "You should take your time to think about it, Simon."

"I've already thought about it for a long time. You know, my father is a firm believer that too many cooks spoil the broth. Quick decision making is very important in a small winery. My brother, Christoph, is the eldest and he's the one who spends the whole day helping in the wine cellar in whatever way he can. While we've often had our differences, I know that Christoph is ambitious, diligent and determined. In my heart of hearts I know it's right of my father to pass the wine cellar onto him."

"Simon, in the two years we've known each other, you've learnt to be matter-of-fact in your decision making. I take off my hat to you for that. That's a great achievement for a seventeen-year-old!"

"You mean, if you were to wear one, that is," snorts Simon, and Jan joins in the laughter. But Simon's expression soon turns serious once more. "I don't have much time left. I have to be in London by the start of June. Besides, I can't calmly say farewell to mum and dad. They won't let me leave just like that. It will have to be done quickly and easily. I can write them a long letter from my grandparents' house in London before I leave for America."

"So you've already made up your mind?"

"Yes," says Simon firmly. He hugs 'the old Dutchman' and gets up from the bench. "You'll hear from me. You were in the East and I'm heading west!"

Jan watches the young man as he walks out through the farm gate, and then he's gone …

The wide world – this notion was always somewhere in the distant future. I was already living out the future in my own mind, while actually dealing with the present. But now I could no longer daydream. The time for dreaming about the future was over and it was time for me to make a decision. Because 7th June, 1829, was the day that Marala wanted to get married. Or at least was meant to.

I knew that this decision would influence my entire life. I was to either emigrate to America via London, or not go to London and possibly also never again have the chance to set off for America.

2. Farewell and a sore shoulder

It should be about five o'clock in the morning on this Tuesday 3rd March, 1829. Simon slips out of bed and slides into his shirt, trousers and jumper. Without a sound, he reaches for his coat, slings his knapsack over his shoulders and slinks downstairs on tiptoes. At the front door he gropes around for Alex, the dark-brown, Braun family hunting dog who always sleeps in this spot.

Alex has already opened one eye and begins wagging his tale as Simon tenderly pats his head.

"So this is goodbye, is it?" thinks Simon, and is forced to swallow hard. "I've contemplated this a thousand times … Now it's time to actually go through with it!" Simon stands up, goes down the steps and along the path to the gate, where he turns around to look back. It could be years before I come back here …

The night is pitch-black, but Simon knows his way around. He marches along a wide, well-worn path – sometimes paved and sometimes sandy – always keeping alongside the Rhine.

Even at this time of morning, the Port of Mainz is bustling with noise and activity, with merchants, coachmen and sailors busy at work. Simon slowly brushes past the big and small ships that are docked along the quay. After a few minutes, he notices a two-masted schooner flying the Dutch flag at its stern. The ship is being loaded with wooden barrels, which are being lowered into its hold with the help of a sturdy crane. Two older men are standing by the hatchway and observing the freight as it enters.

Simon calls out in their direction, "Good morning! May I come on board?"

"Yes, as long as you're not a tax collector!" shouts the older, grey-haired man, and both men burst into fits of laughter.

As Simon carefully crosses the gangplank, he keeps an eye on the crane and the barrels, which are suspended from thick ropes that are grating along their pulleys.

"Well, my boy, what can we do for you, then?" asks the grey-haired man with a slight accent.

"I'd like to go to Rotterdam, I mean, ultimately London, but Rotterdam would get me off to a good start. I thought that perhaps you might need an assistant sailor who can help you out on the way."

"You mean you'll work on board, in exchange for us taking you along? Well, we are sailing to Rotterdam." The older of the two men, who looks like he's probably the captain, throws a questioning glance at the sailor standing beside him. "What do you think, Matthias, could we use another sailor to help us out?"

"It depends on what kind of sailor he is. Can he pull his weight?"

"I can work hard," declares Simon firmly. "My name is Simon Braun, I'm seventeen years old and I come from here – from Mainz. I have to go to London."

The captain looks Simon up and down. "Good, son, we'll take you. You'll work on board with us and if you really can pull your weight, then you'll also receive a few guilders' pay in Rotterdam. Is that a fair deal?"

"Yes, thank you!" Simon smiles at the two men.

"This is Matthias, my first mate, I'm the captain – my name is Friedrich – and Jesse and Daan work below deck. Matthias will show you your bunk now."

A few minutes later, Simon is back on deck and watches as the next barrels disappear into the ship's hold.

"Simon, you can climb down the rope ladder and help Jesse and Daan to stow the barrels in the cargo hold!" shouts Captain Friedrich.

"Yes Sir, Captain!" Quick as a flash, Simon has already climbed down the ladder.

Two sweat-covered faces greet Simon inquisitively.

"Good morning! I'm Simon, the new helping hand on board."

"Good day, I'm Jesse and this is Daan. Lucky we have a new deck hand. We wore the last one out so much that he had to be carried off board!" Not only Jesse and Daan, but also Captain Friedrich and Matthias up on the deck roar with laughter.

Daan gives Simon a tap on the shoulder. "No harm intended. Jesse is just a joker. Now get to it. The barrels are heavy. And watch your feet: you can say goodbye to them if a barrel rolls over them!"

As the sun rises, all the barrels are stowed on board and the five men have truly earned their breakfast break.

"Men, we set sail in half an hour! Daan and Jesse, you show Simon what he has to do. Matthias, you take the helm."

At around midday, Balthasar Braun rushes up the front steps of his house with long, quick strides. A few seconds later, he is standing next to Josephine-Christine in the drawing room.

"He's gone, Balthasar! Simon has left. He's not coming back!" Tears roll down Josephine's cheeks. Fear is written all over her pretty face.

"Now let's take it one step at a time," Balthasar says, attempting to calm his wife down. "Simon is often away. Isn't it likely he is hanging about in a neighbour's cellar, or visiting Jan ter Bruggen?"

"No. Mr. Vonecken told me that Simon didn't turn up for his lessons this morning … Christoph and Josephine haven't seen him either. I went to his room and found this card. Balthasar, he's not coming back – our Simon is gone!" Balthasar notices his wife's despair. He takes the card out of her trembling hands and reads:

Dear Mum and Dad,

You mustn't worry, but when you read this, I'll already be on my way. I love you all very much, but there comes a time when each of us must take his life into his own hands. My time has now come.

My first stop is London. I will visit Grandpa and all the others there and will pass on your regards.

Goodbye for now …

"Josephine, we have to settle down now and work out what we want to do."

"I know exactly what we should do. You have to ride off at once and bring me my baby back!" Josephine looks resolutely into Balthasar's eyes.

"Please sit down next to me here on the chaise longue for a moment." Balthasar puts his arm around Josephine and draws her close. "Now tell me, in which direction should I ride? To the coach station in Mainz or the port? Or did he perhaps go to Nierstein or Worms to board a ship?"

"I don't care where you go, Balthasar," retorts Josephine sobbing into her embroidered handkerchief. "How can you be so calm?"

Balthasar suddenly jumps up and rings for Rosi, who appears with a worried expression on her face.

"Rosi, please tell Joseph he should immediately saddle up Kasimir for me!"

"Yes, right away Mr. Braun!"

"So you want to search for him?" Josephine asks.

"I'll ride to Jan ter Bruggen's house. Perhaps he can tell us more than what we can decipher from this card."

Balthasar Braun takes the shortest route to Jan ter Bruggen's estate, through the vineyards. Will ter Bruggen know how Simon wants to get to London and what he plans to do afterwards? Will he react at all if Balthasar approaches him?

As he rides into the courtyard, Balthasar immediately spots Jan ter Bruggen, who with sleeves rolled up and brush in hand, is bent over a wooden vat.

"Excuse me, Mr. ter Bruggen, my name is Balthasar Braun."

"Good day Mr. Braun. I've been expecting you. You can tie your horse over there in the corner by the drinking trough. In the meantime, I'll bring us a wee bottle of wine and a couple of glasses."

Expecting? Why did he expect me? He must know something!

Just as Balthasar has finished tethering Kasimir, Jan ter Bruggen returns and takes a seat on the teak bench in the courtyard. He offers Balthasar a glass of wine.

"Riesling, Mr. Braun. Here you go!"

"Thank you Mr. ter Bruggen. The fact of the matter is – our Simon is gone."

"I know. He had been speaking about his desire to seek his fortune in far-away places for some time now."

"Do you by any chance know how he plans to get to London?"

"By ship. He wanted to leave very early this morning to catch a ship to Rotterdam so that he can cross over to London from there."

"Very well, thank you. Then I'll be off again," says Balthasar before emptying his glass with one big gulp, and looking at it once more before adding, "A superbly tangy Riesling of outstanding quality!"

"Then wait a few moments and drink another drop with me. I hope you don't mind my asking, but are you of the opinion that you should go and fetch Simon?"

Why is he asking me such a question? Simon is our son!

"Yes of course! We are all worried and my wife is desperate."

"Is it about Simon or about you?"

"What do you mean, Simon or us?"

"Do you want to bring Simon back because it will benefit him or because it'll benefit you and your wife? You know, I've spent quite a lot of time with Simon over the past few years and I think it would be best for you to let him go. It's not that he is unhappy with his family. It's just that the world has become too small for him here. If you fetch him, you will have to lock him up and sooner or later you will lose your son. Don't worry. I'm convinced that Simon will forge his own path, and that one day you will be able to hold him in your arms once more. Then again, there's also Marala's wedding …"

Marala, the little Indian girl? What does Simon have to do with her? Our son seems to have discussed things with this ter Bruggen man that we know nothing about. He has obviously become a confidant for Simon.

"Mr. ter Bruggen, it is a little embarrassing for me to admit it, but Simon has spoken to you about matters that he hasn't told us …"

"But Mr. Braun, you shouldn't be embarrassed about that. I'm just an old man pursuing my favourite pastime of winemaking. I have a lot of stories to tell because I've seen a fair bit of the world. And that's how Simon and I have become friends over the past few years."

"Matthias, I'll take the helm," says Captain Friedrich, stepping up to the big ship's wheel. "There are dangerous currents here by the Loreley."

"Captain Friedrich," yells Daan, "look at that barge over there! It's on the wrong course. It's heading straight into the rapids!"

Slowly but surely, the barge is heading toward the rocks. "Come here boys! You, too, Simon. If that ship up ahead doesn't pull into midstream soon, it'll be forced onto the cliffs by the current. The whole barge will be torn apart," declares Captain Friedrich.

At that moment, Simon notices a faint murmur. "What's that sound?"

"Those are the elves chirping to attract seamen," offers Matthias.

"Simon, don't let him fool you. The chirping is a sound caused by the currents here," explains Captain Friedrich. "The story about the elves is just sailor twaddle. There are often accidents on this part of the Rhine. But now pay attention: we only have one chance to save the barge. We have sails, which make our schooner faster. That means we can catch up with the barge and come right up beside it. One of us has to then jump across onto it with a rope and tie our two vessels together. We can then tow the barge back into centre stream."

"No, I don't want any part in it!" blurts out Matthias on impulse. "I'm too old for such experiments!"

With fear in his eyes, Jesse declares, "Daan and I can't swim. It's much too risky for us!"

"I'll do it," says Simon calmly. "We have to save them; we can't just sail behind them, waiting to see what happens."

Sure enough, the Dutch schooner is soon right behind the adrift barge, which is steadily heading straight toward the rapids. Simon is standing on the starboard side of the sailing ship with Matthias and Jesse with a thick, heavy rope in his hand, which is tied to the ship's stern at the rear. Captain Friedrich is steering the schooner, with its two masts and two gigantic gaff sails close beside the little barge. The ships are now rising and falling more and more forcefully. The currents are already noticeable.

When the schooner is at about the same height as the barge, Simon clambers onto the railing and takes a massive leap, landing pretty roughly on the barge while still firmly clutching the rope in one hand. A sharp pain shoots through his right shoulder, which he has just bumped into the hatch, but Simon has no time to think about that right now. He jumps up and runs forward as fast as he can, toward the ship's bow. Once there, he ties the thick rope to the bollard that is used to moor the barge in the docks. Captain Friedrich turns the steering wheel and the schooner is towed toward the centre of the river. Simon watches as the thick rope begins to tighten. "I hope it doesn't tear," he thinks to himself. Simon runs toward the helm stand. "Steer toward the port side, otherwise you'll end up in the currents and your barge will crash into the rocks!"

Startled, the helmsman springs up from a crate and stares at Simon, opening his glazed-over eyes wide. "Where did you come from?"

"From the schooner up ahead. I jumped on board. We want to help you. Come on, now to larboard!"

"I must have fallen asleep," yawns the helmsman as he moves the rudder.

The barge suddenly lurches and then it slowly rolls toward the port side. A wave of relief washes over Simon. "It's working!"

At the next bend in the Rhine, at Sankt Goarshausen, the Dutch schooner is moored to a jetty so that Simon can get back on board and they can untie the rope. The barge is steered portside to come up beside the schooner and be moored there. Simon leaps off the railing and back onto the schooner, where he is greeted warmly by Daan and Jesse. He is gripping his right shoulder. "Well done, boy! That was a great feat."

"Simon, what's wrong?" Captain Friedrich eyes the young man quizzically.

"My shoulder hurts. I bumped into something when I jumped across onto the barge."

"Let me have a look." The captain pulls Simon's shirt down around his right shoulder to take a look at the bruise. "That's a fine mark, but it won't kill you. It'll be gone in a couple of days. You have my respect, Simon – you fit in well!"

"Let's drink to that with a couple of beers tonight, Captain!" remarks Daan grinning at everyone.

I was now on my way, I had made a start – I knew this was the beginning of a new phase in my life. It was of course difficult to leave, but a decision had to be made. Deciding means choosing one way or the other – certainly not both. And once you have made a decision, you have to stand by it, always looking ahead to the future.

3. Drunk for the first time

No sooner has the schooner been tied to the quay wall in Koblenz when Jesse and Daan are already waiting impatiently on the quarterdeck. They are ready to go ashore. But Captain Friedrich, Matthias and Simon take their time.

"Hey!" calls Jesse in the direction of the cabins below. "Are you nearly finished? Daan and I want to get going – we're hungry and thirsty!"

"Yeah, yeah," comes the booming response from below.

A moment later, Simon bounds onto the deck, followed by the two others.

"Finally! I could eat a horse," sighs Daan.

They set off through the narrow alleyways of Koblenz, Daan and Jesse in front and the others behind them.

"There's a good tavern up there on the corner where they serve delicious roast pork," suggests Jesse. "What do you think?"

"Good, let's go," agrees Matthias after receiving the nod from Captain Friedrich and Simon.

Simon is the last to enter the rustic pub, and he is struck by the formidable noise inside. As he squeezes his way through the space between the densely occupied tables, he remembers that he has been to Koblenz once before – when he was on his way to London with his father. Back then they stopped for a bite to eat at the inn called 'Zum vollen Fass'.

Jesse and Daan have found a free table in an alcove. "What will it be, gentlemen?" A slim young lady is standing before them expectantly.

"A large beer and roast pork and potatoes for everyone," orders Captain Friedrich.

Shortly afterwards, five big beer steins are placed in front of the men.

"Cheers men," says Captain Friedrich. "To Simon and the successful rescue operation on the Rhine!"

"Ah! That went down well and it's so nice and cold! We could do with another round," says Jesse.

"Why do you all speak German so well – you're Dutch, aren't you?" Simon wants to know.

Captain Friedrich grins in amusement. "Well, I've been sailing up and down the Rhine for a good thirty years, so you'd think I would have picked it up by now. Daan and Jesse come from the border region and pretty much grew up speaking both languages. And Matthias speaks German because … Well, you tell me."

"He is German, right?"

"Right!" they all sing out in chorus and raise their beer mugs again.

After a hard day's work, the roast pork tastes splendid. But when a few more rounds of beer have flowed down their dry throats, Captain Friedrich decides, "I think we old folk will have to call it a night. What do you reckon, Matthias?"

"Yes, Captain. We just can't match the youngsters' energy anymore."

When the blonde waitress next approaches their table, the captain picks up the tab and orders another round for the three 'young sailors'. He and Matthias then get up and leave.

Jesse looks at Simon mischievously. "So, Simon, what do you think of the blonde?"

"She's pretty. Why do you ask?"

"Spiffing wench – I could get to like her!" interrupts Daan.

Simon is embarrassed and doesn't know what to say.

When the waitress returns to their table with the next round of drinks, Jesse grabs her by the waist and pulls her onto his lap.

"Hey lass, how about you and me get together?"

"Why not? You're a strapping lad. But you'll have to wait your turn."

"What do you mean about 'my turn'?"

"Well just take a look around the pub. There are another twenty-one blokes in line before you tonight!"

Jesse and Daan laugh out loud as the waitress releases herself and goes straight back to the bar. Only Simon is unsure whether he should laugh.

"Blimey, Daan, she not only looks great, she also has a quick tongue on her!" notes Jesse.

When the next round comes, Jesse spanks the waitress once.

"Hey, who said you could do that?" she snaps at him. "If you still want a chance tonight, you'll have to behave yourself better than that!"

Jesse's eyes widen. "Daan, did you hear that? She wants me tonight. It's my turn again tonight."

"I bet it's not," scoffs Daan.

"But you heard what she said. She'll let me get into her tonight!"

"Jesse, hold your horses. That was just a manner of speaking."

Daan looks at Simon. "Tell us what you think!"

"What exactly are you talking about? What does 'get into her' mean?"

"Have it off," blurts out Jesse. "Don't you know what having it off is?"

"Sure I do," answers Simon hastily. Christoph explained it to me in detail.

"But you haven't done it yet, right?" asks Daan.

How should he answer? For some reason, this is all very embarrassing for Simon. "Yes," is his eventual, rather sheepish reply.

"What do you mean, 'yes'? Have you or have you not had it off with someone?" Jesse wants to know.

"No, I haven't done it yet."

"So you're still a virgin. Oh, well, we were all virgins once," chuckles Daan. "Shall we help you amend the situation?"

"But not with that blonde – she's mine!" interjects Jesse.

"No, no, I don't need your help."

"Then let's order another round of beer!"

"The beer is gradually going to my head," points out Simon. But he doesn't want to reveal yet another weakness right now.

When the pretty waitress brings the next round, she's sitting on Jesse's thigh before she has the chance to put the beers down. Brash Jesse plunges his right hand into her cleavage and runs his index finger over her breast.

"Hey!" she wards him off. "Like I said before, It's not your turn yet. I would have turned a blind eye, if only you had placed a guilder or two between those impetuous fingers of yours. Why do you think the dear Lord put a slot there? But you won't get anywhere the way you're going …"

"Give it up, Jesse," laughs Daan. "You're no match for her."

Two or three rounds later, Jesse and Daan are also starting to show signs that the jolly beer is taking effect.

Crash! Simon's head slams down onto the table. Befuddled, he instantly heaves it up again. At that moment, the pretty waitress comes over. "So, boys, I think the little one can call it a night. You should get going." She puts a hand on Jesse's shoulder. "And we can continue our conversation next time. In case you wanted to know, you made it from number twenty-one to number eleven." She says this with a defiant grin.

Daan pays the bill. Then the two sailors prop Simon up between them and they all leave the tavern.

"Simon, wake up! The sun is already high in the sky!" The yelling sounds muffled in Simon's ears. His mouth is completely dry, he's thirsty and he has a strange, stale taste in his mouth. Simon opens his eyes. He's lying in his bunk. What happened? They had gone to get a bite to eat and a drop to drink; at some point only the three of them were left; they had lots of fun and drank much too much beer. And then – Simon can't remember any-more. What happened? He tries to get up, managing only to raise his head before sinking back into the bunk. It's as if someone came and fitted a solid wooden beam above his bunk in the night. And now he's just bumped against it, because a sharp pain shoots through his head.

"Simon, come on and get up, will you?" Someone's shout from the deck penetrates into the hold.

Somehow he manages to force himself up and climb onto deck. Matthias is the first one he comes across. "Gosh, what a sight! They really got you pickled!"

Daan and Jesse are chuckling away while working on the other side of the ship. Captain Friedrich is standing at the helm. It's clear to Simon that he owes an apology.

"Reporting aboard, Captain."

"That was your first bender, was it Simon?"

"Yes, and it'll be my last."

"That's what you say now, but just wait and see. Find a spot to sit on the deck and let the fresh wind blow into your face. Then you'll be all right again. You're of no use to us in your current state."

"Thanks Captain," mumbles Simon, and he feels like his head is about to explode.

"Tell me, Daan, how did I get on board?"

"Can't you remember anything?"

"No. Jesse was talking to the waitress and all of a sudden, my eyes closed."

"That's what happens when you don't know how to drink!"

Simon is sitting on the deck, lost in thought and watching the picturesque vineyards in the Middle Rhine Valley pass him by. "It's pretty steep," he thinks to himself. "It must be very arduous to work there."

But his thoughts drift further along the Rhine, over the North Sea and all the way to London. Marala! What will it be like to see her again? Will her parents even let him see her? How will she react when she sees him? Will she be happy? What should he tell her?

At noon, Simon's stomach begins to settle down and his headache recedes considerably. At lunch he is already able to eat something and in the afternoon he gets back to work.

Never again will I drink too much, Simon decides. Never.

Late in the evening, they dock the schooner in Cologne and all walk into town together like they did last night. But for Simon, both beer and wine are out of the question tonight.

Josephine-Christine has been in a daze, walking in and out of each of the rooms in the Brauns' villa all day. She can't concentrate on anything; she's always thinking about her youngest. Late in the afternoon, Balthasar comes to tea in the drawing room.

He looks at Josephine dolefully. "What are we going to do now, darling?"

"My dear, after having spoken to Jan ter Bruggen yesterday, I spent quite some time discussing the matter with Rudolf Vonecken today, and have come to the conclusion that we should let Simon go."

"But yesterday we decided that you were going to travel to London as fast as possible to bring him back! Are you turning against me now?!"

68

"No Josephine, I'm on your side. But in our current situation, we have to think long and hard about what to do next. The first solution isn't always the best one."

"But Simon is my son – I want him back! He is still so young!"

"You know, yesterday, Jan ter Bruggen asked me whether we want Simon back for his sake or for our own. I've been thinking about that question ever since and I discussed it with Rudolf Vonecken today."

"And what did he say?"

"Vonecken is of the opinion that we should let Simon go. The boy is so independent and extroverted that we would otherwise have to lock him up from now on. Josephine, we can't stop time and we certainly can't turn the clock back. We'll just have to accept it!"

Tears roll down Josephine's cheeks. "My Simon! But what can we do? What's the right thing to do?"

"I think we should write a letter to your parents letting them know what Simon's plans are and telling them that we are not opposed to them. They have to support whatever he is planning to do."

"I can't do that, Balthasar. I think I'm going mad!"

Balthasar takes his wife in his arms and presses her firmly against his chest. "I know. I feel the same way. But haven't we always done our utmost to ensure that our children are raised into well-educated, confident and independent adults? God will be by his side!"

Over the next few days, Simon works aboard the schooner like an old sea dog. He helps set the sails and haul them in again, scrubs the deck and even polishes the ship's metal parts until they gleam. In his free time, he sits on the deck, watching the changing landscape on the left and right banks of the Rhine. The steep mountains in the Middle Rhine region are followed by the flat area around the Lower Rhine. In this fashion, they sail past Dormagen, Düsseldorf, Duisburg and Xanten, before arriving in the ancient Roman city of Nijmegen in the Netherlands. Here, on the southern branch of the Rhine, the River Waal, Simon catches a glimpse of the majestic Valkhof citadel.

So I, the son of a winemaker, got really drunk for the first time in my life by drinking beer in Koblenz. When in rambunctious, cheery company, one loses track of the amount one has consumed. The lesson? Drink less! It took a lot more attempts and a long time before I had a sense of what the 'right amount' was. But the most important lesson was: never drink so much so as not to know what is happening at all times. I understood that straight away and it never happened to me again.

4. In Rotterdam Harbour

S imon!" shouts Captain Friedrich from the ship's wheel. "Jump on the quay wall and tie the rope to the bollard in front of you! Daan, you jump astern!"

"Yes, Captain!" they chime in unison.

A short time later, the schooner is docked by the quay wall in the port of Rotterdam. Along with Jesse and Daan, Simon slides open the heavy hatch, exposing the view of the neatly tied-down barrels inside.

After Captain Friedrich returns from his leave ashore, a monstrous wooden crane swings over the ship and the three young sailors disappear inside the schooner's hold. A net made from thick ropes is let down from the crane.

"Jesse, you untie the ropes securing the barrels while Simon and I roll the barrels into the net," decides Daan.

Matthias is standing up above by the hatchway, passing on the orders to the crane operator to raise the crane each time Simon and Daan have rolled two barrels onto the net lying flat on the floor. The first mate gives the thumbs up with his right hand and then the crane workers lift the barrels using gigantic pulleys, bringing them out of the hold and onto the quay wall. From there they are rolled into a tall, wooden warehouse.

The barrels are unshipped for hours on end. Simon and Daan have taken off their shirts – their bodies are glistening with sweat. Every now and then, they stop for a large gulp of refreshing water from the ladle in the water bucket.

"Simon, for someone from the 'high society', you sure can muck in!" remarks Jesse and grins in appreciation.

"What did you say, Jesse? I didn't understand."

"You're all right … for a toff," yells Daan, as he watches the last of the barrels sway through the hatch.

In the evening, the crew celebrates Simon's going away at an inn.

"At what time does your ship leave for London tomorrow?" Friedrich wants to know.

"At nine o'clock on the dot."

"You can sleep in your bunk tonight then. We don't want you to get lost tonight, do we?" says Friedrich with a smile.

"We'll take Simon under our wing," declares Daan. "What do you reckon, Jesse?"

"We'll look after him, Daan!"

70

"Do you already know where we're going then?"

"Of course! We know our way around Rotterdam," Daan reassures Simon.

Jesse grins mischievously to himself.

"Simon, we'll see you in the morning." Captain Friedrich and Matthias bid farewell in front of the inn before turning to walk toward the port.

Once they are out of earshot, Jesse says, "So, let's go!"

"Where are we going now?"

"The 'Tall Anna', a cosy pub a couple of streets away," answers Daan.

"But I won't drink as much as you, all right?"

"You don't have to be in on every round, Simon," says Jesse. "Besides, you won't have time for that!"

Simon doesn't get it. As they turn the next street corner, he immediately notices the imposing 'Tall Anna' billboard. It must be over three metres tall. On it is a picture of a tall, slim woman with dark hair, who is raising her ankle-length skirt on one side, revealing an infinitely long, completely naked leg. Her blouse reveals more than it covers. A strange, expectant smile is painted on her face. From top to bottom on the woman's right side, in large, hand-painted letters are the words, 'Tall Anna'.

Before Simon can think about it further, Jesse and Daan have already taken him into the pub and claimed a free table in the centre. Simon is amazed. He feels like he's in a robbers' den. Men and women are crowded close together, while pretty waitresses push their way through the rows to serve drinks. Simon immediately notices that they are all dressed in the same way as the 'Tall Anna' pictured outside: in long skirts and low-cut blouses that leave the shoulders bare. There's a small stage in the centre of the pub, on which a lady is dancing.

"What will it be, sweetness?" the deep voice of a woman tears Simon away from his thoughts. At the same time, Jesse pokes him in the arm. "Beer, Simon, do you want a beer?"

"Yes, I'll take one."

Jesse and Daan are whispering to each other, but Simon's eyes are again wandering around the tavern. The women who are sitting at the tables next to the men have gaudy hairstyles and make-up. It's clear to Simon that they are not their wives.

A large man is sitting behind them in an alcove on the right with one of the ladies on his lap, and he is unashamedly touching her breasts. Both of them are laughing. It seems like everyone is happy here, and a jolly cheerful atmosphere prevails. On the left, not three tables away, a couple is having an animated conversation – sometimes loudly and sometimes very quietly. Each time the man whispers something to her, the woman laughs effusively and somewhat artificially, thinks Simon. She has pulled up her skirt so high with her left hand, that Simon can see her knee and even part of her bare thigh. Then Simon's eyes almost pop out of their sockets as he watches the man put his right hand on the woman's thigh before sliding it out of sight under her skirt. The woman leans forward and bites the man's earlobe gently.

"Cheers, Simon!"

"What? What is it?" Simon jumps with a start.

Daan slaps him on the shoulder with his left hand. "Cheers, Simon. Be careful they don't bewitch you!"

Simon raises his glass to his lips and takes a big swig of beer.

"This is where it's all happening, Simon!" declares Jesse with a twinkle in his eye. "Smashing girls, cracking atmosphere, don't you think?!"

"I've never seen anything like it."

When Simon turns his gaze back toward the pair two tables away, the woman puts an arm around the man's neck and whispers something to him. They both get up from the table, the man puts his right arm around his escort's waist and the two of them disappear through a door at the other end of the pub.

The waitress brings the next round of beer for Jesse and Daan.

"I have to go. Where's the ...?" asks Simon now. Jesse points at the door at the other end of the pub – the one which the couple just went through. Simon heads off and finds himself in a wide corridor with numbered doors on both sides. Which way should he go? He decides to go down the hall, which winds around a few corners, until he finds what he is looking for. Only on the way back does Simon realise that there are voices coming from behind some of the doors, and sometimes groans. "Humph ...," he thinks to himself, "are they revelling or working in those rooms?"

At one point one of the doors opens slowly and a young waitress with an impish smile edges through the gap between the door and the door-frame. Simon hears the sound of a man's loud groans. Curious, he looks past the waitress into the room. There is a large bed in the middle on which the couple Simon had seen in the public bar earlier is lying. The woman is lying on her back with her legs splay and the man is between her legs, his head pressed against her shoulder while he is hard at work – or at least that's what it sounds like. The lady looks straight at Simon and smiles. That's when he realises he is staring at her and is standing as if bolted to the floor. The door slowly clicks shut and the young waitress remarks with a suggestive smile, "So, young man, do you want a turn, too?" And with that, she turns on her heel and returns to the public bar. Simon doesn't know what to say and just follows her silently. Back at the table, Jesse and Daan stare at him. "What's with you?"

72

"Oh, nothing!" To distract them, Simon asks, "What's been happening here?" and takes a big gulp from his beer stein.

"You missed a dance on stage. The lady was wearing a skirt with an outrageous split in it," whispers Jesse to him.

The generally rowdy atmosphere promptly influences Simon and he starts to chat excitedly with Jesse and Daan while they watch the performance on stage. Out of the corner of his eye, Simon sees the couple from earlier on return to the public bar. Just before they sit down at their table, the lady scans the room and her gaze stops when she lays eyes on Simon. She whispers something into the ear of the man beside her, who then sits down without a word. Seconds later, the lady is standing before Simon and smiling at him suggestively. He wants to get up, but is pushed back down gently. The lady sits down on the empty chair next to Simon, leans toward him, places her hand on the back of his neck and abruptly kisses him on the mouth. It's as if a lightning bolt has shot through Simon's body. He's nervous and can feel the tiny hairs on the back of his neck stand up on end. He can feel the woman's soft, full lips on his own. Simon is so perplexed that he's transfixed. But then a warm, pleasurable feeling slowly runs through his entire body.

Jesse can't believe his eyes. "What's going on?" Daan shrugs his shoulders.

"He just sits there and – oops – along comes a tantalising beauty and kisses him?! She's kissing Simon on the mouth, Daan!"

"I can see that!"

"Yesterday I tried everything to get close to a woman once again. I heaped compliments onto her – and what happened, Daan? Nothing!"

"But you made up some leeway, Jesse."

"Poppycock! Look, she's still kissing him!"

The lady unlocks her lips from Simon's and looks deep into his eyes. "You're a real sweetie. What's your name then?"

"Simon."

"Simon, dearie, won't you come next door with me? We could have lots of fun together."

"Um … I don't know …"

"Simon, love, for a couple of guilders I'll give you heaven on earth!"

"Oh no, I don't think so. I don't have that many guilders!" Simon now feels very warm. There is most likely sweat on his brow and the palms of his hands are certainly very moist.

"What a pity, Simon. I think you'd be able to get me off once more, strapping young lad that you are."

The lady strokes Simon gently on the cheek and is about to get up when Jesse grabs her by the wrist.

"I … I'll come with you. I'm better at it than Simon anyway. He's still a virgin!"

"That's exactly what's so alluring. Besides, Simon is also a gentleman. I notice such things."

"But unlike him, I'm willing. And I also have money. How much?" Jesse tightens his grip around the woman's wrist with his coarse fingers.

"Ow! But I don't want to go with you. Now let go of me!" Her smile has disappeared and fine wrinkles have appeared on the woman's forehead.

"Let her go, Jesse," warns Daan sternly.

"No! I want to pay her. It is a transaction after all!" Jesse throws the woman a challenging glance. "Why don't you want to do business? Come off it! My money is worth just as much as anyone else's." Jesse's voice is getting louder.

"I – DON'T – WANT – TO!" screams the woman back in his face.

Her burly companion at the next table jumps up and is there in a fraction of a second. He punches Jesse's chin hard, making him fall backwards onto the chair of another customer, who immediately springs up and hits Jesse, too. Daan grabs his mate and pulls him to safety.

"Simon, pay the bill at the bar and I'll take Jesse and leave. Otherwise we'll go to the dogs!"

A few minutes later, Simon and Daan are guiding a staggering Jesse toward the port.

"That was lucky!" says Daan. "That could have been ugly."

"Especially for Jesse. If they'd really put him through the wringer, we would have had to carry him back on board in pieces."

Jesse opens his bleary eyes. "Man, my head is pounding! I could have finished one of them – but two at the same time is a bit much."

Daan and Simon grin to themselves and Daan reassures Jesse, "You would have won if you were sober."

I was actually very tired from the heavy work I had done. It wouldn't have taken much more beer to make me fall asleep standing up. But what I experienced really stirred me up – excited me on the one hand and unnerved me on the other. Now and then I kept imagining I could see Marala before me. Hopefully I'll see her soon!

5. Reunion in London

The two-master that is taking Simon to London has been sailing along the Thames for hours now. The water is calm; the weather is sunny and warm, as it has been during the entire trip. Simon is sitting at the ship's bow with his legs dangling over the edge. The countryside is sweeping past him, as if it were a theatre backdrop being constantly drawn by a cord. Now and then, smaller and larger towns pop up along the river banks – some of which Simon still remembers.

The same thoughts and questions keep racing around his mind. Marala – what will their next encounter be like? How will she react when he confronts her? Should he visit her as soon as he arrives in London – or should he go to his grandparents' house first? How will Marala have changed? What does she look like now? And will he be able to convince her not to marry the other man, but to instead go with him to America? Simon pushes these thoughts away and instead attempts to concentrate on his surroundings. There's no use in wearing down his mind with all these maybes. It would be best to just wait and see what happens.

"Southend-on-Sea, Canvey Island, Gravesend, Grays, Greenwich, and finally into the Surrey Docks: sailing into London can be so boring," someone with a deep voice says to Simon. "Have you been to London before?"

Simon turns around. A well-dressed, middle-aged gentleman is standing beside him.

"Yes. I went there for the first time a few years ago, when I was twelve."

"And how old are you now?"

"I'm seventeen." Simon sizes up the gentleman beside him: pale face, dark hair, moustache, slim figure, nicely tailored suit.

"Are you travelling with your parents? I may address you informally, may I not?"

"Of course, but I'm travelling alone."

"What do you mean, alone? You're travelling to London alone at seventeen? Where do you come from?"

"I come from Mainz."

"Pardon me. I haven't even introduced myself. My name is Rickmann and I'm on my way to London on business. You haven't run away from home, have you?"

"I'm going to visit a friend in London … and my relatives. My name is Simon Braun, by the way."

"I see. And I thought …"

"Everything is in order. This afternoon I'll be at my grandparents' house in James Street," professes Simon in a firm tone. I wonder what Mum and Dad are doing right now? Are they worried?

"Look over there, Simon – you can see the first signs of London now. It won't be much longer before we reach our destination."

"Careful on the gangway, please. Be careful!" A sailor with a loud, calm voice ensures that the passengers and their luggage reach the pier safe and sound. Most of them look as if they want to be the first ones to stand on dry land once more. Simon waits until the rush is over. As he crosses the gangway, he sees Mr. Rickmann waving at him from his position next to a cab.

"Simon! Over here!"

Simon waves back.

"Even though James Street is not exactly in my direction, you're welcome to come with me," says Rickmann, as Simon walks over.

"James Street is near Covent Garden," answers Simon.

Rickmann gives the cab driver a quizzical look.

"That's almost in the same direction," says he. "We can drop the young gentleman off at Covent Garden."

"Thank you, that's very kind of you, Mr. Rickmann!"

"My pleasure, Simon," says Rickmann, opening the cab door.

It's not long before Simon is standing in the Hill family wine and spirit shop on James Street. He watches as his Grandpa Simon advises an elderly customer on his range of Scottish malt whiskies while his Aunt Betty is recommending a white wine to a lady customer. Simon retains a very calm appearance, even though he's extremely tense on the inside. He has no idea how they will react. The lady finally leaves the shop with three bottles of Chablis in her basket.

"Simon, it's good to finally see you again!" Betty rushes over to Simon and gives him a big hug.

"Hello, Aunt Betty," is all that Simon can utter in astonishment.

Betty kisses Simon on the left and then on the right cheek.

"Aren't you surprised at all?" asks Simon, who is himself surprised. "Surely you haven't been expecting me?"

Grandpa Simon is now standing beside the two of them as the second customer shuts the shop door behind him, leaving with a bottle of Finest Rare Malt Whisky in his hand.

"Indeed, Simon," says Grandpa Simon, "We were told you were on your way." He puts an arm around his grandson's shoulder and continues, "Come

76

with us to the drawing room and we can calmly discuss everything over a cup of tea."

"Charles, you'll be alone in the shop now," calls Betty into the doorway of one of the back rooms. "I'm going to tea with Simon and Father!"

"Hello, Simon," comes the response from the invisible answerer.

On the way upstairs, inside the imposing red-brick house with its little tower, the three of them run into Grandma Mary. "Simon, thank God you've arrived in London in one piece!" By the time she has finished her sentence, she has already drawn her grandson into her arms.

At the drawing room tea table, Simon seems to be the only one who is puzzled. He thought that he would be the one to surprise them when he entered the shop.

"What's going on here? How could you have possibly known that I was coming to visit you?"

"We received a letter from your parents, Simon," replies his grandfather in a calm voice.

"And they told you to graciously welcome me and to not let me leave," retorts Simon abruptly.

"No, no, Simon," reassures his grandfather, "on the contrary. Your parents want us to look after you and to support you, since it's your intention to go to America. And you also wish to meet Marala before she gets married? Isn't that the little Indian girl who had brought you back home once upon a time?"

"Yes, but now I'm completely confused. How do my parents know that I want to meet Marala?"

"From a gentleman named Jan ter Bruggen. He helped your parents come to the decision not to stop you, but rather to let you go. And we are of the same opinion. Simon, you may stay here as long as you like. Your room is where you left it."

Simon notices the tears running down his cheeks. He is impressed by his parents' reaction. He had not counted on such nobleness of character from them.

"What do you think, Simon?" booms Grandpa Simon. "In the next few days you can let me know what exactly you would like to do and how we can assist you."

"I thank you all. For a start I'd like to visit Marala tomorrow …"

The tall block of flats on Jamaica Road is a staggering sight, its white window frames glowing in the already strong March sunshine. Simon stares at the front door. He feels hot, his palms are sweating and his heart is pounding like crazy. But he pulls himself together and enters the building, climbing the many stairs leading up to the correct flat. Simon swallows one last time before raising the heavy, iron door knocker and letting go so that it hammers against the door several times in quick succession. After what seems to be an eternity, the door opens slowly, and Harsha, Marala's mother, appears in the doorway. Simon recognises her straight away.

"Yes?" Harsha looks at the young man inquisitively.

"Hello, Harsha, good day."

"I know you ... Just a moment ... I've got it! You are the young man from Germany, Simon. Abhay found you by the Thames a few years ago after you had been beaten up."

"That's right – that's me. Please call me Simon."

Harsha laughs jovially, hugs Simon, takes him by the arm and leads him inside. "Come in and sit in the lounge room. I'll make us some tea."

Simon feels as if a great weight has been released from his shoulders. After such a friendly greeting, he feels much better. He is now sitting with Harsha at a low table – each of them on a thick mat, and is enjoying his first cup of tea.

"What a pity that Marala isn't home," says Harsha. "She would have been so happy to see you!"

"Isn't she?" Simon's bitter disappointment is so obviously written all over his face, that Harsha has to laugh despite herself.

"She'll be right back. She shan't be long. Tell me: what have you been doing for the past few years? And what brings you back to visit us?"

Simon starts explaining and is quickly absorbed by his stimulating conversation with Harsha, so that he doesn't even notice when the front door opens and shuts. But suddenly, there is a young woman standing in the lounge room. As if struck by lightning, Simon thinks: Marala! There she stands, looking breathtakingly beautiful in a pale-coloured sari that contrasts strikingly with her dark skin. Tall and trim, her thick, jet-black hair is tied back in a braid, and she has a gorgeously delicate complexion with the same fascinating brown eyes. Simon is upstanding in a flash.

"Simon!!!" Amazed, Marala loses grip of the bag she had just been holding, and it falls to the floor. "You're in London?" A beaming smile spreads across her face, making her look even lovelier. She then goes up to Simon and envelops him in her arms without hesitation. Simon can feel her pressed up against him but he falters for a moment before finally daring to put his arms around the young woman. And the resulting feeling is far from unpleasant. Simon is struck by her slim, firm figure in his arms. Harsha's voice jolts Simon and Marala back to reality. "Sit down, you two!"

Marala pours herself a cup of tea and asks, "How long are you staying in London, Simon?"

"A couple of days," he answers, carefully.

"Great, then we can do a few things together!" blurts out Marala.

"Marala, you know that the 7ᵗʰ June is your big day," interjects Harsha, slightly admonishingly.

"Yes, Mum, I know. How could I forget?"

Simon forces a smile. He is anxious. Should he pretend that he doesn't know anything about Marala's wedding plans? Does Harsha even know that he and Marala have been constantly writing to each other over the years?

Marala seems to have read his thoughts. "Simon, I'm to be married on June 7th."

"Oh – and to whom?"

"His name is Meghnad Kapur," remarks Harsha. "He is the gentleman for whom my husband works. He is very well-to-do and will look after Marala incredibly well. She will be living in the lap of luxury!" Harsha smiles with pride and joy.

Simon bites his tongue. He doesn't want to talk about this subject right now, especially not in front of Harsha. So he takes a sip of tea and then says, "Harsha, have I told you how wonderfully refreshing your tea is?"

But Marala interrupts them again. "What have you been doing since the last time we saw you?" She notes that Simon can successfully keep up a neutral and diplomatic appearance, and that he is choosing his words very carefully. He's grown tall, broad-shouldered and athletic, and he still has the same thick, full head of hair. Marala silently examines Simon from top to bottom. His facial features have become more pronounced, but that blue – the glistening blue of his eyes hasn't changed. Marala detects so much in his eyes at the same time: confidence, curiosity and willpower. In his presence, she feels absolutely comfortable and well understood.

Simon talks about Jan ter Bruggen, about his work in the vineyards, his siblings and his parents. Marala also tells of her life in London, her imminent wedding and her future husband … And they both have the same intense feeling that they would rather spend many hours alone discussing what's really on their minds. They feel drawn together like two strong magnets. If they had been alone, they would surely have physically touched one another without hesitation.

She is so beautiful, so gentle and so elegant. Simon is completely overwhelmed and Marala can sense it. At the same time, she is impressed by how well he can contain himself. They lose all sense of time, and it's only when Abhay comes through the door that the two youngsters realise how late it is.

"Simon, you're here in London?"

"Abhay, you recognised me immediately? I'm impressed!"

"I've never forgotten you, my boy. Let me take a look at you – you've grown tall and strong."

Despite the joy of their reunion, the time eventually comes for Simon to leave.

"Be careful on your way home," grins Abhay, "especially along the Thames!"

"I'll see you to the door!" Marala gets up and instinctively reaches out for Simon's hand. They leave the flat together and walk silently down the stairs. At the bottom, Simon pauses shortly in determination and turns to face Marala. His heart is in his mouth as he gently cups her face in his hands and then just as gingerly kisses her. He can feel Marala's lips responding, and she then wraps her arms around his neck and presses her mouth more firmly against his. Simon closes his eyes and lets his thoughts wander, lost in another world. He could stay here for hours, but Marala gently pulls away from him. "I have to go back upstairs."

Simon continues to hold Marala tightly in his arms. "Will I see you tomorrow?"

"Yes, tomorrow at around twelve on our bridge!" She then pulls away completely and turns toward the staircase.

"I'm looking forward to it!"

Simon is overjoyed on the way back to James Street. The walk gives him time to sort out his thoughts and feelings.

His family is sitting at the drawing room table sharing a bottle of wine.

"Simon, sit down and have a glass of wine with us," calls Uncle Charles.

"What are you drinking, then?" asks Simon, looking around at everyone's faces.

"You have to try it and tell us." Charles places a wine glass in front of Simon and his cousin, Janet, pours his wine.

Simon picks up the glass, holds it up to the light, and concludes, "Bright garnet red in colour, with medium intensity." He then holds the glass cautiously up to his nose and deliberately takes in the aroma from the wine goblet, before swishing the wine around the glass and sniffing at it again. "The fragrance reminds me of strawberries and cherries, with a hint of toasty notes." Simon takes a sip and lets it roll over his tongue before moving it around his mouth, all the while sucking in some air. "Medium-bodied, soft, round tannins, and the taste of strawberry and cherry; extract, acids, woodiness and alcohol are very well balanced."

"Now," asks Charles impatiently, "what kind of wine is it?"

"I once tasted such a wine at Jan ter Bruggen's house. It was a Pinot Noir. But this wine is not typical in Germany. I also drank such a wine with

80

Grandfather last time I was here, and it was from Burgundy. So I would say it's a Pinot Noir from Burgundy, from a Premier cru vineyard, because the wine tastes very concentrated and intense."

"Well done, Simon. That's exactly right. It's an 1812 Pinot Noir, from the premier-cru field called 'Clos du Chapitre' in Gevrey-Chambertin."

Elisabeth and Janet are just flabbergasted. "How did you recognise it? How can you remember all the different wines?"

"I don't know." Simon shrugs his shoulders.

"I keep telling you, you have to taste lots of different wines and try to remember them all!" exclaims Grandpa Simon.

"Tomorrow is another day," concludes Grandma Mary. "That's enough for today!"

I was now back in London. This time on my own – which made me proud of myself. I was very happy about the positive reception from my family, but also from the Roshans. I had been simply bowled over by Marala's good looks, and if I hadn't already had butterflies in my stomach before, they definitely would have started by now ... I was so, very arrested! I had suddenly regained my courage and confidence with regard to Marala. Maybe she really would like to go with me to America! Jan ter Bruggen may have told me not to get my hopes up. But after that kiss ...?!

6. Lovesickness and a ticket to America

Simon is up early. After breakfast, he visits Grandpa Simon in the Hills' wine and spirit shop. Today, his grandfather is introducing him to the world of fortified wines: Port, Sherry, Madeira, Pineau des Charentes, Floc de Gascogne ... They talk about vineyards, grape varieties, various styles and notable producers. Every now and then, Simon casts an eye on the huge grandfather clock: 10:10, 10:22, 10:29, 10:32 ...

"Fino sherry and Manzanilla are both the colour of straw," explains his grandfather. "It matures in wooden barrels under a layer of yeast known as flor. That layer protects the wine against oxidation. There is no flor layer over Oloroso or Cream Sherry, allowing the wine to come into contact with oxygen, which gives it its dark, amber colouring."

"And what about Amontillado Sherry?"

"The flor layer floating over Amontillado dies off. This sherry does indeed end up being amber in colour, however not as dark and intense. And it tastes lighter and finer than Oloroso or Cream."

Simon's gaze falls on the clock again and it is now 11:38.

"Grandpa, I have to go now. We can talk further this evening!"

"Simon …" Simon Hill is speechless, but he refrains from commenting. He can imagine where Simon would like to go. "Be careful!"

Simon bounds into the family home, grabs his jacket and is back on the street in no time at all.

He quickly strides towards Covent Garden, avoiding the crowd around the market stalls, and then searches for a way around all the hustle and bustle. He purposefully cuts through the little alleyways and reaches the bridge at almost exactly twelve o'clock. Simon's gaze sweeps across to the opposite bank of the Thames, where he spots her sitting: Marala is wearing a dark blue sari with a white sash. Simon starts to feel queasy. And the feeling is getting stronger and stronger the closer he gets to Marala. They are now facing each other. Marala smiles at Simon and he suddenly feels much lighter. They hug without hesitation, but when Simon attempts to kiss Marala, she turns her head to one side.

"Simon, this can't go on. We're not allowed to kiss. In a couple of weeks I will be married to another man."

"Marala …" Simon would like nothing more right now, than to list every argument as to why Marala should not marry a man who is so very much older than her, but he has already decided to tread very carefully on this subject with Marala.

She beams at him. "But it's wonderful that you're here! What shall we do today?"

"Let's go for a walk – over the bridge and then along the Thames, toward the Tower."

"Yes, the weather is very inviting!"

It's a beautiful, warm, spring day. The sun is shining over the river and is gently warming the backs of their necks.

"I'm walking beside the prettiest, most sincere and agreeable woman in the whole world," thinks Simon.

Marala interrupts his thoughts. "Simon, I want to explain something to you. In our culture, it's normal for parents to marry off their children. My father owes a duty of thanks to Meghnad Kapur. And so they have agreed that I shall be given to him as a bride."

"But do you have any feelings for this man?"

"My mother says that my feelings will develop over time."

"Do you really believe that?"

"There is nothing I can do to change it. My father and Meghnad Kapur would both lose face otherwise. I must not and cannot let that happen!"

They slowly walk along the riverbank, enjoying their time together. Simon grabs Marala's hand, and she doesn't resist. Silently, they continue to walk along, hand in hand, for a while. Then Simon can't contain himself any longer – no matter how good his intentions may be. He stops walking and turns to face Marala before embracing her and kissing her soft lips. At first, he notices Marala's attempt to push him away, but she soon stops resisting.

"I love you," says Simon finally. "We belong together, Marala. Can't you see that?"

"No, Simon, it's out of the question."

"But I know you love me, too. You can't just ignore that!"

Marala strokes Simon's face with her gentle hands. "Simon, you mean a great deal to me. But I will nevertheless marry Meghnad Kapur. It can't be helped."

"But it can, Marala. You can come to America with me. We would be free to establish ourselves there and to start a new life together."

"No, it really won't do. And if I truly meant so much to you, then you would accept my decision."

"Of course I respect your decision – even if I see things much differently. But think about it, Marala – when you're twenty five, he will already be sixty!"

"I've already thought about it, Simon, and things will go ahead as planned."

Marala smiles at Simon reassuringly. "Let's walk on a little further."

Simon looks out over the Thames. He grasps at Marala's hand and they continue to stroll along the riverbank.

It now occurs to Marala that Simon mentioned the word 'America'. She had been so preoccupied with convincing Simon to accept her marriage, that she had not been paying attention earlier. "What about America?"

"I'm going to emigrate there."

"You mean, you won't be going back home?"

"No. I told you about it in my letter: Christoph is the eldest and is more interested in the winery than I am. Sooner or later, I would have had to find something else to do anyway."

"And your parents …? Do they know about your plans?"

"Yes, my parents and grandparents know about my plans. But they're not exactly rapt about them!"

"Aren't you much too young to migrate? And besides, it's probably very dangerous; you don't know a soul there and you don't know what awaits you!"

"Don't worry about me. I'll manage."

Simon looks at Marala and is shocked to see tears rolling down her cheeks. He freezes. How should he console her? "You're right, Marala. I don't know what to expect. But I think I know what you should expect, and I'm much more afraid of that."

With his fingertips, he carefully wipes the tears away from her cheeks. "But whatever happens, you can always reach me via my parents in Germany or my grandparents here in London. You know it's the Hill family on James Street. I've promised to write to them about where I'll be staying and what I'll be doing."

"Does this mean we'll never see each other again?"

"Why do you say that?"

"You sound as if you're ready to leave tomorrow."

"I'll be staying in London for a few days longer. First I need to find out when the next ship leaves for America. My grandfather will help me prepare."

That evening, Simon retires to his room early. He had been quiet, solemn and withdrawn, even at the dinner table. Elisabeth and Janet had attempted to encourage him to play cards after dinner, but Simon turned down the offer because he wouldn't have been able to concentrate. He is now lying in bed and thinking of Marala. When he closes his eyes he can see her before him – her beautiful face, her tender, soft skin and the unbelievable depth of her brown eyes. He knows that he has failed, and that she won't go to America with him. Marala is so impressively self-assured and so disciplined, and she's already made up her mind. Simon feels ill and his stomach is churning. There are tears in his eyes, but he has never really learnt how to cry. His thoughts are racing so much that he has a headache. Until now, he has always been able to find a solution to every problem, but there is no solution for this one. Marala will always remain unreachable – his true love won't be his. She will marry that old man.

Marala, too, is lying in bed in her parents' house and crying bitter tears into her brightly-coloured pillows. All the letters she has written to and received from Simon, and all their conversations prove that he understands her better than anyone else has ever understood her. And aside from that, he has turned out to be a tall, good-looking man. How she would love to drop everything and immigrate to America with Simon! But she couldn't do that

84

to her father and Meghnad Kapur. She wouldn't be able to live with the guilt.

Harsha has silently slipped into the room. "Marala, why are you crying?" she asks, worried, and sits on the edge of the bed.

"It's nothing!"

"Are you in pain? Did someone hurt you?"

"No!" comes the strained response, muffled by the cushion.

"You're nervous about the wedding!" remarks Harsha with a smile.

"I'm just not feeling very well today!" offers Marala curtly, suddenly highly strung. By no means shall her mother find out that she has been meeting Simon – otherwise she will forbid it. She is not allowed to meet up with another man so soon before her wedding. But Marala is determined to spend every spare moment with Simon until he leaves.

'Wilcox & Shaw Shippers & Co.' is written in large letters on the massive sandstone building with the gigantic windows. Simon walks into the shipping company building in the Port of London with his grandfather. A tall, wide hall stretches out before them. There are countless counters and desks, behind which employees are sitting, and many people are already waiting in queues. Three majestic chandeliers are hanging from the ceiling, and the walls are decorated with paintings of ships and seascapes. Impressed, Simon slowly follows his grandfather up to one of the counters, behind which a noble-looking, older lady is working.

"Good day, gentlemen! What can I do for you?" Her voice is friendly, but assertive.

"Good day! My name is Simon Hill and this is my grandson, Simon Balthasar Braun, from Germany. We would like to book a passage to New York for Simon."

"New York? We have a ship heading there the day after tomorrow. Hmm … but the ship is booked out and it looks like the next are as well."

"Is there another option?" Simon Hill would like to know.

"If I may be so bold, may I suggest Boston? That's north of New York."

"Grandpa, Boston is very good," chips in Simon. "Abhay once told me that a lot of tea is transshipped there and also that it's generally a nice place."

"If you say so," murmurs his grandfather. "Then we'll book a ticket to Boston."

"Very well," says the lady, cheerfully, "the ship is called the 'Whitecap', and is a full rigged, three-master under Captain Johansson, one of our most experienced captains."

"Johansson – that sounds Scandinavian," says Simon.

His grandfather shrugs his shoulders.

"True," nods the lady, "Captain Johansson is a Swede, but his wife is English. The 'Whitecap' leaves London at midday on 2nd May. I just need a few more details … Would you like a cabin or a dormitory?"

"We'll take the cabin," answers the grandfather.

The lady fills out all sorts of forms with a fountain pen, before finally handing them over. "Here are your papers, Mr. Braun."

Simon is confounded when he hears how much his trip will cost. One can almost buy a coach for that price!

Simon Hill pays for the passage, and then he and his grandson leave the big building. Once outside, Simon's grandfather turns to him and says, "The date is set, Simon. You're leaving on 2nd May – a Saturday. Do you know how long such a crossing lasts?"

"Yes – between 45 and 55 days – Jan ter Bruggen told me. It depends on the elements."

"Let's assume that your passage will be a safe one."

"Thank you once again for everything, Grandpa!"

"Don't mention it, Simon. In the next few days, we'll also have to buy you a waterproof knapsack, sturdy shoes and durable clothing."

"But Grandpa …"

"No ifs or buts! What you are about to embark on is no small matter, Simon, and you must get off to an optimal start. Now let's go through there into the coffee house across the road and have something to drink."

From their table in a corner of the coffee house, Simon orders a Yunnan black tea. He likes its malty, bitter flavour. Grandpa Simon celebrates the occasion by drinking a cognac. "This is a VSOP Cognac from the Domain Chainier in the Petite Champagne region, and it's wonderfully smooth," he explains to Simon.

"You're always on the job, Grandpa," grins his grandson in jest. Once they have each savoured their first sips, Simon Hill asks, "Tell me, Simon, how are things going with your Indian friend, Marala?"

"Not well."

"What do you mean? Haven't you met up with her again?"

"I have. But she is to marry on June 7th. Her husband will be much older than her … He is the tea merchant that her father works for."

"Well, I suppose her parents feel a sense of duty toward him. Marriage is not about feelings, Simon. Our two cultures are not very different in this matter."

"But two people cannot be married if they barely know each other. Marala could be his daughter!"

Simon Hill can see the disappointment in his grandson's eyes. He looks at the young man, full of energy – an optimist who has come up against an obstacle for the first time in his life.

Yes, that's exactly how it happened: for the first time, I was stopped in my tracks. No matter what I did, there was no way I could prevent the wedding. But I had a ticket to a mysterious future, a ticket to the 'New World'. However, I could barely think about that. My thoughts were on Marala, and I realised how many headaches and how much nausea can be caused by lovesickness.

7. Off to America

How do you know this coffee house? It's quite hidden, isn't it?" Marala's sharp, direct gaze pierces straight into Simon's eyes.

"I came here with my grandfather yesterday. We are hardly likely to see people who know you here."

"I'm pleased that you're so concerned about me. But what were you doing in this area?"

"Take a look across the road. What do you notice?"

"Nothing – just large, imposing office buildings."

"Look more closely!"

"What am I meant to notice then, Simon?" Marala impatiently wants to know. But then the scales fall from her eyes and she is slowly able to read out the words 'Wilcox & Shaw Shippers & Co.'.

She swallows and starts to look pale about the gills. She is obviously shocked to the core. The time has come for him to leave!

"I didn't know how to tell you," explains Simon. "So I thought it would be best to bring you here."

Marala reaches for her teacup and attempts to bring it to her lips. Simon notices how much she is shaking. He places his big, strong hand over her fine, delicate fingers to comfort her.

"Marala, we both know that we have to move on and that we only have a few more weeks together. My ship sets sail on 2nd May at around noon and a month later you will already be married."

"Yes, but …" Marala sounds despondent.

"No buts'! Let's order another piece of cake and then we can go to the British Museum on Great Russell Street – perhaps we can find some exhibits from India," suggests Simon in order to change the subject.

"Apple pie?" Marala asks, her voice trembling while she tries hard to force a smile.

The following spring weeks just fly by. Marala cleverly plans her days in such a way that neither her parents nor anyone else notices how many wonderful hours she is spending with Simon.

But eventually the 2nd May comes around. Simon is woken by the sound of a large bell ringing. Janet and Elisabeth are standing in his room and shouting, "Get up, sailor – land ahoy! Breakfast is ready, sleepyhead! We're taking you to your ship at midday."

Simon sits up sluggishly. He is still tired, so terribly tired. He farewelled Marala yesterday – they held each other close and kissed endlessly. At the same time, Marala had been trembling from head to toe and she had wept bitterly. Simon had spent the best part of the night awake, collecting his thoughts. He had only fallen asleep in the morning.

His grandparents and two cousins are waiting for the traveller at the breakfast table. Mary and Charles are already down in the shop.

"Good morning, Simon," comes the greeting from his grandfather. "Did you sleep well?"

"Not bad."

"You look tired, my boy," says Grandma Mary worriedly.

"I'm fine."

"Have you packed your knapsack, Simon? You haven't forgotten anything?" throws in Grandpa Simon.

"Yes, everything is packed."

"You'll be sailing over the ocean for almost one and a half months," says his grandfather. "You must be sure to eat as many fruits, vegetables and potatoes as possible so that you don't get sick."

"What will you do if you fall ill regardless?" asks his grandmother. "Is there a doctor on the ship?"

"I don't know, Grandma." Simon stands up and retrieves a small bottle from his knapsack. "Look at this magic potion. Hopefully it'll work!"

"Magic potion?" Puzzled faces are staring at Simon.

"Aunt Betty made this for me. She bought some fresh lemons and we filled this bottle with their juice."

"And that's supposed to be an elixir?" Grandma Mary is sceptical.

"Jan ter Bruggen was in South Africa for a long time. He told me that many sailors are taken ill with scurvy. It's the most common cause of death in sailors."

"What is scurvy?" Elisabeth wants to know.

"It's an illness one contracts when one doesn't eat enough fruit and vegetables – that is, when one has an unbalanced diet. That's what Grandpa meant just now. And when you're at sea for a long time, the fresh foods don't last very long. Jan told me that sick sailors felt better very quickly after they ate oranges or lemons."

"And how does one know when one has scurvy?" asks Janet, afraid.

"One is always tired, the gums start bleeding, and later the teeth fall out. That's followed by fever, diarrhoea, wasting of the muscles – and if one is injured, the wound doesn't heal properly." This had all been described thoroughly to Simon by Jan ter Bruggen.

"Ugh, that really sounds very terrible!" Elisabeth is appalled.

But Grandpa Simon smiles approvingly. "Aha! Thus the squeezed lemons. Lemons contain many vitamins and their juice lasts for a long time because of its acidity. Very clever, Simon!"

Delightfully radiant sunshine and agreeably warm temperatures make the drive from James Street to the docked 'Whitecap' terrific. Simon draws in all the views and impressions and it becomes clear to him that this will be the last time he will be in London for a long time. As they make their way to the dock, he sees the 'Whitecap' looking majestic in the water. The ship looks very new – it's so clean, elegant and gigantic. Its massive, mighty hull exudes the type of strength the ship will require to cross the rough Atlantic. Its three masts soar simply infinitely high into the blue summer sky.

Standing on the square by the ship, Simon feels as if he's in an anthill: It's teeming with people. Sailors are loading all sorts of crates and barrels on board. Simon can see people standing at the ship's railing who are very well dressed, but also modestly dressed passengers and sailors in smart uniforms. They are all watching the farewells that are going on around Simon for all to see.

"Simon, do you have your knapsack?" asks Grandma Mary for the hundredth time.

"Yes, of course."

"Now it's time to say goodbye," says his grandfather. "Come, let me give you one last proper hug, my boy."

One by one, they each say farewell to Simon, hug him, and kiss him on the cheeks.

"Simon, it would be better if you were to line up over there!" Janet points at the queue in front of the gangway.

"Do you have your documents, lad?" is Grandma's next nervous question. "You look after yourself and don't forget to write!"

"Yes, Grandma, I will try to write regularly."

It takes a long time before Simon has worked his way to the front of the ticket control queue. It's finally his turn, and he shows the two sailors his documents. Alongside other travellers, he then crosses the steadily rocking gangway, turns around once more, and searches for his family among the many people standing by the ship below. Then he sees them and calmly raises an arm, even though he is almost bursting with excitement. It won't be much longer now before he has left London behind him. I wonder how Marala is, what she is doing at the moment, and whether she is well?

Grandpa shouts out something, but Simon can't hear it over all the noise. One by one, the family disappears into the coach before they drive off. Simon slings his knapsack over his shoulders and goes to search for his cabin. The entrance to the twin cabins is located at the stern. Simon marvels at the superstructure made from fine teak, which indicates the ship's high quality. A fairly wide staircase leads below deck. With one hand, Simon holds onto the robust, brass-finished banister. He is soon standing before the door numbered 'six'. He grins. Six – just like on his first trip to London. Simon knocks on the door and receives an immediate reply. "Come in!"

A well-dressed man stands before him. He looks like he's in his mid-thirties, with blond, somewhat thinning hair and he is smiling at Simon amicably. He seems to be kind and likeable.

"Good day. Will you be my cabin-fellow on this long cruise?" The man examines Simon from top to bottom.

"Yes, my name is Simon Braun." Simon offers him his hand.

"John Parson, pleased to meet you." The gentleman grips Simon's hand in a vigorous handshake. "You look very young. May I ask how old you are?"

"I'm seventeen."

"Seventeen! What's such a young man doing on this ship?"

"I'm going to Boston," replies Simon laconically and they both have to laugh.

"There'll be plenty of time for us to relate our life stories during this long voyage," says John Parson. "I've taken the liberty of claiming this bunk. Is that all right for you, Sir?"

"Yes, of course. But you don't have to call me 'Sir'."

"Very well then – call me John. Let's get on with the unpacking and then go up onto the deck! There is more going on up there. And besides, we'll have plenty of time to be bored later."

Simon takes a look around the cabin, which isn't any bigger than the one he slept in on the 'Repatriate', on his way to London. Two bunks, two narrow cupboards, a table, two chairs, a mirror and a small wall closet. All in all though, the interior leaves a first-class impression.

Soon afterwards, Simon is standing at the railing with John Parson and they are watching as crates and barrels disappear into the ship's hold. At the stern stands a small, older, somewhat plump-looking man in uniform. He has a thick, blond beard and is wearing a peaked cap. Simon looks at him more closely. That must be Captain Johansson. He is standing so confidently beside the sailor at the ship's wheel.

The most diverse goings-on are taking place down below, by the ship. People are hugging each other – some crying, some laughing. One woman is standing on the quay wall with two girls and is waving a white handkerchief at an officer standing on the ship.

"Where in England are you from, Simon?" John Parson would like to know now.

"I'm not from England at all. I'm from Germany, but I have relatives here in London. And now I'm emigrating to America."

John raises his eyebrows in astonishment. "But you speak London English perfectly!"

"My mother comes from London."

"Oh, that explains it, then. I come from Cambridge, by the way, and I'm an architect," says John. "Would you like to look around the ship? Will you come to the bow with me?"

But Simon isn't really listening. He's thinking about Marala. He's becoming more and more aware of the fact that he will lose her forever – that he might never see her again. Suddenly the bellyache he's had for days returns. The pain always returns when he thinks about her. Simon can see Marala's face before him. He looks into her beautiful, warm brown eyes.

"I'm going then, Simon … I'll take a walk around … see you later?" John shakes his head uncomprehendingly over Simon's distraught behaviour.

Simon runs his eyes over the ever-dispersing crowd gathered on the square by the ship. Lost in thought, he absent-mindedly looks ahead. Suddenly, like magnets, his eyes are attracted to something. Marala! She is standing there, off to one side, leaning on a wall and looking at him steadfastly.

She came! His heart swells. She came to say goodbye and to show him that she is thinking about him.

Simon raises his arm and waves at her – and Marala waves back, her figure small in front of the large wall.

There are only a few minutes left; the gangway is being pulled in, work-ers are untying the ropes and the 'Whitecap' begins moving slowly.

"Simon, you look like you're rooted to the spot! Haven't you moved in all this time?"

"No." Simon looks briefly at John, who is now standing beside him again, and then focusses on Marala once more. The ship draws away from the quay. More and more water fills the space between Marala and Simon. He raises his right hand high above his head to show that he can still see her. In doing so, he has to fight back the tears and his stomach ache gets more intense.

"I say, is that pretty, young woman with the dark skin down there waving at you?"

"Yes, that's Marala." Simon swallows hard.

"Your sweetheart?"

"It's much more complicated …"

The 'Whitecap' leaves the dock and moves out into the waters of the Thames. Simon's gaze is fixed upon Marala, whose silhouette is getting smaller and smaller until she is smaller than a dot, and then invisible.

I wonder how long she was waiting on the riverbank? It must have been hours … many hours!

"Come on, Simon," John attempts to distract him, "I'll show you the ship. That'll help take your mind off things." But then he realises it would probably be wiser to leave Simon alone for a while, and leaves.

Simon stares at the riverbank sweeping past before him, but his thoughts are on Marala. Everything around him is sinking into a deep, dark void.

I never would have imagined that saying goodbye would be so difficult. Knowing that I couldn't change anything caused me pure, thoroughgoing pain. At that moment, I wasn't interested in anything anymore: not in the adventure of crossing the Atlantic, which was now beginning, not in the many new people on board and not even in what I was to expect to find on the other side of the ocean.

8. First acquaintances on board

Scenery or homesick?"

"Sorry?"

A young man in uniform leans on the railing next to Simon.

"The way you stare at the banks: are you looking at the scenery or are you homesick?"

"I'm thinking about someone."

"Homesick then." The sailor takes a silent moment to look at the banks of the Thames as they slide by.

"I'm George – who are you?"

"My name is Simon."

"Simon – we're off to America!"

"Have you been over there before?"

"Yes, this is my third crossing!" There is a trace of pride in George's voice. "Were you visiting someone in England?"

"I'm emigrating."

"Alone?"

"Yes."

"Hmm – you're probably the youngest person on the ship who is travelling alone. Exactly how old are you then?"

"I'm seventeen."

"Seventeen! That's pretty brave."

Simon is also curious. "You wear a uniform. Are you important on the ship?"

"The captain is important. I'm the second officer."

"You're still pretty young for that, aren't you?"

"I'm twenty-two."

"Then you left home early as well."

"True, but it wasn't entirely my choice. My mother died when I was seven."

"And your father?"

"My father was an officer in the Royal Navy. He lost his life four years ago."

"Was it an accident?"

"He was serving in the Mediterranean on the HMS Dreadnought, a 98-gun frigate with three decks, a formidable ship!"

Simon can sense how much George is affected by telling the story. There is a lump in his throat, and he cannot speak.

"They were following pirates in the Mediterranean," George continues. "They were operating out of Northern Africa, and did a great deal of damage to the merchant ships. When my father's crew captured one of the ships, there was a fight – my father was hit in the head by a bullet. He died instantly …"

Simon can barely look George in the eyes. A single tear falls slowly down the young officer's cheek.

"I'm sorry, George."

"It works – I mean, it was four years ago. And it gets better every month."

"Why did you go into the navy too?"

"I have no relatives – back then I had just turned eighteen, and friends of my parents helped me. Some of them were in the Royal Navy. I always wanted to do what my father did, and the sea fascinates me just as much as it had fascinated him. Fascinating, the way he sensed it. The merchant navy seemed to me to be less dangerous. But it can get pretty exciting with us as well – you'll see."

"I can't wait to find out."

"And? Have you met anyone here on board yet?"

"Yes, my cabin mate, John Parson, and now you."

"You're in a cabin? Can you afford that?"

"The crossing was a gift from my grandparents."

"You were very lucky." George takes a closer look at Simon. "Although I guess I should have known – I could have guessed from your clothes."

Simon is suddenly confused. He doesn't want to be judged by the wealth of his family.

"Most of the passengers are billeted in the large berth." George points to the middle of the ship. "And do you see the hatchway in front of the forecastle? Those are the crews' billets."

"I would love to see the whole of the ship sometime," says Simon. "Is it allowed to take a look around?"

Right then, a dark voice reverberates over the deck. "Mr. Boyt to the quarterdeck!"

"Oh, that's me. The captain – I have to go! It was nice to meet you, Simon."

"You, too, George! See you later."

Simon wanders along the railing to the bow of the 'Whitecap'. The ship sits calmly in the water of the Thames, on a steady course towards the North Sea. Simon observes the people who are on deck with him. He sees a few well to nobly dressed people, lots of couples, but also a number of people who seem to be quite poor, including a few families with children. Are they emigrants, just like him? Or tradesmen? Maybe even people who have already emigrated, and came home for a visit? Simon smiles at the different people on board, a few of whom greet him in return.

"Hey, Simon, what are you doing out here then?" John Parson has walked up to him. "How long is it going to take until we are on the open sea?"

"We should reach it this evening," Simon answers. "Have you ever wondered why exactly all the people here on board are travelling to America?"

Before John can reply, a shrill woman's voice answers the question. "We were visiting our home in Oxford, and now we are going back."

The voice belongs to an old, stoutly built woman. She is standing next to a gaunt man who looks to be about the same age. The couple seems to be quite well off.

"Excuse us please, for butting in like that," says the gentleman to the two young men. "My name is Curtis Tremaine and this is my wife, Henrietta."

Simon and John also introduce themselves. But after that, neither they nor Curtis Tremaine can really get a word in edgewise. They can take part in the 'conversation', which the communicative Henrietta now leads, only by nodding or shaking their heads. Everything simply bubbles out of her, all the way from her birth to her marriage, then their emigration, and right up to the latest gossip. Simon's gaze wanders more and more. His attention lands by a group of boys that are throwing a ball between themselves. It reminds him of ball games with his brother Christoph in the garden of his parents' Villa.

Suddenly, a big blonde man grabs the ball with a grin on his face. He says something to another man standing nearby, and then they both walk away. They throw the ball between themselves as they do so, while the boys run behind them and attempt to win it back. Then, quite suddenly, the blonde man throws the ball into a high arch and overboard. One of the boys starts to cry, while the other one runs away, to appear seconds later with a simply dressed woman in tow.

"That's the man, Aunt Shayne!"

"Which one? The one with the blonde hair?"

"Yes, him, him!" The boy stretches out his arm and points at the culprit.

"Excuse me – can you tell me why you threw these boys' ball into the sea?"

"Because I wanted to … cow!"

"Impertinence! Why are you cursing at me?"

"Be careful who you talk to!"

"And who is going to replace the little ones' ball?"

"It wasn't worth anything anyway … Now go to hell!" The blonde man moves threateningly towards the woman. She pulls the little one close to her and turns away, frightened.

"That's right, get lost!"

Simon watched the scene tensely. He would have preferred to step in, but the ball was lost forever. Simon is sure that there will be another opportunity to teach the man a lesson.

"Simon, have you seen the Tremaines yet?"

"No."

John and Simon are sitting in the mess room, where passengers and officers of the 'Whitecap' are waiting for the evening meal.

"If they sit down at our table, then the journey is done for us," John smirks. "We will most likely be entertained until we're in America."

Simon leans over towards John. "Say, do you know that blonde man, three tables over?"

"His name is Flynn Corwin, an unsavoury person. He elbowed me out of the way as I came on board."

"A short while ago on the deck he just took a ball from two small boys and threw it overboard."

"That sounds like him. I'm going to stay out of his way as much as possible. I don't know the dark haired man beside him. But the other two at his table are Alastair Rowley and his wife Lindsay."

"They're married? But he's so much older than her – at least twenty years!" Simon bursts out. Right away, he thinks of Marala. Soon she too will be the wife of a much older man.

"True, but once you are that rich, you can take your pick of women. Alastair Rowley is the director of a bank in Boston."

"How do you know that?"

"I met them both on the pier before we cast off."

"Oh how nice that you saved places for us!" Simon and John barely flinch as they hear Henrietta's voice.

"Well, now nothing else can happen to us during the crossing," John mumbles quietly. Simon bites his tongue, but is unable to suppress a smirk.

Within seconds Henrietta is sitting next to Simon at the table, and has already made eye contact with the waiter. "Is this your first overseas journey?" she wants to know.

John joins in with, "Yes, I …"

"You should know that the ship won't necessarily sit as calmly on the water as it does now once we make it to the Atlantic. When we came over from Boston, my Curtis spent half the journey with his head in a bowl … Have you ever experienced a storm at sea, Simon?"

"The first time that I …"

96

But Henrietta is already interrupting Simon. "Well, when we sailed to London …"

Nothing remains for the three men to do except to look helplessly at one another and provide at least the appearance of listening to Henrietta. Curtis' face is turning noticeably red.

John leans over towards Simon. "My God, is it going to be like this for the next few weeks? Can't we turn her off somehow? Take a look at poor Curtis, he's already turning red! Any second now he's going to burst!"

Henrietta keeps on talking, turning herself around and raising her hand in greeting at the Rowleys as she does. Then she says to Curtis, "Have you seen them yet, Curtis?"

Her husband shrugs his shoulders and grumbles, "Who do you mean?"

"Alastair Rowley with his young wife!"

"Do you know the two of them, Henrietta?" John wants to know.

Curtis joins the conversation for the first time. "That's Alastair Rowley, the director of the BBBC, the Big Boston Bank & Co., a well respected banker. The woman at his side is his wife, Lindsay – isn't she a sight for sore eyes?!"

"I should have guessed that you would like her, Curtis, typical for a man!"

"What do you want from me then, Henrietta? Lindsay Rowley really does look very attractive!"

"This trollop is so much younger than he is – and I've already heard a great many stories about her!"

"What type of stories then?"

"Just take a look at how tarted up she is … those type of stories!"

"Always tattling! She is very attractive, and maybe she's nice as well, but then of course you get these stories – it's terrible!"

"Oh, you're all men, you don't want to hear this sort of thing. But I do have to tell you one of those stories, just once …"

Curtis Tremaine is clearly embarrassed by his wife's behaviour. But he already knows from experience that he can't stop her. Who knows what discussions he would then have to have with her later.

Simon turns to Henrietta: "I have heard that you are bankrupt?"

"Who told you something like that?" Henrietta's eyes widen.

"I heard what two of the other passengers were saying about you. They said that you only undertook the journey from Boston to London so that you could borrow money from your relatives, in order to avoid the worst of it."

"That is a story out of whole cloth! Curtis, say something! You can't allow such a rumour to go unanswered!"

"What exactly do you want me to do, Henrietta?" Curtis seems helpless and subdued.

"Nothing. You can't do anything," Simon explains calmly. "In two days the whole ship will have heard that you're bankrupt."

"But it's not true!" Henrietta yells angrily. "It's all made up!"

"One of the men did say that, too," Simon confirms.

"And – did the others believe him?"

"They said, when rumours like that are going around, there's always a tiny bit of truth to them."

John stares at Simon, as though he isn't quite sure what he should think about his behaviour.

Simon continues, "Henrietta, I don't know this Lindsay Rowley. From what I can see, she looks good. But I can't say anything about what type of person she is. So I have to trust the opinion of someone I know who knows her."

"Simon, I don't understand. What does that have to do with the rumour about us?"

"First it's just small stories that people tell themselves. But then the stories get bigger and bigger, like blowing into a balloon – depending on who tells the best story. It depends on the imagination of the teller."

"Yes, but …"

"Maybe to begin with it was only a hat that didn't sit straight, then an old fashioned hat, and then a hat that wasn't paid for. A little while later your whole wardrobe is unpaid for and at the end you're bankrupt."

"Once again, Simon: That's just not true!"

"There's always something to the story."

"No, nothing, absolutely nothing!"

After this outbreak, silence falls over the table for long seconds, and then Simon says slowly, "You're right."

"What do you mean by that?" Henrietta is clearly extremely agitated, but looking very scared at the same time.

"Henrietta, nobody was talking about you. I made it all up. The Tremaines are not bankrupt."

"What impertinence! How could you do something like that to us, Simon?"

Simon looks calmly into Henrietta's eyes. "Isn't it a relief to hear that there is no rumour? It's nice when someone has the guts to admit that they made it all up, isn't it?"

"You can't just go around making up rumours about us for the whole world to hear!"

"Or re-tell? Henrietta, you shouldn't say anything about Lindsay Rowley that isn't actually true. But that also means that you have to listen to people if you want to get to know them."

"Are you trying to say that I talk too much?"

"I'm trying to say you should listen sometimes, which will give other people a chance to say something."

John and Curtis can no longer hold in their laughter, and, thank God, even Henrietta giggles in relief.

"Hey, you oaf, can't you look where you're going?" The call comes suddenly from another corner of the mess hall. Flynn Corwin had turned on someone in uniform. "Look at that, now I've stained my shirt because you bumped into me! You're like a bull in a china shop!"

"Excuse me please, my good Sir; that was not my intention," the uniformed man answers politely. As he turns around, Simon recognizes George Boyt. With a bright red face, he leaves the mess hall.

John nudges Simon. "What do you think about going up on deck to see if we've already reached the English Channel?"

"Good idea, it's pretty stuffy in here."

They meet Alastair and Lindsay Rowley at the door of the mess hall. Simon and John follow them out, and Flynn Corwin and his companion strike off in the same direction. For the second time in a row Corwin runs into John and elbows his way past him. As they climb up the stairs, Simon sees how Flynn, thinking he is unseen, grabs Lindsay Rowley's behind. Shocked, she turns around, but Corwin only says, "I thought she was going to fall down the stairs."

Alastair Rowley takes his wife's arm. "Careful, Love." To Flynn Corwin he says, "Thank you for helping my wife."

"But of course I wouldn't hesitate to help such a lovely lady!" Corwin grins, flicking his blonde hair to the side.

Outside on the deck it is gradually getting dark. Lights from a town shine along the banks.

"That must be Margate," says John. "So now we are sailing into the English Channel. We'll soon be able to see Ramsgate." He points at the coast, disappearing in the sunset.

"There are almost no clouds," Simon realizes. "We'll be able to take a look at the stars later on." He takes a quick look around. "Look over there, John. The Rowley's are standing with that Flynn Corwin and his friend."

"That's cheeky of him." John grins, almost in recognition.

"What do you mean?"

"Simple: While they were eating he certainly talked to both of them normally, as much as he is able to hold down a sophisticated conversation at all. Afterwards he grabs her bottom to show her that he's interested in her. And now he is certainly flirting with her further."

"But that's indecent!" Simon finds.

"Correct. But don't we want to find out if his scheme to impress her is successful in the next few weeks ..."

9. A day at sea

Simon inhales deeply, taking in the first fresh breeze of the day. It is barely five o'clock in the morning, but he can't stay in his cabin any longer. It's stuffy under the deck and the smell of whisky also pervades the cabin – the whisky that John Parson had taken the liberty of consuming shortly before going to bed.

Up on the quarterdeck, two sailors hold the 'Whitecap's' helm firmly in their grip, while George Boyt stands behind them as officer on duty. Simon nods at him and climbs up to the upper quarterdeck – also known as the poop deck. At the same time, he hears a bell chime twice, but cannot place the sound.

It's still misty, but it looks like it'll be a fine day, so that he will have a great view from here later on. Simon leans back on the railing and gazes up into the sails. The 'Whitecap' is sailing comfortably on a close reach. The regular creaking of the woodwork gives a sense of how powerfully the sailing ship is working its way through the sea.

"Good morning, Simon. Did you sleep well?" Suddenly, George is standing beside him.

"It was all right for the first night on board. George, what were those chimes all about?"

"You mean when the bell was struck – the ship's bell?"

"Yes. I don't know what it means – what the ringing means. When it rings twice or three times. I think it can strike up to eight times."

"On the quarterdeck, behind the rudder, is an hourglass or more precisely, a half-hourglass. It's the most important timekeeper on board. It is turned over ever half an hour."

"Why don't you just use a normal clock? Why something so antiquated? An hourglass!"

"The hourglass runs completely steadily, no matter whether the sea is calm, as it is now, or whether a storm is rocking the ship to and fro. The

100

hourglass also doesn't mind whether the temperature is below freezing, or whether we are crossing the equator at 100 degrees Fahrenheit or 120 degrees Fahrenheit."

"What's Fahrenheit?"

"Don't you know? Don't you come from England?"

"No. While it's true that my mother is English, I was born and raised in Germany."

"I'm surprised to hear that! Well, then you couldn't know about it, could you? You measure temperature in degrees Celsius – we measure it in Fahrenheit. 100 degrees Fahrenheit are roughly 40 degrees Celsius."

"And what about the chimes?"

"That's the ship's bell I was just talking about. We have six watches on board – each one lasts four hours. Each time the hourglass is turned over – every half-hour – the bell is rung once more than the last time, which results in one to eight rings per watch."

"Very well, I understand now." Simon nods in satisfaction. "What actually happened between you and that Flynn Corwin character at dinner last night?"

"After having eaten, I wanted to leave the mess hall and had to walk past him and another gentleman. That Corwin man had drawn his left elbow back and that's why I bumped into him, causing his arm to fling forwards abruptly. Well – whatever had been on his fork ended up on the table – but you surely noticed that part. Since he began protesting immediately, I wasn't able to reasonably explain myself. So I decided to just apologise and leave."

"Wise decision."

"Boyt, don't you have anything to do?"

George flinches. "Of course I do, Captain." In the blink of an eye, Captain Johansson has appeared on the quarterdeck.

"Take it easy, Boyt. The water is calm and it's going to be a fine day."

"Thank you, Captain."

Just as George has finished introducing Simon to the captain, the ship's bell rings six times.

George throws Simon a questioning look. "What time is it now?"

"It's now the morning watch, which goes from four to eight o'clock – six chimes means three hours after the watch started, so it's seven o'clock." Captain Johansson looks amazed. "Correct! Are you somehow involved in sailing?"

"No, Captain. My parents own a wine cellar on the Rhine in Germany, and my grandparents run a wine and spirit shop in London. But I find everything to do with sailing very interesting. And I like your ship. With its many sails, the 'Whitecap' appears at once mighty and elegant."

"That she is, Simon, an elegant ship. But when it's stormy and the waves are high, it can feel like you're standing on a cockleshell. Boyt, keep your eyes open!"

With that, Captain Johansson turns and leaves the poop deck.

"Gosh, George, you really jumped when we suddenly saw the captain standing before us," whispers Simon.

"I'm not really allowed to talk to passengers while I'm working. But since there's hardly anyone on deck, the captain decided to turn a blind eye. He may be tough, but he's fair."

"It sure is bright out here, damn it!" a sleepy voice interrupts them. John Parson climbs up onto the deck to be met by two grinning faces. "What's wrong? Who are you making fun of?"

"Of the many people out here," says George, keeping a straight face. John takes a look around. "But there is no one here."

"There is one person," explains Simon.

"You mean me, right? Um, well, yesterday I ..."

"... inhaled a couple of whiskies," finishes Simon. "Perhaps that's why I woke up so early, you were snoring like a sawmill."

The sun is now high in the sky and the deck is teeming with people. Simon is sitting on the hood of the central companionway, watching the sailors work.

"Hey, can you pull me up?" On the deck before him stands a black-haired boy of about ten years. He is smiling and stretching out his hand toward Simon. Simon takes it and helps the boy climb up onto the hood.

"Thanks – you have a good view from up here. I'm Tom."

"Hello, I'm Simon."

"Are you emigrating to America?"

"Yes."

"Where is your family?"

"I'm going alone."

"There are four of us. Dad, mum, my little sister Anna and I. What are you doing up here on the roof?"

"I'm watching the sailors work. I think it's fascinating how it all works. Setting the sails, hauling them in, adjusting them according to the wind ..."

"It's boring now that we don't have our ball anymore."

"Oh, that was you."

"I was who?"

"You know, the one that tall blond man took the ball from and threw it into the sea."

102

"That nasty feller! If I were bigger, I would've hit him, but my dad told me to leave him alone. That man also kicked my friend Oliver. He now has bruises!"

"Tom, my boy, come down from there!"

"Oh no, it's my mum!" Tom quickly slides off the hood. Simon also jumps down onto the deck and politely introduces himself. "Hello, my name is Simon Braun."

"Elisabeth Rushfort. I see you've already met my son, Tom. Are you staying in one of the cabins?"

"Yes, why?"

"I haven't seen you down below, Mr. Braun. But maybe there are just too many of us."

"You're welcome to use my first name. And the cabins aren't particularly roomy, either."

"Simon, come with me! I'll introduce you to my father and sister," calls out Tom.

The upper deck is the longest continuous deck aboard the 'Whitecap'. It's a large hall in which countless hammocks dangle from the ceiling and people sit together in small groups, some on crates and some simply on the floor. Due to the sparse lighting and the dark oak beams that make up the ship's structure, the room looks gloomy, almost scary. Adding to that the air is oppressive and stale, and infused with the musty smell of many people's sweat mixed together.

A black-haired man jumps up and stretches his hand out toward Simon, obviously wondering what such a well-dressed young man is doing here. The man is quite tall and thin, almost lanky. His black, curly hair looks exactly like Tom's, and stands in stark contrast to the pale tone of his skin. His worn-out trousers and brown shirt make him appear even paler. Like most people on this deck, he is walking around barefoot.

Elisabeth does the introductions. "This is my husband, Arthur, and the little girl over there is my daughter, Anna."

"You were right, Elisabeth," says Simon, "there is much more space in the cabins than there is here."

And there's much more privacy.

"We'll manage for one-and-a-half months," says Arthur.

Elisabeth makes a completely different impression than Arthur. Her skin-tone looks much healthier, and that's only emphasised by the colourful clothing she is wearing.

"Would you like to sit down, Simon?" Elisabeth points at a crate.

"Thank you."

Simon finds out that Arthur and his wife come from the English Midlands, where Arthur used to work underground as a miner, where he toiled hard for hours on end. But since his pay was not enough to feed the family, Elisabeth was also forced to work. She would earn a few pounds as a washer woman and cook's maid in a factory owner's household. A while ago, they read in the newspaper that people such as themselves were able to establish their own livelihoods in America. So six months ago they made the decision to emigrate.

"Is this your chest here? It's so nicely decorated."

"Yes, that's our luggage. Inside is everything that we are taking with us to begin our new life," explains Elisabeth in a voice tinged with pride. "There's clothing, some porcelain and cutlery and a few personal items in there."

"That's not much for a whole family," thinks Simon and says, "But you've brought much more with you than I have. I only have my knapsack."

"And, Simon, what do you actually want to do in Boston?" Arthur wants to know.

"Honestly, I don't know! But I know what I'm capable of."

"How old are you?"

"Seventeen!" interjects Tom. "He already told me that on the deck. And mum, he can also speak German, French and something else."

"Spanish," says Simon. "But not as well as English and German."

During the conversation, Simon notices more and more about his surroundings. How closely people live beside one another here! Some of them even have to stand up to let others walk past. People are dressed completely differently here, and their looks and faces tell new and interesting stories.

In the afternoon, Simon is again sitting on the hood of the central companionway. He is no longer watching just the sailors at work, but also paying attention to all the different people on board. Up until now, Simon had thought that he and John were living in very tight quarters, but the constriction he witnessed when visiting the Rushforts below deck had left him speechless.

"You and your husband were in London on business?" That voice sounds familiar to Simon, but at the moment he can't place it.

"Yes, my husband visited his correspondent bank in London to discuss business matters, and we were also invited to a few receptions and balls."

"You must have been the prettiest woman at those events!"

"You're flattering me."

"Is that any wonder? You're the most attractive woman on the entire ship!"

104

"Oh, don't be silly ... There are several others."

"It may not have occurred to you, since you are at liberty to look at yourself in the mirror every day, but your figure is wholly exceptional, if I may be so bold. And along with your choice of clothing and elegant hairstyle ... It's really very difficult for a man like me to retain his composure."

"I make you nervous then, do I?"

"Of course it's not easy for a man in his prime to contain himself."

Simon carefully takes a peek over the edge of the roof. He gets a glimpse of a lady's head and sees straight down into a low-cut neckline. It takes him a couple of seconds before he recognises the woman. Lindsay Rowley! In contrast, he only needs to smell the man in order to identify him: It's Flynn Corwin. Simon returns to his spot, from which he cannot be seen. At the other end of the deck, he can see Alastair Rowley standing with Curtis and Henrietta Tremaine.

"Lindsay, are you able to always resist all of your suitors?"

"What do you mean?" From the sound of her voice, Simon takes it that she is smiling mischievously.

"I'll try to keep the stallion away from the mare for as long as I can!"

Then it's quiet. Only a moment later, Lindsay Rowley walks toward her husband and the Tremaines. Simon peers over the edge once more. Corwin is also gone. Like a weasel, Simon slides down off the hood and retires to the ship's bow. What was it that John had said? "But don't we want to find out if his scheme to impress her is successful in the next few weeks ..."

"Hey, Simon!" a voice calls out from the forecastle, the uppermost deck at the bow.

"Hello, George!"

"Have you met our figurehead, yet?"

Simon shakes his head and makes his way toward the bow. Brimming with pride, George points at the noble, wooden lady painted in white, whose body appears to be wrapped in the finest of cloths.

"This is our 'White Lady', our figurehead," declares George.

"She's bigger than a person!" marvels Simon.

"And look at how delicately she's been carved. Each fold of the silk cloth has been carved out with precision. The 'White Lady' is our lucky charm."

Simon gazes out into the distance at the line that separates the water from the sky.

"There's only water as far as the eye can see! George, what's the actual distance between England and America?"

"From London to Boston we cover a distance of about 4,000 sea miles."

"That doesn't mean anything to me. We use kilometres where I come from."

"That would be roughly 7,300 kilometres."

"That's a long way!"

"From London, we first sail to Funchal," George continues. "We pick up new provisions there, and then we cross the Atlantic."

"Funchal is on the island of Madeira, right?"

"Right, Simon, you know your geography. Funchal is the capital of that volcanic island in the Atlantic. It belongs to Portugal."

"I've already heard about that," relates Simon. "Rudolf Vonecken, our tutor, who comes from Belgium, had been there once and had told us about it. And aside from that, there's a special wine in Madeira that doesn't exist anywhere else. I tasted some of it when I visited my grandparents in London."

"Madeira wine," agrees George. "There'll most certainly be some of that in our provisions when we leave Funchal to head for Boston."

"And when do you think we'll reach Madeira?"

"It's about 1,600 sea miles from London to Funchal, that's a good one-third of the whole journey. Assuming we'll be at sea for fifty days, depending on the wind and weather conditions, then we should get there on the 20th May."

The sea kept enchanting me more and more. With what seemed to be a never-ending expanse, it just seemed unfathomable to me. Added to that was the adventure of migration, that magnificent ship, and the new, interesting and so very different people on board. I was very shocked to see how some of the passengers had to live on the ship. And until that moment, I had thought that I already had such little space in the cabin. But I learnt my lesson: To inform myself as thoroughly as possible before taking on a position and beginning to profess it.

10. Wine and fury in abundance

Hey, Simon, which island is that over there?" John points into the distance, where land has been visible for a short while.

"Madeira, isn't it?" Simon is unsure.

Under steady wind conditions, the 'Whitecap' cuts through the waves of the calm sea. It's the 22ⁿᵈ May, 1829.

"How could we find out?" ruminates John.

"We'll just ask the captain. He's standing back there."

"Simon, you can't just …"

"It's worth a try!"

Absolutely calm and collected, the Captain is standing at the quarterdeck railing, as Simon approaches him.

"Excuse me, Captain. We have a question."

"Ah, Messieurs Parson and Braun. What can I do for you?"

John stretches out an arm and points in the direction of the island before them. "Is that Madeira up ahead?"

"No, gentlemen, that is the island of Porto Santo. It lies about twenty-three-and-a-half sea miles north-east of Madeira." With broad, sweeping gestures, Johansson explains, "We'll pass by Porto Santo on our right-hand side and then approach Madeira on a south-westerly course. Funchal, our destination port, is on the island's south east. Before we reach it, you will see the 'Ilhas Desertas' or 'Desert Islands' on the left-hand side, south-east of Madeira."

"What will the weather be like on Madeira, in the middle of the Atlantic?" John immediately asks the next question.

"Has George not told you that yet?"

"No. Where is he, anyway? Did he sleep in?"

"George was on the graveyard watch last night," answers Johansson.

"The graveyard watch?" John looks puzzled.

"That's the watch from midnight until four in the morning," Simon already knows, "the second night watch."

"George seems to have taught you well, Mr. Braun. Now back to Madeira. The island is located on latitude of 32 degrees north and longitude of 16 degrees west, thus being closer to Africa than Europe. Its climate is thus fair and warm. Luckily it's mostly not too hot, because there's almost always a cooling breeze there," reports Johansson. "We will pick up supplies in Funchal and plan to set sail again three days later."

In the afternoon, the passengers believe they have landed in paradise. From a bay surrounded by thick greenery, stretches out row after row of neat, whitewashed houses with red-tiled roofs. Most passengers are standing on the deck and watching intently as the crew manoeuvres the majestic ship up to the quay wall. John and Simon are standing with the Tremaines on the quarterdeck and watch as the first onlookers and merchants start to gather by the ship, while up above, the first passengers are beginning to wait for the gangway to be positioned so that they can finally set foot on solid ground once more.

"John, what are your plans?" asks Henrietta Tremaine. "I hear we're staying here for three days."

"I don't know yet. What are you doing, Simon?"

"I'd like to get a closer look at the vineyards and visit a wine-growing estate where Madeira is produced. One of my acquaintances in Germany, Jan ter Bruggen, advised me to seek out a Mr. Robert Henriques here. His family is supposed to own an estate in Camara de Lobos."

"Could you take me along?" pleads John. "Or would it be better if I weren't to go with you?"

A steady stream of people is alighting the ship at a snail's pace. As if guided by invisible hands, the unruly mass of people magically files into an orderly queue. Suddenly there is unrest at the end of the queue. Again and again, individuals are being shoved aside. Then Simon realises why. "Look over there! That Flynn Corwin is pushing his way through the rows with his friend in tow."

"How outrageous! Arrogant pig!" curses Henrietta Tremaine.

"Imagine what that would be like on the gangway − how's that meant to work?" John raises his voice.

Horrified, the four of them watch as the two men recklessly tear through the crowd, accompanied by loud groans and profanities. Then, in the middle of the gangway, a man is suddenly dangling over the safety net and can only just manage to hold on. At the same time, a little boy with a shock of curly, black hair is pushed down under the ropes. There's a short cry before the child disappears under the water between the ship and the quay.

Everything seems to freeze. With looks of horror on their faces, the people all seem to be rooted to the spot, with screams being heard here and there.

In one motion, Simon is standing on the railing, his eyes fixed down-wards. The 'Whitecap' is roughly two metres away from the quay wall. There is no sign of the boy. But thanks to the concentric circles on the water's sur-face, Simon can figure out where he must have fallen. If he surfaces right now as the 'Whitecap' bangs against the quay wall, he won't survive.

"I have to grab hold of him underwater," is the thought that flashes through Simon's head as he jumps. In the blink of an eye, he has dived into the cold bay water.

"Help, Mr. Braun!" Henrietta instinctively covers her face with her hands. "Curtis, John, did you see that? The young Mr. Braun just jumped into the water!" Leaning over the railing, the three of them try to make him out in the water. But to no avail – in the shade of the ship, the water deep below looks like a black hole.

The 'Whitecap' moves about a metre toward the quay wall. "They'll be squashed! The ship will press them against the wall – you'll see!" screams Henrietta. Meanwhile, George Boyt and Captain Johansson have joined them. Curtis briefly explains the situation to them. As opposed to Henrietta, he appears to be calmness embodied. John, on the other hand, is visibly worried.

"Captain Johansson, you have to do something!" shouts Henrietta.

"But my dear lady, what should we do?" objects George Boyt. "This ship weighs over a thousand tonnes. One cannot simply push it away from the quay with a broomstick." That was a little cheeky of the second officer. But the captain is obviously pondering a solution and does not rebuke George's conduct.

The terror on John's face is clear for all to see. "Is there no chance at all, then?"

"Help! The ship is about to hit against the wall!" comes a scream from the ship's bow. There is a furious and hectic cacophony of voices. Fragments of sentences are shouted to the quarterdeck. Great throngs of people push their way to the ship's railing while others gather on the quay wall. All eyes are on the water. But there is nothing to be seen.

"They can't survive this!"

"They'll be crushed against the wall by the ship!"

"The boy will drown, he can't even swim!"

"Poor parents!"

"No. Whether the two of them come out of this unscathed now rests solely in the hands of Simon Braun," mutters Captain Johansson.

"Over there!" Suddenly a woman's voice rings out from the quay. "There they are! Behind the ship!" A murmur of relief goes through the crowd gathered on the pier. Several men are already throwing a rope with a loop at the end out into the water. And, as a matter of fact, behind the ship's stern, Simon is swimming on his back while gripping the boy tightly under the arms. He now reaches out for the rope with one hand.

As Simon slings the rope around the boy, he sees his face for the first time. In the past few minutes he has had other things to think about. In no time at all, he had decided on the only possible way of saving the boy's life: by swimming underwater along the length of the ship toward the back.

"Tom! It's you!" he shouts, astounded.

"Simon … Thank you … The water is so cold, brrr!"

"Now that you mention it ... You did well, Tom!"

"Ready?" Simon hears an invisible, deep voice from above.

"Yes, haul him up!" he shouts back.

Only a few minutes later, Simon is standing on the quay wall and looking down at himself. Before any of the many people staring at him has the chance to say anything, he walks past all of them, boarding the ship and disappearing into his little cabin to change into some dry clothes.

But he is given no chance to have a break.

"Hey, Simon, come out. You're the man of the moment!" John barges into his cabin. "The people want to see you!"

"But I don't want to see them!"

"Why not? That was really great, how you managed that. I wouldn't have dared to try!"

"John, I just wanted to rescue the boy. I don't want ... I don't like what's coming now!"

"But Simon …"

"Please just leave me alone, now!"

A bewildered John shuts the door behind him and climbs back up to the deck. Never before has he met someone who doesn't wish to be thanked for his assistance.

"Over here, John," Henrietta waves him over. "Where is our hero, then?"

She is standing there, full of expectation, along with Curtis, Lindsay and Alastair Rowley, Captain Johansson, George Boyt and the first mate, John Triggerman.

"He's not coming. He wants to be left in peace," explains John.

"We have to applaud him! Simon saved little Tom's life!" asserts Henrietta.

"No, I think that's exactly what he doesn't want!" observes George thoughtfully. "Simon does not like to be the centre of attention and also doesn't allow others to place him in the limelight."

"You mean, he is a man of action, but isn't able to present himself," offers Alastair Rowley in his own, analytical way.

"No, no, I don't mean it in that way! I've had the chance to get to know Simon a little better here on board. He has a strong character and is incredibly self-assured. He very carefully weighs up right and wrong, good and evil against each other. But once he makes up his mind to do something, he carries it out."

"Yes, but he couldn't have weighed anything up or have thought about it for very long," finds Curtis Tremaine. "He was in the water immediately."

110

"I think Simon is able to accurately assess a situation very quickly. And on top of that, he appears to know no fear … Or at least he can hide it well."

"You're right, George. Simon really knows no fear!" confirms John.

The next morning, Simon is again the first on deck and at breakfast. He then goes to the upper deck, where the Rushforts are staying. As opposed to the last time he was down here, the people are not looking at him mistrustfully. They appear rather friendly and some of them even smile at him.

"Simon, Simon, Simon!" Little Tom runs up to him and leaps into his arms. "Mummy told me I should say thank you to you … But I would have done so anyway!"

"Good morning, Tom. It's good to see that you're well again!"

In an instant a crowd has gathered around Simon – the rest of the Rushfort family is also among them. Arthur steps forward and says with a slightly tremor in his voice, "Good morning, Simon. I'd like to very sincerely thank you for your engagement. Without you we wouldn't have our Tom anymore."

"Simon, how can we ever repay you for what you have done for us?" An emotional Elisabeth gives Simon a hug.

"Wait just a moment. There is nothing to repay. I didn't even know it was Tom when I jumped into the water. I would have rescued anyone as a matter of course."

Less than two hours later, Simon and John are wandering around the vineyards near Camara de Lobos. Simon is paying attention to the finest details: the vineyards laid out in terraces, the soil composition, the types of retaining walls, the grapes, and how they've been pruned. John is meanwhile gazing into the distance with the aid of his right hand as a sun visor.

"Simon, just look at that never-ending water!"

"You can gape at that every day at sea, John, from morning till night."

"Yes, but from this height the view is much better. Besides, I'm standing on solid ground and I'd like to savour it."

As if from nowhere, a suntanned elderly man is suddenly standing before them. "Hello! Who are you? What are you doing here in the vineyards?"

"We're looking for Mr. Henriques", explains Simon. "We are passengers on the 'Whitecap', which is anchored at Funchal. Simon Braun and John Parson."

"There are many Henriques here," mutters the old man. "Do you know his given name or his address?"

"Robert, Robert Henriques is his name."

"That's fortunate – he has his adega, his estate, here in Camara de Lobos. It's not far from here." The man points in the right direction.

"That white house there?" asks John.

The old man grins. "Almost all the houses here are white."

Robert Henriques is a friendly man of about fifty years of age, short of stature and with a thick head of black, frizzy hair. Simon and John have barely introduced themselves before he takes them on a tour of his vine-yards and estate, explaining all the details of Madeira wine to them. After this 'dry lesson', John is now looking forward to tasting the wines. In the cellar of his estate, Robert Henriques offers the two young men one good drop after the next. While Simon always spits the wine into a tin bowl after tasting it, as he learnt to do in his grandfather's cellar in London, John swallows glass after glass of wine.

"John, don't drink so much!" warns Simon. "Remember, we still have to get back to the ship."

"Don't worry, it's cool here in the wine cellar, so I'm fine," says John, raising his glass. And then takes a big gulp.

Simon turns to Robert Henriques. "So did I understand that correctly? For the most part, there are five grape varieties on Madeira: Sercial for dry Madeiras, Verdelho for the medium drys, Bual for the semi-sweets, Malm-sey for sweet wines, and finally the Tinta Negra Mole – or 'Velvety Black' – which you believe is only of average quality."

"Right," confirms Henriques. "If, for example, I want to produce a sweet Madeira, I interrupt the alcoholic fermentation, so that a residual sweetness remains in the wine, as in a Bual or a Malmsey. Then I let the skins ferment along with it. This interruption in the fermentation is caused by the addition of aguardente, a kind of brandy, so that there is then between seventeen and twenty percent alcohol in the wine. It is then placed on the roof of my adega in wooden barrels to age, in that the young wine is exposed to a carameliz-ing effect there due to the heat."

"Cheers," exhales John loudly. Then his eyelids droop shut and his head falls onto the table. At the last moment, Simon reaches for John's wineglass before it has a chance to fall out of his hand.

"Your friend seems to have had a few too many," grins Robert.

"Yes, and now I have to figure out how I'm going to get him back to the ship. Do you have a cart or something with which I can move him?"

Henriques is beaming. "I'll give you a wheelbarrow. But don't imagine it's so easy to get from here to the port!"

"I think I'll manage that. And I'll bring the wheelbarrow back tomorrow."

"Fine, Simon. Then let's taste the rest of the wines and you can tell me how Jan ter Bruggen has been going over the past few years."

Pushing the old, heavy wheelbarrow with John in it through the narrow alleyways of Funchal is quite a demanding task for Simon. Sweat is dripping from his chin and pouring down his back, down to the waistband of his trousers. John lies cosily in the barrow, mumbling unintelligible sentences to himself. While it is generally downhill, there are however a few steep, uphill sections to get through on the way. The closer he gets to the port, the more furious Simon becomes, with both John and himself. Why did John have to drink so much and why hadn't Simon done a better job of looking after him?!

Suddenly, there are three young boys standing in front of the wheelbarrow. Before Simon can react, they are rifling through the helpless John's pockets and have already taken out something golden – a watch.

Great, that's all I need now! When it rains, it pours!

Simon lets go of the barrow handles, which then hit against the cobblestones with a loud thump. The back of John's head slams down hard against the wheelbarrow's wooden edge. In a matter of seconds, Simon confronts the three young lads and plants a punch on the chin of the one in the middle. As that boy loses his balance, one of his accomplices squeezes past the wheelbarrow and flees. The other one, the one with the watch, turns around and starts running too.

After him! Simon breaks into a sprint. In a wild chase full of twists and turns through the alleyways, they run down the hill until Simon is on the thief's heels. By this point he is boiling over with rage. With one quick, strong blow to the back, Simon pushes the lad into a doorway. Without thinking about it, Simon starts punching. His fist hits the other bloke in the face, making blood shoot out of his nose. On top of that, he then knees him in the stomach. The chap wails and doubles over, but Simon kicks him once more, and then he is out cold on the ground. Simon reaches for the gold watch.

Only now does he become aware of what he has just done. He had been so furious at John for drinking too much, that he just exploded and released his rage. It slowly dawned on him that he had overreacted and had lost control of himself. Simon takes out his handkerchief and kneels down next to the boy. He then grabs him gently from the back of the neck and raises his head a little in order to carefully wipe the blood from his face.

The door next to them creaks open and an old woman appears with a bowl of water and a towel.

"I saw what happened!" she booms.

"Everything?"

"Yes! He stole a gold watch from you. You retrieved it."

"I overreacted. It was wrong of me. I shouldn't have hit him like that."

"But you're still here … If he had won, he would have run away. I know him and his friends."

The old woman crouches next to Simon and holds the bowl of water out for him. Simon takes the wet towel and uses it to clean the boy's face. The thief slowly regains his senses and opens his eyes in slow motion. Simon forces himself to not avoid his gaze, but instead to stare wilfully into his eyes. Confused, the boy sits up and continues to stare at Simon. Simon in turn gets up and pulls the old woman up with him.

How will the young man react?

Slowly, very slowly, he creeps backwards before turning around and running away.

"You showed him!" declares the old woman with satisfaction. "Those boys are always threatening us oldies and stealing from us. There are three of them."

"True," confirms Simon. "But I still shouldn't have allowed myself to explode like that."

"Why don't you come inside and have a drink?"

"That's very kind of you. However, the friend they tried to steal the watch from is waiting for me a few streets away. I have to return to him."

"Goodbye, young man," says the old woman. "You're very brave … You didn't run away!"

So that's how we landed in the 'Paradise of Madeira' in the best weather, and in a matter of seconds, little Tom found himself in a life-and-death situation. In that situation, I reacted exactly in the right way. I worked out what the situation was like, calculated the risks, saw a chance of rescuing him and single-mindedly used that chance. But when the three boys stole John's watch on the following day, I wasn't in control of the situation. I followed my instincts and just let out my rage without thinking about it. I was appalled so much by my behaviour that I learnt I should never let it happen again. At such moments one is no longer in charge of the situation; one becomes vulnerable and subject to defeat.

That adventure on the way back to the ship is something John would not remember. Only the bump on his head was something he would carry around for a while yet. And me? I spent that night lying in my cabin, thinking – about Marala. Her wedding day was getting closer and closer.

11. Learning to listen and toughen up

When Simon returns to the 'Whitecap' late in the afternoon of the following day, the sensation caused by his rescuing little Tom seems to have died down. He had left the ship very early this morning, returning the wheelbarrow, and then spent the day in the vineyards with Robert Henriques.

John is sitting on the poop deck, full of expectation. He's been looking for Simon all day. His headache has now subsided and the fresh air on deck is doing him good. He then sees Simon climbing up to the uppermost deck.

"Simon! Where were you all day? I've been searching for you!"

"You look much better now, John."

"My watch is gone! We have to look for it!"

"Gosh, you snored loudly last night!" replies Simon, laconically.

"Did you hear? My gold watch is gone!"

Obviously agitated, John stands before Simon, gesticulating wildly. From far away, it probably looks as if the two of them are having the fiercest of arguments.

"Simon, don't you understand me? I have lost my gold watch. It's a family heirloom – the only thing that really means something to me!"

Simon grins, then reaches into his trouser pocket, pulls out John's watch and dangles it in front of his face.

"My watch!" Tenderly, John strokes the metal object with his fingers. He then inspects the watch in minute detail. Suddenly, but slowly, he lifts his gaze to meet Simon's eyes. "There's blood on it."

"Oh! I didn't notice it."

"Where did it come from?"

"John, can't you remember anything that happened yesterday?"

"I can remember a lot! I still remember that we were at Robert Henriques' house, and then I somehow managed to come back to the ship. Then I woke up and had an enormous headache. I thought I was going to die. At some stage, I got up. But it was already well into the afternoon."

"Well – as you could probably gather from your headache, you drank so much at Robert Henriques' that you fell asleep on me. We put you in a wheelbarrow and ..."

In a strikingly matter-of-fact way, Simon continues to describe the events of the previous day. When he is finished, John touches the back of his head with his hand. "So that's where this gigantic bump comes from!"

"Unfortunately there was nothing for it. I had to act fast!"

"Thank you, Simon. Never before has someone defended me like that!"

115

Astounded, Simon sees tears welling in John's eyes, which eventually run down his cheeks. How odd to see a grown man crying!

"John, it was really nothing special!"

"Yes it was, Simon. They could have robbed us of everything … or worse: they could have harmed us!"

"Please, John, calm down. Everything turned out well."

"Yes, thanks to you! You took matters into your own hands!" John gets more and more impassioned. "A boy falls off the ship, right between the ship and the quay wall – and before I even have the chance to notice, you're already in the water. Then three brutal chaps confront you and a drunk, helpless John, rob him – and you don't retreat even one barleycorn. You know no fear, Simon, and I admire you for that! And you're only seventeen years old while I'm already thirty-five."

"But John, everyone is different. You have your advantages in other areas."

"Oh, Simon. You're simply following your path in life without fear or trepidation. But you don't have any idea how I feel or why I'm on this ship at all." During this speech, John's face has turned bright red and his facial expression has become more aggressive, almost frozen.

"John, settle down and I'd gladly listen to you. Otherwise … you'd bet- ter just keep it to yourself!" Simon gets up and goes to sit down a few yards away, on the other side of the poop deck.

John follows him. "Please forgive me. You're right. My tone of voice was inappropriate." He clears his throat once again and swallows before continuing, "I told you that I'm an architect, that I come from Cambridge, and would like to explore the big, wide world …" John's voice sounds calmer now, even though there is still a certain degree of tension visible on his face.

"Yes," nods Simon.

"But that's only half the truth," continues John. "I come from a respected family of architects in Cambridge, and have a younger brother. I've always wanted to be an architect. My brother, on the other hand, wanted to be everything – except an architect."

"That works out well! So you became an architect and your brother is doing something else. Why don't you take over your father's business?"

"Simon, there's one thing you should know: We were raised very strictly, by both my father and my mother. As a child, I wasn't allowed to do any- thing, and later on I was meant to be able to do everything! As an architect, my father was always patronising and correcting me – he never really believed in me and therefore never assigned any great responsibility to me. In hindsight, I think I wasn't able to mature on my own at all. Up until now,

116

I've always lacked the courage to go my own way, to develop my own style, and to think beyond Cambridge as an architect. In the end, my father made sure that my brother also became an architect and took over the office, and thus took my place."

"I don't understand that. Why did your father prefer your brother? Didn't he have problems with him?"

"My brother is good at adjusting to and complying with the wishes of others. I've never been very good at that."

"Humph … well," mumbles Simon.

"You don't know what to say, right?"

"What do you want me to say? I'm listening to you. It was very different for me. I guess I've always had a mind of my own and I often used to cause my parents great distress. Whenever I hear about how others grew up, it becomes clear to me how downright tolerant my parents were. They very rarely stopped me."

"Yes, that's what makes us different. You have learnt to deal with different types of people and situations – I haven't. You have no reservations, you know what you're capable of, and I don't."

"Slow down, John! You're making it sound like I'm a hero. But I'm not!"

"I don't want to be a hero either, Simon. But I want to try my luck in the New World and prove to my parents that I'm capable of being a good architect and of courageously taking my life into my own hands."

"You'll manage to do that, John," declares Simon, smiling confidently. "Now let's go and see whether dinner has been served yet."

"Thank you for listening to me, Simon," says John and wipes the tears from his face. "And – please, keep it to yourself!" He takes another look at the watch before putting it in his inner jacket pocket. "This watch is the only thing I brought with me from home to remind me of my family and to spur me on to succeed!"

Later that evening, Simon is sitting on the roof of the central companionway, looking up at the bright, starry sky. The stars are twinkling like buttons on a black curtain. From the harbour of Funchal, Simon can make out individual lights leading all the way up into the mountains. The conversation with John really got under his skin, and is still bothering him. He never would have thought that his friend had such problems. Up here, Simon can reflect in peace. The only sound that reaches his ears is that of the Atlantic. Aside from those on watch on the quarterdeck, Simon feels like he has the whole ship to himself.

But then he hears a quiet, tremulous voice. "Leave me alone, please!"

Simon looks around. There are three shadows moving at the front of the ship. Simon turns his head to one side and places a hand behind his right ear. He puts all his concentration into listening to find out what they are talking about.

"Rushfort, you told the captain on me! You told him that I pushed your stupid son off the gangway!"

"No, I didn't." Arthur Rushfort's voice sounds choked and distressed. "I didn't say a word!"

"We'll see about that! I'll wipe that smile off your face!" threatens the other man.

"Corwin, that's Flynn Corwin," thinks Simon. Silently, he slips down off the companionway and sneaks, crouched down, toward the shadows. Suddenly, he hears two or three dull thumps that sound like punches. Simon rushes over in time to witness Tom's father being held fast by Harold, Corwin's constant companion, while Corwin punches him in the stomach. Arthur Rushfort is now doubled over and gasping desperately for air.

"Corwin, what are you doing? What did he do to you? Let him go!" As if from nowhere, Simon emerges from the darkness. Shocked, Harold releases his grip on Arthur, causing him to fall down to his knees. Quick as a flash, Flynn Corwin grabs Simon's arm and twists it up behind his back. From the corner of his eye, Simon notices Arthur get up and hobble away. But Harold's fist is already connecting with his stomach. Simon squirms in pain.

"So much as a peep from you about this, Braun, and you'll really get to know what we're made of!" hisses Flynn Corwin in Simon's ear. Harold's fists continue to hit Simon's stomach and face. Finally, Simon runs out of strength and he slumps down like a sack of potatoes. Corwin lets him sink down onto the ground, and then finishes him off with a couple of kicks. Then everything around Simon is engulfed by darkness.

Pain, strong pain. In the belly, face and back. Simon's head is pounding. He slowly tries to open his eyes and can vaguely make out an oak ceiling above him. Then his eyelids shut once more. A short while later he attempts to open them again, and this time he finds himself looking at John's face.

"Simon, by Jove, you're opening your eyes!" gasps John. "We have been very worried about you. How do you feel?"

Simon tries to say something, but he can't speak.

"Just stay in bed, everything will be fine," John reassures him and turns around. "That's right, Doctor Baker, isn't it?"

"Your friend will get well again, Mr. Parson. It's mostly just bruising, meaning he will be on his feet again in a couple of days."

The ship's doctor leans over Simon and presses his stethoscope against the boy's chest.

118

"He's opening his eyes again, doctor!" calls out John. "He's awake."

The doctor raises his head and scrutinises Simon's eyes.

"Mr. Braun, where do you feel pain? Could you describe for me how strong it is?"

"How … did … I …" It's difficult for Simon to answer. Doctor Baker reaches for a cup and holds it up to Simon's lips. Once he notices that it's water, he takes a big gulp. And then he lets his head fall back on the pillow.

"How did I get here?" Simon finally manages to get out.

"Arthur Rushfort and three other men brought you here," explains John, visibly relieved that Simon can now answer clearly and distinctly. "He also reported that it was Flynn Corwin and his friend who made such a mess of you."

"Let it be," mumbles Simon. He wants to push the matter aside.

"You can't just let it rest! The captain will also want to question you about this!"

"Leave it alone!" repeats Simon.

John wants to continue, but Doctor Baker stops him.

"A couple of days' rest and then you will be able to do anything again – even dive into the Atlantic," says he, packing his things before saying good-bye.

John now wants to know more. "Simon, Arthur Rushfort said that you stood up for him so as to try and stop Flynn Corwin and that Harold fellow from beating him up …"

"Please, John, I don't want to talk about it anymore," mumbles Simon, and closes his eyes.

Over the next few days, John proves to be a genuine guardian angel. He gets rid of everyone who wants to visit Simon – only Captain Johansson and George Boyt are allowed in. However, Simon continues to refuse to make a statement against Flynn Corwin and Harold, until the Captain declares that he is unable to take action and is therefore forced to let the matter rest.

For the past two days, the 'Whitecap' has been back in the middle of the Atlantic. For the first time, Simon takes his dinner in the mess hall as before.

"Simon, it's great to see you back in the land of the living!" exclaims Henrietta Tremaine, adding with curiosity, "Now tell me what really happened."

"Henrietta, just forget about it. I don't want to talk about it."

"Yes, but you could at least suggest that the two of them were the culprits. You must be black and blue all over! And you're surely in a lot of pain." She pauses for a moment. "Or are you afraid?"

Simon knows very well that he is being observed by Corwin and Harold. So he just puts on a fake smile. This pretence continues over the next few days.

Then, one evening, after a beautiful, sunny day at sea, something happens. A crowd of people, who want to go to their cabins before dinner, has gathered around the rear companionway. Corwin and Harold are among them. As they are about to go down the solid oak staircase with the brass bannister, Simon and John happen to be standing in their way while having a conversation. Corwin gets ready to push Simon out of the way. He obviously feels superior and on the safe side. But Simon just turns his head to stare directly at him completely straight-faced. The two men have one another fixed in their gaze for what seems like an eternity. Finally, Simon says in a steady and quiet voice, "Touch me again, Corwin, and you'll make an enemy for this life and the next. Whenever something befalls you, you will have to look over your shoulder and wonder whether Simon Balthasar Braun isn't behind it."

With deliberate slowness, he walks past Corwin and disappears in the direction of his cabin. He gently closes the door behind him, but a moment later, John comes in, "What was that, then?!"

"What do you mean?"

"Don't deny it, I was standing pretty much beside you. Your facial expression, Simon – it was so ice-cold! That's exactly how I would imagine a killer, a gun fighting hero during a duel!"

"John, I just want him to drop it. I just want him to leave the people on board alone."

"I'm glad you didn't stare at me like that. I would really be afraid of you if you did, Simon!"

I'm not sure what had unsettled me more back then: What John had told me about his relationship with his father, or the fact that he had cried in public. A man who cries in front of others – unimaginable!

Never again did I want to be beaten up as I was then. During the next few days, I could feel every bone in my body aching. In order to be able to avoid such situations in future, I needed to behave and negotiate more shrewdly. And in case there was no alternative, I would have to learn to be faster – with my thoughts as well as my movements. And now I knew what it was like for the other person if I injured them – something that was not always avoidable. Sometimes it would even be necessary for survival. That was the lesson I had learnt from this confrontation with Flynn Corwin.

12. The thrill of a moment

"Mr. Braun, please wait a second!"

Simon is about leave to the mess hall – first as usual – straight after breakfast as the first officer addresses him.

"Good morning, Mr. Triggerman."

"The captain is awaiting your company up on the quarterdeck!"

Simon hurries to the deck with swift steps. Captain Johansson is standing between the helmsman and another sailor, the compass in sight.

"Good morning." Simon steps into the circle and Captain Johansson nods at him.

"Mr. Braun, I had promised that you could work for us," the Captain mutters into his beard, his eyes wandering towards the sail. "The weather is promising to be glorious again today. Therefore, Triggerman and I have agreed that we should place you at Alan's side. He is an experienced sailor."

He turns to look at the gangly man standing next to him. "Alan, you are to be responsible for looking after Mr. Braun's well-being. Are we understood?!"

"Yes Sir!" Alan gives a curt nod to Simon. He doesn't have much hair on his head and Simon notices two scars, one on his right cheek and one on the left shoulder.

"Mr. Braun, we'll be climbing up the main mast to the rigging and clamber onto the yards to set sail."

As soon as they are out of earshot of the Captain, Simon says, "Alan, you don't have to address me so formally. Just call me Simon. If I may work here, then I wish to be treated exactly the same as all the other sailors."

"Listen up lads!" Alan shouts to the other sailors at work on deck. "You all know Simon – he's the one that rescued little Tom. Today he will be working with me up in the masts."

As Simon looks at the crew, he sees friendly but also rather sceptical faces.

What must they think – a passenger from a good home, freely volunteering to work with them, performing lowly tasks?

Less than ten minutes later, Simon is on the footrope moving up to the highest spar of the main mast, setting the sail with Alan and another sailor. Alan shouts against the wind, "How are you feeling, Simon? This isn't your first time up in the sails, is it?"

The other sailor yells at Alan, "He's no idiot."

"I was up in the sails once during the crossing to London," Simon shouts back. "But the masts weren't by any account as high as the ones on the 'Whitecap'. It's a marvellous feeling! How high up are we here?"

"We are more than forty metres above the sea. The wind blows differently up here than it does down on deck. Make sure that your feet are always securely in place and that you are always holding on with at least one hand. Otherwise you won't be up here much longer when the next storm brews."

"Alright," nods Simon and then shouts enthusiastically, "Just look at the endless horizon! It's incredible!"

And he looks on: water and horizon. The wind blows away all of Simon's concerns and he enjoys his day up in the sails.

As the sailors receive their helping of stew on the upper deck, Simon stands with them in the queue.

"Why don't you go to the officer's mess to eat?" asks Alan. "They are surely serving up something good for the fine folk there."

"Alan, are you at loss for my portion here? Or have I not earned it yet?"

"No, no, of course you have, but here there's only stew with some crackers."

"If I work here, then I shall also eat here!"

A smirk spreads across the faces in the queue.

Captain Johansson and John Triggerman stand beside each other on the quarterdeck. "Triggerman, can you see Braun over there? Now he's even eating stew with the lads."

"I'm surprised he's lasted the whole morning. I was convinced that he would have given up by now."

"Not me – not after he saved young Tom. Hats off to Mr. Braun. The lads seem to respect him. He has the charisma of a nautical master."

"I wonder if they will really accept him?" Triggerman wonders doubtfully.

"Probably not all of them, but he's already battling for his place. He has a very straight-forward view of things. He'll always be alright, anywhere he goes – you can be sure of that, Triggerman. Just let him carry on a little longer if he wants to."

"Yes Sir."

The days unwind slowly like a rope from a roll – boredom starts to spread. Captain Johansson ends his regular log book entries with "Nothing particular to report." The 'Whitecap' cuts evenly through the quiet waves of the Atlantic and the constant wind ensures their steady progress.

The sun is high in the sky with most of the passengers spending their days on the upper decks in order to enjoy the good weather. The crew has placed folding chairs and teak tables on the poop deck. John Parson, Curtis

122

Tremaine and Alastair Rowley are seated at one of these tables and while away their time playing cards under the watchful eye of Henrietta Tremaine, who, along with Simon, stands close behind her husband at the railing.

"Curtis, surely not that card!"

"Henrietta, would you like to play?" asks John with a feign smile.

"Curtis, deal the second black card from the left!"

"Henrietta, would you kindly hold your silken tongue?" Curtis snaps, his cage somewhat rattled.

Simon whispers to Henrietta, "Curtis is right. The other players shouldn't assume that whilst they are playing, their spouses are helping them to cheat. Anyway, it might be that he already has this game in the bag."

Henrietta removes her hand from her mouth and whispers back, "I hadn't thought of that. My Curtis is no fraud! I didn't say anything about the other players' cards!"

Then she turns to look out at the Atlantic and sighs. "It is so boring here! It's difficult to occupy oneself with anything."

"That can change in a moment," says Simon. "Who knows when we'll find ourselves in the midst of a full-blown storm ... I prefer to be bored with nothing to do."

Simon continues to watch the card players for a while, but then remembers George's suggestion: that he should take a closer look at the ship, particularly the workmanship of the beams, especially at the bow. George had informed him that one could access a storage room by means of a steep set of stairs in the rear storage deck. Behind this is located another storage room, one lined with rows of shelves and through which one could re-enter the cabin area.

On the spur of the moment, Simon makes his way towards the middle hatchway. Whilst doing this, he must be careful where he steps as people are to be found everywhere: lying, sitting, reading books, playing board games or simply bored stiff. He descends the stairs, arrives at the upper deck and looks about. No-one here ... I haven't seen that before – most of the time it's teeming. Simon makes his way towards the storage deck. Here are the provisions that are required for a journey as long as this. Large barrels and cases are stacked on top of each other and moored.

Simon moves forth slowly and in doing so notices the branding on the barrels. For example, one cask is branded 'Madeira', produced by Henriques & Henriques, dated 1819 and contains 600 litres. However, there are also barrels filled with port and whisky. As Simon approaches the bow, he notices small dribbles of water running down the inner side of the tailboard and disappearing down through the floor. That means the ship is not completely watertight. Simon remembers George explaining to him that there are two pumps on deck that are in operation the whole day, around the clock. Thus the intruding water is pumped out of the ship's belly.

After having studied the massive bow with its thick oak beams, Simon orientates himself slowly towards the rear, passing further rows with more boxes. Finally he stands before the extremely steep stairs and begins his ascent. The door at the top has a knob. As Simon turns it, the door opens with a short creak. Suddenly – a scurry: Two small grey mice seek shelter below a shelf at lightning speed.

The smell of cheese and ham penetrates Simon's nostrils. So this is where the provisions are stored! Bottles are lying on one of the shelves. Simon carefully draws one out. Written on the bottle in white paint is, "Grant's Whisky, Scotland 1807." Simon respectfully puts the Whisky back and looks around some more. Suddenly he hears a quiet noise – it sounds like a person groaning. Simon stands still and quiet to locate its source. It must be coming from the storage room next door. Quietly and slowly, Simon moves towards the door, his ears sharply tuned. The groaning is not constant, rather it sounds rhythmic. It doesn't sound like someone in pain or who is scared – instead it sounds like someone straining themselves.

Where have I heard this before? Simon tip-toes towards the door, quietly grasps the doorknob and slowly begins to turn it. No creaks, that was lucky! As Simon opens the door carefully, he observes something else: a light whimpering that complements the moans. So it is coming from two people. In Simon's mind a scene develops, one that he has seen before: In the saloon in Rotterdam. But by now he is already standing in the room. The room is large with protruding shelving units that are filled top to bottom with bed linen and other cloths. Maybe it's sails? As Simon peeks around the first shelf, he sees Lindsay Rowley leaning with her back to the wall. In front of her stands a man, whom Simon recognises, even from behind: Flynn Corwin. Lindsay Rowley has her eyes shut, her face is sweaty and her hair is tousled. Simon is spellbound by the sight of her naked knee. Her feet are not touching the floor, her legs are wrapped around Corwin's hips. His trousers are dropped and his boots stand abreast from them like two stiff posts. Corwin moves his hips with an even rhythm – the deep groans and light whimpering sounds undulate at exactly the same pace. Simon is rooted to the spot – in actual fact he would love to leave as quickly and quietly as possible, but he is too fascinated by what he is witnessing. His brother had a crude expression for this game. But he'd also been sure that it was only possible to do it lying down.

124

Simon's body is extremely tense, this scene makes him feel strange. Then he gets a shock: Lindsay Rowley opens her eyes, first gazing at him with a misty look, but then suddenly wide awake. She says nothing and the scene seems to freeze. Tiny little dimples start to form beside her lips. Simon feels his face starting to flush. He wants to turn away but he cannot. It's as if his body were blocked.

The moans and whimpers intensify and Lindsay's eyes become misty once more. Simon notices that something is happening to him, too. That's enough to shake him up. Silently, he leaves the room. The corridor to the passengers' cabins starts behind the storage room. Simon stands at the end of this corridor in front of a large mirror. This is where the ladies on board come in their pretty dresses to critically observe whether their hat and hair-style are correctly in place. Simon slowly looks himself up and down – his arousal can still be clearly seen in the mirror. He tears himself away and disappears as quickly as possible into his cabin.

At dinner, Lindsay Rowley takes her usual place beside her husband, Alastair. She is careful to ensure that she can keep Simon in full view. The young man immediately feels embarrassed and he evades her eyes. He then tries to pretend as if nothing has happened. As Henrietta, Curtis and John Parson discuss the card game that her husband lost against Alastair Rowley, Simon glances intermittently across at Lindsay, unnoticed. He had already noticed the pretty lady at the start of the trip, although he hadn't paid her particular attention after this. Now he looks at her with different eyes. She is tall, has a slim figure and her dark, thick hair falls in curls around her shoulders. Lindsay seems to have good taste: at least Simon likes the way she dresses herself. However, he is most of all impressed by her bright blue eyes. Those same eyes that had just before faced him.

"Pardon me, Mr. Braun." Simon has managed to avoid Lindsay Rowley for a few days. He obviously noticed that she wanted very much to speak with him. Now she stands beside Simon at the railing on the boat's deck.

"Yes?" Simon starts to notice himself tensing up again.

"You have kept your mouth shut," she whispers.

"Sorry?"

"You didn't tell anyone about what you saw."

"Why should I?"

"You don't care about gossip – that is fitting to your character."

"How on earth would you know what is fitting to my character?" asks Simon. " You don't know me at all."

"I have been watching you."

Lindsay plays with the rope, which she is holding to keep herself steady, and gazes out across the dark blue ocean.

"Because I saw you. I noticed that."

"No, already before – I already noticed you before that. You save a young boy's life or you return the stolen watch to your friend."

"How do you know about the watch?"

"I asked John Parson, because I had heard something about it. He told me the story. He truly admires you."

"Is that so?"

Simon leans on the railing in order to keep a firm footing. His gaze follows that of Lindsay's, out across the sea.

"John told me your entire life story." Simon doesn't know what to say. Finally he explains, "I can keep a secret, Mrs. Rowley, I can assure you of that."

"I had never a doubt in my mind of that."

"Can he as well?" Simon wishes to know.

"I think so. He is a noble man."

"I doubt that very much," Simon says decisively and looks Lindsay in the face.

"You don't like him!" Her blue eyes flash.

"I find him to be a careless show-off."

"Flynn is charming."

"That's only because he wants something from you. And that he's already achieved – however his real triumph will only come when he has told the 'right' people."

"I was wondering about something else," Lindsay abruptly changes the topic. "What are you planning to do in Boston?"

"I do not know."

"So you are travelling to Boston and do not yet have a notion of what you want to do there? Do you know anyone there?"

"No."

"Then you are completely on your own! Maybe I can … we could help you."

"How would you help me?" asks Simon bitingly. "Oh, but of course – you know me so well!"

"Exactly," confirms Lindsay Rowley with an impish smile. Then she turns around and leaves.

Simon looks at her wistfully as she departs.

"Simon."

Lost in thought, he turns. John has approached him.

"What was it that Lindsay Rowley wanted to discuss with you?"

"She wished to know what I have planned to do in Boston."

"Simon, she has already interrogated me twice about you!"

126

"Yes, I know."

"Why is that?"

"I sussed that out during our conversation. She knew things about me that only you would know."

"I beg your pardon!" John looks a little confused.

"It doesn't matter," Simon explains.

"Are you sure?"

"She doesn't know anything she shouldn't know. But John, in the future do be careful to whom you tell things."

"I promise."

During these days, when I was bored or took a rest, I was always con-fronted with a vision of Marala and had to think of her marriage. There were just a few more days left – and I was here, on my way to America. How would she look? What would she be wearing? A dress or a sari? Would she be happy with a man who was so much older? Would she be his only wife or would she have to share her husband with other women?

The situation with Lindsay Rowley bothered me, however. I had been turned to stone as I had caught her with Flynn Corwin. I hadn't been able to budge. My head had been telling me 'go' but my body refused to follow. This short moment absorbed me in numerous respects.

13. One door slams shut – another swings open

Already in the night, a twinge starts in the belly. By morning it has grown into a full-fledged nausea. Simon wallows in his bunk. Finally he gets up and clambers on deck. Air, fresh air to breathe! He drags himself to the bow and sets himself there on a beam. With each wave, the 'Whitecap' rises and falls calmly and evenly. Indeed, today everything seems to suggest that the weather will be sunny and pleasant.

Simon knows very precisely the reason for his queasiness. It is the 7th of June, 1829. Today, Marala will marry Meghnad Kapur. Simon had already felt this sickness once before, when he had to leave Marala behind upon his departure from London. Today their parting will be sealed: On the present day there lays not only some thousand kilometres between Marala and himself, but worse still their door to a shared future slams shut.

The sun rises, bit by bit the deck comes alive. The crew begins working as ever more passengers arrive, more or less well-rested. But Simon would rather be away, far away and all alone.

"Good morning, Simon." John lightly slaps a hand on his shoulder.

"Morning," mutters Simon.

"What's ailing you? So downtrodden?"

"I'm sick as a dog, and honestly I'd rather spend today on a deserted island."

"Why, for goodness' sake?"

"Why? Today is the 7th of June, and it's all over!"

"What is over? Tell me already!"

"But you've seen her, Marala, the girl who stood on the wharf as we left London."

"Yes, now I remember. But why is it over with? What's changed? Are you operating a carrier pigeon service on board here?" John attempts to cheer up his friend.

"Please, John, don't make jokes. Today is the day that Marala marries another man."

John wants to put his arm around Simon's shoulder, but he holds off. "Please, John, just leave me in peace."

"All right, I'll see who else is prowling around on deck."

Simon's glance falls on the net under the bowsprit, that wooden pole which juts from the bow like a spearhead. Simon climbs over the figurehead, the 'White Lady', and springs into the net.

"Yes, here things are bearable," he thinks to himself. "So long as the weather stays like this. And how do I get back from here? Well, we'll see."

The fresh sea air and the even swayings of the ship make it so that Simon eventually falls asleep like a baby in a cradle.

On the poop deck the second officer observes the passengers killing time.

"Hello John, have you seen Simon?" he asks John Parson.

"He's sitting up front on the bow."

"I was just there, and I didn't see him."

"What is it then?"

"Nothing out of the ordinary, the captain wants to see him."

"He certainly won't be in a state for that today."

"Why's that?"

"Well, he should probably tell you that himself. The reason is very pretty and named Marala."

"Marala, the Indian girl? Let's see if I can find him yet."

Hardly has George Boyt gone when Lindsay Rowley is standing right next to John.

"Marala, what a peculiar name. Who is that?"

"She's marrying today in London – and Simon's sure got problems with it."

Lindsay steals a glance at her husband Alastair, whose rapt attention is absorbed in a game of cards. "Alastair, I'm going for a little stroll."

Alastair Rowley briefly raises his head and watches his wife saunter away, twirling her umbrella in her hand.

"Simon, hey, Simon!" calls George over the 'White Lady'. The figure down there in the net seems to be in a deep, sound sleep.

"Simon!" screams George with all of his voice. Slowly movement comes to the sleeping body. Simon looks up, looks briefly confused and shakes himself.

"George! Good that you've come. Give me your hand and help pull me up."

"How did you ever wind up here?"

"Jumped … I wanted to have some privacy. Brrr, I'm chilled to the bone!" Simon barely feels his stiff limbs.

"No wonder. Up here the wind booms in your ears," confirms George and adds, "What's happening with Marala?"

"She's marrying today," answers Simon curtly, climbs from the top of the figurehead onto the bowsprit and jumps down.

"So that's why you want your privacy," nods George. "I can understand that. Inform me in case you need something." Soon only the second officer's back is visible. As Simon straightens himself out, he finds himself looking directly into Lindsay Rowley's luminous eyes.

"Good afternoon, Mr. Braun."

"Good afternoon, Madam," answers Simon and sits down on a thick beam.

"Please excuse me for speaking so plainly to you. I overheard Mr. Parson tell Mr. Boyt that you weren't feeling well."

"Mrs. Rowley, I ... Why are you interested in that?"

"Couldn't you just call me Lindsay?"

"Pardon?"

"I mean it!"

Simon requires a moment to reflect, being quite preoccupied. Then he answers, "Good, Mrs. Rowley, ehm ... Lindsay."

"So, Simon, what is going on with Marala?" she asks, now visibly unburdened.

"Now what do you know of Marala?" asks Simon astonished.

"The name Marala appeared a short while ago – and apparently she is the reason for your bad mood."

"Marala is a young Indian girl I met when I was in London for the first time with my father. We've kept contact ever since that time, written to one another ... Marala is the best friend that I have. And she is wondrously beautiful. When I came back to London for a few weeks, on my way to America, we immediately got along with one another ... We kissed ..."

"You fell in love with one another, you are in love!"

"In love – what does that mean? When we were together, I always had a queasy feeling in my stomach, and when we weren't together I wanted to see her again as soon as possible."

"But that is the most unmistakable sign that you are in love!"

"But now it must come to an end!"

"Because she is marrying another?"

"She's marrying a much older man. Her father works for him."

"Why not? My Alastair is also much older than me."

"But Marala is marrying him out of deference to her parents."

Simon hesitates, and then speaks anyway, "And you are not truly happy either, are you?"

"What makes you think that?"

"You know already ... I saw you two together ... under the deck." It embarrasses Simon to say it out loud, and his face flushes with heat.

"Oh, you mean that!" Again the tiny dimples form near Lindsay's lips, just as in the situation of which Simon had spoken. "You can't understand the situation," explains Lindsay. "I don't want to speak about it with you now ... perhaps later."

130

"Please excuse me. I don't want to intrude."

"Simon, I'd actually like to suggest something else to you. Recently I've been speaking often about you with Alastair. When we arrive in Boston, you'll have no one to turn to. We feel that you could really amount to something, given the right support. Could you conceive of accompanying us and living with us?"

"But you hardly know me at all! We've conversed just a few times, and then you invite me to live with you?"

"You need not be shocked," states Lindsay, smiling. "We came to know you as a friendly young man who comes from a good family. Your manners are excellent, although you don't make much of it. But what's learned is learned. We've heard that you've mastered multiple languages. You have courage, and the fact that you took your life into your own hands at just seventeen has extremely impressed Alastair and me. Therefore we would like to help you to a good start in your new life."

"Nonetheless: You can only judge from appearances. You have no idea whom you bring into your house."

Lindsay doesn't answer right away. Then she looks Simon directly in the eyes and says, "Alastair and I cannot have children. We've been thinking for a long time that it would be nice to foster someone. Just reflect on it. Give yourself time, after all you don't have to decide tomorrow."

"Lindsay, I thank you for your proposal. I will give it consideration."

"Very well. If you have questions, then please come right to us." Lindsay briefly lays her hand on Simon's. "There, and now I'll leave you in peace."

There sits Simon now. He feels completely overwhelmed and so many thoughts are whirling through his head. Marala … marriage … done and gone … Lindsay Rowley … Boston … a new life …

"Excuse me, Captain Johansson, one word please."

The captain stands next to John Triggerman on the helmstand. Now he looks to the side at Alastair Rowley, who has just spoken to him.

"Good afternoon, Mr. Rowley. You would like to speak with me?"

"Yes, but confidentially."

"Then may I invite you into my cabin. This way!" Captain Johansson approaches Alastair Rowley and points in the direction of his cabin.

"Thank you."

As he enters the captain's cabin, Alastair immediately notices the luxurious furniture, predominately finished from the finest mahogany. Then a round table, perched on four artfully carved legs, catches his eye.

"Please take a seat." The captain courteously pushes a comfortably upholstered chair to Alastair Rowley. "May I offer you something? Madeira, Port?"

"A Port, please."

With a precise grasp Captain Johansson retrieves two crystal glasses and a dark bottle from the cabinet. "How about a ten year-old Tawny Port? One of my passions."

"Sounds terrific, many thanks."

The captain takes the time to slowly fill both glasses with the Port wine. Then he asks, "What can I do for you?"

"For a start: Can we keep our conversation in confidence?"

"Mr. Rowley, so long as the things about which you'd like to speak do not either violate the law or slander another, I don't see a problem."

"On the contrary, Captain. It concerns Simon Braun."

"Simon Braun?" Astonished, the captain raises his thick brows.

"What do you think of him?"

"Mr. Rowley, you ask me what I think of Simon Braun? Now you have to explain why you're interested in my opinion."

"Ah well, for that I have to reach back a bit. As you know, I am one of the directors of the BBBC, the Big Boston Bank & Co. My wife Lindsay and I essentially lack for nothing: We have a beautiful great estate directly in Boston and lead a varied and joyful life. But, you see, we cannot conceive children. You know, time flies, one grows older and at some point one asks oneself: Was that it? It's much too late to adopt a baby, but nonetheless we would like come to the aid of a younger person who proves himself worthy, whether through education or better still by the structuring of his life."

"I can follow that," nods the captain. "And for this you've chosen Simon Braun?"

"Yes, perhaps. He is just seventeen year old, travels into a foreign country far from home, knows no one, doesn't know what he wants to do."

"Mr. Rowley, all of what you say is true. But one can also observe all of these points from another perspective. Simon Braun is just seventeen years old, it's true, but he speaks at least four languages, of which he knows German and English natively; he wants to go to a foreign and far-off country that he has himself sought out, and if I'm not mistaken he's already covered more than three quarters of the way. And your argument that he knows no one is false! I don't know any one on board here who knows more people than he, or conversely: Here on board there is certainly no single person who doesn't know Simon Braun. More still, I know only few people who are as curious for knowledge as him."

"But captain, my wife and I would only like to help him."

"You have noble motives, as I understand it. What I'd like to say is: You'll have to 'sell' these motives differently to Simon Braun, or he won't get involved. He is a very independent young man and he isn't eager to accept help."

132

Alastair Rowley pensively swirls his Port glass. "So would you basically confirm our impression that Simon Braun is a loyal and honest person from the ground up?"

The captain has to smile benignly. "Well, Mr. Rowley, if I had to choose one person to accompany me on a journey across a desert or sailing around the entire world, Mr. Braun would be one of the few to even come under consideration. You've heard of course, how he saved the life of young Tom. There are hundreds of people aboard the 'Whitecap', but Simon Braun was the one who responded within seconds and acted."

"Thank you, Captain," Alastair Rowley arises. "You have helped us a great deal. That we keep this conversation between ourselves …?"

"Only natural, Mr. Rowley."

Restlessly Lindsay Rowley had been pacing back and forth on the boat's deck, repeatedly stopping to watch the door of the captain's cabin on the quarter deck, and resuming her nervous gait. Finally Alastair comes on deck.

"There you are, Lindsay!" With quick strides Alastair approaches her.

"And?" She looks at him expectantly.

"To keep things short: The captain feels exactly as we do."

"I already told you, you can trust in my knowledge of human nature."

"Yes, yes, but now I am satisfied. When a person of such integrity as Captain Johansson confirms your judgement, it can only strengthen us in our enterprise."

"I am so glad that your mind's at ease!" Lindsay Rowley takes her husband in the arms and smiles contentedly.

"I have an appointment with the Tremaines on the poop deck," says Alastair. "Curtis wants to win his money back. Will you accompany me?"

"Happily, my dear." Merrily Lindsay links arms with her husband.

I still remember this day as if it were yesterday. The twinges in my belly stayed with me the entire day. I had the feeling, such as never before, that I had lost something permanently. Marala was married. It was as though a door was slammed directly before my nose. Persistently I had the thoughts: Should I have sought my happiness in London? Would I have had a chance with Marala? Would there have been a future for us both?

I had hardly given any thought to Lindsay Rowley's proposal. Why I hadn't, I still can't say. Then I began to give it serious consideration. What were the aims of the Rowleys? Why had they precisely chosen me? Had a new door truly been opened for me?

14. Through the storm on a knife's edge

Yet another lovely day at sea draws to a close. On the boat deck, John Triggerman and George Boyt stand and watch the ascending moon. Most of the passengers are already below deck; up here it is very calm. The impressive panorama of the starry sky shines above both officers.

"Good evening." Simon Braun comes to them out of the semi-darkness.

"Hello, Simon."

"Isn't that an exquisite night sky?"

"Yes, exceptionally," agrees George with Simon. "And with it the rising moon, which reflects in the water. Everything is black as pitch, yet the moon's glow is so comforting."

"I don't want to scare you, gentlemen …," out of nowhere appears Captain Johansson behind them, "… but we experienced precisely this situation on the 29th of June, 1815 here in the Atlantic. The night began with a gorgeous sunset, the moon stood above the bilge just as today … And then came the storm. For all my life, I will never forget this night!"

"Captain, do you mean to say that we will have a storm tonight?" asks John Triggerman with a concerned look. "But the night looks so peaceful!"

"Yes, you said it, almost too peaceful … that can change very suddenly, and then we'd have a violent thunderstorm. Not necessarily, but it's possible," says the Captain. "We had better prepare ourselves for it."

Simon awakes in the night, as his forehead hits the edge of the bed. Immediately he notices how turbulently the 'Whitecap' is rocking.

"Simon, are you awake?"

"I am now." Simon touches his forehead.

"What's going on there?"

"I would say the weather has taken a turn."

"You mean there's a storm?"

"Hats off to the Captain!" murmurs Simon.

"How do you mean?"

"Last night I was standing with George and John Triggerman on the railing of the boat deck. We were admiring the moon and an incredibly beautiful night sky."

"And – what did the Captain say?"

"Storm. Not necessarily, but it's possible!"

John's ears prick up visibly. The sea rages deafeningly, and the woodwork of the 'Whitecap' moans and groans eerily under the force of the ocean.

"Simon, I feel sick. Do you think we're going to sink?"

"Madness, John. I'm going up … Maybe I can help!"

In no time at all Simon is dressed, reaches for his thick jacket and stands before the door which leads to the deck above. Besides the sailor guarding the door, no one is here.

"Good morning, Liam," greets Simon.

"Simon, I can't permit anyone to pass through here," the sailor apologises.

"But I might be able to help!"

"If I let you on deck, I'm in for trouble."

"But you can say I claimed that John and George would expect me on deck … Or better: Just say that I escaped from you!"

Liam grins, turns around, and Simon sneaks past him. Already on the stairway he hears the wind roaring. A shiver runs down his spine and the tiny hairs on his arms stand on end. He feels no fear, but he is tense and nervous about what is to come. Right before he reaches the top step, the ship swings so strongly that he is thrown forcefully back and forth; but he can still just barely clasp the handrail.

Always keep a hand holding on.

Safety ropes have been stretched crossways all across the deck. Carefully Simon peeks around a corner; he wants to see what's happening on the bow of the ship. A violent rush of noise pounds at his ears as the 'Whitecap' rises and falls heavily. When the bow lifts from the water, Simon only sees the open sky; as it sinks with a wave back into the water, the 'Whitecap' itself seems to be headed directly for the ocean floor. Simon turns around and climbs slowly towards the helmstand. There stands George, who gazes back at him in astonishment.

"Simon, what are you doing here?" he yells. His hood almost covers his whole face. Simon can only recognize his eyes and nose.

"I want to help. What can I do?"

"You can hold on!" George barks back. "Don't stay standing in the middle. Back to the wall!"

"Braun, why aren't you under deck?" the Captain bellows at that moment, standing in a dark corner in front of the quarter deck.

"He wants to help," assures George.

"And where is Triggerman?"

"He's at front … Making sure the sails at foremast are hauled inboard."

"Boyt, all sails must be hauled inboard!" The storm immediately blasts through each word, and the noise of the sea drowns out the rest.

"Take care that it happens quickly!" orders the Captain. "I am taking command here now!"

George tries to make his way across the few meters to Simon. At that moment something large and heavy slams on deck directly between them. It is a sailor. He lies lifelessly on his back. His right leg is sticking out of his body in a completely unnatural way. On the back of his head a red puddle has formed, which is immediately flushed away by seawater and swashes over the deck.

"God!" George screams and jumps to the sailor. He kneels down, lays the finger of his right hand on the jugular vein of the lifeless sailor and looks to Simon, who is at his side in a flash.

"He has to go below," calls George. "He fell from the main mast. While you help there, I'll go to the mizzenmast. Do you think you can do it?"

"Definitely," cries Simon. "Don't worry."

"You heard the Captain, the sails need to be hauled inboard. I'll take this man under deck, the doctor will look after him."

Rivulets of water are streaming over George and Simon's faces. Is it rain or seawater? Whichever it is, there's far too much.

"You can rely on me, George, I can do it!"

George takes the lifeless sailor by the collar of his shirt and pulls him over the deck. As Simon watches after him, a wave snatches his entire body, sweeping his legs up from under him. Luckily he had been clinging to one of the security ropes with both hands. He lands on his behind and jumps back up as fast as lightning, before the next wave can hit him. Then he grapples his way to the main mast. There, he grabs hold of the rigging as the next wave swooshes over the deck. Simon jumps onto the railing and clambers up the shrouds of the rigging. Fortunately it is slowly becoming day. Though grim clouds darken the sky, Simon can at least see where he is going. The water still pours as if from buckets. Meanwhile Simon's jacket is soaking wet. Carefully but single-mindedly he climbs up. Higher and higher still, until he recognises three sailors on a yard, one of whom is Alan.

"Simon! Good that you've come!" calls Alan. "We've already lost two men. Stay out and help us reef the sail."

Up here the wind is even stronger than below on deck, and it whips the rain at one's eyes like needles.

It must be far worse for the sailors up here in the masts than for the people under deck. On account of the enormous heights, the swinging movements and also shifts in direction are even more extreme. "Riding wild horses must be child's play compared to this balancing act," Simon thinks. But finally, after a long period of intense struggle, the sails of the main mast are indeed secured and the sailors find themselves back on deck. One wave after another pummels into the ship.

136

"Alan! Alan!" screams Captain Johansson, gesticulating wildly.

"Simon, come with me!" Alan clutches Simon by the jacket.

Side by side they scramble to the helmstand.

"Alan, go with Mr. Braun to the storage deck and help the others tie up the barrels and boxes," orders the Captain.

"Aye-aye, Captain!"

"How many men have we lost on the main mast?"

"Two sailors have fallen," Alan explains, grasps Simon by the sleeve and points in the direction of the middle hatchway.

Stooped, Simon works his way along a rope over the deck. After a few meters he encounters two sailors pulling forcefully on a rope winch. Again, a massive wave hits the deck with full force. One of the sailors is able to hold on, while the other is swept along by the wave to the other side of the ship. Thinking on his feet, Simon lets himself fall on his stomach and slides after him. He is able to grab the other by the pant leg right at the railing, before he can be washed overboard. With his free hand Simon reaches for a belaying pin rail and finds a protruding pin to take hold of, on which a rope is moored. In only a few seconds Alan is there. The other sailor gets back on his feet, and forces out a smile despite the biting wind and the heavy rain. "Thanks!" he calls and hurries on.

Alan and Simon make their way in the other direction, into the hold of the 'Whitecap'. On the upper deck the passengers cower together, fear in their faces. Children hide themselves in their parents' arms. A whimper sounds through the deck and the smell of vomit is in the air.

Further down in the ship on the storage deck, the woodwork creaks and moans; it must endure an enormous pressure. Simon and Alan join the sailors working here and help secure the stacked barrels and crates two- and threefold, so that they cannot tear loose in the turbulence and become ungainly missiles. Dexterously Simon climbs above the tall stacks of barrels to distribute the ropes. It's a breeze for him, who after all used to compete with Christoph climbing around the barrel storage cellar back home.

Finally Alan calls up to him, "Hey Simon, we're done here. Come up with us!"

"I'll come right after you," Simon answers. "I want to check on a few people on the upper deck!"

"All right!"

With determination Simon balances on the upper deck on his way to the Rushforts' encampment. For these scarcely twenty-five meters, he needs far more time than usual. Finally he lowers onto the tarpaulin of the Rushforts, who have tied up all of their belongings to prevent them from shifting around. Little Anna, seeking help, has cuddled next to her mother.

"How are you all?" asks Simon.

"All right," says Arthur. "But up there all hell must be breaking loose. Will we ever survive it? Will the ship endure the storm?"

"Don't be worried," Simon reassures him. "The ship is no nutshell, and the captain is an old warhorse who knows exactly what to do. He's very calm."

"Were you above?" asks Tom with wide eyes.

"Yes, I was even high up in the main mast. Up there a real devil of a wind blows into one's ears."

Again already Simon is jostled into the air. Elisabeth takes hold of his hand and squeezes forcefully. "Watch out, Simon!"

It is only around late afternoon that the storm noticeably subsides. But for the sailors there is hardly a break: now it's time to clean up.

Simon, who has been helping the entire day, finally turns back exhausted into his cabin. "John, you look a sight!" he says as he sees his friend.

"I'm not doing well, Simon, I've never been so sick in my life," answers John. He is pale as a ghost and he seems to struggle to keep his head up. "Is it over, Simon? Is the storm past?"

"Yes, and as far as I can judge, the 'Whitecap' has withstood everything well."

Briskly Simon slips into a dry pair of pants and a fresh shirt. The stench below deck is hardly bearable. He retreats as quickly as possible back above. More and more people are congregating there. In the crowds Simon encounters Henrietta Tremaine.

"Simon, how are you?"

"Thank you, Henrietta, good. Where have you left Curtis?"

"He's on his way, but he's had a rougher time in these sea conditions than I have."

Simon nods sympathetically. At this moment he sees Flynn Corwin and Harold at the railing. Corwin turns around, his face quite sallow. Simon can't hold back a grin. Then someone bumps into him: the first officer.

"John!"

"Oh, Simon. Excuse me!"

"It's nothing. Are there any dead or wounded?"

"Eight sailors dead or missing and one passenger, an older man; his wife says he had a heart condition. In addition, countless injured among the crew and the passengers."

"That is not good," says Simon, but John Triggerman already hurries onward.

The next day, the captain has arranged a funeral service at noon. The flag of the British Empire lies carefully folded before the helmstand next to the compass. The bodies are lined up next to one another on the deck and sewed into sailcloth. Captain Johansson begins the funeral service with prayer. In following he pays tribute to the deceased sailors. When he has finished, a loud chorus of "God save the King" rings out over the ocean. Each body is laid on a wide teakwood plank, which projects over the railing of the 'Whitecap' towards the sea, and is covered with a British flag. One after another the dead slide slowly into the Atlantic, their final resting place.

Simon stands next to John Parson and Curtis Tremaine, and obliquely before him he spots Lindsay and Alastair Rowley. Due to the crowding Lindsay stands slightly behind Alastair. Next to her Simon sees Flynn Corwin, who whispers something to Lindsay, grasping her arm as he does. She is evidently trying to get rid of him, and whispers hastily back. Lindsay seems serious, even worried. She can't manage to extract herself from Corwin, there are simply too many people standing in the crowd.

Simon wants to know what's going on there, and pushes himself closer to the group. Now he can hear clearly as Corwin speaks to Alastair Rowley. "Mr. Rowley?"

Alastair turns around, "Yes?"

"I absolutely must speak with you!"

"But not now," Lindsay pushes herself in between. "Mr. Corwin certainly has the patience to wait until the end of the funeral service." She tries to manoeuvre her husband somewhat further to the front of the crowd, clearly as far as possible from Flynn Corwin. Without keeping a straight face, Corwin gives her one more pat on the behind.

"That looks like blackmail," Simon thinks to himself. He takes it upon himself to speak about it with Lindsay at a suitable moment.

After Captain Johansson has spoken the last prayer, the crowd disperses. Simon looks around for the Rowleys and for Flynn Corwin, but they are nowhere to be found. But then Simon recognises Lindsay Rowley below on the boat deck. "Perhaps now is the right time," he thinks to himself and goes speedily down to her.

"Hello, Lindsay."

"Simon!" Lindsay turns around. Simon is shocked to see that she has tears in her eyes.

"Is everything all right?" he asks.

Silently she shakes her head.

"What did Flynn Corwin want from you?"

"I don't want to talk about it," Lindsay declares.

"Lindsay, he also spoke to your husband, I heard everything." Simon paused. "You can't avoid Flynn Corwin."

"But I can't talk about it!"

Simon summons all his courage, "I'm just telling you what I think. I believe, Corwin wants once more to … you know already. And he's putting you under pressure by extortion, threatening to tell your husband everything if you don't succumb."

"Simon, please …"

"Or not, it could be otherwise: He says that you also had fun with him and therefore it's only normal to repeat it, is that right? Lindsay, I saw you then, you enjoyed it!"

"Where are your good manners, Simon?"

Now Simon is becoming vexed. "You want me to move in with you in Boston and live with you, but you don't trust me? Lindsay, I told you first thing what I think of this Flynn Corwin. He doesn't mean well to you, he's a villain!"

"No, I do trust you," says Lindsay quite meekly. "But please, let me try to speak with him one more time."

"You won't have any success," asserts Simon.

Lindsay looks sadly at him. "Simon, please don't let this situation decide whether you move in with us … Please!" she implores. Then she briefly strokes Simon's hand as it rests on the railing, and turns to go.

At that moment John Triggerman appears standing beside Simon.

"Simon, would you please follow me? The captain desires to speak with you."

"Now?"

"Yes, at once."

Simon follows the first officer under deck. In the captain's cabin the first thing he notices is the large map table in the middle of the room. A large window front inserted in the stern of the 'Whitecap' allows a wide view over the once-more friendly ocean. Yesterday's storm seems like a distant dream.

Just then Simon notices that the room is full of people. Captain Johansson, John Triggerman, George Boyt, the ship doctor Dr. Baker and Alan stand in a circle along with two other sailors Simon doesn't recognise – and finally, the sailor who he had caught by the pant leg yesterday and saved from being washed overboard.

"Gentlemen," begins Captain Johansson, "this is a sad day for us, but we can also be thankful. We're still alive, the ship sustained only little damage and is in good condition. We could save the majority of the sails, and for that we have one person to thank – who isn't even part of the crew." The

140

captain pauses and looks into the circle of people. "We are gathered here below and not on deck, because if I know the person who has brought us here, he doesn't want any commotion. You can well imagine: I am speaking of Simon Braun."

Simon is confused, almost shocked, when he hears his name. He hadn't expected that.

Now Captain Johansson looks at him directly. "Mr. Braun, on behalf of Fred, too, I would like to give you my sincere thanks." He nods to the sailor who Simon recognises from the morning of the storm. "Fred is only here today because you grabbed hold of him before a wave could drag him into the ocean."

After the captain has shaken his hand, Fred too approaches Simon with a wry, bashful smile. "Simon, how can I thank you?" he asks.

Simon thinks for a moment, then his eyes light up. "I have an idea," he smiles whimsically. "But I'd like to talk about it confidentially with you and Alan."

That afternoon in a quiet corner of the ship, Flynn Corwin suddenly sees three sailors of the 'Whitecap' opposite him. One of them, a lanky chap with a scar on his face, speaks to him.

"Mr. Corwin, how are you doing? Have you weathered the storm well?"

"All right, thanks," answers Flynn Corwin cautiously. There are three powerful men before him.

"A ship can only survive that if it has a superb crew," the other continues.

"That seems clear to me." Corwin looks inquiringly from one to the other. What do the sailors want?

"There has to be one hundred percent cooperation, and everyone must be able to trust one another."

"Certainly."

Amicably and calmly, the ostensible spokesman continues. "There each is responsible for the other and they protect one another mutually ... as well as their friends!" It remains unclear to Flynn Corwin what the three are getting at. But they appear quite resolved.

"I understand," he declares. "But why are you telling me all this?"

"Because of Lindsay Rowley," replies the sailor. "Be friendly to her, but reserved ... Do we have an understanding?" His tone is slow and relaxed, but no less threatening for it.

Corwin is speechless and gulps. The three seamen are already turning away when the hulk turns once more and asks, "Mr. Corwin, do you know the newest member of our crew?"

"What new member?"

"Simon Braun."

With an open mouth Flynn Corwin remains behind alone in the hatch-way, petrified as though turned to stone.

The weather on the sea can change as quick as lightning and within sec-onds dangerous situations arise. The storm taught me that it's important to plan for all eventualities and to prepare oneself as well as possible.

This menacing storm, the 'little Whitecap' on these insanely high waves, the massive volumes of water, this ice-cold wind and the ear-shattering noise – that is when I realised that there is sometimes hardly a shoe's width between life and death. I learned that it's always worth struggling, that one can't give up, even when there seems to be no way out. Besides, I experi-enced something which I had never known before as such: The experience of camaraderie, or simply put: teamwork. During the storm I experienced for the first time what a good crew can manage together.

15. Setting foot on a new continent

Out there … Boston must be somewhere out there.

Lindsay Rowley stands lost in thought on the bow of the 'White-cap' looking over the 'White Lady' towards the sea. In the dis-tance, the horizon is still all that can be seen.

It won't be much longer now before we are finally there, back home after more than 130 days! Lindsay has to think of Simon. When will he call another place "home"? Can her house become this place?

Not far away, Lindsay hears the murmuring of men's voices. She turns around. Flynn Corwin and his constant companion Harold are standing a few meters away. This is my chance!

Lindsay breathes in deeply and approaches both men.

"Mr. Corwin, can I ask a minute of your time?"

Shocked, Flynn Corwin looks up and lifts his hands as if to protect him-self. He almost gives the impression that he is afraid of Lindsay.

"Huh?" she thinks to herself, but continues anyway, "Could I please speak with you alone for a moment?"

"That's not necessary," replies Flynn. "It's much better if no one sees us together."

"Excuse me?" Lindsay asks, astonished.

"Well," intones Flynn, "you have a friend on board who is dearly concerned about your reputation."

"A friend?" Lindsay is stunned, but the two men have already walked on by. "… crew," she hears Flynn say as he hastily departs.

"Lindsay, here you are!" Still perplexed, Lindsay looks toward her husband. What was the meaning of Flynn's reaction? But she has no more time to give the matter thought. "We ought to begin talking bit by bit with Simon," says Alastair. "Or else we'll be in Boston before the issue's been decided."

Lindsay nods silently.

"Oh, by the way, have you heard?" Alastair adds. "Simon is now part of the crew."

"He's now part of the what?"

"Yes, Captain Johansson mentioned this morning that since yesterday, Simon Braun officially belongs to the crew of the 'Whitecap'," nods Alastair, lifting his hand to wave. He has discovered the Tremaines on the other side of the deck.

Unnoticed, Lindsay lags behind a few steps. She has to think. Different strands of thought hang in the air – but she cannot bring them together. But fortunately the second officer, George Boyt, and John Parson approach her just then.

"Excuse me, Mr. Boyt, may I briefly interrupt your conversation? I have to ask something – in private."

"Naturally, Mrs. Rowley. How can I be of assistance to you?"

"It concerns Simon Braun. My husband just told me that Simon now belongs to the crew of the 'Whitecap'. Is that true?"

"Yes, Mrs. Rowley. Simon Braun has proved himself as a full crew member, not least during the storm. Thus the captain wanted to decorate him … in a way that Mr. Braun could accept."

Lindsay nods comprehendingly. "Thank you, Mr. Boyt. That was all I wanted to know." As she follows Alastair, it goes through her head, "You have a friend on board who is dearly concerned about your reputation." Flynn Corwin had said that, and then came the word 'crew'. Now Lindsay understands, as though the scales were falling from her eyes. Simon Braun, how did you manage it? She shakes her head, smiling.

After lunch Alastair Rowley waves Simon over to his and his wife's table. "Mr. Braun, please take a seat with us."

Simon sits and looks back at two expectant faces. "You can surely imagine why I've asked you to join us."

"Yes, Mr. Rowley."

"Lindsay and I have considered that you could begin your new life in America in our house. What do you think of that idea?"

"Mr. Rowley, I've already told your wife that your offer surprises me. Indeed, you hardly know me."

"And you hardly know us," responds Alastair. "We'd rather speak of what we can offer you. We live in a large house with plenty of space, where you would feel anything but confined. From our house to my bank in Boston is around fifty minutes by coach. Boston's economy is growing tremendously, and later you will have outstanding opportunities to develop yourself."

"What do you mean by later?" Simon looks from Alastair to Lindsay, who smiles at him encouragingly, and back at Alastair.

"My bank, the BBBC, is one of the major financial sponsors of Harvard University, of which we are very proud. It was founded in 1780. The way in would only require a few minutes of your time."

"Do you mean that I should study at the university?" Simon's eyes widen in amazement. He had never thought of this possibility until now. "But Mr. Rowley, in my whole life I've never seen a school from the inside."

Alastair Rowley smiles benignly. "Should I assume that you'd like for once to see Harvard from the inside? Or are you concerned that you couldn't cope with the demands?"

"I can't say that," replies Simon earnestly and contemplatively. "I would in fact be interested in the university ..."

"Wonderful, then we are in agreement on this point!"

"And what is taught there?" Simon now wants to know.

Here, too, Alastair has an answer ready. "Theology, law and political economy are the most important faculties there. In your case, Mr. Braun, I wouldn't think of theology."

Simon shakes his head in amusement. "For that I'd have better stayed in Germany."

Alastair treads onward, "I see that you want to become a businessman, and in that case law wouldn't hurt. But political economy would be much more interesting and useful for you. An exciting field!" raves the banker.

Rapt in attention, Simon has followed the explanation. But now he says, "Mr. Rowley, that is all doubtless very exciting and stimulating. But where's the catch? What do you expect from me?" Involuntarily he begins to speak faster. "It seems to me that we're already in the midst of a deal.

But unless each side brings benefits to the table, it can't be a fair exchange. You've already spoken of the advantages for me, but what about yours?"

Smiling, Alastair Rowley looks at his wife. Lindsay makes a surprised face, but says nothing.

"Cripes, this boy is good! He scrutinises the circumstances! He has instinct!" His gaze returns to Simon. "Mr. Braun: On the one hand, we'd really like for you to live with us and quite simply to help you. On the other hand, as a businessman I cannot help but think further. I am of the opinion that your furtherance will have effects which will be most rewarding for myself as well as you. The better I get to know you, the more certain I am that what I invest in you in the coming years will be, now, let's say: returned fifty-fold."

"One to fifty, that sounds enormously profitable," replies Simon amicably. He remains businesslike, but inside he is tense down to his toes.

Alastair Rowley straightens up in his seat and smiles mischievously. "Please understand me correctly, Mr. Braun. You mustn't do what displeases you. I will not compel or force you, and you don't have to sign anything either. I don't want you to pay me back any of what I invest."

Lindsay has been looking back and forth between the two men for a while already. Now she turns outraged to her husband, "Alastair, why bring up all of that? Why must you start off with business deals once more? We want Simon to move in with us, and you're scaring him off!"

"Lindsay, please let your husband speak. I'd like to hear what he has to tell me," Simon insists, anxious to reassure Lindsay.

"I have thought for a long time," Alastair now continues, "about what could possibly prevent Simon from moving in with us. I think the issue is that he cannot pay anything. Thus I found it better to suggest a business to him which he would find agreeable."

"Yes, and how does this business look?" asks Lindsay, dumbfounded.

Alastair briefly raises his hand and turns back to Simon. "Mr. Braun, I do not want to use you, and you have nothing to fear. We solely want you to join us in our house, and all the rest will follow by itself. I am certain that the business will then start off on its own … just so … You are not obliged to actively do anything in particular. I promise you – and you too, my love – that I will tell you when the deal has been fulfilled. But until then it will remain my secret."

Simon is still unsure what he should think of the offer. It sounds too good to be true. "What if, after a few months, I want to move back out?" he therefore asks.

"Then you move out," explains Alastair firmly. "There are no obligations for you." He pauses briefly and then clarifies, "I am convinced that you will learn many new, exciting and necessary things with us."

Simon looks Alastair Rowley earnestly in the eyes, then stands up slowly, extending his hand to the other. "All right, I'll come with you!"

Alastair lifts himself and grasps Simon's hand spiritedly. "The right decision, Mr. Braun! Then I would like to also propose we speak on informal terms, Simon."

"Thank you, Mr. Rowley, proposal accepted!"

"Call me Alastair, please."

Lindsay's whole face is beaming. Her relief is clear to see. She pulls Simon to her and embraces him.

The door to the mess hall flies fitfully open, and in the next moment John Parson stands in the room. He raises his arms high and cries, "Land … Land in sight!"

The passengers jump up and a mob of people streams through the corridor and up the steps to the deck. Everyone is chattering excitedly. As Simon sees the many people, he takes a step back. This mob is not for him. A look towards the poop deck tells him that no one else will find room there. But in the lower part of the main mast rigging, he sees Alan. Simon struggles his way over to him through the turmoil. Alan stretches a hand to him. "Hey, come up, Simon! You'll get a much better view from up here."

"It's full on deck!" Simon remarks in astonishment.

"It's always like this," says Alan. "Everyone's excited that we'll be docking in a few hours. Just climb all the way up to the top. From there you'll have a stunning look-out and no one will trample on your feet."

In a flash Simon stands on the top and holds a hand over his eyes. Truly, far in the distance he makes out land, hills and perhaps the outlines of buildings. As Simon looks below in the meantime, it seems as if he is looking at an anthill. Somewhere in its midst are the Tremaines, John Parson, George Boyt, Alastair and Lindsay Rowley – people with whom he has spent the last weeks in a confined space.

A few hours later the 'Whitecap' enters Boston Harbour, a mere formality for a man as experienced as Captain Johansson. Slowly and patiently the ship passes the various wharves, the warehouses and shipyards on its way to 'Long Wharf', the largest wharf in Boston. The passengers on deck are thrilled and overjoyed. For so many days they had been on board, on these wavering planks. Now they will finally have solid ground back under their feet.

"Simon, where were you the whole time? I was looking for you!" cries John Parson through the turmoil. Simon grins from ear to ear and points to the sky with his right hand.

146

"I could have thought so, actually," grumbles John and jostles Simon jokingly on the shoulder. "What are you going to do now? Shall we go on land together?"

"No, John, I'm going to move in with the Rowleys. It's the best decision I could make. They are very friendly people, and I feel like I can trust them."

"Definitely, Simon, you've really had good luck. And if ever someone asks if you know a good architect …"

"John Parson," answers Simon with a smile. "I only know one, and he is dear to my heart."

At precisely 2:38 o'clock in the afternoon, this Wednesday the 24th of June, 1829, the 'Whitecap' moors at the 'Long Wharf' in Boston. The first passengers quickly surge of board through the narrow gangway. With all their luggage, they can only move forward very slowly. Simon observes the action on the wharf from the boat deck. To Alastair Rowley's question when they should disembark, he had answered that he'd be in no hurry at all, as though he had all the time in the world.

Coaches are waiting, and many people carrying heavy loads depart on foot. A crane heaves barrels from the 'Whitecap' onto land.

"Hey …," calls a child's voice below Simon. He has a pretty good idea who it is. Already the boy jumps up to him. "Simon, my friend!" Tom Rushfort faces him with a big grin.

"Tom! Now we've finally made it. We're in America."

Seconds later the rest of the Rushfort family is standing before Simon.

Arthur clasps his hand firmly.

"Simon, take care of yourself, and stay as you are."

Elisabeth furtively wipes a tear from her eye. "We will never forget what you did for our Tom," she whispers. Then she takes Simon in the arms and presses him close to her. "Good luck in America!"

All of a sudden half of the crew is circling them. All grasp Simon's hand and pat him powerfully on the shoulders. Captain Johansson is also there. "Mr. Braun, I too would like to personally bid you farewell. And one thing is certain for you: If you ever travel on my ship again in the future, your voyage will be courtesy of the shipping company."

Simon has to laugh. "Captain, I have your word!"

Suddenly a thought comes to him. "Where is George Boyt?" He looks around and then discovers George, who is standing a few meters away and grins broadly back. Simon goes up to him. "George, now we also have to say goodbye. It was nice to have met you."

"Take care of yourself, Simon. You've had a real stroke of luck for your start in the New World … Congratulations."

"Yes, I am excited about the opportunity which has been offered to me."

"Make something of it!" says George insistently.

"You can rely on me, George," responds Simon earnestly.

"And I can always visit you when I come to Boston; now I know where to find you."

"You are always sincerely welcome to my home, George!"

A shining black, elegant coach stands on the wharf. A tall man with dark hair has dismounted from the coach box and begins to stow the Rowleys' many trunks.

Alastair Rowley lays a hand on Simon's shoulder. "Simon, before you get in, I'd like to introduce you to our loyal coachman and steward, Karol Rudzinski – Karol, the young man here is Simon Braun. He will be living with us from now on."

"Very well, Mr. Rowley," answers Karol somewhat stiffly and with an unusual sounding accent.

"Good day, Mr. …"

"Just call me Karol, Mr. Braun," responds the other, already seeming a bit more relaxed.

"Simon!" someone calls from the 'Whitecap' in this moment. George Boyt comes storming down the gangway. "Wait! What is your new address? I want to visit you and be able to write you."

Simon turns to Lindsay, who responds immediately. "Quincy Street in Cambridge, Massachusetts."

"Thank you, Simon, and much luck in America!"

"May there always be water beneath your keel," replies Simon, as would be expected.

A little later, Simon sits in the coach across from Lindsay and Arthur Rowley, while Karol drives the horses on. For Alastair and Lindsay it is now headed home, but for Simon it is leading to an unknown future.

You know, the situation with Lindsay Rowley and Flynn Corwin … My solution wasn't exactly in the delicate English style, but an end simply had to be found. And one which would not harm Lindsay, at that.

I've spent many days and long nights deliberating whether I really should have taken the chance of moving in with the Rowleys. Today I see it as the right decision, but in hindsight it's always easier to say what was right or wrong.

148

At innumerable points in my life I've made acquaintances and formed friendships. Many of these people have left just as they came. But there are exceptions. Then one meets a person with whom one is bound one's entire life, though one sees one another only seldom. For me, George Boyt would become such a friend.

BOOK 3

1. A new home

Horses' hooves clack along steadily over the cobblestones. Simon's gaze drifts over the houses rolling past. They are large and made of stone, and seem very familiar to him. And those street names which he can recognise in passing don't sound so foreign.

"Here it looks just like in England!" Simon exclaims in bewilderment.

Alastair nods. "Our area is called New England. These states were the first regions in North America to be populated by the English. Here you find place names like Dover, Newport, Worcester, Exeter, Plymouth or Cambridge – that's where we're going now."

"How long is the way?"

"About an hour," explains Lindsay. "By the way, we call those first English settlers here in New England the Pilgrim Fathers. In 1620 they came on the Mayflower from Southampton in England and landed at Cape Cod, roughly a hundred miles south of Boston. In Europe the Pilgrim Fathers were persecuted because of their religion, and so they left the 'Old World'. They broke away from the English state church because the reformation of the English church wasn't strict enough for them …"

Simon listens attentively, then asks, "Why can't people just believe what they want to believe? Must everyone always be the same? "

"That, I fear, will never change!" sighs Alastair.

At last the Rowley's coach leaves the city behind. A slightly hilly landscape now extends before the window, with forests and green meadows in its midst – everything bears a striking resemblance to England or Germany.

Then they reach Cambridge and Quincy Street. As the coach makes a turn, Lindsay announces proudly, "That is our home."

Behind carefully trimmed bushes and tall trees, Simon can see a white house with a red tiled roof encircled by a neatly clipped hedge. A small

151

canopy stands over the entrance, and the windows have dark blinds. Simon himself comes from a lavish familial home, but this building surpasses all his expectations.

"What are you looking like that for, Simon?" Alastair wants to know.

"I am overwhelmed."

"You unfortunately can't see your area from here, since the windows look out onto the other side," Lindsay eagerly explains.

"Do you live there all alone? I mean, with the servants?" Simon asks in astonishment.

"No," Alastair responds smiling, "the servants live in that building, back to the right."

"Ah, I see it, and next to it?"

"That's where our horses and coaches are held."

Lindsay playfully lays a hand on her husband's knee. "Alastair loves horses," she says, "and he likes to go out riding when there's enough free time."

Now the coach halts before the entrance with two columns. Simon quickly jumps out to offer Lindsay a helpful hand.

"Simon!" she cries out. "What a gentleman you are!"

The heavy, powerful entrance door opens and an older man with sparse white hair and a serious demeanour strides toward them. He is wearing a sort of uniform.

"Good day, sir and madam. Was your journey satisfactory?"

Simon is amazed. How formally he expresses himself! He is as stiff as a poker.

"Thank you, Mr. Snyder," Alastair nods to the butler. "Everything as expected. And how have things been here in Cambridge?"

"In due form. There were no unplanned incidents," is the again very formal response from Mr. Snyder.

"Many thanks, Mr. Snyder. We will discuss everything else later."

"How old can this Snyder be?" Simon asks himself. "In his late fifties? In any case he makes a very stern impression."

"Come, Simon," Lindsay pulls him out of his thoughts. "I'd like to show you the premises."

They enter a large, high entrance hall. Simon looks above: He can see up to beneath the roof, which is carried by massive oak beams. Two women come toward them; one of them is very young and pretty with long brown curls, tall and very slender. With an open, curious glance she examines the guest. The other woman is clearly older, redheaded and a bit chubby. She seems very friendly and somewhat maternal.

"Good day, sir and madam," they both greet the newly arrived.

152

"Simon, may I introduce you to the heart and soul of our house? Mrs. Molly Jones, our cook. And that is Lilly Owens, our housemaid," explains Lindsay.

Simon nods cordially, still a bit reserved in the new surroundings.

"And this young man, my ladies," Alastair continues, "is Simon Braun from Germany. He will be living with us from now on."

"Good day, Mr. Braun," the duo answers so simultaneously that Simon has to refrain from grinning.

"Lilly, would you please unpack our luggage immediately?" Lindsay orders.

"Of course, madam." Lilly curtseys, casts another stolen glance at Simon and hurries off.

Lindsay takes Simon by the arm and points to the left. "Simon, at the front here you will find Alastair's study. As the director of such a large bank, he rarely has a regular day and often brings work back home with him. Behind the study there is a small salon where we normally take our meals. Over there," Lindsay spins around, "is the servants' common room, behind it the kitchen. And so, now we'll go back and see the large salon."

Lindsay walks straight ahead and opens a great double-wing door. It opens onto a gigantic room. The right side of the salon is dominated by a huge table, which could certainly seat more than twenty people. To the left, comfortable armchairs invite one to linger before a large fireplace of warm brick. On the walls hang tastefully selected paintings, and the ceiling is decorated with stucco. The most imposing thing, however, is the huge window wall on the back wall. Through the window Simon sees a terrace, beyond which a seemingly endless garden is visible.

"Simon – you aren't saying anything at all!" Lindsay remarks.

"What a view!" Simon responds. "I'm simply speechless."

"But we're not done yet," Lindsay impishly points out. "Now we go up to the first floor."

Shortly afterwards Lindsay stands with Simon on the balustrade of the gallery on the first floor. Lindsay explains and explains … Reading room, guest room, bedroom, dressing room … "Dressing room?" Simon blurts out in between.

"Yes," laughs Lindsay, "a room for my clothes, shoes, hats and so on." Simon is still speechless – even in his wildest dreams he would not have imagined what he sees here.

"Over here," Lindsay continues, "we have another guest room. That's where I sleep when Alastair snores too loudly. And as a good finale, you will find the bathroom over there."

"A bathroom?" Simon interrupts, astonished. "You have your own bathroom?"

"This way," Lindsay requests, "I'll show you."

Simon's eyes widen when he sees the bright, tiled room.

"Simon, don't you know something like this? You surely must have also bathed at home."

"Yes, but we don't have a unique room for it. I don't know anyone who has a bathroom. At home we put a tub in the kitchen once a week, where everyone bathes one after the other. In our rooms we have little basins and a mirror on the wall."

"This is much more comfortable, Simon, you'll see."

Simon points up toward a pipe coming out of the wall. Below it is a small tub. "And what is this here?"

"That is a shower. When you want to refresh yourself, you stand beneath it and let the water run over your head and body."

"I've never seen anything like it! It's like rain falling from the ceiling."

Lindsay can't help smirking at Simon's childlike wonder. "Simon, now I will show you your new realm. That is one floor higher."

Soon Simon is standing in the attic, in a large room with one wide window and two narrow ones to one side. A further window opens onto an exquisite view over the garden and the landscape behind it. Simon likes the expansiveness up here.

"I'm sorry," says Lindsay now, "the room is still only sparsely furnished. Before our departure to England we didn't know yet that you'd be living with us now. But in a few days it will look completely different. I will naturally see to it that some more nice furniture is installed here for you."

"It's already fine, Lindsay," answers Simon. "That's more than enough for a beginning."

"The other rooms on this floor are storage rooms," Lindsay comments further. "I hope that you will settle in well with us."

Still a bit dumbfounded, Simon perambulates the large room. "I've never had so much space all to myself."

Later in the day, tea and biscuits are served in the small salon.

"Now, Simon," asks Alastair, "what do you think of our house?"

"Honestly, I'm overwhelmed. I feel like I'm in paradise."

"Will you be able to feel comfortable in your new room?" Lindsay inquires with some concern.

"Naturally! You know, Lindsay, back home I already had it very good, but here … It's all really very generous."

"Tell us a little about your past," asks Lindsay, "do you have brothers or sisters? I am quite excited – we still know so little about you!"

Alastair also looks at Simon with anticipation.

"Well," Simon begins. "I was born in Mainz, which lies directly on the Rhine ..."

Simon narrates and narrates – and all of a sudden it's evening.

"Already dinner time!" cries Lindsay and claps her hands.

Mr. Snyder serves a chicken soup as an appetiser, with Lilly Owens alongside to help. Simon unmistakably notices that she is smiling surreptitiously at him. He reaches for the silver cutlery, and becomes conscious that he is holding something very valuable in his hands. Also plates, bowls and the rest of the porcelain are undoubtedly of high quality and high price. Mr. Snyder unerringly pours white wine in their glasses from a bottle wrapped in a champagne-coloured cloth. The butler seems distanced, but absolutely confident and precise at what he does.

"Simon," Alastair says to his young guest, "as the son of a wine cellar owner, can you tell us exactly from which German wine-growing region the Riesling comes which we have in our glass now?"

Lindsay gives her husband an almost angry look. "Alastair, why do you have to provoke Simon like that? On the first day, too, you really shouldn't!"

Alastair brushes her objection aside, shakes his head softly and looks back at Simon inquisitively.

Simon smiles. Then he examines the wine in the glass, sticks his nose in deep and closes his eyes. Next he purses his lips and takes a sip on the tongue, swishes it around, breathes in the air and lastly swallows. Quite slowly a smile spreads over his face. He declares, "The wine has a light-golden colour and a clear complexion. To the nose it exhibits a complex flavour characterised by white fruit. It reminds me of peaches and apricots, along with mineral tones, traces of earthiness and a hint of petrol. On the palate it is full-bodied, with lots of fruit ... Here too its aromas recall peach and apricot." He pauses and takes another sip. "The alcohol content is not slight, but it's well incorporated into the extract of the wine. Residual sugar and acidity are also well balanced." Simon looks at his host. "Alastair, this Riesling comes from a qualified winemaker and from a vineyard of high quality. The wine is clean, its components are finely coordinated – a work of good handicraft. However this wine comes not from Germany, but from the French Alsace. If I should still more precisely locate it, then I would say: from the region 'Haut-Rhin'."

Alastair jumps up and grabs the wine cooler, strips the cloth from the bottle and looks at the label. "Cripes!" he cries out. "Lindsay, he's right, it's a Riesling from Alsace and – you won't believe it – it comes from Eguisheim, region 'Haut-Rhin'."

"Simon, how are you able to do that?" asks Lindsay. "Why are you so well-versed in wine?"

Simon's glance falls on Mr. Snyder, who has stayed standing in the corner and lost his countenance for a moment. He stares at Simon with an open mouth. He has to pull himself together to keep his facial expression from slipping away. Simon wants to avoid laughing at Mr. Snyder and thereby offending him. Thus he answers without hesitation, "My grandfather Simon Hill is a wine and spirits dealer in London. From him I learned most of what I know about wine."

As Simon wakes up in his new bed the next morning, the first thing he hears is the twittering of birds in the garden. The sun shines brightly on his face. He stretches himself. He has had a wonderfully deep and dreamless sleep. His gaze meanders to the windows, behind which the new day awaits him. A new exciting day …

Below in the small salon, Alastair Rowley is already sitting at the table reading a newspaper – at any rate, Simon surmises that it is Alastair since the newspaper blocks his view.

"Good morning, Simon," comes his voice from behind the rustling paper. "Did you sleep well on your first night in America?"

"Good morning, Alastair. I slept wonderfully, like at home. It's marvellous to sleep in a real bed again."

"Well," Alastair folds the newspaper up, "then let's begin with breakfast."

"Where is Lindsay?"

"She's coming, she always takes a bit longer in the morning." Alastair reaches for the coffee pot and asks, "And – what will you do today? Any plans already?"

"First I'd like to take a look at the surroundings and get oriented."

"Then next week we'll ride to Harvard and see if we can accommodate you there."

"But first Simon is coming with me to Boston!" comes with force from the door where Lindsay now stands. "We must buy you a few things to wear. You can't run around like that."

"Lindsay, you don't also have to buy me clothing, too."

"You can't have much a wardrobe in your backpack," Alastair now interjects. "Viewed in this light, we are bound to outfit you for a start."

"So it's settled, Simon," says Lindsay conclusively. "Tomorrow we'll go to buy clothes!"

"In addition I'd also like to write two letters," says Simon.

"Naturally!" Alastair responds. "I'll have paper, quill and ink brought to your room immediately."

"And if you've written the letters by tomorrow, we can send them off in Boston," adds Lindsay.

156

It was lovely to have a home again. I was truly very graciously taken in and felt well from the start. But the luxury with which I found myself confronted made me anxious. Can one live in such riches, when other people don't know how they will find food to eat? Would the excess go to my head and make me into another person? And if I should later have to renounce it – could I do it? I couldn't answer any of these questions, since the answers lay in the future; but I believe it was good that already back then I was grappling with these questions. For in fact, there came back to me other times and other circumstances.

Naturally it was clear to me that I should initially accept many things from Alastair and Lindsay, but at times I had a hard time dealing with it. I would pay it back down to the last penny, there was no doubt in my mind.

2. Black is not quite white

Bright rays of sunshine stream through the alley's lush greenery, as if through a clear tunnel. Simon stands before the doorway of the Rowleys' house and for a moment he feels almost blinded. Then he walks down the alley, through which he arrived in the coach yesterday. He wants to walk to Harvard College. Curiously, Simon observes his environment. After a few hundred meters on Quincy Street he passes a church, and then the vista opens onto many more tall buildings. Some are built from red brick, others are covered with plaster. In the middle is a building crowned by a tower. This must be the College. Impressed, Simon considers the complex for a while before turning south ... Through the streets and alleyways of Cambridge he seeks a route down to the Charles River. During his walk he encounters the most diverse people of different skin colour and ancestry, as he knows from London before. Where is it that these people come from? Are they born in America or did they migrate like him?

Simon drifts around extensively, and eventually tries to find the way home. For this he is quite certain that he can rely on his sense of direction. The return route leads him over a narrow path bordered by high hedges and low trees. It is dark and cool here, almost a bit eerie.

157

At the end of the path stands a huge, thick bush. Simon circles it and finds himself suddenly on the Rowleys' spacious property once more. In the distance he sees the residential house, and the stalls before it. As Simon still hasn't seen them from the inside, he is intrigued. The stalls are clean and well-kept, like everything here. In the first lie different coaches, from open landaus to ample travelling coaches. In the back of the building Simon recognises various agricultural equipment. Clean and arranged in orderly rows, just like he remembers from home.

There being nothing more to see here, he turns to the second stall building. People must be conversing here, for Simon can hear several voices. Just about four to five meters before the slightly ajar entrance gate, he hears a clamour behind him. He turns around: A small black boy runs right past him. He has very short hair and wears a dark blue jacket. Simon guesses the boy is around ten to eleven years old. Quick as lightning, he disappears into the stall through the gap in the gate without looking around.

As though grown out of the ground, in the following few seconds there stand two sweating figures before Simon: a tall man with light blonde hair and a small, plump man who gives off a grim air. Both are unshaven, and together make a shabby impression. They hold rifles in their hands, pointed towards Simon.

"Out of the way!" bellows the big blonde. Simon has to think of something – now, right this second, something has to come to him. The two men are presumably after the little black boy. Simon doesn't know what they want from the little one, but he gleans that the boy is in a precarious situation.

"Pardon me, I do not understand you," answers Simon amicably in German. The men look at him, baffled.

"We want the Negro bastard, is that clear? To the side!" shouts the smaller man, seeming completely out of breath.

Win time, I've got to win time for the little boy. Still in German, Simon answers, "I cannot understand you, gentlemen. I am German and unfamiliar with your type of manners. I implore you, please, to put your minds to rest and explain peacefully what you want."

"We'll shoot!" cries the blonde. "Make way or we'll put a bullet in your belly!"

Simon's heart races like mad; he has never looked into the barrel of a gun before, but his exterior gives nothing away and he doesn't budge one inch to the side. Unruffled he directs his gaze at the two scurrilous attackers. Behind him he hears the stall gate sliding fully open, and he senses that many people stand there without being able to see them.

The blonde loses his patience. In a flash he turns the rifle in his hands around and rams Simon in the pit of his stomach with a powerful thrust of the rifle butt. A dull pain passes through Simon and he loses control of his legs. As if in slow motion he falls to his knees.

Don't let them out of your sight, look them in the eyes! Don't look at the ground! Simon sees that the tall fellow is aiming his rifle butt anew, this time directly in his face. In the last second Simon turns to the side so that the rifle butt only strokes his cheek. Then suddenly three men are standing by him; Simon recognises Karol Rudzinski the coachman from the corner of his eye.

"We want the little Negro bastard, get out of our way!" bellows the small fat man.

"You shall get nothing more here today," enunciates Karol with a determined voice. "What after all has this little boy done to you strong men, that you are hunting him with weapons?"

"He stole an apple. Let us through!"

"The boy slipped out back a while ago already. So get lost."

Against their will the two men draw back, but the little fat one cannot resist spitting at Simon.

"Can you stand up, Mr. Braun?" Karol Rudzinski bends down to Simon, grips him under the arms and helps him stand up straight.

"Thanks, I think I can already!" Simon looks around, slightly dizzy. Next to him are standing two men unknown to him, a white and a black one. Without a word they turn around now and go into the stall. Karol follows them together with Simon and helps him to sit at a table in the entrance hall. The other two have disappeared into the back part of the stall.

"Comb through every horse box," Karol calls out to them.

"What are you looking for?" asks Simon.

"The little black boy."

"I thought he ran out through the back of the stall?"

"The stall has no door in the back at all, but I had to say something to those two." Astonished, Simon sees the hitherto stiff-seeming Karol smile. "If the boy has crept into a horse box, it can be dangerous for him; the horse could baulk at him and kick."

Simon nods and looks at the other. "Mr. Rudzinski, you can call me Simon. It's only right, since you rescued me."

"Rescued? We rescued you? You saved that boy's life. I don't think that we could have helped him if the two miscreants had already made it into the stall. But it was an adroit idea of yours to respond only in German. The two had no clue how they should react."

"At that moment nothing better came to my mind," explains Simon. "The whole time they had their shotguns pointed at me."

"Yes, we were afraid for you, Simon," answers Karol seriously.

"Here he is," a powerful voice now calls out from the dark. "He was sitting behind the bales of straw."

The two men lead the little boy forward and seat him at the table with a friendly push.

"So, little guy, what is your name?" Karol asks the boy.

"Tyson La-Ron," stammers the boy, totally frightened.

"That's right," nods the black man next to Karol. "He is the son of Latisha La-Ron. Tyson lives with his mother on a farm about two miles west of here. His father was a slave and worked in the cotton fields in the South. He was killed, and Latisha managed to flee north with Tyson."

Little Tyson keeps his head sunk low during this narration.

"What I don't understand," Simon interjects, still holding his hand to his stomach, "all that brutality because of an apple?"

Karol turns around and reaches into a shelf on the wall, takes an apple and puts it in Tyson's hands. Then he explains, "Here people have been killed for much less. The slave trade is forbidden in the North, but that still doesn't mean that blacks have even remotely the same rights as we whites."

Simon strokes Tyson carefully on the head and says, "One must not steal, Tyson, under any conditions. Stealing brings mistrust and uncertainty. Next time say you're hungry and ask politely for something to eat."

"Hopefully he doesn't starve," Karol bursts out.

"You can always get something from me, that is a promise!" explains Simon emphatically.

Without saying a word, Tyson leaps up and is gone.

Karol grins and looks around the room. "Well, back to work, boys, or we won't be done at all today."

To Simon he adds, in German, "Respect, Simon, very few would have had the courage. You can believe me."

"How is it that you speak such good German, Karol?"

"I come from Poland ... And you?"

"I come from Mainz on the Rhine," replies Simon.

"And what wind blew you to America?"

"I emigrated, because I believe my prospects for the future will be better here. My older brother Christoph will inherit our parents' wine cellar."

"That is very audacious," intones Karol.

Simon shrugs his shoulders and asks, "And why are you here, Karol?"

"I emigrated with my family."

"Your family?"

Karol sights lightly and continues, "That is a long story. My parents and I lived in the beautiful town of Lemberg on the Poltwa in Poland.

160

Lemberg lies in Galicia and is the seat of the region's central government. The Russian czarina Catherine II wanted to take our land, and arranged to split Poland with the Hapsburgs and the Prussians. There were three Polish partitions and before we knew it, in 1795 Poland was history and wiped completely off the map. So much for the theme of stealing ..." Karol looks in the direction of the stall door through which little Tyson had disappeared. "My homeland Galicia was taken over by the Hapsburgs. Emperor Franz II occupied many posts in public offices and in schools with his people, so that the German language became increasingly more important. My father is a teacher and couldn't stand the occupation and the changes that came with it. So we left Galicia one day, when I was nineteen years old."

Simon had listened spellbound to Karol's narrative. Now he says, "My homeland was also occupied. Until the Vienna Congress in 1815, Mainz belonged to Napoleonic France. But that's over."

"That's enough history for today, Simon," declares Karol firmly. "You must go to the house and have Molly bandage your cheek."

Simon had almost forgotten the wound already. Cautiously he touched his cheek, and blood stuck to his fingertips.

"As far as I can see, the wound is neither long nor deep, " Karol reassures him. "Your cheek is just a little split. You have an excellent reaction capacity. Otherwise the matter wouldn't have turned out so mildly."

Simon shakes hands farewell with Karol and goes on his way to the main house. Pebbles gnash beneath his feet as he passes by brightly-coloured flower beds and rows of high trees. The Rowleys' garden seems perfectly peaceful and betrays nothing of the brutality of the men who had previously hunted down a young boy.

"Simon, what happened to your cheek?" asks Lindsay at dinner with concern in her voice.

"Just a cut, nothing more," answers Simon and brings a slice of roast to his mouth on his fork.

Lilly Owens, who serves at the table, looks half-astonished at Simon. Earlier in the kitchen she seemed very agitated when Simon came to Molly with the wound.

"Did you stumble against something?" Alastair asks, and can hardly restrain a grin.

"A piece of wood," elucidates Simon dryly, and also has to smile a little.

"What sort of a piece of wood?" Lindsay begs in confusion.

"Oh, it was in front of the horses' stall," says Simon with composure. "The object was the butt of a rifle."

"The butt of a rifle?" Lindsay shrieks piercingly. "What happened?" Fear could be read on her face. Alastair and Mr. Snyder, too, look at Simon as though petrified. Lilly furtively bites her lip – she knows Simon's story already. Matter-of-factly, Simon now relates his encounter with the two armed thugs and how Karol Rudzinski and the two other men helped him.

"Be careful around such people," Lindsay pleads. "Promise us that, Simon!"

"Pardon me, Lindsay, but when an injustice occurs I must intervene. The little boy couldn't help it. The two men acted completely unreasonably."

"Alastair, say something to him!" Lindsay tries her husband for help.

But he isn't quite of her persuasion. "Lindsay, in all honesty … That is just how we came to know Simon at the beginning: courageous and ready to help. But nonetheless, Simon," he turns now to his guest, "it is a tribute to you that you cannot endure injustice. But you must learn to judge where it can go well or where it is simply too dangerous. Justice unfortunately doesn't always get its due." With these words Alastair makes a grim face.

"What do you mean by that?" asks Simon, taken aback.

"From your home, you are used to people following law and order," answers the man of the house. "It should also be thus here, but there are people who don't much value a human life. With his weapon, one or another tries to get the law on his side. And with the question of 'black' and 'white', the souls of the United States are deeply divided. You know that we in the northern states have forbidden slavery. But there are still many who consider black second-class humans – or worse still. In the southern states slavery hasn't been abolished, and it looks like it will remain that way – its whole economy is based on it."

"What exactly are slaves?" Simon wants to know.

"They are Negroes, that is, blacks from Africa or the Caribbean who are purchased by plantation owners or factory owners and must thereafter serve them. In economic terms, they are an asset, and object."

"An object? Not a person?" Simon shakes his head. "On my parents' land there also live families who work for us. They help with the grape harvest or with other activities. I know servants and attendants, but they are still people … like us. My father always said: 'Respect every person as if they were yourself, no matter who it is.'"

"Your father had then a very progressive perspective, Simon," judges Alastair. "But now let's not spoil our fine meal any further, shall we?"

One travels halfway around the world to America, to this young, forward-looking nation without emperor or king. And then one has to realize that many things still do not change: Arrogance and pride, greed and envy, lack

162

of respect for one's fellow man because of their position, their nationality or the colour of their skin. What did Alastair Rowley say? "Justice unfortunately doesn't always get its due!" I had to ponder over these words once in peace. Every person who lives in a society or nation must follow law and order; that is why laws are enacted. I came to the conclusion that everywhere in the world it is of decisive importance who makes the laws and how they are enforced. That is the measure of justice.

3. A missed cue

He has stayed up writing letters late into the night, lighting a candle to see by after the last daylight faded. First to his much-missed family back in Mainz, then to his grandparents, uncle, aunt and cousins in London. He has hesitated somewhat over how the third, and longest, letter should be addressed. Should he direct it to Marala's parents? But he does not know their new address, and cannot be sure that his letter will reach them.

In the end he has resolved to dispatch the letter under separate cover to Elizabeth and Janet his cousins, and entreat them to deliver it to Marala. Only by this means can he hope she will receive his letter, and even this is far from certain. But he has to let her know how painful it had been for him to take his leave of her. And he wants to tell her about everything that had happened on the crossing, and how he is faring here in Boston.

That night Simon sleeps only fitfully. Having been caught up in his long letter to her, Marala seems to appear before his eyes, so intensely he can almost touch her. With a stitch in his chest, and a kind of tingling in his fingers, he tosses and turns restlessly in bed. His heart thumping, he relives again and again the last precious days and hours with Marala, seeing and feeling again each moment as before, until, finally worn out, he drops into sleep.

"Good morning to you, Simon, good morning Alastair!" Lindsay is fresh and radiant as she sits down to breakfast with the two men.

Bone-weary after his sleepless night, Simon returns her greeting as cheerfully as he can.

Alastair peers over the top of his gazette with an air of bemusement. "Is there something particular today, my dear?"

"Surely you've not forgotten? Simon and I are going into Boston today to pick out a new outfit for him."

"Of course, my dear, we mentioned the matter only yesterday. I fear I may be growing forgetful!"

"Pray do not let it trouble you," says Simon, "We were talking of quite a different matter just now ..."

Now Alastair almost interrupts Simon, and starts to explain, "My dear, Simon is wondering whether while he is here in America he should continue to be known by his German name, Simon Balthasar Braun, or whether it would not be wiser to simply use the English form of Simon Brown."

"I believe I must decide the question before applying at Harvard College," Simon adds. "I shall after all be a part of the English-speaking world from now on."

"What do you say, Lindsay?" Alastair asks his wife.

"Well, so many new immigrants to our land seem to choose a new name, for so many and differing reasons – either out of a wish to reinvent themselves, or to conceal something ..."

"But such is not the case for Simon," Alastair interjects. "After all, his intention is not to give himself an entirely new alias, but merely to, shall we say, adapt his name to the circumstances in which he finds himself."

"Simon Brown," Lindsay enunciates the new rendering delicately. "It has a nice sound ... so manly! I believe Simon Brown will be easier for him as he goes about his new life."

"I believe so too, my dear," Alastair affirms, and turns his attention back to his reading matter. "Better the changes should come right at the start."

Chattering merrily with Lindsay all the way, the journey into Boston town seems to Simon to last no time at all, and in what seems like moments the carriage has drawn up in front of a Milk Street tailor's shop. Even from the street, the establishment makes an elegant impression, with the words "Alexandre Gilot – Tailleur" written in large letters over the doorway, while high up from the gable an insignia with two huge crossed sewing needles swings underneath a wonderfully ornate beam. As Simon follows Lindsay inside, the noise of the busy shop-lined street is left behind, and an atmosphere of quiet activity takes its place. In the front of the store a handful of assistants are displaying lengths of cloth, which are examined closely by the

164

customer and, if they pass muster, cut to size. Other customers are having measurements taken, and admiring and even trying on garments made up for other people. The back section of the store is screened with panels and curtains, and Simon has a clear impression of nimble fingers hard at work, just out of sight.

"Bonjour, Madame Rowley, Bonjour, Monsieur!" A striking brunette from whom the first bloom has not yet faded comes out to greet Lindsay and Simon.

Lindsay replies with a "Bonjour, Pauline!" and turns to Simon. "Simon, this is Pauline, an excellent dressmaker, with an exquisite taste for cloth and for colour. She is a Parisienne of course, but she has worked here for Alexandre Gilot for years." She turns back to Pauline and continues, in French, "Pauline, may I introduce Simon Brown. He is a German gentleman, who came to Boston on the same ship as my husband and I. He will be living with us from now on. We shall need one or two coats, with trousers and shirts to match."

Pauline lifts her right arm, and glances over with a coquettish regard. "Madame, if you would be so kind as to follow me, then we shall be undisturbed." The dressmaker points to a corner curtained off from general view.

"Simon, we are to continue there. Shall you come?" Lindsay translates, already following Pauline.

Simon nods a trifle absently. He wonders if he should make clear that he is perfectly able to understand the women? Back at home his Belgian tutor Rudolf Vonecken had made a point of instructing Simon and the other children in the French language. But he would hate to be thought to be swellheaded or arrogant. Better to stay with English for the time being.

Pauline closes the curtain, turning to Simon and revealing an enchantingly accented English. "So we may proceed to measure you up, Mister Brown?" She casts a wink to Lindsay, and chatters on in French. "Mon Dieu, for such a creature to cross one's path! So young, strong, and handsome ..."

"For shame, Pauline!" says Lindsay slightly outraged. "I shall have to ascribe such a remark to your French upbringing, I'm sure!"

Pauline contents herself with a snicker, as Simon bites his lips and tries to pretend he is unaware of what is passing. Should he have said something after all? But now it is, too, late, and the only thing is to continue in seeming ignorance.

Pauline is confronting Simon armed with a pencil, paper and measure. "Mister Brown, if you will please to stand up straight, with the back nice and upright, and the arms out to the sides?" The dressmaker takes down lengths, widths and circumferences with a practised air, all the while making notes, and muttering in French an occasional clipped, dry-sounding comment to herself, which causes Lindsay to raise her brows with a wry look. "Such thighs … a stomach like a board, I declare … this back, with these strapping arms … why it would be a pleasure to …"

"Pauline, you forget yourself!" complains Lindsay, repressing a smile.

"Eh, Madame Rowley," Pauline purrs, "to have the chance of such a prince coming into one's home!" Then addressing Simon again, "Please to face the glass Mister Brown, then we can take the measurements of the back." And in her dry native tone, "Oh-la-la … Such perfection in the gentleman's posterior as we have here! He pleases you, too, Madame, I am sure of it!"

Simon steals a glance at Lindsay, who quickly turns away – but not before he has spied her flushed cheeks and caught a light, barely audible "Oui …"

"Pauline, I believe I shall pass an eye over your new cottons a while," Lindsay exclaims, and disappears through the curtain.

In the looking glass, Simon's gaze falls onto Pauline's upturned face, smiling up at him as she kneels to measure his leg. As she leans slightly forward he has a glimpse of her bosom spread below him, and becomes aware of a rising arousal. Pauline's suggestive remarks and Lindsay's reaction to them have not left him cold. "Keep your composure," he enjoins himself. "Just try to concentrate on something else. Think of Harvard College and all you will find there …"

Finally Lindsay and Simon are again ensconced in the carriage on the way back to Cambridge, and a wave of relief washes over Simon. I got through it!

"We shall go by way of the postmaster's office so you can send off your letters to your people at home," announces Lindsay, with a relieved smile. She is evidently anxious to forget about her indiscreet exchange with Pauline.

"By the way Simon, we shall have company for dinner this evening. Not a big thing; we have invited some friends to whom we would like to introduce you."

Simon nods, his head still full of her quiet "Oui."

Later, as the sun flames red over the western horizon, in its last farewell before surrendering to the night, Simon sits on the veranda, enjoying the quiet glory of the view.

"Simon?" Lindsay appears in the door. "Here you are!"

Behind her are Alastair and a tall, blond man of around fifty, whose decidedly attractive companion has a dusky complexion and a confiding smile. Her bright gown shines against her husband's more sober garments.

166

"Simon, may I introduce Mr. Cameron Wood?" Lindsay continues. "He is a director of the BBBC just like my husband, and this is his lady wife Isabella, my dearest companion." And as she says this she clasps Isabella's waist.

"A very good evening to you both," Simon politely returns. "My name is Simon Balthasar … erm … Simon Brown."

"Indeed," Alastair adds. "The young man hails from Germany, and is come to our shores to begin a new life."

"A new life no less!" smiles Cameron Wood, with a certain ironic air. "Was his old life then so very terrible?"

"We would hardly have welcomed him into our house if that were the case!" Alastair counters dryly, and is echoed by Isabella's heartfelt "Of course not!"

"Not only is she lovely, she is also quite charming," thinks Simon. Her friendly manner however can perhaps be attributed to the warm alto tones of her voice. At first glance the Woods seem to Simon a pleasant couple, and he can well understand the intimacy between Lindsay and Isabella.

Lilly Owens comes over to the group. "Beg pardon, Mrs. Rowley ma'am, there are more ladies and gentlemen arriving."

"Welcome, friends!" calls Alastair, going over to the newcomers. "Simon, this is Harvey Barton and his wife Alice. Harvey is a director at the New England Bank of Boston. And here may I introduce Leon Taylor and his tiny wife Sarah."

Sarah Taylor is indeed childlike in figure, but responds with an indulgent smile to Alastair's jocularity. With a wink of an eye, he continues, "Leon is our physician here in Cambridge. And a fine pair of hands he has too, as I have had reason to confirm myself."

Yet more faces can be seen through the door to the veranda, and Alastair pulls Simon by the sleeve before he can say a word to the doctor and his wife. "We shall plough on, Simon. A very good evening, Alexander … Alexander Rickleby with his wife Ashley, and Oscar and Daisy Thickstone."

This foursome seem to Simon rather less pleasing. The Ricklebys have a haughty air, as ones highly persuaded of their own superiority, and it is evident that they think the Thickstones quite beneath their notice. The latter pair appear somehow out of place in this company, with Daisy Thickstone's eager peering of her head to make out every detail of the other arrivals.

These ponderous presentations are somewhat embarrassing to Simon, unavoidable as they are. As the newcomer to the Rowley's set he is the natural object of scrutiny for the others. As Mr. Snyder enters bearing a salver with small crystal glasses of some ruby wine, Simon has a shrewd notion of what is to come. Scarcely has every guest received a glass when Alastair raises his own. "My dear friends! I am honoured by your most kind company tonight. And it is my pleasurable duty to introduce to you, my dearest friends, Simon Brown, who will be our guest from now on. Ladies and gentlemen, to his very good health."

The company dutifully takes a sip, then Alastair nudges Simon. "Well then? What exactly would you say we are drinking?"

The answer comes to Simon almost instantly. "A port wine from the Douro valley, in Portugal. More exactly I would call it a tawny port, a ten-year old."

Everyone looks at him. The guests sniff at their glasses, and turn and turn about the port which is passed reflectively over the tongue and held critically up to the light. Then finally Dr. Taylor addresses Simon, and the company holds its breath. "May I ask how you come to that conclusion, Mr. Brown?"

"Well, seen against the light, the wine does have a dark red tone, but not such an intense one, indeed the colour rather seems to shade into the brick-red – a sign, I believe, that it has matured slowly, and in a wooden barrel. Then in the nose, the aromas recall ripe, dark berries, with notes of spice, and a gentle hint of a roasted flavour. On the tongue one notices at once the wine's powerful character, and its bounty of fruit, and warmth – a warmth by the way that relates to the wine's undoubtedly elevated alcohol content. One notes also the spicy, roasted aromas that develop on the palette. It is a port which fills the mouth entirely, without being in any way heavy or dull. An effect attributable to its rich load of fruit and the natural sugar. And the finale is extremely complex: long and nuanced. Undoubtedly, in my own opinion, an exceptionally good, well-matured tawny port."

Silence – one could hear a needle drop. Simon feels rather awkward. Then at last Alastair clears his throat and asks, "Snyder, what do we have in our glasses this evening?" The butler swiftly advances to Alastair's side, and holds out a dark bottle. The wine's identity has been simply written right on the bottle in white lettering.

"Burmester's 10 Year Old Tawny Port," Alastair reads.

"Why sir, that is quite simply impossible!" cries Oscar Thickstone. "A sensation! Can he do that with any wine?"

"I must say I do not know," Alastair replies. "But certainly the feat has been achieved with every wine we have tried together."

Simon is the centre of attention for some while longer, much to his discomfort, but soon enough supper is served on the long oak dining table. The gentlemen thereafter retire to the small salon, to savour their good cigars and a whisky or brandy or two in comfort. Simon sits among them, paying more than usual attention when the conversation turns to overseas trade, and the latest in ship building. Alastair, sitting next to him, leans over confiding, "You ought to know, Simon, that our Alexander is a naval architect, and owner of Rickleby & Smith Co., one of the foremost yards in Boston."

This pleasantry is overheard by Alexander Rickleby. "Give me just two more years and I shall have made the company the largest shipwright's in Boston – and soon enough the largest on the whole East Coast," he blusters.

Cameron Woods replies in his usual quiet manner, "Be mindful of what you assure us there so confidently, Alexander. One never knows what fate has in store."

"Pshaw, and what should fate do to me?" Rickleby is evidently a very model of aplomb. "Just a few more years and merchant shipping will be prosperous beyond all recognition. Ships will be in demand as fast as we can build them – and we will build them."

Oscar Thickstone puts his oar in. "There are however other shipyards than yours, my friend."

But Rickleby will hear none of it. "Oscar, I'm afraid you have very little notion of commerce on such a scale. You would be better occupying yourself with your best beef and pork sides."

Oscar Thickstone reddens. "My wife and I have a respectable enterprise, sir. Small it may be, but we serve our patrons nothing but the best!"

Alexander Rickleby dismisses this with a wave of his hand.

"Alexander, for all love." Cameron Wood is conciliatory. "Let us treat each other like gentlemen, after all."

Not long after this exchange, the door opens and Lindsay summons Simon over. "Gentlemen, you must allow me to deprive you of Mr. Brown for a while, the ladies are most eager for their share of his company."

Simon hesitantly looks round the assembly and then to Alastair. "By all means, Simon," he encourages the young man, "don't keep the ladies waiting, their curiosity must be satisfied."

In the larger salon the ladies have gathered cosily on a cluster of sofas set round a low table. Through the doors to the veranda a slight breeze refreshes the spacious chamber.

The first salvo of questions comes almost before Simon has taken his place amongst them.

"Do you have brothers and sisters at home?"

"How, pray, could you possibly be brave as to journey so far alone?"

"What must your parents be thinking, what must they be going through! To know one's son venturing alone all across the world!"

"Why America of all places?"

"Are you perhaps attempting to escape from something or someone?"

For a while Simon patiently gives each question its proper response. He has the feeling of seeing his whole life pass in review before him.

Then Isabella, in an aside to Lindsay, is heard to remark, "But how brave of you, my dear, to offer your hospitality to this young man! Were you aware of his story? Had you perhaps had opportunity enough on the crossing to discuss the matter in full?"

"Of course we often came into conversation, most especially towards the end of our journey," replies Lindsay. "Although I must admit that much of what we are hearing tonight is as new to me as it is to you."

"I declare, I believe much of what the young man says sounds like the sheerest fantasy," Daisy Thickstone objects. "I do wonder how much we are supposed to believe?" The small, plump butcher's wife appears to have only just noticed that she is not after all the centre of attention.

"Daisy, I do assure you, everything that happened to Simon on board of the 'Whitecap' I saw with my own eyes. And I'm sure that everything else our guest has related must be equally true; Simon's habit is to understate the matter rather than the reverse."

But Ashley Rickleby cannot resist a tease, murmuring in French, "Lindsay my dear, it is scarcely a puzzle to any of us why one would procure such a fine, comely young man as a house guest!"

"This cannot pass without remark," thinks Simon. "Impossible to carry on any longer pretending that you don't understand."

Isabella is on the point of a retort, when Simon interjects smoothly in his elegant, idiomatic French, "Mrs. Rickleby, although we are so slightly acquainted I would allow myself to observe that one often ascribes to others motivations which one may rather in fact be harbouring oneself."

The general amusement seems to save the moment. Ashley Rickleby at first looks very grave, but is then persuaded to laugh over her indiscretion and Simon's adroit reply. But Lindsay jumps up without a word, and not once looking round disappears through the veranda doors into the darkness.

Ashley Rickleby calls after her, "Lindsay, I do beg your pardon! Do excuse my rudeness!" But to no effect. "Isabella, will you go after her? What can be the matter? I hardly meant it."

Isabella is vexed. "Must you always plague her so, Ashley! You go too far sometimes, I must say."

The only person in the room under no illusions just why Lindsay has fled the room sits perfectly still, in an agony of indecision over what to say or do.

170

Then Simon stands up. "Ladies, if you will permit me, as I am the object of this discord I will myself go to find Lindsay." He disappears in turn into the night.

Away from the light of the windows, the blackness is absolute, and Simon hesitates. As his eyes slowly grow used to the darkness, he can make out a silhouette in the depths of the garden. As he cautiously approaches towards it the figure takes on a familiar form.

"Lindsay, I must beg your forgiveness."

She spins around. "You startled me! What do you want?"

"Forgive me."

"Forgive you? But what for? Because you understood every word that passed between Pauline and I? Or because you deceived me in keeping me in ignorance? You purposely led me into this position!"

"Please, Lindsay, do allow me to explain. I was afraid you would find me boastful or conceited if I had said that I understand French. I could not know what turn the conversation would take, and by then it was too late. And then I convinced myself it would be better to hold my tongue."

"You have caused me much mortification, Simon."

"Lindsay, there are only two people who know of what has passed: yourself and I."

"And Pauline!"

"No, she does not know that I speak French."

"Nor must she learn it. Is that understood?"

"Of course."

Lindsay looks at him soberly. "And what other revelations are we to expect from you? Is there anything else I should know before I compromise myself again?"

"I cannot recount to you in just a few weeks all the events of seventeen years. If you must know I do speak some Spanish, although more imperfectly. I have no other languages."

Simon can just about make out Lindsay's cheeks start to dimple in the darkness.

"I could never mean to do anything to compromise you, Lindsay."

Raising her right hand she stroked his cheek lightly. "Oui, I would hope not. Now let us return to the salon, our guests will be wondering what is become of us."

Looking back on the incident I could of course have sidestepped much discomfiture if I had disclosed promptly that I understood the foreign tongue. But ultimately I was glad to have dared the disclosure that evening, as had I not, the misapprehension would not have disappeared but rather grown,

and would have been a hindrance in my relations with Lindsay. My rela-
tions with Lindsay ... I could feel there was something between us ...
"Oui." I found myself often thinking of the encounter in Alexandre Gilot's
rear quarters, dwelling less on Pauline's charms than on Lindsay's words
and actions. The remembrance of the rendezvous that I had unintentionally
witnessed, between Lindsay and Flynn Corwin back on the 'Whitecap', cast
its habitual spell.

4. The enterprise takes shape

Mr. Brown! What can you can tell me about our new president?"
The little man with the white hair glowers from the podium
down at his students in front of him. With his immaculately fitting dark suit, furrowed brow and heavy spectacles, Professor Hicks looks
authoritarian, almost intimidating.

"Sir, his name is Andrew Jackson. He was born in March 1767, was
admitted to the bar in 1786; then served for some years as a prosecuting
officer in North Carolina. In 1798 he was elected a judge of the Tennessee
Supreme Court. He became a national hero having defeated the English in
January 1815 at the Battle of New Orleans, as major general of the Tennessee militia. Since January this year he has been the seventh President of the
United States of America."

Professor Hicks nods contented. "Thank you, Brown. A respectable
showing, considering you have only been here for a few weeks."

Simon lets his tense body sag discreetly back against the back of his
chair, as his thoughts wander back to his first day here at Harvard College.
He and Alastair had been granted an audience with His Magnificence, and
apparently just a few words from Alastair were enough to gain him entrance
here. That had deeply impressed him. The subsequent guided tour of the
buildings gave him an even greater sense of respect. He later spoke to the
first students and professors, and felt quite at home after only a few days.
Simon had immediately realised that he would have a lot to learn here. But
he is ready to work, he is indeed!

"Mr. Brown! Daydreams? Are you still with us?" The Professor's voice
snaps him out of his thoughts. "I asked you if the Code Civil has any mean-
172

ing for you. Your colleague MacShaw has a problem at the moment: Perhaps you are capable of saving his head?"

Simon goes to jump up, but first looks around him alertly, and sees a tall blushing student standing behind him. Simon feels that all eyes are upon him.

"The Code Civil is the French book of private law, and is one of the most significant legal works of our times. It was introduced by Napoleon Bonaparte."

"MacShaw, you are fortunate, you may sit."

After the lecture, the student MacShaw comes over to Simon before he can stand up. He bends down slightly to him and whispers, "Thank you."

"Not at all ... but what for?"

"You can't know yet, but Professor Hicks can become exceptionally angry and mean when he realises that we have not memorised material that he has already covered. We went through the Code Civil a few weeks ago, but today I had a complete lapse."

"That can happen," Simon replies.

"Hicks thinks not, if one has reviewed the material diligently. He asked you because you have only been at the College a short while."

"And if I had not been able to answer?" Simon wants to know.

"He assumed that would be the case. That would have cost me days of extra work."

"Extra work?"

"For example a paper on America's path to independence. At least a week of work!"

"Hey, in that case I have really done you a favour!" Simon smiles.

"Yes," MacShaw grins. "Thank you again. But how is it that you are so familiar with the Code Civil, if you have only recently come here?"

"I come from Germany, and have only been in America for a few weeks. The region I come from was occupied by Napoleon, and so we were subject to French law. MacShaw, what was your first name again?"

"Theodore."

At evening, when Simon returns to the Rowleys' house, Molly Jones greets him with her warm, quiet alto voice, "Very good evening to you, Mr. Brown."

Simon has to grin as Molly stands in front of him as sturdy as an oak. "Good evening, Mrs. Jones."

"Have you had a hard day?"

"Exhausting."

"Your expression speaks volumes, even though you smile, Mr. Brown. Dinner will cheer you up again. I'm sure you'll like it," the cook says, and turns back to her kitchen with a smile.

Simon knocks on the door to the dining room, and hears Alastair's curt "Come in!"

"Simon!" Lindsay beams at him. "How was your day?"

"Tiring. It is not easy to constantly give your attention to following the lectures."

"I'm sure you'll get used to it." Alastair is sitting with his paper in an armchair at the window.

As Simon is reporting the situation with Theodore MacShaw, Lindsay interrupts him, "MacShaw? Is that the son of Angus MacShaw, the architect?"

"I don't know," replies Simon. "We didn't talk for long. Most of the students seem perfectly nice, but at the moment I am still the new one."

"But you are managing, I hope?" Lindsay wants to know, concerned.

"Of course, please do not worry. I was just thinking that I ought to give the students time to get to know me, and not barge in amongst them like a bull in a china shop."

With his eyes still concentrated on his paper, Alastair comments, "Lindsay, Simon is capable of coping. The father is also called Theodore, by the way."

"Whose father?" Lindsay turns to her spouse.

"Angus MacShaw's father."

"Then the father of my classmate could be the architect," concludes Simon, his eyes brightening.

"What are you thinking of?" asks Lindsay.

"Of my friend John Parson. He is an architect, as you know, and he is looking for work. John wrote me a letter which gave me his address in Boston. He would like to come to visit me next Thursday in the late afternoon. I wonder how he has got on?"

"Do you think I didn't see that?" Molly Jones grasps Lilly, who is going out of the kitchen, firmly by the arm.

"Leave me alone, Molly! It is not what you think!"

"Lilly, it is obvious for anyone who knows you even a little. You have a soft spot for our young Mr. Brown."

Lilly widens her large brown eyes. "A soft spot?!"

"If you aren't careful you will fall in love with him. That would not end well. Believe me!"

"In love, Molly? Are you crazy?" The young girl shakes her head energetically, but Molly remains serious and firm.

174

"No, Lilly, I am not crazy, and I want to save you from …"

"But I am not in love with him!" Lilly's mind goes back a few days. On the terrace Simon had come into conversation with her and had enthused about the scenery of the Rhine valley, with its vineyards. There had been such a light in his eyes …

Molly does not let the matter drop. "Girl, I've seen you looking after him when he goes by, smiling at him when he says something to you. Get him out of your head before it's too late!"

Suddenly the kitchen door bursts open, and Mr. Snyder appears in the door frame. "Ladies, vite, vite! The family are waiting for their supper!"

In seconds the women spring apart, and a minute later Mr. Snyder and Lilly Owens are serving the meal in the dining room. As practised and deft as ever, Lilly glides through the room, and her frequent stolen glances at Simon and the light smile on her lips are hardly to be noticed.

The next day there are no lectures and Alastair takes Simon with him to Boston in the coach. Simon wants to take a closer look at the port and the ships at anchor there. The previous evening Alastair had told him of the great shipyards, that were turning out sailing ships of ever-greater size and speed, and were growing in influence for Boston.

The day is bright and clear. Simon leaves his host in front of the BBBC, and threads his way through the bustling streets to Hutchison's Wharf. Going south, he passes countless quays – Clarke's Wharf, Butler's Wharf, Long Wharf and all the rest. He peers curiously at all the vessels fastened to the walls of the quays, at their unloaded wares and their flags that give information on the origin of the ships.

Simon's route finally takes him past the South Battery and various other moorings until he arrives at the Gibbon shipyard. Alastair had suggested to have a look at two new ships that were being built on the wharf and were nearly finished. He'd been told to keep towards Orange Street or South End. Just before his destination, Simon is wandering lost in thought by a long, high wall, when he suddenly hears a deafening yell from a wide open iron door. Simon stands still, glances through the door when a hard blow on his head knocks him to the floor. Dizzily Simon probes for the source of the pain and feels a lump forming. A glance at his fingertips relieves him, no blood is sticking to them. His scalp seems to be fine. By him lies a rough block of wood, which evidently struck him. Simon stands up and grabs the block. He briefly sees only dimness, but fortunately this condition only lasts a few seconds. He looks round. Where could the block have come from? Simon doesn't have to search long: between two smaller ships, probably here for repair, a mob of twenty or thirty men have driven a single young man into a corner, and are threatening him with heavy clubs. They are all shouting at once, Simon can make out English and Spanish words.

All against one! With the block of wood in his hand, Simon sets off right through the shouting crowd. At first no one notices him, but as he stands next to the young man, and looks into the eyes of the attackers, they pause astonished.

"Hey, who are you?" cries a voice from the crowd.

"Simon Brown," answers Simon loudly, but calmly and slowly.

"What do you want here?" comes from another corner of the group.

"You invited me!" Simon points to the lump on his head and lifts the block of wood up high. "Here is the invitation."

"Then you can go again now!" a quite squawk voice makes itself noticeable.

"Pardon me? First you invite me and now you dismiss me? What impolite manners are these?"

"You don't even know what is going on here!" cries yet another.

"Oh I do …" Simon's voice remains calm and reaches normal volume again. "That is recognisable to anyone from outside: a single person is being cornered by a large crowd."

"What did he say?" comes from the back of the mob.

"If you would be quieter we could all understand each other better," Simon explains, and repeats his last sentence.

As if from nothing, an elderly man now stands between Simon and the young man. Then a dark, threatening voice from the crowd yells in Spanish, "Shut up and disappear, otherwise we'll stretch your neck, too!"

Simon retorts, likewise in Spanish, "In a crowd you can have courage. But come out here so we can speak face to face. Or do you have to hide because there is nothing behind your voice?"

The older man and the young man stare at Simon, the older asks, astonished, "You speak Spanish?"

Before Simon can answer, the crowd parts, and a large, bear-like man steps forward. He declares, again in Spanish, "Here I am. And what do we do now?"

"I would like to know that too," Simon answers. "What is this about? We surely cannot be intending to come to blows."

"We want our pay for the last two weeks," the bear growls.

Simon turns questioningly to the two other men. The elder says, "We cannot pay at the moment, although we would like to pay. But who you are anyway?"

"My name is Simon Brown. I happened to be passing by here."

"You can speak Spanish," says the other now. "Tell the men they should be patient for a few days more, then we will take it from there …"

"We don't want to wait any longer, we want our dollars! Now!"

176

"Gentlemen," Simon interrupts, well aware that he now has to create a resolution, so that the situation does not escalate again. "Give me two hours. I will retire with these two gentlemen here and attempt to clarify the situation. Then we can gather again here and talk to each other. I would like to ask you to now return to your work."

The workers exchange uncertain glances, begin to exchange a few words with each other, and finally turn away. Next to Simon, the young man crumples, and sits on the floor.

"That was close! I have never been so afraid in my life," he stammers, and holds out his shaking right arm to Simon. "My name is David Lewis. I am the co-proprietor of Ringfield & Lewis. Maynard Ringfield is the senior director, and my partner."

"Please calm yourself a moment," answers Simon. "But we cannot rest too long. I have promised that these men will have an answer in two hours, and that they must have."

"Mr. Brown," the old man now gives Simon his hand, "First I must thank you for coming to our aid. We should continue the discussion in the office."

Simon and Mr. Ringfield take David Lewis under the arms, and help him to his feet.

In the office Mr. Ringfield brings Simon a towel soaked in cold water. "Here, use this to cool the injury," he says. "It will sooth the pain. And please take a seat."

Simon presses the towel to his lump. "Please just call me Simon. Mr. Ringfield, your workers are waiting for two weeks' pay. Why do you not pay? The situation out there was quite dangerous."

"You are right," agrees David Lewis, who appears to be feeling better. "In recent years we have acquired some Spanish workers. Unfortunately they speak only poor English, and we speak no Spanish. As most of the Spaniards are good shipwrights, and we are talking about the same work, the language barrier was not a big problem. But now we are having difficulties completing two ships, and hardly any money is coming in. Therefore we are two weeks behind in paying their wages."

"David, let me explain," the senior interrupts his partner. "The cause lies further back, when you were not even employed here. Do you know, Mr. Brown, the Ringfields have been shipbuilders for generations, we come from Scotland in fact. I came to Boston with my wife and established this shipyard. It is not among the largest in the business, but we are known for good quality. Everything was running well, until a large shipyard from Boston, Rickleby & Smith Co., made contact with me. They intend to take us over. As I have taken young David Lewis into the shipyard, and he has advanced our business with new ideas, the purchase will become more and more expensive for Rickleby & Smith. Now they are attempting to put pressure on us, by making it difficult for us to buy materials from our suppliers or to borrow money from the banks."

"Is the yard otherwise working profitably?" Simon asks David Lewis.

"Yes," he answers. "Simon, please call me David. I first worked as an employee for Maynard Ringfield. His way of working and his comprehension of quality pleased me. The working climate was always characterised by fairness."

Now Ringfield again cuts his partner short. "I am very satisfied with David, and as my wife and I have no children, I made him an offer to enter the firm, and later take over it entirely. The young man has excellent ideas, as you can see from the two ships in dock at the moment." Now Ringfield's eyes begin to brighten up. "On paper there exists a new type of merchant vessel with a concave bow, simply revolutionary! If we can realise it, we will be unbeatable ... I mean of course, our customers will be unbeatable."

"Look, Simon, from this sketch you can see what I mean." David is now also notably enthusiastic. "The bow has a negative curvature; is cut concave. So it will cut the water and not primarily push it aside. We, Maynard and I, believe that with this we can achieve speeds that are some miles per hour faster."

"That sounds good," nods Simon. "But now we must find a solution to the wages, otherwise you will have trouble again."

"Why are you helping us?" Maynard looks into Simon's eyes. "I mean, you came by here by accident, and have taken on our side, have indeed risked your life ... who are you?"

"I come from Germany and emigrated to Boston some months ago by way of England ..." Simon tells of his parents, siblings, and relatives in England, briefly and concisely. He also tells of Jan ter Bruggen, the mysterious Dutchman who had first made him really curious about the world. "Here in Boston I am living with Alastair and Lindsay Rowley, and I am studying at Harvard College."

Ringfield's face darkens. "With the Rowleys?"

"Do you know them, Maynard?" David Lewis interjects.

"Not personally, but Rowley is director of the BBBC. That is where Rickleby & Smith have their accounts."

"Mr. Ringfield, give me a day. I will try to get a new line of credit and take the time pressure away from you, so that Rickleby & Smith can no longer exercise any pressure."

178

"How is that supposed to work?" asks Maynard Ringfield sceptically. "I don't see how you or I have any chance!"

"I will go out with you, talk to your workers, and will ask them to keep quiet for another 24 hours, until we can present them with a solution for the wages. If I should fail, you win a day. But if I do get approval, then give me the chance to gather experience in shipbuilding business from you, alongside my studies, and involve me in the plans for your new ship."

"Maynard, he is right," David declares. "It doesn't make any difference for us whether now or in 24 hours – we can try it. In any case, it would be good if we had someone who speaks Spanish, wouldn't it?"

"Very well, Mr. Brown," nods Maynard Ringfield. "So into battle."

After an hour and a half of intensive discussion, Maynard Ringfield, David Lewis and Simon Brown are again standing in front of the office. David strikes the heavy ship's bell by the door with a hammer to summon the dockworkers. Then Simon explains to them briefly and diplomatically why the wages cannot be paid, and sets out in headwords the plan to diffuse the situation for the shipyard, without betraying too much of the exact procedure. He has a suspicion that Rickleby & Smith could have infiltrated a man into Ringfield & Lewis. A heated debate follows, and the workers want to know if Simon can be trusted and also if he will return. Eventually they appear to be persuaded, and a meeting is set for the next day at 5 o'clock in the afternoon.

"Simon, what are you doing here?" Alastair springs up behind his desk as Simon enters his office.

"Have you a few minutes' time for me, Alastair? I must speak to you about something urgent."

"Yes certainly, otherwise my secretary would surely not have allowed you through."

Alastair indicates the chair in front of the desk, and Simon sits. Coolly he relates what has happened to him today. Then he comes to speak about the heart of the matter. He knows that he must not give too much away. "Alastair, Alexander Rickleby is a friend of yours, and therefore it is out of the question that the BBBC takes action on this matter. But your friend Harvey Barton is after all on the board of the New England Bank of Boston. Perhaps it is possible for him to help Ringfield & Lewis. I do not want to drag you into it, but perhaps you could give me a few tips."

"Do you not think we could invite Mr. Ringfield and Mr. Lewis here to BBBC, and discuss a loan, or securities, or perhaps a possible surety with them?"

"No, Alastair, no chance." Simon remains consistent. "As the BBBC manages Rickleby & Smith's account, it appears from my point of view that a collaboration with Maynard Ringfield is impossible. It should be difficult to build up a relationship of trust."

"Have we then gone against him in any way? Could we not after all form a business relationship with Ringfield & Lewis?"

"Alastair, no. But could you please ensure that your friend Harvey Barton talks to me before the end of the day?"

"Hmm," says Alastair, "in view of the apparent urgency I will write you a few lines which you can present yourself to his secretary. My compliments to Harvey."

Simon rises. "I thank you, Alastair."

The other just nods. "Just speak to one of the two doormen in front of our bank and have yourself taken to NEBB with one of our coaches."

As Simon closes the door of Alastair's office behind him, he has a smile on his lips and the quiet hope that he can help Ringfield & Lewis.

On the other side of the office door, Alastair Rowley leans back in his armchair and lights a cigar, while a grin spreads on his face. "Simon Brown, who would have thought it … My enterprise is already underway!"

The time in Harvard was really exciting, from the first day on. I met many interesting people, some of whom were to accompany me through my whole life. At the college I not only was imparted a lot of knowledge, but also received the 'tools' that helped me in my later life, to keep an overview, to master many of my problems, and to use opportunities.

When I think back to my first encounter with Ringfield and Lewis, as I stood before this mob: Actually, I was not afraid at all. Strange – somehow I was confident that the situation was controllable. Only much later did I ask myself if that was arrogance, confidence in my own capacities, or simply intuition ...

5. Various goals are followed

As Simon dismounts from the coach in front of the New England Bank of Boston, his gaze turns first to the massive stone facade and the large entry door. With just a few steps, he is standing inside the bank in front of a counter, behind which sits a gentleman smiling in a friendly manner, looking at him expectantly.

Simon introduces himself. "Simon Brown. I would like to speak to Harvey Barton."

Now the gentleman examines him attentively, almost piercingly, as if in slow motion from top to bottom. "Cannot I be of service?" he asks.

"No, Alastair Rowley from the BBBC referred me specifically to Mr. Barton and recommended that I speak with him today!"

In an instant the smile returns to the gentleman's face. "Mr. Rowley? Of course, Mr. Brown. Please, follow me!"

The way takes them through wide corridors, over elegant staircases, into bright hallways right up to a rustic desk, behind which an elegantly dressed woman sits.

"Please wait a moment!" says the man from the counter, stepping up to the woman and exchanging a few words with her, which Simon does not hear. Then the gentleman takes his leave and goes.

"Good day," the woman turns to Simon. "What can I do for you?"

Simon gives her the carefully folded note from Alastair. "My name is Simon Brown. I would like to see Mr. Barton, and I am to give you this message."

The woman scans the note. "I will ask Mr. Barton, if he has time for you right now." After knocking softly she disappears behind a heavy oak door, to reappear before Simon seconds later. "Go on in, Mr. Brown."

Simon thanks her and is immediately greeted by a powerful voice, "Good day, Simon Brown, how do you do? Would you prefer to bank with us instead of with the BBBC?"

The small, chubby Harvey Barton in his massive chair with the overly long back rest seems almost to disappear behind his desk. His friendly, rounded moon face is further emphasised by his bald head.

"Good day, Mr. Barton," Simon answers. "And – yes."

"What do you mean, yes?"

"I would like to do some banking with you."

Harvey Barton looks uncertainly at Simon. "Does Alastair know of this?"

"Yes, I just saw him. Mr. Barton, it concerns a particular deal."

"You have my attention."

"Do you know of the shipyard Ringfield & Lewis?"

"Maynard Ringfield's shipyard?"

"Exactly. Maynard has taken on the young ship builder David Lewis as a partner and business manager of the firm." Simon explains the situation to Harvey Brown calmly, including all the details.

Barton interrupts him suddenly, "You must know that Alexander Rickleby is a good friend of mine."

"Yes, Mr. Barton, but during our meeting at the Rowley's I had the impression that Alexander Rickleby … let me put it this way: that you don't believe everything he says, and that you don't think all of his words or all of his deals are good."

Harvey Barton is obviously astounded for the second time in the conversation. "How did you come to this conclusion?"

"Gestures, body language, and choice of words. By the way, Alastair asked me if I wanted to make the deal with him, of course. But the BBBC is the bank of Rickleby & Smith, so this is not an option."

"And what are the exact details of this deal?"

"We agree on a realistic price for the two ships which are just about to be completed. You pay one hundred percent of this amount in credit to Ringfield & Lewis and receive the two ships as collateral. We will meet at the shipyard tomorrow at eleven o'clock to discuss the details with Maynard Ringfield and David Lewis."

"Hm …," says Harvey Barton. "What is the general financial situation of the shipyard? Are there already any credit arrangements?"

"I can't tell you that at the moment. I want everyone sitting at the same table. As far as I know, the shipyard does not have a house bank, they conduct their business here and there as they see fit."

"Does that mean that if we successfully close the deal then all further bank business will be done with us?"

"The first request may well go to your bank," Simon nods. He knows that even in this matter he cannot make any promises. "Mr. Barton, one more thing: I am thinking of an interest rate along the lines of six percent per annum."

Harvey Barton chokes, coughs, and his face begins to turn red. "And what about our profit? The market price is eight percent per annum."

Simon smiles. "We all have to make an effort, Mr. Barton. Particularly in the current situation."

"Can we agree on seven percent?"

"We agree to six percent and have faith in the capabilities of the NEBB!" Simon jumps up and holds his hand out to Harvey Barton. "We meet tomorrow at eleven, and you will have your foot in the door at Ringfield & Lewis!"

Harvey Barton reaches out and shakes Simon's hand. "Agreed, Mr. Brown."

Once Simon has left the office, Harvey Brown has to take a seat. Had this young man, not even twenty years old, just taken complete control of the conversation and achieved exactly what he wanted …?

Over dinner at the Rowley house, Alastair wants to know everything about the day, Ringfield & Lewis, and the conversation with Barton. Simon, however, does not want to give away too much of his strategy. He excuses himself early, to go to his room and work. He still has to review the content of his last lectures at the college. He is finally deep in mathematics, politics, and history when someone suddenly touches the back of his neck. He looks up, shocked. Lindsay stands behind him. He had not even noticed as she walked through the door.

"Still working at this hour?"

"Just another half an hour, and then I'm finished."

"You need to sleep, just like everyone else," says Lindsay, sitting down nonchalantly in the armchair next to the desk. Her slender body is sheathed in a flimsy night gown, over which she wears an open silk dressing gown. Simon risks stealing a glance at Lindsay's noticeably attractive figure. The thin material of her night gown drapes over her body like a second skin, and Simon catches glimpses of the contours of her breasts, her rolling hips, and her slim legs. The sight moves and excites him, singular and irresistible. He feels a tightening in his pants. For fear of being discovered, he moves his chair closer in to the desk.

Lindsay appears to smile faintly in the candlelight. Had she seen through his manoeuvre and noticed, that her signals are achieving the desired result?

"Simon," she says, "I want to ask you again to be careful with yourself. Don't get caught up in affairs which you won't be able to keep track of later."

"Don't worry, I hope at least, that I have found a solution, with which all parties can be satisfied."

Lindsay coquettishly crosses one leg over the other and dances her dainty slipper on her toes. She is obviously enjoying having Simon's attention on her, but at the same time there appears to be a certain unease running through her. They speak casually for a few minutes about the college and the students that Simon has met so far. Then Lindsay stands, moves behind Simon and begins to lightly massage his shoulders. Simon closes his eyes for a moment.

"I am very impressed with how you have planned the whole business with the shipyard," he hears Lindsay say, then she takes her hands away, and the door to his room is slowly drawn to a close.

183

It was a strange night. Simon could barely keep the thoughts from running through his head. The next day played out in his head. Would it all go according to plan? And then the situation with Lindsay … He was not sure what to think about that. She looked wonderful, sitting there in the arm-chair bathed in candlelight, and he had enjoyed her soft touch, no question.

You could almost mistake Simon for a burglar, the way he creeps onto the premises of Ringfield & Lewis early that morning. He can observe the premises in relative anonymity from his position behind a large pile of oak planks. He had resolved to observe the people and the operations exactly, in order to get a picture of the firm's routine.

Simon remembers an advice from his father, "If you cover a distance of ten meters while working, then that is immaterial. If you go the same way a hundred times, you have covered a thousand meters. Therefore, you should consider in advance the best way to shorten the distance. Time means money."

For a few hours, Simon follows the ways that the workers take. He tries to commit to memory who works with whom, and how cooperation pro-ceeds: calm and businesslike or loud and with lots of gesticulation. Sud-denly a coach turns into the drive, and Simon has no problem guessing that Harvey Barton sits inside. Simon uses the general excitement over the arrival of the lordly coach to reach the office, arriving just in time to intro-duce Ringfield, Lewis, and Barton to one another.

"You are right on time, Mr. Brown!" says Maynard Ringfield and turns to Harvey Barton. "May I show you into the office?"

David Lewis uses this opportunity to whisper to Simon, "Were you able to make any progress?"

"We will have to see what Mr. Barton has decided, after my discussion with him yesterday."

David Lewis takes hold of Simon's coat sleeve and asks, still whisper-ing, "You spoke to him yesterday personally? How on earth did you get an appointment with Harvey Barton?"

Simon simply grins and follows the other two men into the office. Harvey Barton gets right to the point, "My dear sirs, Mr. Brown here came to visit me at the bank yesterday, and proposed a deal. We are to provide you with a loan for the two new ships. Mr. Brown is of the opinion, that we will be able to accept the two new ships as collateral. Are the ships currently serving as col-lateral, or are there loans on them from other banks or institutions?"

"No, Mr. Barton," Maynard Ringfield answers, "there are no prior loans at hand. Until today Ringfield & Lewis have always paid for everything in cash. We have a signed purchase contract from a New York shipping company for both unfinished ships."

Simon pays close attention to the conversation and the conduct of the men around the table.

"What type of ships are they? Freighters or fishing boats?"

"They are lightweight, speedy freighters."

"So they are ships which will transport more expensive goods," concludes Harvey Barton. "If you already have signed purchase contracts, then deciding on the sum of the loan is not complicated. I would say: To avoid exhausting your final reserves, we will set the loan amount at sixty percent of the agreed upon sale price. Do you agree, my good sirs?" Harvey Barton looks around the room.

"That sounds fine", nods Maynard Ringfield, while David Lewis breathes a barely noticeable sigh of relief.

"What are your other conditions?" Maynard Ringfield wants to know. "We have to be able to afford the loan. How high will the interest rate be?"

"Mr. Brown drove a hard bargain yesterday. We agreed that one hundred percent of the loan will be paid out, with an interest rate of six percent per annum."

"Six percent!" David Lewis raises his eyebrows. "That is favourable is it not?"

"That is a decidedly favourable interest rate. In general we receive at least eight percent," says Harvey Barton with a glance in Simon's direction. "Before I forget: We would like to take a look at the books for the last few years, in order to get an accurate picture of the shipyard. Apart from that there is nothing to stop the deal going forward."

David Lewis jumps up. "We've done it, the work can continue!"

"Ah, I almost forgot." Barton raises his hand. "If the deal is a success for both parties, then I would ask that, in the future, we act as Ringfield & Lewis' bank."

Finally, the business partners part with a firm hand shake and an agreement to sign the contract the following week. Just a few minutes later, David Lewis pounds on the ship's bell with a hammer. The impatient shipyard workers gather together in a hurry, and the two business managers announce that salaries will be paid by the next week. Suddenly the large, burly Spaniard from the previous day steps in front of Simon, who had kept to the back.

"I want to thank you, Mr. Brown. You promised that you would return today, and you kept that promise. You are a man of your word."

"You won't get rid of me that quickly," Simon grins, and turns toward Maynard Ringfield, "Maynard, if you would do me a small favour?"

"Anything!" Maynard calls exuberantly.

"You could confirm in writing that I was unable to make it to class at Harvard College today, because I was doing business for Ringfield & Lewis."

"Not a problem, Simon."

The next day, Simon makes his way towards Harvard with a queasy feeling in his stomach. Without being asked, he calls in to Professor Hicks before the first lecture of the day and hands him the letter from Maynard Ringfield. Just then a student appears next to him, and informs Simon that he should attend His Magnificence immediately.

The college rector looks sternly at Simon. "Mr. Brown, where were you yesterday? Here at the college we had neither sight nor sound of you for the entire day!"

"I beg your pardon, yesterday I was at Ringfield & Lewis' shipyard."

"So you spent the day gadding about in the harbour of Boston! You can't be serious! You have only been with us for a few months and you are already letting yourself go? Becoming unreliable? Think that you have better things to do?"

Simon is not sure what he should do at this point. The letter from Maynard Ringfield, which he could offer as an excuse, is with Professor Hicks. What could he possibly say which won't strain the already tense atmosphere?

Just then there is a knock on the door.

"Enter!" The rector looks impatiently at the door, which opens forcefully. Professor Hicks stands in the door frame.

"Magnificence, I believe I owe you an explanation."

"Not now, Professor. As you can see, I am busy. Mr. Brown, who has only been with us for a short time, does not find it necessary to attend his classes, to say nothing of informing us of his absence."

"But that is why I am here. I forgot to inform you, that Mr. Brown received an assignment from myself."

"What type of assignment?" His Magnificence wrinkles his face in astonishment.

"Ringfield & Lewis, a shipyard in the Boston harbour, needed a loan to finance the building of two new ships. The loan was to be provided by the New England Bank of Boston. Mr. Brown here was supposed to document the communication between the parties, as well as determine the legal

186

requirements and background for accepting the loan. Yesterday he observed the negotiations on site. It was thus impossible for him to attend his lectures."

"Professor Hicks, I am worried about you. You are starting to become forgetful."

"I know, we spoke about Mr. Brown's absence this morning in the circle of college lecturers."

His Magnificence clears his throat. "Good, then let us leave it at that, shall we. You may go, Mr. Brown."

"Thank you," Simon replies simply, bows, and goes past Professor Hicks into the hallway.

Professor Hicks closes the door behind himself and turns immediately to Simon. "Brown, what Mr. Ringfield wrote to me … You did very well! Come to my office after the lecture and tell me the whole story!"

"Thank you, Professor."

"What for?"

"I have the feeling you just saved my skin."

"Ah, Brown, things are never as bad as they seem," Professor Hicks replies, and although he looks quite serious, there seems to be a twinkle in his eye.

I found the negotiations with Harvey Barton and the conversation at the shipyard exceptionally interesting and instructive. First you set a goal – here it was the loan and its conditions. Then you have to decide the best way to achieve this goal. Once you have decided on the path, you have to attempt to reach the goal you have set, using diplomacy, empathy, and determination.

What was Lindsay's goal, as she sat next to my desk wearing her alluring night gown? I was excited by what I could see, or, more accurately, what I could imagine. Did Lindsay just happen to come into my room, or was she really worried about me? She, too, had a goal in mind, that much was clear.

6. Hostility and friendship

A loud crack echoes through the evening quiet of the Rowley house. Simon sits at the desk in his attic room, absorbed in his calculus studies. Now he listens alertly downstairs. What was that? A gunshot? Or … no … the slamming of a door, a heavy door. He can already hear the shouting: A dark voice, loud, furious, and bloodcurdling. "Brown, where are you?"

Simon jumps up and is already on the stairs, taking them two or three steps at a time until he is standing in the foyer in front of Alexander Rickleby. "You're here late, Mr. Rickleby." Simon looks at his counterpart as if he had been expecting him.

"What were you thinking, mixing yourself up in my affairs?" Rickleby yells. "It's absolutely scandalous!" The shipyard owner stands before Simon, his face glowing red, and angrily swings his black walking stick with its silver knob through the air. "How dare you?! You will come to regret this!"

Molly Jones and Edward Snyder, startled by the loud noise, have hurried out of the kitchen into the foyer. Lilly Owens stands rooted to the spot in the entryway, one hand over her open mouth, with fear in her eyes. From the corner of his eye, Simon can also see Lindsay. She must have just come from the small salon, and still has the door handle in her hand. She also seems shocked, however, with a forced smile on her lips, is doing her best to project calm. "Good evening, Alexander. How nice to see you," she welcomes the guest in a surprisingly quiet voice. "Alastair has not yet returned home."

"I am not here because of Alastair. I'm here because of your little bastard there!" Rickleby answers, pointing at Simon with his walking stick.

"Alexander, you cannot speak like that about our guest!"

"I couldn't care less! Brown, open your mouth and apologize! Afterwards we will see how you can fix the situation."

Simon still hasn't made a move, so Lindsay decides to take the matter in hand. "Alexander, Simon, please follow me into the large salon, we can talk with each other there." Lindsay walks toward Simon, takes hold of his shirt sleeve and pulls him in the direction of the salon door.

"What on earth were you thinking?" Rickleby yells as he follows the other two.

Once they are in the salon, Simon turns to Rickleby and says in a calm voice, "Mr. Rickleby, what are you talking about?"

"You know exactly what I'm talking about! You concocted a plan to muddle up my business … together with Harvey Barton. But you will be sorry, you'll see."

"If you are talking about the shipyard," Simon answers, "then my goal was not to harm you, but rather to help Ringfield & Lewis. The shipyard had a problem and I was able to help a bit with the solution."

"That's ridiculous, and even a Greenhorn like you must have known it right from the start! Ringfield & Lewis were almost finished, they were just about to go bankrupt, they couldn't even pay their workers anymore." Rickleby paces back and forth in the salon, obviously angry. His face has turned dark red, pulsing veins are visible in his neck and on the hand which holds his walking stick. "We were in a perfect position to take over the shipyard … and then along comes an ignorant German and spoils my entire plan! Brings the NEBB on board and secures financing for Ringfield & Lewis for the whole year." Alexander Rickleby stops pacing, breathes in and stares darkly at Simon.

"Mr. Rickleby, I stand by my words: I had no intention of harming either you or your shipyard."

"Poppycock! You don't just pull a finance deal like that out of your hat! It was all planned. I say you wanted to injure me, you and Barton! Ringfield & Lewis won't sell any more, of course. Why should they? There's no need to anymore. The value of the shipyard has probably increased tenfold in the last few days!" Rickleby inches a little bit closer to Simon. "Do you have any idea who you are dealing with?!"

Lindsay wants to calm the furious shipyard owner and places her hand on his arm. But Rickleby rebuffs her. "Don't touch me, Lindsay! I don't want to calm down. In the past few days I have lost an asset. You don't just forget something like that!"

"But Mr. Rickleby," pleads Simon, since it is clear to him that Rickleby can barely control himself, "Ringfield & Lewis was never yours. If you had acquired the shipyard at a low price due to bankruptcy, then you would have taken away everything Maynard Ringfield and David Lewis have earned with their hard work." He positions himself between Lindsay and Rickleby as he says it.

"Are you unable to see that, or do you just not want to?" Rickleby's words are almost tumbling over themselves. "I practically had the business in my pocket, and now you have ruined everything."

The shipyard owner raises his right hand, balled into a threatening fist. Time seems to stop for a moment, each of the three is breathless. Then Lindsay yells with fear in her voice, "Alexander, how can you!"

As if in a trance, Rickleby turns toward her and lets his fist slowly fall, as if only now comprehending whose salon he is standing in. "Oh, leave me alone," he mumbles.

"Alexander, I think it would be better if you would leave now," Lindsay says, now with astounding composure.

Rickleby stares at Lindsay as if stunned, then turns towards the door. "Brown, you'll get what's coming to you! This isn't over yet." Turning to Lindsay he adds, "No offence, Lindsay. I don't hold you and Alastair accountable."

As Alexander Rickleby disappears into the foyer, Simon says calmly, "I am glad that I was able to help Ringfield & Lewis."

The door opens and a frightened Edward Snyder enters the salon. "Can I help, Mrs. Rowley?"

"Yes, Mr. Snyder, Mr. Rickleby would like to go now," Lindsay explains. Once Snyder has disappeared again to bring the uninvited guest to the door, Lindsay says to Simon, "I've never seen Alexander like that before. I am truly appalled. Thankfully Alastair is sure to arrive soon."

Barely a quarter of an hour later the master of the house has arrived. With hurried steps he enters the salon.

"Alastair!" Lindsay calls, relieved. "You will never guess who was here just a few minutes ago."

"Alexander Rickleby. Mr. Snyder told me already. I expected him to come after Simon!"

"You took that into account? I thought he was going to beat Simon up." Lindsay is still very pale.

Simon joins the conversation, "Lindsay, Alastair said that he expected that to happen ... so did I."

Alastair nods, his face solemn. "Indeed, Simon, you ruined what would have been a very lucrative deal for him."

"You think that Simon made a mistake too, then?" Lindsay asks.

"No. Simon acted exactly the way I would have, if I had been in his position. That is why I helped him get the appointment with Harvey Barton. But the truth of it is that a very good deal has slipped through Alexander's fingers." Alastair is unable to hide his smile. "But everything went all right, didn't it?"

"Yes," Simon nods. "Mr. Rickleby pulled himself together."

"And what about Alexander?" Lindsay wants to know.

"Oh, he'll calm down eventually," says Alastair. "That's business for you – sometimes you win, and sometimes you lose."

"What on earth is that lad doing up there?" Maynard Ringfield stares spellbound out of the office window. Simon sits high atop a pile of wooden

190

planks and scribbles with a lead pencil onto a relatively large piece of paper.

"No idea," says David Lewis in reply. "That makes the third day that he has sat up there for hours and hours."

Maynard Ringfield frowns. "David, we have so much to do right now, he could help us a little bit with the work, instead of painting up there on high."

"Somehow I don't think that he's just aimlessly drawing," opines David. "He's thinking something through again, I'm fairly certain about that."

"Hey?" Maynard calls out. "Where did he go? He was sitting up there just a minute ago, right?"

With the large piece of paper on his knee, Simon had been watching the operation of the shipyard and making notes with his pencil. He missed nothing, not even the way a small hand pulled a hammer towards itself behind the back of the bearish Spaniard, and then plunged under the hull of one of the new ships like a shadow to disappear completely – in the direction of the gate. Simon, as fast as lightning, stuffed paper and pencil between two planks and, with a few quick, quiet jumps, disappeared behind one of the two thick gateposts.

Suddenly a small black boy scampered around the corner with the hammer in his hand. Simon smoothly grabbed the boy by the front of his shirt and pressed him against the wall. With his free hand he took the hammer away, so that the boy could not hit him with it.

"What are you doing, sonny boy?"

"Let go of me! Let me go!" The little boy squirmed, and tried to kick Simon. He simply took a step backwards, without letting the boy go. At that moment Simon recognized the boy. "Hey … aren't you Tyson? The boy who was chased on the Rowleys' property by those shady characters! Of course …"

Little Tyson simply stared at him.

"Now you are speechless? Didn't I tell you that you shouldn't steal? And now I catch you here with a hammer in your hand!"

As the boy remained silent, Simon took him by the arm and dragged him over the entire shipyard to the office. Tyson fought with tooth and claw and yelled, "I don't want to! No, let me go!" But Simon held onto him with his hand as tight as a vice.

Accompanied by Tyson's loud shouts of protest, Simon sits the boy in the office on a chair in front of Maynard Ringfield's desk, and presses his shoulders against the back of the chair. Then he turns to the two business managers, "Maynard, David, I caught this boy on shipyard property, in the act of stealing this hammer and running away with it." Simon places the hammer on the desk.

Maynard and David have sprung out of their chairs, shocked by the noise that Tyson is making. "It's you then." Maynard is the first to find his voice. "You have been stealing tools from us for some time, true? That will cost you, my boy." With Tyson still fidgeting, Maynard turns to Simon and continues, "I wondered where you had got to. You sit for hours on top of those wooden planks and then, from one second to the next, you disappear."

"Of course, my 'painting'. In the excitement I forgot all about it. David?" asks Simon, "can you hold on to the little thief here? I'll just quickly jump up onto the planks and fetch my sketch."

"Can't the sketch wait?" David objects. "Let's just deal with one thing after the other, first the boy, then the sketch."

"No, I've just had an idea. Maybe we can kill two birds with one stone." Simon has already left the office, and David is just able to grab little Tyson before he can escape once more.

When Simon returns, the boy is sitting stiff and quiet in the chair. "And? What did you do to him?" he asks incredulously. "How come he is sitting so still and not moving?"

Maynard grins. "We told him that you know him, and that you know where he lives."

"And that worked?"

"Maynard added that you are stubborn and persistent before all else. If you want to breathe down someone's neck then they'll never get rid of you."

Tyson cowers in the chair during this exchange, staring at Simon all the while. Simon spreads his sketch onto David's desk. "Excuse me, David, but I've had a few thoughts that I would like to share with you both."

Maynard looks sceptically at the drawing. He only sees numbers, dashes, and arrows. The paper is almost torn from use in some places. "What does this all mean?" he asks. "Well, it's no work of art."

"But it might be worth a few thousand dollars all the same!" says Simon with a laugh. "I already spent almost two hours up on those wooden planks on the morning before Harvey Barton came to visit. Since that day I have been thinking about what I saw from up there."

"Well, what did you see?" Maynard wants to know.

"I've documented it all in this sketch. The numbers represent different procedures, the dashes represent the locations at which individual crafts are carried out, and the regular lines mark the distance that the individual work-ers travel to carry out their tasks."

192

"It's all just total chaos!" David exclaims.

"That's exactly what I thought. If the work flow was better organized, then the workers wouldn't have to walk as far to get tools or materials. They would save a lot of energy and labour. The time it takes to build a ship would decrease significantly, which means that the ships would be less expensive to build."

Maynard looks at the diagram critically. "What changes would you make?"

"I would store materials and tools closer to the individual work areas. We can divide the workers much more strictly into different working areas, so that they don't all work here and there all over the ship, but instead each concentrate on a single area."

"Hm … that seems to make sense," says David, scratching his chin with one hand.

"There should always be one person responsible for each of the working areas, who will also make sure that there are always enough materials and tools available," Simon adds. He turns to Tyson. "Which is where we come to our little delinquent here. We'll assign a Tyson to every … let's call them organisation masters, who will be responsible for running around or other dispatch work."

"Can you read and write?" Maynard asks Tyson chuntering.

"A little bit," is the restrained answer.

"Do you go to school, boy?" Maynard wants to know now.

"Y … No."

Maynard looks doubtfully at Simon.

"Of course he'll have to learn to read and write!" Simon explains. "But if Tyson grows into this assignment, then we will be able to offer him a real chance later on, with a permanent position at the shipyard."

Maynard makes a suspicious face. "A permanent job for a thief?"

"Yes," smiles Simon. "If he's working for Ringfield & Lewis, then he won't have to steal any more, am I right?"

"Can we be sure?" David also seems to have misgivings.

"I think so. I'll take Tyson home to his mother now and have a talk with her. In the meantime, you can rack your brains thinking about my sketch. We'll see each other again tomorrow afternoon."

"All right Simon," nods Maynard. "I'll have a think about how to organize lessons for Tyson. He won't be able to go completely without them."

Not too long afterwards, Simon stands with the obviously nervous Tyson on the veranda of a simple cottage. Simon knocks on the door, which opens straight away. In front of him stands a delicate, dark skinned woman. She is still very young and has a pretty face, but her expression is fearful. Her fine, elegant appearance and her long, silk black hair directly contrast her simple, humble dress. She stands shyly in the doorway without saying a word.

"Good day, Mrs. La-Ron, my name is Simon Brown. I live with the Rowleys here in the neighbourhood, and I would like to exchange a few words with you about Tyson here."

"What has he done now then?"

"May I come inside?"

"Oh, excuse me, of course." Latisha La-Ron steps to the side and opens the door. "Take a seat at the table, Mr. Brown."

Simon surveys the room as he sits down. It seems to function as both kitchen and living room. It all looks very humble, but also very clean.

"May I offer you something to drink? I'm afraid there's only water."

"Yes, please," Simon answers, smiling.

Latisha La-Ron picks up a pitcher of water and attempts to pour some into a glass. But her hands shake so much that she almost knocks the glass over.

"May I?" Simon takes the pitcher from her hand and pours the water himself. Then he looks his host in the eyes. "He stole a hammer."

"Sorry?" Mrs. La-Ron makes a face, as though she must have misheard.

"You asked me what Tyson had done this time. He stole a hammer from the Ringfield & Lewis shipyard."

"My God, Tyson, how many times have I told you not to steal!" Latisha La-Ron turns imploringly to her son. Tears run down her cheeks. Then she suddenly drops her head into her arms on the table and begins to cry bitterly. Tyson stands behind his mother, with his tail between his legs, and strokes her hair softly. "Oh Mama, don't cry. I only do it so that we can buy something to eat … please!"

"Mrs. La-Ron," Simon intervenes with a friendly voice, "You don't have to be worried. I'm not here to complain, or to cause trouble for you. I want to offer your son a deal – and you, as well."

Latisha La-Ron raises her head very slowly, and looks at Simon with her teary eyes, without making a single sound.

"I think I have a job now, Mama," Tyson chatters excitedly.

"A job?" Latisha La-Ron looks disbelievingly at the boy. "Tyson, you are far too young to have a job."

"That all depends," says Simon. "I had to start helping my parents in their winery when I was very young. Of course, Tyson shouldn't have to work like a grown man. The job has to fit the worker, that's the most important thing. I believe that your son has a lot of nonsense going on in his head …" Simon tells of his first meeting with Tyson in front of the Rowleys'

194

barn, and of the events of today. Then he continues, "Tyson will start at the shipyard helping with the organization. The job means regular work that he can cope with and also a regular salary. On top of that, Tyson won't have any time for his foolishness and will learn to work with wood and iron. I have already spoken with the shipyard owners, Maynard Ringfield and David Lewis. They are willing to accept my proposal, provided that Tyson learns to read and write and that you, Mrs. La-Ron, agree to the idea."

Latisha still looks at Simon disbelievingly. "Who are you? Why are you helping us?"

"I am an immigrant from Germany ..." Simon roughly describes his history and explains his current position to Latisha, in order to put her mind at ease.

As he comes to the end of the tale, Latisha lays her hand on Simon's, which is sitting on the table. "When Tyson was three years old, his father was murdered," she says. "He, like me, was a slave on a gigantic cotton farm in the South. With a lot of pain and effort and the help of friendly people, I was able to flee to the North with Tyson. Since then we've had to manage our lives alone ..." Latisha swallows hard, then tears roll down her cheeks once more. "Thank you, Mr. Brown."

"You certainly haven't had it easy," Simon answers. "And Tyson deserves a chance." He stands up from his chair. "So, Tyson, early tomorrow you will be at Ringfield & Lewis to report to work on time, with greetings from myself. I will also be there tomorrow, late in the afternoon."

"All right, but is everything already sorted out?" Tyson wants to know.

"The sketch that I gave those two in the office is your ticket in, and I don't think that you will be refused entry. We'll see each other tomorrow afternoon."

Simon walks to the door, but Latisha La-Ron grabs him. "I don't know what to say ..."

"Nothing," Simon answers and removes her hand. "It's all up to Tyson now."

I infuriated Alexander Rickleby against myself. I would have to deal with his hostility again. That's the way life is sometimes: Although you do the right thing, some people take offence, simply because they see things differently. Or, in this case, because they place their own well being before the fate of others. You have to learn to deal with things like that in life, but it's not easy when you are young. At the same time, I knew that supporting Tyson La-Ron was the right thing to do. He would feel the same when he grew up, I was certain. But the friendship which I would form with Tyson years later was not something I could have predicted.

7. A step too far?

Mountains of books are stacked on the writing desk in Simon's attic room. The biggest stack are the works that he needs for his studies in Harvard. Text books for mathematics, physics, legal science and economics. Beside them are piled the weighty tomes that Simon has borrowed from David Lewis, and some more that he has found in Harvard's library. These volumes deal with the oceans, sailing, ship-building, and navigation. On a small side-table stands a teapot and a used cup – Simon has not had anything else up until the evening. There is still so much to read!

Simon looks up briefly and throws a glance out the window: The sun, a glowing red ball, vanishes leisurely behind trees on the other end of the property. Simon has not even noticed how quickly the time has passed. But his eyes quickly find their way back to the numbers and letters on his writing desk, and his thoughts become immersed in the calculation of the speed of ships on the high seas.

Suddenly, he feels a soft, warm breath on his neck. The hair on his nape stands on end and a shiver runs down his spine. Shocked, he wants to look around, but tender fingers grab his head and hold it tight. Then Lindsay's quiet voice asks Simon, "Did you see the sunset? Romantic, wasn't it?"

"Hello, Lindsay," answers Simon hesitantly. "Yes, a wonderful sunset. Is Alastair already on his way to New York?"

"He left this morning," answers Lindsay, as she softly massages his cheeks with her thumbs. "He'll come back again next weekend."

Simon feels the erotic tension between the two of them. What indeed is going to happen? Since the last time she visited him late at night in his attic room, there have always been these moments where his attractive hostess has crept into his thoughts.

"One hasn't seen you for the whole afternoon, Simon," Lindsay continues. "Lilly told me that you fetched a teapot from the kitchen and disappeared again immediately."

Finally Simon is able to free himself from the tender hold and turn around. It hits him like a blow: Lindsay is only wearing a short silk nightdress that flows around her figure in gentle curves. The straps are so thin that Simon fears they could rip under the weight of her breasts. The cleavage is also so low that it borders on a miracle how everything stays in its place. Lindsay smiles at him, takes a couple of steps backwards, and sits on the bed.

"Simon, come to me, please." Very gently she pats beside her on the mattress.

How can her voice just sound so seductive? Simon hears his heart pumping like a power station and feels a quiet pressure in his ears. He gets hot and he cannot stop staring at the woman on his bed. As if in a trance, he rises and goes slowly towards her. Even before he has reached the bed, Lindsay rises, takes him in her arms and begins to kiss him. Her soft lips touch his, at first just very cautiously. Then her pressure becomes more intense and Simon feels Lindsay's hands on his cheeks. Slowly he kisses her back and a pleasant feeling of warmth passes through him.

Skilfully and incredibly fast, Lindsay frees him of his shirt and trousers and pushes the two wafer-thin nightdress straps down from her shoulders. Like in slow motion it slips down her body. Like the way dear God created them, they stand before one another, Lindsay's kisses become more and more overbearing and her hands stroke Simon on his whole body.

But now he returns to his senses again. "Stop, we can't do this!" he calls out and pushes Lindsay away from him.

She remains very calm. "It is your first time, Simon, isn't it?"

"Alastair ... Lilly ... Mr. Snyder ...," stammers the young man.

"Everybody is gone," explains his counterpart. "Alastair is in New York and the others have their free evening." Without a spark of arrogance she looks at him and skilfully steers the conversation in the desired direction. "You are frightened of your first time!" Her gaze glides pleasurably over Simon's body. "Look at yourself, how powerfully you are built, how good you look!"

But Simon is still determined. "We're not allowed to do that." At the same time he still has to admire Lindsay's naked body: her well-formed breasts, her firm, flat stomach, her narrow hips and legs.

"You find me desirable too," she ascertains with a satisfied smile. "You cannot deny it, I see it on you!"

"Yes, but ..." Hardly has Simon started to speak, when Lindsay's lips are back on his. Very slowly she sinks onto the bed and pulls him with her. Simon's resistance crumbles. Lindsay's familiar, tender way, her lips and her shining eyes do not miss their effect.

At some stage, Simon's hands begin hesitantly to move and feel out, in astonishment, the curves and secrets of her figure. Surprised, he notices how Lindsay trembles at his touch. A soft sigh escapes from her lips. Skilfully, she brings her body into position underneath Simon: She knows exactly what she wants and what she is doing. Simon gives up wanting to think clearly, his body evades his reason and does what he has wanted to do for a long time. Single movements find a rhythm and steer towards the unavoidable. Lindsay's groans give way to a panting, while something in

197

Simon's head seems to explode. At the same time, there flashes through his body a well-known and yet so new feeling. He eases himself down on Lindsay and buries his face in the pillow beside her head.

Tenderly Lindsay strokes him on the neck and whispers in his ear, "Thank you, Simon!"

Simon still needs a moment to find his breath again and return to reality. Then he murmurs, "We shouldn't have done that. That was not right!"

"But it was beautiful," answers Lindsay gently. "Don't worry. You make me very happy – that can't be wrong."

Simon sits up and looks at Lindsay. "Does Alastair not make you happy, so?"

"Not in this way – in his own way, yes. Every now and then I miss something. But you can't understand that."

"Explain it to me!"

"Not now, Simon. Now we both need our sleep." The beautiful lady of the house rises, stands for a short moment completely naked in front of Simon and then slips her nightdress over her head.

After Lindsay has gone, Simon lies awake for hours and ponders what has taken place. What has he done? Will he be able to look Alastair in the eyes ever again? Has he betrayed his trust? So this was now his 'first time'. This is how it feels – bad. Why must he now think of Marala, of all people? She is so far away – and Lindsay so near. Too near. It takes a long time before the tiredness overcomes Simon.

The next morning Simon has reached a decision: He must absolutely speak with Lindsay about last night: Something like this can never be repeated. But when he steps into the small drawing room, only Lilly Owens smiles at him pleasantly. "Good morning, Simon. I'll bring you the tea immediately."

"Thank you, Lilly. Where is Mrs. Rowley?" Simon notices that only one place has been laid at the breakfast table.

"She went away in the coach very early this morning. I cannot say when she will be back."

Disappointed, Simon sits down and sips at his tea. "I must go to Harvard now," he says. "But I can talk to her later as well."

The day in Harvard seems to drag on endlessly. Simon spends hours there in lectures and seminars, but thoughts and images of last night keep passing through his head. He must speak with Lindsay … absolutely … today still!

In the afternoon Simon meets Mr. Snyder in the entrance hall of the Rowley villa. "Ah, good day, Mr. Brown, it's good that I've met you here. Mrs. Rowley is expecting you at the stables."

198

"Right now?"

"Yes, you should please visit to the stables immediately."

"Already on my way." Simon places his briefcase on the stairs and turns on his heel. At the stable he meets Karol, who is just leading out a saddled-up brown stallion by the reins.

"Hey, Simon, how are you?" the coachman greets.

"Very well, thanks. Have you seen Mrs. Rowley?"

"Of course. She wants to go for a ride and you should accompany her. This is why I've already saddled-up the brown stallion for you."

"And where can I find her?"

Karol grins and points to the courtyard entrance. Lindsay's white horse trots, with flowing mane, along the road leading north from the Rowley estate. Simon stands before the brown stallion, strokes his blaze, pats his neck lightly and speaks calm words to him. With a great leap he swings himself into the saddle, allows Karol to give him the reins and gallops off.

A few minutes later, he has caught up with Lindsay, and without exchanging a word they both allow their horses to fall into step. Lindsay is sitting in a lady's saddle with both legs hanging from the horse's left side, all the time she is watching Simon. Finally she begins, "I have already waited for over half an hour for you. I would like to show you something. Besides, we can speak with one another here without being disturbed."

"I missed you this morning. You were already away," answers Simon.

She smiles slightly. "So you missed me? I like that!"

"I didn't mean it like that. I have to speak to you."

Lindsay nods. "I with you, too. I would like to explain some things, so that you don't reproach yourself even more. You know, Simon – I love Alastair. I have always loved him and will always do so. But he is just years older than me." She hesitates briefly. "And as well as that, he was once seriously ill."

"What was wrong with him?" asks Simon, shocked.

"He doesn't want to talk about it."

"And what has that to do with me?"

"Please allow me to continue," says Lindsay. "You can ask me questions later and express your opinion."

"Fine." Simon nods. Perhaps he should really first listen to what Lindsay has to say.

"Well, due to his illness and his age, Alastair and I can no longer come together like the two of us did yesterday. You understand what I mean, Simon." Still Lindsay watches him steadfastly and seems to register every change in his face.

Simon briefly returns her look and answers with a curt "Yes."

"I can't do without it though. I need it every so often. Can you under-stand?"

"Yes … But what about Alastair?"

"He knows about it. We have spoken about these things, he accepts my needs … not least because there is no other way. But he doesn't want to know the details, and he absolutely would not like anything to become public."

"Alastair agrees to it??" Simon is amazed.

"Yes, he does," explains Lindsay with a happy smile. "You must believe me!"

"Yes, I certainly must – I can hardly ask him."

"No!" is the unexpectedly sharp return.

"Lindsay," Simon wants to know now, "yesterday: did that just happen or did you plan it?"

"Does it make a difference for you?"

"I don't know … I see myself a little like a target."

She smiles. "Yes, Simon. You were my target."

"Since when?"

"Is that so important?"

"For me, yes. Since when have I been your target?"

"Let me think … Since the crossing on the 'Whitecap'." Now she does go a little red.

"For months so!" Simon is shocked. "You have been thinking the whole time how you can get me into bed?" Now he wants to know exactly. "From when exactly has this been on your mind?"

The conversation now seems to be going in a direction that Lindsay does not like. "Simon, I did not allow you live with us, because I, as you so coarsely put it, 'wanted to get you into bed'. I wanted to help you from the start. I really like you. And you know that, too. Between us there is a lot of trust. On the other hand, it is exactly this which moved me to choose you as my … let's say, companion. You are very reticent, conscientious and trust-worthy. As well as that, you are young, handsome and strong." Now she has to grin again. "My God, there was nothing else I could do. It was inevitably going to lead to this."

For a while they ride silently side by side. By now the road has become a bumpy farm track, lined by high grass. Houses and barns have been left behind. The nature gets more unspoilt, they approach a dense wood. "Where are we riding to?" Simon wants to know.

"Let yourself be surprised."

After some more quiet minutes, the farm track leads into nothing and Lindsay guides her horse to the right, to nowhere it seems.

"Lindsay?" asks Simon, "do you know the way?"

200

Suddenly, she gives her horse the spurs and just cries, "Yes, I know the way!" Simon has no other choice, but to follow her. A dark path goes deeper into the wood. All of a sudden, it seems the sky opens and they reach a big clearing. A sluggish river flows through the middle, leading to a lake. At the shore of the river Lindsay dismounts and takes a tin from her horse's saddle bag and seats herself on a scraggy old tree trunk. After Simon has got off his horse also and has sat beside her, Lindsay holds the tin under his nose. It is full of magnificently smelling biscuits. "One of my favourite places," says Lindsay. "Here I can relax and unwind wonderfully."

Simon looks around, astonished. "It is beautiful here." He bends over, holds a hand in the river's fresh water and cools his brow with it.

Lindsay moves nearer to him and, with one hand, strokes his cheek. "Simon, do you think you can get involved with this?"

He looks at the river and answers objectively, "I'll think about it."

For a long time they sit quietly side by side. Every now and again, one of them reaches into the tin for one of Molly's amazing biscuits. Finally Lindsay says, "I think we should go. Can you help me onto the horse?"

"Of course." Simon jumps up, takes the horse by the reins and pulls it over. Then, with both hands, he takes Lindsay by the waist and lifts her into the saddle. She grins, but doesn't say anything, about which Simon is very happy. But just in the moment when he is mounting his brown stallion, he hears a hissing on the ground beside Lindsay's horse. A snake!

Even before he can warn Lindsay, the horse shies and rears up. It takes a few steps back and is now standing up to its knees in the river. Lindsay can no longer hold on and falls backwards off the saddle, so that she is hanging headfirst from the horse. Everything happens so quickly that Simon cannot react in time. Lindsay keeps getting pulled with her head under water. Simon comes to his senses, jumps out of the saddle and makes towards Lindsay's horse. He knows that the animal is panicking more and can drag Lindsay hundreds of meters through the water behind it. With a steady grip he grabs the saddle, with his free hand he tries to free Lindsay from the stirrup. He pulls her to him with a yank on her shoe and, at the same time, pushes the stirrup in the other direction – and behold! Lindsay comes free. Simon lets go the saddle and grabs her with both hands. He holds her as tightly as he can. Like a reflex, Lindsay puts her arms around his neck and gasps greedily for air.

"What was that? Simon, what happened?"

"A snake. The horse got a fright and you weren't prepared."

Simon has completely forgotten about the snake, but it is obviously satisfied with scaring off the supposed intruders. It has probably retreated long ago into the nearest bush.

Simon holds Lindsay very tightly in his arms, carries her to the shore and sits her on the tree trunk. The water flows in streams from their bodies. Luckily, the horse has by now calmed down again as well, so that Simon can lead it without any problems out of the river. He sits beside Lindsay, who has already taken some deep breaths and has calmed down relatively quickly.

"Soaked to the skin …," she mutters. "We are soaked to the skin."

"Therefore we should set off soon and ride home to put on some warm clothes." As soon as Lindsay has recovered somewhat, they remount and set off on the return journey.

"Oh my God, Mrs. Rowley! What has happened?" Karol dashes towards them and grabs hold of the reins.

"A snake," answers Lindsay. "The horse shied and I fell into the river. Luckily Simon was able to free me." Simon has found a horse blanket in the stable which he now lays around Lindsay's shoulders. It is clear from the way she looks that she is freezing.

"Come, to the house," she says, "I'll ask Lilly to draw you a hot bath."

In the entrance hall soon only single drops on the floor bear witness to the misfortune that has befallen the two of them.

As Simon sits in the hot bathtub, he lays back his head pleasurably and tries to relax. Comforting warmth spreads through his body. The quietness makes him only now notice how tired he is. But then tender fingers glide through his hair, he springs up and a stream of water splashes out of the bathtub.

"It's good that we've tiled everything here," giggles Lindsay and steps – again completely naked – into the bathtub opposite him.

"Lindsay, what's the meaning of this?" cries Simon. "What happens if Mr. Snyder or Lilly burst in here?"

"I have made provisions, don't be scared. Besides I'm cold!"

Simon observes Lindsay sitting opposite him with her hair pinned up, who with a smile on her lips starts to rub along his legs. Time seems to have stood still, then Lindsay's hands wander further upwards until they have reached their target. Just as Simon really starts to enjoy her touch, Lindsay suddenly lets him go. Simon opens his eyes with a questioning look. "What's up?" comes from his mouth, but Lindsay doesn't answer, just steps slowly out of the bathtub. At the wash basin she stays standing.

Simon cannot see enough and notices how he is losing control again. He slowly steps out of the bathtub and goes across to Lindsay to kiss her. Her lips respond to him with passion. Lindsay draws back, pulls him with her and leans against the wall next to the wash basin. Seconds later her thighs clasp around Simon's hips. Without thinking he holds her tight and begins to move with the eventually familiar rhythm. Suddenly the moment on the 'Whitecap', when he caught Lindsay with Flynn Corwin in the sail locker, shoots through his head. The same situation ... This time it does not take long either until the tension is released like an explosion.

In the night Simon lies alone on his bed without again being able to sleep. What a crazy day!

So that was my 'first time': a journey of discovery for me and my body, sudden and unexpected. It was planned by Lindsay strategically and with military precision, like she confessed to me one time. Later I had to think about whether I could have prevented this 'hostile takeover'. But I was in this respect way too inexperienced. The feeling of going behind Alastair's back was terrible and upset me, but Lindsay put a spell on me and her words calmed me. Nonetheless, I decided on something at that time: I had to learn to keep control, even in seductive moments.

8. In the right place at the right time

Early on Saturday evening Rowley's villa is festively lit-up. One elegant coach after the other drives up the pebble path in front of the main house. Lindsay already announced in the morning that she expected Alastair home by midday and that company was invited for the evening.

Simon returns from a long day at Ringfield & Lewis. In an unobserved moment, he quietly pushes through the entrance door and retreats to his room. Quickly change the sweaty clothes and freshen up! Hesitating, Simon throws a glance in the mirror. Yes, it is good that today the house is full. It will be easier for him to approach Alastair in company than to have a private conversation.

When he finally clasps the handle of the salon door, a confusion of loud and soft, high and low voices invades his ears. Simon opens the door and looks at the gathering. The atmosphere is boisterous and cheerful in the festively decorated salon. A reception at the Rowleys' home always promises to be a pleasant evening. None of the guests have seen Simon until now, and so he can allow his gaze to wander through the room for another moment. He sees that the guests are mostly friends of Alastair and Lindsay, many of whom he has already often met. Among them is also Alexander Rickleby … What a surprise!

"Good evening, Mr. Brown. May I offer you a small glass of something?" Suddenly, Mr. Snyder is standing before Simon with a tray full of crystal glasses in his hand.

"Good evening, Edward," he answers, takes a glass of wine and quietly joins the circle that has gathered around Alastair. Simon holds the glass under his nose, closes his eyes and inhales the wine's aroma deep inside him. The aroma is so typical that Simon believes for a moment that he is back on Madeira Island again. The bright blue sky, the fresh, salty air of the Atlantic, and behind him the vast volcanic rocks of the island! He places the glass to his lips, takes a strong gulp and allows it to encircle his tongue. When he opens his eyes again, he notices that everyone else in the circle is watching him expectantly. Harvey Barton addresses him cheerfully, "Good evening, Simon. How are you?"

"Fine," answers Simon, while he registers Alexander Rickleby stepping up to them with dark looks.

"Simon!" Alastair, who is standing directly beside him, places an arm around Simon's shoulder. His body tenses involuntarily. How often, over the last few days, he has imagined this first encounter 'afterwards'! But he will master the situation, has firmly resolved to do so.

"Did you have a good journey?" he asks innocuously.

"Yes thanks, absolutely no problems; and luckily it was a success, as well. Thanks by the way for being there when Lindsay needed you!"

For an instant, Simon's breath catches, but luckily Harvey Barton interposes, "What do you say about the wine, Simon?"

Relieved, Simon lifts the glass to the light and begins to describe it, "It sparkles like amber in a chalice. In the nose there is an enchanting bouquet, with the aroma of flowers and raisins; lots of caramel; fine scents of salt and flintstone. On the palate one tastes an elegant sweetness, intensity and full flavour; the same aromas congregate here as well. The wine has been fortified; brandy was added to it during the fermentation. This interrupted the fermentation and retained the sweetness. The high alcohol content is swallowed wonderfully because of the intense extraction of the wine, so that it is absolutely not perceived as disturbing. Its lingering on the palate is decidedly long, very pleasant, and multilayered."

Simon makes a dramatic pause and takes another small mouthful.

"So – what is your conclusion, Simon?" asks Harvey Barton.

"A wonderful Madeira, typical for the Malmsey grape variety; ripened for a long time – I would say at least ten years."

Alastair looks around the room and discovers Edward Snyder at the buffet. "Mr. Snyder, please bring me a bottle of the aperitif."

"Certainly, Mr. Rowley!" The butler is immediately standing in the circle with the desired bottle.

"We will just have a look so to see what we have here," mutters Alastair and then reads aloud, "Madeira, Malmsey, 10 years old, Robert Henriques, Camara de Lobos, Funchal."

"That is truly amazing," the butcher, Oscar Thickstone, remarks. "Time and again, I am both delighted and astonished at all the things that one can taste. Imagine I had a ham in front of me and could tell you by smelling and tasting it, where the pig had lived and what it had eaten, if it had grown up in a field or pigsty and with which type of wood it was smoked with in the oven." Laughter pervades the salon. Eventually, all become engrossed back in their conversations.

Alastair takes hold of Simon's arm and says, "Simon, many thanks that you looked after Lindsay with such attentiveness." Immediately, Simon's tension returns. Everyone in the circle is watching Alastair. He explains, "Do you know, Lindsay went riding last week and luckily Simon accompanied her. Lindsay's horse shied in front of a snake and threw her into the river. Her shoe got caught in the stirrup, and she was dragged under water again and again. Thank God that Simon was able to free her out of this situation."

"Lindsay was surely riding with a lady's saddle?" Leon Taylor, the doctor from Cambridge, wants to know. "These lady's saddles should be forbidden; they are much too dangerous! The horse just cannot be brought under enough control."

"But Leon, don't start on about that again!" his wife Sarah complains. "A gentleman's saddle is improper for a lady. She cannot sit like a man on a horse – impossible!"

But Leon Taylor counters, "Reason has to stand above fashion or propriety, Sarah. You really must agree."

"Balderdash!" Sarah is getting worked up. "Customs and decency should be valued and defended in our country!"

Harvey Barton might have a feeling that the discussion could develop into a serious marital row and tries to manoeuvre the discussion in another direction. "Where are you actually coming from at this late hour, Simon? From your first workplace or your second?" He winks at Simon mischievously.

"From Ringfield & Lewis," answers Simon.

"Developing well, our shipyard, isn't it?" says Harvey Barton, visibly amused.

That was enough to get Alexander Rickleby into action. "They talk about development and drag blocks of wood through the water. That is just ridiculous!" he mocks.

"What? Blocks of wood?" Harvey Barton asks, baffled.

"Yes," laughs Alexander Rickleby. "One sits in a rowing boat and pulls wooden blocks on strings behind him. The other lies on the grass at the shore and has fun watching the whole thing."

Everyone in the circle laughs loudly and Simon joins in. Then he says, "How we spend out work breaks, you can safely leave up to us." Inside though, he is very tense and does not let Rickleby out of his sight. He registers every gesture, every word. How does the other know about the tests with the model ships? Only four people are aware of these tests: Maynard Ringfield, David Lewis, with whom he performed the tests, himself, and Ricky Eckstein, a technician from the shipyard.

There can only be one answer: Ricky Eckstein must be the mole, of this Simon has no doubt. For a long time, he has already had the feeling that Alexander Rickleby is getting information directly from the shipyard. How else would it have been possible for him to purposefully turn suppliers and the authorities against Ringfield & Lewis? And Ricky Eckstein is the only one who comes into question as a mole.

Simon does not allow anyone to notice his inner restlessness. He talks with the others, laughs with them and has fun; his mind, however, is racing. What information could Eckstein have already given away, and how will it be possible to stop him? No question: Eckstein has to go!

After the meal, Simon retreats to a remote corner of the veranda. Nobody can see him here, and he can think of Ricky Eckstein without being interrupted while he watches the starlit night sky.

Suddenly the door from the salon is opened, and the confusion of many voices forces its way outside. After a few minutes, Simon hears the clicking of heels on the tile and the voices of two ladies who walk onto the veranda and sit at a garden table not far from Simon.

"It's wonderful to feel the fresh air this mild night, isn't it Daisy?" That is clearly Ashley Rickleby.

"You can say that again," answers the second – unmistakably Daisy Thickstone. "Ah, at Lindsay's we always get a meal like in a high-class restaurant. I cannot get enough of it."

"One can see that on you," comes the slightly sharp answer. "But don't worry about it. I have eaten too much as well."

"Ashley, you cannot complain! With your figure, you are still able to turn every man's head. And you can wear what you want: It always looks very elegant."

"I say! You are just lacking a little taste. But still I find you very likeable."

"Lindsay is looking stunning again tonight: such a great dress and what radiance! I am totally impressed."

"Psst, not so loud!" hisses Ashley and lowers her voice. "What do you think? How much is that due to her young lover?"

Simon cringes. Is Ashley Rickleby merely speculating, or does she know something?

"Ashley, just how can you say something like that?" Daisy flares up in rage, but Ashley does not seem to be impressed by this.

"What do you think? Can you imagine that Lindsay is just living with this young Simon, without anything happening there?"

"You couldn't do that?" asks Daisy, piqued, but audibly curious.

"No, of course not," laughs Ashley. "This Simon looks good and is strong. Nothing more is needed. I would teach him the rest, you can be sure of that."

"But Lindsay is not like that," says Daisy energetically.

"What do you mean with 'like that', Daisy? Alastair is not the youngest anymore – there is surely nothing much still happening there. A young chap can stir up a lady's blood completely, you can believe me. But of course you know nothing about that. Something like that you have certainly never experienced in your whole life …!"

"What are you trying to say?"

"Ah Daisy, don't be insulted – but such a young boy does things to you that lie beyond the limits of your imagination. I know what I am talking about."

"Your Alexander is not a young boy anymore though, is he?"

"Who is talking about Alexander?" Over where the ladies sit, dresses rustle as if Ashley Rickleby is taking a quick look at the salon door. Simon stays completely silent in his corner and continues to listen.

"My Alexander is ambitious, successful and rich. He spoils me with money; that is a completely different story. But between you and me, Daisy – he is often travelling and that makes the thing easier for me."

"What thing then?" Daisy Thickstone is acting really very naively, and Simon wonders why Ashley is confiding these details in her, of all people. But on the other hand … with Sarah Taylor or Isabella Wood, the educated wife of the second bank director of BBBC, she could hardly be talking about it.

"Daisy, you are slow on the uptake! Alexander spoils me with money and ... the young men just spoil me in other ways. Do you understand now?"

"Oh, yes, but what young men?"

"One is a student, son of a lawyer. I often meet him in a hotel. And Daisy," Ashley is almost whispering now, "he can be lecherous, you couldn't imagine! The other one works for us in the stable."

"How did you come across him then?"

"Alexander employed him and I noticed him immediately: tall, blond and strong. After a couple of months I had got him so far."

"How far did you have him?"

"Sometimes I have the impression that you really don't understand anything! Dirk, that's his name, just couldn't keep his fingers off me any longer. Of course I lent him a little hand. You know ... and then, one evening, it happened. Everyone was out; I went to the stable, just me and him, in the hay ... I don't need to say anything else, do I?"

"No, of course not. How exciting!"

"Yes, Daisy: it is. Now and then I bring him into the house with me. The risk increases the thrill."

Ashley's revelations have evidently left Daisy speechless. "Please excuse me," she rises. "I am so excited that I have to drink something!"

"Fine, I'll follow you in a moment," replies Ashley. "I want to enjoy the peace and fresh air for a little longer."

With a fine clicking sound, Daisy departs. She has hardly disappeared inside the house, when Simon seizes the opportunity, slinks across to Ashley's table and sits on the seat where Daisy was still sitting just a few seconds ago. Ashley is leaning back with closed eyes in her chair. After a short moment she opens her eyes again and her face drops.

Simon smiles amiably at her shocked face. "Hello Ashley."

"How long have you been sitting here?"

"Well, I have been longer on the veranda than you and Daisy."

Ashley's facial expression distorts even more, and into her voice there comes something fearful and shaky. "Did you hear everything?"

"Everything!" Simon confirms, in a quiet, matter-of-fact way.

"You have difficulties with Alexander," says Ashley. "He is angry with you, because you ruined a business deal on him. Now you will use me against him ... correct?"

"No."

"Do you want to blackmail me? Do you want money from me? That's it, an immigrant needs money!"

"No."

208

"Say it, Simon," Ashley begs, tormented, "what do I have to be scared of? What do you want?"

"Ashley, I don't know why, but somehow I like you," replies Simon. "I just want one thing: that you never again make insinuations regarding me or people that I know."

"But … you have me at your mercy!" cries Ashley, astounded. "You could completely ruin my position in society."

"Yes, I could. But I won't." Simon waits a moment then adds, "Now we both have a secret."

"And will you keep it well?" The attractive entrepreneur wife looks at him in doubt.

"You will just have to take your chances on it."

Simon stands up and, unnoticed by all the others, enters the garden from the veranda to get through the kitchen into the stairwell and from there to his room.

"David, I have to speak with you!" Two days later, Simon bursts into the office of Ringfield & Lewis.

Fortunately, David Lewis is alone in the office. "Simon, what is wrong? Your look shows that something bad is up."

Simon grabs a chair and sits opposite David. "It's about Ricky. He is spying on us and passing on the information to Alexander Rickleby."

David furrows his brow. "That is a serious accusation. I really cannot imagine that. I have known Ricky for many years."

"It corresponds to the facts though," insists Simon. "Two days ago, the Rowley's had company and Alexander Rickleby was there as well. He mentioned our trials with the model ships, even if he was more or less ridiculing them."

David's eyes widen in shock. "How can he have found out about them?"

"Well, we carried out the trials on a Sunday morning. There was nothing happening here; I didn't see anybody. I was especially watching out if somebody else was here. So: Just us two, Maynard Ringfield, and Ricky Eckstein know about the trials. What do you say to that?"

"Yes … Looking at it that way …" David hesitates still. "Then Ricky is really the only person who comes into question."

"That's what I am saying!"

"And now? What will we do now?"

"He has to go! We have to get rid of him as quickly as possible!"

"But Simon," David sways his head. "Ricky is a nice guy and a really good ship-builder as well."

"He is and remains a traitor. David, I cannot stand traitors!"

"Is there no other solution? Should we not speak with him first?"

"He will deny everything and lie to us," says Simon. "What else can he do?"

"There must be another possibility! Let us think it over," entreats David.

After a few moments of silence, Simon explains, "David, you have known Ricky for a very long time. This is why you think he is honest and loyal. But the fact is that he can only be a mole. It can be supposed that Alexander has something against him or that Ricky has financial troubles and can be blackmailed."

"Hm – then we have to find out where Ricky's problem lies. That is what you mean, isn't it?"

"Yes, exactly. We must find out what is going on there. Then we can maybe find a solution for Ricky's problem and speak some plain language with him."

"That is it, Simon. That is how we will do it!" David springs joyfully from his chair.

"You'd better sit down again," says Simon. "Think about it – Ricky could have come to you or Maynard with his problem as well. He should especially trust you, if you know each other for so long. But he did not do so. This matter must be approached with extreme caution. Listen: You give Tyson a few days free. I'll speak with him and put him on Ricky's trail."

"Tyson?"

"Yes, he is exactly the right person for this task. He should write down for us what Ricky is doing, where he is going and who he meets. I easily can determine on the side, if he is making progress with the writing."

David sighs and looks a little desperate. "Simon, why do they make our lives so difficult? We just want to design and build ships. So, when do we want to start this thing?"

"Right now … Never put off until tomorrow what you can do today! I will talk immediately with Tyson, will find him somewhere." Simon springs up and goes to the door. Before he leaves the office, he turns around again. "David, not a word to anybody, not even to Maynard. This will remain our secret for now!" Simon can no longer hear what David answers to this.

What a happy circumstance that I was on the veranda at exactly the right time! So I had something on Ashley. I did not want to use the situation to hurt her or Alexander. But it could have made sense to use my knowledge to steer Ashley. As it later turned out, I was one of the few people, about whom she sometimes spoke positively and who could have been able to influence her.

The issue with the mole could have been resolved relatively simply: get

210

him out of the company, get him away, it's over! But David absolutely wanted to keep Ricky. Seen professionally, this was without doubt the correct decision. But how could we prevent him from spying for Rickleby again and build back up the trust in his character?

9. A cunning plan

The old cottage sits still and picturesque in the middle of a huge, wild garden at the edge of the woods. It looks dilapidated, but the roof, at least, looks solid. Simon knocks on the old, twisted door. He wants to speak with Tyson, but it is Latisha who opens the door and whose face immediately lights up.

"Good day, Mr. Brown, step inside! Tyson is not home yet, but he will surely come soon. May I offer you a cup of tea?"

"Gladly, Latisha." Simon steps into the small, by now familiar, small living quarters and sits himself at the kitchen table.

"I would like to thank you from my heart, Mr. Brown," says Latisha, as she wipes off her hands on her apron. "Tyson is like a new person since he has been working at the shipyard. He talks about it every day, even when he is not there. And he gladly goes to lessons and does his homework, what really astounds me." She turns to the oven and says over her shoulder, "I think that now he has something that he can be proud of. Tyson even takes care of things that crop up around the house and is happy to give me a hand."

"Latisha, you don't have to thank me," answers Simon. "Tyson is a bright fellow, and we need somebody like him. If he can stay committed, he will go a lot farther in the shipyard."

The kettle on the oven begins to whistle and the aromatic flavour of tea is already filling the kitchen. "We have of course been doing a lot better financially as well, since Tyson has been getting wages," Latisha continues. "You make me very happy." With these words she takes hold of Simon's hand. Simon is moved. He has really helped this woman – and it wasn't so difficult at all.

Now the house door is roughly pulled open, and Tyson bursts in. "Hello Simon, have you been waiting long for me?"

"I was able to enjoy a cup of tea with your mum and have a nice chat with her," explains Simon, rising from his seat. "Let's step outside for a while; I would like to talk with you in peace."

Latisha takes a couple of steps towards the door. "You can stay here. I still have to see a friend of mine anyway. That way you won't be disturbed."

A few minutes later, the kitchen table is covered in lots of notes of various sizes that are more or less crumpled. "Your handwriting is very legible, Tyson. It is impressive." Simon has to smile at the confusion, but he does not say anything.

"I practise diligently," answers the boy. "Mum always says: The future belongs to those who can read and write."

"She is right there. Have you discovered anything about Ricky Eckstein?"

"I'll quickly sort out the pages and then we can begin." Tyson engrosses himself very keenly in his notes. "Well, Ricky lives just a few miles from the shipyard. Various other people live in the house as well. Ricky has a wife and two children – they are a lot younger than me though. His wife hasn't gone outside for months now. Sometimes a neighbour buys bread, milk and other things for her. She must be very sick. Ricky often has to look after the house-keeping as well."

""Who told you this, Tyson? Are you careful enough, too?"

"Yeah, sure," Tyson assures him beaming, and continues proudly, "I asked a boy on the street; he knows the family. Sometimes a fine gentleman with a big bag comes; the boy thinks this is the doctor."

"Tyson, you have done good work there." Simon pats Tyson on the shoulder; seated on his chair, he seems to grow with pride.

"There is something else that could be important," Tyson continues. "Yesterday after work, Ricky met a man a few streets away from the shipyard. He sat beside the man in a black coach and then the curtains were drawn. The coachman kept a good eye on who came near the coach. That's why I didn't get close enough and couldn't hear what they were speaking about."

"Did you see the man?"

"Yes, he waited in front of the coach until Ricky was there. I don't know him though. He is not fat."

"You mean slim – more thin?"

"Yes, exactly. Slim is the same as thin?" asks Tyson, curious for knowledge.

"Correct."

"The man was tall. He had a top hat on his head, wore a black coat with golden buttons, and held a walking stick in his hand. He was looking very sinister. That frightened me a little."

212

"Hm … I have absolutely no notion who that could be," mutters Simon to himself, as he rubs his chin.

Tyson is thinking intently as well. Then something else comes to his mind. "I am not completely certain, but I think the gentleman's walking stick had a golden knob and a special shape; that's why I noticed it too. It looked like …"

Simon interrupts him, "Was it in the shape of a dragon?"

"Yes, exactly. How do you know that? Do you know the man?"

"Maybe, Tyson. Pity that you weren't able to get closer, otherwise you could tell me if the golden buttons on his coat looked like little dragons as well."

"They were not round and smooth at any rate. I know that for sure!"

"You have really helped the shipyard with this, Tyson. I have to remind you again though that your task is extremely important and that you are not permitted to speak with anyone about it. Do you hear? With nobody!"

"I give you my word of honour!" Tyson promises with an earnest expression.

It is pouring rain and the wind is blowing around his nose as Simon marches through the shipyard to the office, under a dark cloudy sky. Now and again, Simon makes a skilful leap over a puddle. His neck is completely buried in his jacket's collar, his cap pulled down over his face. His mood lightens a little when he sees that light is burning in the office. A blazing, warm fire in the fireplace receives him there.

"Good morning, Simon," David Lewis greets him. "What sort of weather have you brought with you?"

"Morning, David. You're in good spirits!"

"The reason for that is just that I came here very early because I have so much to do still, and it was hardly raining at all then. With this weather absolutely nobody is going to stray over here on a Sunday."

"That is probably true."

"It's better like this, because we can talk without being disturbed. Come on, sit down! I've put on some fresh tea."

Simon obeys the request and takes the cup that he is offered. "Tyson has brought us forward. Ricky really seems to have problems: His wife must be seriously ill. A doctor visits at regular intervals and looks after her. And: Last week Ricky met a noble gentleman in his coach at a quiet place. Tyson says that the curtains were drawn. He couldn't find out what it was about, but his description of the stranger exactly fits Alexander Rickleby."

"Hm … this doesn't augur well," says David, furrowing his brow. "And how do we behave now?"

"Well, I'm thinking about this all the time. I have already gone through different possibilities in my head. The following seems to me to be the best …"

The next morning Simon is already sitting at Maynard's desk when David enters the office with Ricky Eckstein. Ricky looks somewhat disconcerted, but follows David's silent command and sits down.

"Simon, what are you doing here?" the technician jokes. "Not in Harvard at all?"

"I was looking for something," Simon answers briefly.

"And did you find it?"

"Yes, I did."

"What were you looking for so?"

"For you, Ricky … and for a long time, too."

"What, for me?" Ricky's face looks more and more amazed. "But I am here every day."

"Yes, that's true," nods Simon. "But I didn't know that you were the person I was looking for."

"You are speaking in riddles, Simon. Who should this 'person' be?"

Simon keeps a straight face and explains quietly, "The traitor!"

Crash, that hit home. David Lewis sits there with a stony mien and doesn't move. All the colour leaves Ricky's face; he sits there chalk-white before the other two. "Traitor?" he then stutters, "Me, me … I'm not a traitor!" Even if Ricky gives out an appearance of security – there is no mistaking the shaky insecurity in his voice.

"Ricky," says Simon, "we are far beyond this stage of the investigation. You were shadowed over the last few days. We know enough and have sufficient sound evidence to put you behind bars for the next few years."

Ricky opens his eyes wide. "But you can't do that! My wife …"

Simon interrupts him, "We know that, Ricky. Your wife is sick. But you should have thought of that beforehand. And also, that your two children will miss their dad really much. And when your time in jail is behind you, you certainly won't find any more work, especially not in Boston or the surrounding area. So things will be interesting for you. What does the future have in store for you?"

"But …"

"No buts! Ricky, you have betrayed the entire workforce of Ringfield & Lewis! You are endangering the livelihoods of all the men who make a living here, just like you, for their wives and children. Do you think Alexander Rickleby is using the information you have supplied him with to help us? No, he will try to destroy us."

214

When the name Alexander Rickleby is mentioned, Ricky's neck quivers and his hands begin to shake. Simon is certain that he is following the correct course.

"David," Ricky now turns to his boss, "we know one another so long by now, almost forever. I've always done good work for Ringfield & Lewis."

David's face is sympathetic and he wants to answer, but Simon intervenes, "David is very disappointed that you didn't come to him with your family problems, precisely because you know each other so long; instead, you chained yourself to Alexander Rickleby. We cannot trust you any longer, Ricky!"

"What do you mean that I have chained myself to Alexander Rickleby?"

"You don't seriously believe that you can just go to him, and explain that from today you don't want to work for him any more?"

"Hm … I hadn't thought about that yet," says Ricky. "But somehow I'll get out of it. Please let me work for you still! I won't betray anything else either … definitely not!"

"It's not as easy as that, Ricky." Simon looks seriously at the person opposite. "David and I fear for your life. Somebody like Alexander Rickleby who puts himself above the law and who is always just trying to exploit advantage, is surely capable of all types of things."

Shocked, Ricky allows his gaze wander from Simon to David, and back again. "Do you think that he will kill me?!"

"We don't know – but we cannot rule it out. If we want to avoid this risk, we have to think now about how we should proceed. David and I have thought of something."

Like an empty sack, Ricky crumples up more and more in his chair. Obviously, he is now beginning to have serious worries. It is clear that he got into this situation unexpectedly and never thought about the possible consequences.

"Let's start again from the beginning," Simon continues. "If it were up to me, you would just be thrown out. You would have certainly deserved this and we would be rid of the problem. For the shipyard, a simple, sharp cut. But you are lucky: David wants to keep you – because he knows you so long and because he values you. Maynard Ringfield knows nothing about this business, and he should not know anything for now. That would just complicate solving the problem. All the others know nothing either, of course. Ricky, we will financially support you and your family. Everything will be done so that your wife gets healthy again. But that won't be done officially; officially we will fire you."

"Fire me, after all?" Ricky's confused mien shows that he is no longer keeping up.

"Listen until I've finished, please," Simon replies. "David and I see just one possibility of extracting you safely from this situation: Ricky Eckstein must become worthless for Alexander Rickleby. If we fire you because of a mistake at work, he will not get suspicious that we know about your spying. And you will no longer have any information that is of interest to Rickleby. After a year or half a year – depending on how things develop – we'll bring you back to the company because of your good knowledge about ship-building. During this time you will maintain contact only, and I emphasise, really only with David. You can look after your family and we'll help you make ends meet financially. When you return, we will keep a small part of your wages every month, so that the shipyard will get back the money that was advanced. Ringfield & Lewis will not charge you any interest."

"You would do that for me?" asks Ricky in disbelief. "My God, how have I earned that?"

"From our standpoint you are just good at your job. On top of this, David still has trust in you and wants to help you personally. But I warn you: Don't disappoint us."

"No, I won't do that." Gradually, a little hope returns to Ricky's face. "Thank you!"

Simon now pushes a piece of paper across the desk to Ricky. "From today, you are struck off the wage list. Everything else will be communicated to your personally by David in the next few days. We have already drafted the letter of dismissal, you just have to sign it." Simon hands Ricky a fountain pen, but the man is still hesitant.

"What guarantee do I have that I will get the money and that I can start again here in a few months?"

"Absolutely none," says Simon abruptly. "You can only trust us. But do you have any reason, even only the smallest reason, to doubt in David or me?"

"No." Ricky shakes his head. "So, where should I sign?"

Ricky has hardly left the office, when David leans over his desk and whispers to Simon, "Do you think it will work?"

"Yes, most certainly. Nonetheless, we have to take into account that Rickleby will try to look into the matter, especially the dismissal."

"But then he can get on our trail!"

Simon nods earnestly. "Alexander Rickleby is a crafty fellow. For this reason, we should set up a reserve for a compensation claim concerning one of our new ships. So at the same time, we have the money available for Ricky Eckstein. We'll set up a new bank account, into which we'll lodge

216

the money; you can then take it out in cash and pay it to Ricky. In this way, we document all payments made to him, and afterwards we can explain everything to Maynard, and provide written evidence. I do not wish to endanger Maynard's trust in us."

David looks at him approvingly. "Simon, you really know exactly what you are doing!"

"Mr. Rickleby? Excuse me, please." Irene, the young secretary, cautiously sticks her head through the office door.

Rickleby looks up from his papers. "Yes, what's up?"

"A Mr. Howard is standing in the outer office; he badly wants to speak with you right away."

"My God, can one not even have half an hour of peace?" the ship-builder grumbles. "How is one meant to concentrate?"

"The gentleman says it is of great importance."

"Fine so, send him in here. And Irene, close the door; I don't want to be disturbed any more! Have you understood me?"

"Yes, Mr. Rickleby."

An untidy looking, brawny man pushes roughly through the door past Irene, without neglecting to give her a slap on the bum.

"Irene," he says delightedly, "nice name, pretty figure!" Without making a sound, Irene leaves the office and closes the door. But if looks could kill, Mr. Howard would cease breathing this very second.

Mr. Howard lets himself fall into a leather chair in front of the huge oak wood desk and with, the same movement, flings his worn out coat over the armrest of another chair.

Alexander Rickleby is visibly annoyed. "Howard – why have you turned up here in my office? We agreed that nobody was allowed see us together!"

"I know, but I must tell you something, Mr. Rickleby. It is extremely important even!"

"What is so important on a Tuesday morning?"

Howard drops the bombshell, "Ricky Eckstein has been fired from Ring-field & Lewis."

"What? That cannot be true! I only just met with him last week. Are you sure about this?"

"Yes, completely sure," explains Mr. Howard. "It is official. I have it first-hand. Yesterday he was fired without notice."

"But why?" ponders Rickleby. "What could have happened to have him get fired without notice? Did they find out, maybe, that he was spying for us?"

"No, that can't have been it," says Howard. "They say he deviated from the construction plan during the manufacture of one of the newly delivered ships, and that the cargo was damaged because huge amounts of water came in through the hull. A compensation claim has been made against Ringfield & Lewis." Howard folds his arms across his chest. "What will we do now?"

"Let me think it over." Alexander Rickleby allows his gaze to wander out the window. "If Ricky Eckstein has been fired because of a serious mistake, then we can take it for granted that Ringfield & Lewis are not on our trail. He is of no importance to us anymore – but also of no danger. Find him, and tell him that we are stopping the payments."

"And what if he tries to blackmail us?"

"That he won't do. After all, he is one of the main players in this matter. Besides nobody would believe him if he revealed himself to be a mole."

"And if they did?"

"Hm," Rickleby considers this briefly. "Maybe you are right. Please make it clear to him in a friendly way, what we will do if he sings." For a short moment, Alexander Rickleby balls his right hand into a fist.

"I will go visit him, Mr. Rickleby."

"Eh, Mr. Howard, before I forget: Try to find out what is happening at Ringfield & Lewis in respect of the compensation claim. And another thing … Never come to this office again! Do we understand one another? You will never again visit me in my office!"

"Yes, Mr. Rickleby." Mr. Howard rises and takes his coat. "I'll be in touch with you."

Back then I was uncertain if we had made the correct decision towards solving the problem with Ricky Eckstein. The matter was not without danger, because he could have gone behind our backs. On the other hand, it was clear to me that if we put our trust in him, we would have an employee who was solid as a rock when the situation had, at some point, been overcome. He would never again allow himself be 'led astray'.

Alexander Rickleby, however, would increasingly become someone who I would have to keep a close eye on. It seemed that he would stop at nothing to achieve his objective.

10. Death for a few sheets of paper

03.02.1830: After the Greek War of Independence, the founding of Greece is declared by Great Britain, France and Russia in the London Protocol.

13.05.1830: Ecuador secedes from Gran Columbia and becomes an independent republic.

28.05.1830: With the Indian Removal Act, US president Andrew Jackson decrees the compulsory resettlement of North American Indians.

09.08.1830: The Duke of Orleans becomes Louis Philippe, King of France.

21.08.1831: During a slave revolt under the leadership of Nat Turner, a total of 55 whites are murdered in the USA. In the same year, the New-England Anti-Slavery Society is established.

08.09.1831: Wilhelm IV. becomes King of Great Britain and Hanover.

Simon is woken by loud birds' twittering. The vital life spirits slowly crawl into his body. Eventually he is awake enough to get up and step across to the window. Two sparrows are sitting on a corner of the window sill and seem to be fiercely scolding one another. Simon has to grin, then he pulls himself together: a new day at the university awaits him.

In the small salon, Alastair and Lindsay are already sitting at the breakfast table and are engrossed in an animated discussion. They involuntarily remind Simon of the two arguing sparrows and hardly seem to notice that he has arrived. Puzzled, Simon joins them at the table and interrupts the conversation, "What's wrong?"

Lindsay holds the daily newspaper open in front of him. Simon reads under the date, 22nd March 1831: Bank Robbery in New York City. Baffled, he looks up. "Are you discussing the bank robbery?"

"Lindsay is annoyed that there are so few security measures in the banks," explains Alastair. "She fears that something like what happened last weekend could also occur to us in the BBBC."

"It really isn't any wonder that a person gets annoyed about that!" Lindsay interrupts. "Somebody strolls into a bank in the middle of the day and steals 245,000 dollars. That is just unbelievable! And the robber wasn't caught – he has disappeared. It won't be any surprise if that tempts even more criminals. And at some stage there will be fatalities."

"And now you are frightened for Alastair," Simon observes. "That is of course very understandable."

"Yes, exactly!" Lindsay feels acknowledged. "A repeat offence cannot be ruled out, or can it?"

"What exactly happened, so?" Simon now wants to know from Alastair.

"Last Saturday, a bank robber strolled into the City Bank of New York in Wall Street during opening hours and did indeed steal this enormous sum – one would really have to be brazen. But I'm sure that the robber will be

219

caught. As far as I know, this is the first bank robbery ever carried out here in America during opening hours."

"Now just imagine, Simon, if that had happened in the BBBC!" Lindsay interrupts again. "Lots of money has a magical pull on criminals."

"But what do you propose, Lindsay?" Alastair is visibly impatient by now. "Should every bank in America be closed now, or should the police open up their quarters in the banks?"

"No, that wouldn't work either."

"See. There we have it so. There is no solution!"

Confused, but not any less worried, Lindsay looks at her husband.

"Alastair is right." Simon wants to reassure her. "If it really was one of the first bank robberies during opening hours, then the possibility that this will happen to him as well is really small. The probability that he is injured on the way to or from work is much greater than being robbed in the bank."

"And this should reassure me now?"

"Yes, I ask this from you. Besides, I am one of the directors, and therefore I am only very seldom at the till," explains Alastair and resolutely changes the subject. "Simon, what are you doing today?"

"I have to go to Harvard now. That will be a stressful day today – Professor Hicks has some exams scheduled for next week and we still have to go over some of the material."

"How are your studies going, actually?" Alastair wants to know.

"It's not bad. When it comes to results, I am somewhere in the middle."

"That is so nice to hear." Lindsay is pleased. "You started at Harvard almost seamlessly after you arrived in America. So I think that being in the middle is a huge achievement."

Alastair nods. "On top of that, you work on the side – or should I perhaps say, mainly – at Ringfield & Lewis."

"No, Alastair," Simon interjects decisively. "Harvard has priority. But the work at the shipyard is just very educational."

"Do other students have additional jobs as well?" asks Lindsay. "Not that you might over-exert yourself."

Alastair interrupts, "This MacShaw, what is his name …? Theodore MacShaw, he surely works in his father's office, or what?"

"Yes, Theodore helps out there now and again. That reminds me, John Parson wants to visit me in the late afternoon. He says he has important news."

When Simon returns in the afternoon, an unfamiliar horse, still saddled, is standing in front of the Rowley villa – a sure sign that John has already arrived. Simon goes around the house and enters through the servants' entrance so that he can reach the kitchen directly. He knows that Alastair does not like seeing this.

"Hello, Molly," Simon amiably greets the cook. "How are you?"

"Oh, Mr. Brown, what a surprise! You have a visit – a gentleman from England is waiting on the terrace; he was here once before. Mrs. Rowley is keeping him company. Lilly is about to serve tea."

"Thanks, Molly. To be honest, I'm dying of hunger. Do you have something small in advance for me? Otherwise I will reserve the whole cake."

Molly's smile completely covers her wide face. "Here, a piece of a sandwich with ham, for the first hunger – the ham is really fresh."

"Thanks, Molly. You have rescued me!"

As Simon walks across the salon, he hears loud laughter from the veranda. John and Lindsay are sitting outside, engrossed in animated conversation.

"Hello, you two," Simon greets them. "You seem to be amusing yourselves well."

John jumps up and embraces Simon. "Long time, no see, my old friend!"

"It hasn't been such a long time at all," Simon parries. "Just a couple of months."

Lindsay has been observing the two friends contentedly. "Lilly's about to bring the tea," she now says. "You surely haven't eaten anything yet, Simon."

"I would like to have it so good as well some time," sighs John. "Everyone is taking care of you, Simon."

"Don't keep me in suspense." His counterpart changes the subject. "Did you get the job at MacShaw's?"

"Did you apply at MacShaw's, Mr. Parson?" asks Lindsay, interested.

"Yes," nods John. "Simon spoke about me to Theodore MacShaw some time ago. He told me about this and said, if I still didn't have a job, he would specifically ask him about it again."

"But surely Theodore cannot decide about jobs in his father's office?" Lindsay wants to know more details.

"No, not that. But he can of course make a recommendation to his father. At any rate, he said to Simon that I should officially apply to MacShaw, and that is just what I did."

"And what has been the result of this, Mr. Parson?"

"When I presented myself, there were still five other applicants there, and my heart sank to my boots. When my turn came, I was amiably greeted by Mr. MacShaw and a colleague, and I was astounded how well they were already informed about me. The job interview itself was quite short for this reason, and very soon we were talking about personal matters."

"That means …?" Lindsay is almost bursting with impatience.

"I have got the job!"

"That is magnificent!" Lindsay is delighted, and Simon is beaming, too. "Congratulations, John!"

"Without you, I wouldn't have got the job, absolutely not!"

"Who knows …" Simon dismisses the idea.

"No, definitely not. I would never have applied to an office with such an excellent reputation."

At this moment, Lilly Owens enters the veranda and brings a huge tray full of thick sandwiches and different sorts of pastry. After everyone has been given tea, John Parson needs to impart the next piece of news. "Do you know, I have already got my first project."

"How exciting!" Lindsay stirs in her tea cup with a silver spoon. "What type of project is it?"

"I am allowed to design and build the new offices for a shipyard."

"A shipyard?" Simon leans back in his seat with an apprehensive look.

"Yes, here in Boston. The shipyard is called Rickleby & Smith Co.," explains John, full of pride.

"That's the biggest shipyard here in the area," observes Lindsay. "Alexander Rickleby and his wife Ashley belong to our circle of friends … Simon has also become acquainted with them," she adds, after a short hesitation.

"You know them, Simon?" marvels John, and then continues, "But not that you might think that you have to help me with Mr. Rickleby as well. I will do this on my own! You have to promise me that!"

"Don't worry. That is your job."

Lindsay opens her mouth to say something, but Simon is quicker and throws her an admonishing glance. He wants John to approach his first project impartially. "Rickleby & Smith Co. is the biggest shipyard in the area and, seen in financial terms, a reliable customer," he explains. "I will stay out of that completely, without question."

"Now let us talk about something different," says Lindsay, to end the subject. She does not want to spoil the good mood at the table either. "Do you actually know the area around Cambridge, Mr. Parson?"

"No, I have only been here once and then just at your home, Mrs. Rowley."

"Then we should prepare a ride for Mr. Parson's next visit, Simon, so that we can familiarize him with our area."

"A good idea," nods Simon. And the three of them are already engrossed in their excursion plans.

After John Parson has departed that evening, Mr. Snyder steps up to Simon and Lindsay. On a small silver tray, he presents Simon with an envelope.

"Excuse me, Mr. Brown. Please allow me to deliver you a letter from London. It arrived at midday today."

Simon grabs the letter and takes a couple of steps towards the salon door. "Excuse me, Lindsay."

As quietly as possible, Simon climbs the stairs to his attic room, allows himself fall onto the bed and opens the envelope. As he unfolds the sheets of paper, a smaller envelope falls at his feet. Without observing it closer, he places it beside him on the bed and begins to read. Dear Simon, all of us here in London hope that you are doing well ...

After several pages he comes to the end of the letter. I am to convey special greetings to you from grand-father. P. S. Your parents want to visit us in the coming months, by the way. Everyone is looking forward to this already. When are you coming to London? Many dear greetings, Elisabeth.

Simon has a thick lump in his throat. He is once again aware of how far away his family is. Eventually he takes the small, inconspicuous envelope in his hand. Written there in a fine, delicate hand is: My dear Simon. Simon begins to breathe with difficulty: that is Marala's handwriting. Slowly and cautiously, he opens the envelope, takes out the pages and unfolds them carefully, almost tenderly. His heart thumps hard as he begins to read. Marala inquires about how he is, and reports on what has happened in the last months.

She writes about daily life in the lordly house of her husband, together with him and his two other wives – for Simon still an unimaginable situation. Marala also describes two big receptions that Meghnad Kapur held for acquaintances and friends from the London society, raves about an extravagant shopping day that she enjoyed with the two other women and about how well she gets along with them.

It is almost two years since the last time we saw one another. I have your face exactly before my eyes, Simon, and I would love to know how it has changed – your forehead, your cheeks, your mouth. If your eyes still shine with exactly the same beauty as at our last meeting? Look after yourself, Simon, Marala.

Simon lets the letter sink and stares, lost in thought, at the ceiling. He noticed this with her last letter as well: Marala does not speak about herself or her feelings, about her joy, her suffering. She only writes about her husband, the other wives, her house and her surroundings, or about special events. Simon does not know how Marala is really doing – and this depresses him.

He returns from his dreaming as somebody sits beside him on the bed and places a hand on his forehead. Simon immediately recognises the tender fingers and the velvety palm. Wordlessly, he presses Marala's letter into Lindsay's hand. She reads it for a while and then says, "Everything all right? Nothing special seems to have happened. So far everything is fine, Simon. Don't be worried!"

Simon sighs. "I have received several letters from Marala, but she says absolutely nothing about herself. How is she really doing? How does she feel, what's going on inside her? What concerns her, what moves her? Nothing!"

"What do you expect, Simon? She is married. Can she be sure that what she writes will remain the secret of this envelope? Is it certain that nobody else will read the letter? What would happen if they did?"

"Then … Hm … You are right: that would be a catastrophe!"

Lindsay bends down to Simon and kisses him tenderly on the forehead. Then she stands up and goes. At the door frame she turns around again. "You know that I am always there for you, Simon."

As Simon enters the office of Ringfield & Lewis several days later, he is greeted stormily by David. "Hello, Simon – good that you have come. We have a customer for two new ships: for two ships with our newly developed bow, in fact. What do you say about that?" David's eyes are shining full of pride.

"Who is the customer?"

"Henderson Transatlantic New York."

"Hey, a great success!"

"That it is," comments Maynard Ringfield from behind his writing desk, where he is studying sketches.

"But, Maynard, you are not really so delighted!" Simon ascertains.

"You know, Simon, with prototypes it's a bit tricky. If it works out, we'll ring in a new era for the shipyard. But if problems crop up, then they will be two of the most expensive ships that Ringfield & Lewis have ever built."

"You are right," David agrees with his co-partner, "but Simon and I carried out the tests with the model ships in order to minimize the risks."

"I know, David," nods Maynard. "And I trust you. It is just that I have already experienced very many defeats in my life. One becomes more sceptical and risk-averse with the years." Maynard Ringfield sighs, looks up and removes the reading glasses from his nose.

"Henderson Transatlantic New York," ponders Simon. "Do you know them, David? From whom did they buy their ships in the past?"

"No idea." David shrugs his shoulders and looks at Maynard questioningly.

"That is an old-established shipping company in New York," he explains. "As far as I know, until now they have bought from Moretti & Sons in New York and, here in Boston, from Rickleby & Smith Co."

224

This could get tricky! Simon's look becomes more serious. Now he wants to know details. "Have the contracts been signed already? Have they accepted your prices, or do you still have to negotiate?"

Now David is back in his element. "Yes. They accept out prices, and Maynard and I are travelling to New York some time in the next few weeks to sign the contract. The appointment for this has not been fixed yet, though."

"That does indeed sound good," says Simon, sounding more confident again.

Lost in thought, Simon strolls along a narrow alleyway in the suburbs of Boston. He likes this quiet back road after a long day in Harvard. Suddenly, and without warning, somebody grabs him by the sleeve and drags him into a dark doorway. Shocked, Simon's eyes widen. Two men are standing before him, their faces covered with dark cloths. They have come so close to him that Simon has no way of fleeing.

"Well, Brown, how's it going?" growls one of them with a dark voice.

"Who are you?" Simon tries to appear calm, but his voice sounds anything but steady.

"That doesn't matter," says the other one now – a small, fat man. Both men appear clean and well-groomed, are wearing jackets and shirts. "You'll get the plans for us," declares the fat one.

"Which plans?"

"The plans for your new ships."

"New ships?" Play dumb first.

Then a fist hits him in the solar plexus. The pain forces Simon to bend forward, whether he wants to or not. In this moment, the small fat man wants to kick him in the face with his foot, but his tall accomplice prevents him from doing so.

"Only in the soft parts, the boss said! Everyone will see it in his face." He pulls Simon up by the shoulders once more and immediately hits him in the stomach again with his fist.

"So that it's clear to you, Brown: we know about the new ships. You will get us the plans by Sunday, otherwise you can really experience something. Have you understood?!"

Simon rights himself with effort and tries to recognise the men's eyes and to stamp them onto his memory.

"Where will I find you?" he pants out.

"We'll find you!" explains the little fat one and hits him again, so that Simon is busy with himself for a while. The men use this moment to disappear just as suddenly as they appeared.

Simon still needs several minutes to recover. Eventually he brushes down his jacket, picks up his leather bag that has fallen to the ground and carefully continues his way home.

For the rest of the day he broods over the two men and the situation with them. Could he have seen them once before? They didn't give the impression of having come down in the world, are certainly not bandits. Who do they work for, and who at all can have interest in the plans for the new ships? In short: what should he do now? Should he tell David and Maynard the story, or would that cause too much unnecessary fuss? Would it be of advantage, to first see what lies ahead of him and who is behind the matter? Or would it perhaps be even better to see the problem through on his own?

Not even a week later, again on his way home from Harvard, Simon is jostled by a little boy. Only just can he keep his legs and prevent his leather bag from falling on the ground. The boy has already continued onwards, without turning to look at Simon. Was this an accident or intentional? Simon decides to continue his way home. Only that evening in his attic room does he think again in peace about the encounter; he has the idea of looking in his jacket pocket – and right there he finds it too: a note. Scrawled there in big letters is: Tomorrow 6 pm at the harbour – Warehouse 7 – We expect you to come alone!

At exactly 6 pm the next day, Simon pushes soft-footedly through the door of warehouse 7 in Boston harbour. In his right hand, he is holding a cardboard roll like the ones used for big building plans. He takes a silent leap to the side and gets on his knees to remain unrecognised. Slowly his eyes get used to the darkness and the warehouse's internal area gets contours. High stacks of barrels and boxes are piled up in long rows. Simon already knows this picture from early morning. He came here already at 5 am – he just could not sleep any longer – and meticulously examined the warehouse, both inside and out.

Now Simon crouches beside the warehouse's door and thinks about the innumerable times that he and his brother Christoph practised gymnastics on the barrels of wine piled high in the cellar of their parents' winery. They used to play cops and robbers back then …

He slowly straightens up and sidles farther to the right. Suddenly, steps can be heard from another corner of the warehouse; they seem to be coming in his direction. Simon moves on swiftly and disappears behind a row of barrels. Curiously, he listens to the darkness.

Already this morning, he considered which strategy he wants to achieve his objective with. And the objective is certain for him: he may not give

226

away the ships' building plans and he wants to see the faces of the men who are waylaying him here in the warehouse.

Simon sidles carefully to the second last row of barrels, far right on the side of the warehouse, goes into the twenty metre deep aisle and stays still when he reaches around the half-way mark. He observes the highly stacked barrels left and right, with the cardboard roll held tightly. Suddenly a masked person appears at the back end of the aisle. Simon recognises the tall, thin man, who hit him a few days ago. With his legs apart and a danger-ously long dagger in his hand, he blocks Simon's way. Simon turns around and sees, at the other end of the aisle, the small fat man; he too is armed with a dagger.

"Brown!" the tall man calls now. "Do you have the plans?"

Simon holds the cardboard roll up high. With slow, short steps, the two masked men approach Simon.

"Now, he's trapped, Ha! Ha! Ha!" laughs the tall one in mockery.

Simon, extremely tense, looks back and forth between the two men.

"How does it feel to be so close to the end?" the small one mocks.

"He's about to wet himself, you'll see," jokes the tall one.

"Why my end?" asks Simon, trying to appear as naive as possible. He is very aware that the two masked men are slowly but surely starting to breath down his neck.

"We don't want any witnesses," the small one explains. "And we never have witnesses." From one second to the next, the two men run towards Simon with their daggers raised. He can almost feel the brutality hanging in the air.

Bank robberies, violence and death were a topic of conservation one morn-ing at the Rowleys' breakfast table. Lindsay's fear for Alastair was clearly noticeable then. We were talking about how people can get into dangerous situations completely coincidentally. And only a few days later, I suddenly found myself in a life or death struggle. I hadn't counted on this: the two men wanted ship-building plans, basically just a few pieces of paper. Sud-denly, my life threatened to end ...

11. A hard blow

In the last moment, Simon steps back two paces. Directly behind him, several barrels were removed from the row, so that a V-shaped hole has been created in the high wall of barrels. In a few seconds Simon leaps up the massive oak barrels as if they were a staircase with extremely high steps. Reaching the top, he balances from barrel to barrel until he is standing under the thick chain of a pulley, which – fastened to a massive steel girder – runs a good way across the hall.

Simon jams the document tube under his belt, takes a running jump and throws himself with both hands onto the chain. The pulley begins to move, and Simon, who is hanging on the chain, crosses several rows of barrels accompanied by loud rattling and squeaking. Half a metre in front of the next row he comes to a halt, swings to and fro taking aim, then jumps off: exactly on target, Simon lands on a big oak barrel. In the last moment, he gives the pulley's chain a light swing upwards; the locking mechanism is released and the chain now moves downwards. It now reaches from the steel girder high up under the ceiling to the dusty warehouse floor below.

As quick as lightning Simon makes a 180 degrees turn, rips the document tube open and lets its contents slide out. Besides several oversized sheets of paper, a huge iron bar of about one metre length also appears. The papers flutter down through the air and Simon throws the document tube after them. His two adversaries already appear at the entrance to the aisle, in the middle of which the building plans are now lying on the floor.

"Hey, have a look at that!" the taller of the two cries. "Brown has made us a present – the ship-building plans have slipped out of his hands."

"Let's take care of them before we destroy him!" replies the smaller one, and already they are rushing to their target.

Simon jams the iron bar behind his belt and turns again to the pulley. With a big leap, he jumps onto the chain which is hanging over the next aisle, and in only an instant he descends five or six metres on it until he has the ground under his feet again. Immediately he creeps to the start of the row of barrels and presses himself tightly against the barrels, the bar raised high above his head. From the other aisle, voices can be heard. Simon presumes that the two scoundrels are now rolling up the plans and stashing them in the document tube. He is not at all hopeful that afterwards they will just withdraw. They have made their position unambiguously clear with the phrase, 'no witnesses'. Simon pricks up his ears. He hears how the two men begin to move and rapidly draw closer to him. "So we have the plans, now let's take care of Brown."

"Where's he got to, so?" jokes the tall one, who has the darker voice of the two. The smaller one laughs sleazily, "Ha ha, which corner has he crawled into?"

When Simon believes the two masked men to be hardly two metres from him, he jumps out of the aisle and is suddenly standing directly in front of them; their arms are outstretched and their daggers held in front of them. Without uttering a sound, Simon lets the heavy iron bar come down with full force on the taller man's right shoulder, just missing his ear. There is a dull crack and in the same second the scoundrel's arm sags down. His dagger falls to the ground, and from behind the cloth an agonised exclamation of pain streams out. As quick as lightning, Simon skips a short step to the side, so that he can now concentrate on the other one. The small fat one has lost his composure for a few seconds, and above the cloth his eyes are opened wide in shock. While his companion, face distorted by pain, clutches his shoulder and sinks to the dusty ground, the fat one backs off. Simon pursues him step by step.

"Don't come too close, Brown!" the fat one screams at him. "I'll stab you to death!" Simon does not react. "Stay still, Brown. I'll ram a hole into your belly," the scoundrel barks in despair.

Simon throws a quick glance at the tall one, who cowers, doubled up on the floor, pulling the document tube over to himself. Without moving, he holds the iron bar to the right behind his body, which is strained to its limits. Suddenly, the fat one leaps a step towards him and lunges with the dagger, which makes an arch around Simon's face. Almost simultaneously, Simon plunges down with the upper part of his body and swings the heavy iron bar with all his might forwards from behind. A sharp hum fills the air and ends in a dull crack. The iron bar hits Simon's adversary almost in the centre of his left thigh. The fat one just falls away to the side with a painful scream. With a powerful swipe, Simon kicks the dagger out of his hand and puts it into his jacket pocket with an agile movement. Then he bends over again and, as quick as lightning, grabs the cloth that his adversary has been covering his face with.

"Aah, aah … Brown," he whimpers, "you have broken my thigh bone!"

With a stony mien, Simon looks him in the face for a moment, then goes across to the other one who is still holding his shoulder. Crying with pain, he flings the document tube and the dagger at Simon's feet to keep him at a distance. "Brown, let us live," he pleads. "We have families!"

Simon sinks to his knees before him and takes the document tube as well as the long dagger. Then he rips this scoundrel's cloth from his face, too.

"How are we going to get away from here now?" the tall one groans at him.

229

From behind, the fat one screams in a frightened voice, "My thigh bone is broken! I can't stand up. It hurts so much!"

"Who hired you?" asks Simon calmly. "You didn't think this all up yourselves."

"We don't know him," answers the tall one. "An acquaintance … aaah … Henry Miller … approached us in the pub and hired us. He gave us the advance payment as well …"

"Aah … my leg … aah!"

"Let us live, Mr. Brown, please!"

Henry Miller. Is their acquaintance really called Henry Miller? Simon runs the name quickly through his head. No, they would have made up such a common name. He can't check up on it anyway. He throws another long glance at the two whimpering men, so that he can remember their faces, then calmly puts the iron bar back in the document roll and goes to the exit. At the door, he turns once more to the two scoundrels, but doesn't say anything; then he continues on his way.

Almost a week has passed when Simon visits the shipyard one late afternoon. He wants to find out how the contract negotiations with Henderson Transatlantic New York have gone. Maynard Ringfield and David Lewis travelled to New York at the start of the week to conclude the deal. In the office Simon meets Maynard, who greets him joyfully. "We've got the contract!" he announces, beaming with delight. "They accepted everything as we prepared it – the prices, the completion dates, just everything. David did a great job."

"That sounds excellent." Simon is thrilled. "That's a weight off my mind."

"And off mine too, you can certainly believe me. How is David, by the way?"

"David?" Simon looks at Maynard, astonished.

"Yes, exactly."

"How should I know that? You were in New York together. What kind of a question is that?"

"No, David was not with me in New York," explains Maynard.

"What? But you wanted to travel together!"

"True. We wanted to meet on Monday morning at the coach station and take the coach from there to New York. But David never came. So I travelled alone. Have you not met him in the shipyard over the last few days?"

"No," says Simon pensively, "but I was only here sporadically as well. I had an awful lot to do in Harvard." He thinks for a moment about whether he should tell Maynard of his encounter with the two masked men, but discards this thought again.

230

"Is David ill perhaps?" considers Maynard and stands up. "Wait here, Simon, I'll be right back." He leaves the office and returns again after a few minutes. "Simon, David has not been here for the whole week. He must be ill ..."

"Strange," mutters Simon to himself. "David would surely try to let us know if he was ill."

"Ah, he is sure to come back again after the weekend. Maybe he has a cold."

"I'll call in on him at home," decides Simon. "Just to see how he is doing." He does not want to make Maynard anxious, but the matter seems extremely strange to him. David would never miss something as important as the contract negotiations with Henderson Transatlantic New York. And just because of a ridiculous cold? No way!

Just half an hour later, Simon is standing in front of a small, neat-looking terraced house. David has already invited him a couple of times to visit his family – he is married and his wife had a baby some time ago. But until now, Simon has never got around to it. He has not yet met David's wife either.

Simon knocks on the black painted door and waits patiently until steps can be heard. A young, dark-haired woman opens the door and looks at the visitor questioningly. "Good evening ..."

"Good evening. Excuse me disturbing you. Mrs. Lewis?"

"Yes."

"My name is Simon Brown," Simon introduces himself. "I come from Ringfield & Lewis."

"Ah, you are Simon! David has already told me a lot about you." A smile begins to form on her face; it becomes even prettier because of this. "I imagined you completely differently." Now she remembers herself and opens the door wide. "That's why I didn't recognise you at once. Do come in!"

"Thank you." Simon smiles back, although he feels anxious. Is David at home perhaps, and he has been worrying for no reason?

Mrs. Lewis leads him into a small living room. "Simon, may I offer you a seat. Here maybe?" Simon sits down and allows his gaze wander around the room. It has been tastefully furnished and is kept very clean and correctly, exactly like he knows David.

"What can I do for you?" asks David's wife now. "Ah, I haven't introduced myself yet: I am Camilla. Would you like some tea? I have just put the kettle on."

"Yes, gladly."

Simon observes how Camilla places the crockery on a tray and then proceeds into the kitchen to pour the water. She is slim, has a delicate figure without being small and makes a very friendly, warm-hearted impression. David is really to be envied.

"How is your son doing?" asks Simon, as Camilla comes back into the room. "He's called George, isn't he?"

A loving smile appears on Camilla's face. "He's doing well. He's sleeping right now." She pours the steaming tea into the cups. "Tell me, Simon. What can I do for you? David wanted to return from New York today. Has something got in the way?"

The shock goes straight through Simon. David has not been at home for almost a week! What should he say to Camilla? That something has got in the way and David has to stay a few more days in New York? Or the truth? He takes a mouthful of tea and then decides on the truth. "Camilla, I am here to enquire about David."

"Enquire? Why?" She raises her eyebrows in astonishment.

"Maynard Ringfield returned from New York today and told me that he travelled alone. David did not appear at the coach station on Monday."

"But that cannot be," stammers Camilla. "On Monday, David left the house in very good time. He certainly wanted to travel to New York. For days he had not been talking about anything else. My God, Simon, what does this mean?"

"I don't know," answers Simon. "I especially came here this evening so that I could have certainty."

"What should I do now?" Camilla wrings her hands. "Might he have had an accident?"

"This evening we can do absolutely nothing," says Simon.

"But what if something has happened to him? We need him – the baby and I." Camilla stands up from the table and begins to walk around the room restlessly. Fear and despair stand written in her face and now tears are also running down her cheeks. She gasps for air, but no sound comes out of her mouth. Simon stands up and, without thinking, takes the young woman in his arms.

"Camilla, you are not alone, regardless of what has happened. I will speak to Maynard Ringfield first thing tomorrow and enquire at all the infirmaries nearby if David is or has been there." Simon loosens the embrace slightly and looks Camilla in the eye. "Tomorrow you go to the police and register David as missing. Perhaps they've heard something there. Have you understood me?"

"But what should I say to them? I don't know anything myself either."

"Say that you have been missing your husband for five days, submit a personal description and report when David left the house and where he wanted to go."

"Fine, Simon, I'll do it ..." Camilla seems a little calmer by now. "Oh God ... Just what has happened to David?"

For a time, Simon remains with David's wife, in order to calm her down. Finally he sets off home, on his way running various scenarios through his mind, from accident to fatal armed robbery.

The next morning Simon and Maynard meet for a briefing.

"Damn it – what's going on here?" Maynard asks himself, after Simon has reported to him about his visit to Camilla.

"I don't know, Maynard." Perplexed, Simon shakes his head. "Today I will first look around all the infirmaries in the area. Perhaps David had an accident. And Camilla will go to the police and register him as missing."

"That is good," nods Maynard. "Now we are getting places."

Then Simon tells about his meeting with the two nasty characters in Boston Harbour. Maynard is visibly shocked by this story. "Simon, I am really glad that nothing happened to you. But the building plans for the new ships are extremely important for the shipyard. Where are the plans now?"

"In the safe," replies Simon. "They couldn't have left it either: just the two of you – you and David – have a key for it."

Now Maynard makes a baffled face. "But you said you had the plans with you in a document tube."

"That is correct, but the plans that I found here in the office were old, and they had nothing to do with the new ships. I was hoping that the two men would not notice with all the excitement."

"Very smart," says Maynard approvingly. "The two ships are of course very important for our shipyard, but at Rickleby & Smith Co., they will be especially angry about possibly losing a decades-long customer in Henderson Transatlantic New York. Not too long ago, Rickleby & Smith Co. wanted to buy up our shipyard, and now we have made this advance ..." Maynard pauses briefly, then widens his eyes in horror. "Simon, what if somebody ambushed David and found the key on him?! The plans are no longer safe then."

"That's true," nods Simon. "The best thing is that I take them home with me. They won't suspect them there. Your place is where they would search first, Maynard."

At night Simon lies in bed with his eyes open and broods over David's whereabouts. Half the day he spent riding through Boston, asking about his friend in every infirmary and at every central place, but nobody was able to help him any further. Nobody has seen David – it is like he has just vanished from the earth's surface. Towards evening, Simon was at Camilla's again, where she told him about her visit to the police. They wanted to take the up matter, but they did not give her much hope. Every day people went missing, but only a few turned up again after a few weeks. Camilla was in complete despair and wept bitterly; Simon could hardly keep her calm.

He now stares restlessly at the ceiling of his room and runs through the various possibilities of what may have happened. David could have got to know another woman and may have eloped with her. – No, impossible, he loves his wife and son far too much for that. Simon can also confidently dismiss the thought that David was hanging out in pubs or saloons for the whole week. His friend is far too conscientious and orderly for such a thing. Somebody could have ambushed, robbed and killed him – Simon would prefer not to think about this scenario at all, although he knows that killing people for a few lousy dollars is an everyday occurrence. Though somehow this answer does not satisfy him. There has to be another reason for David's disappearance. Could it have something to do with the ship-building plans?

Over the next few days, Simon's thoughts keep wandering to David and Camilla, but he has a lot to do for his studies and only gets the chance to call by Camilla towards the middle of the week. She looks bad and Simon hardly dares to ask her for any news. The dark rings under her eyes stand out especially in her flawless face.

"Nothing," she sighs. "Just absolutely nothing. Even the police have not been in touch yet. At least Maynard has promised to keep me covered financially. I feel so useless! I sit around here, looking after George and the household, and my David is somewhere out there and perhaps needs urgent help."

Simon nods understandingly. "I feel very similarly: in the last few days I've constantly thought about what may have happened and where David could be."

"Simon," asks Camilla falteringly. "Do you think … he is dead?!" Big tears run down her cheeks without her being able to do anything against them. Simon takes her tightly in his arms.

"Camilla, everything will be fine!" he tries to reassure her. "David will come back."

"Are you sure?" murmurs Camilla.

"Yes, completely certain."

Camilla releases herself and goes across to the cradle which is standing in the living room. Simon steps beside her. Little George sleeps peacefully and unsuspectingly. Strange, thinks Simon, that this small wooden box seems totally untouched by bustle, fear and violence – a picture of contentment that has in fact a calming effect.

But the calm does not last. The very next evening, Simon is received by Lindsay in the small drawing room. "Simon, at last you are here!" Lindsay greets him with great excitement. "I've already been waiting an hour for you. A messenger from Ringfield & Lewis was here: you should come immediately to the shipyard. It is extremely important."

Simon knits his brow. "Did he say what it was about?"

"No, only that Maynard Ringfield has to see you today."

"All right." Simon puts down his briefcase. "Then it's to the stables."

"I'm sorry," says Lindsay. "You must be very tired already."

Simon tries a smile, but this doesn't succeed so easily. His worries about David are taking up his thoughts completely, and if Maynard summons him so urgently, then something must have happened.

"Karol has already saddled the horse for you," explains Lindsay and briefly strokes his hair. "He's waiting at the stable."

In the case of the two masked men I got away, not least because they under-estimated me. Getting an overview of the surroundings beforehand gave me a decisive advantage. For this reason, David's disappearance hit me so much harder. I felt so helpless: he was simply gone and we were completely in the dark about what had happened and even if he was still alive or not. As Maynard had especially sent a messenger for me, I suspected that it was about David. The journey to Boston dragged on endlessly. Was David still alive?

12. A first suspicion

With foam on the mouth, the stallion comes to a halt in front of the office of Ringfield & Lewis. Nervously he shifts from one hoof to the other. Simon jumps out of the saddle, rubs the brown horse across his sweaty neck approvingly and ties the reins tightly to a post in front of the building. He has not even taken a seat in front of Maynard Ringfield's writing desk, when it is already bursting out of the old man. "Read that through, Simon." He waves a dirty piece of paper with ripped edges around in the air. "You were right. It is about the ship-building plans.

Whoever that may be – now they are trying it with kidnapping. If we don't hand over the plans to them, they will kill David!"

Simon takes the page in his hand and carefully studies the scrawly handwriting, word for word. If you want to see Lewis alive again, hand over the building plans for the new ships. You will hear from us.

"At least David seems to be alive," Simon observes and looks up at Maynard, who is watching him furiously as if he would like to ask, "Are you sure there?" Aloud he only answers, after a brief pause, "Hopefully."

"And what will we do now?" Simon wants to know.

"Hand over the plans of course. Or are you of a different opinion? We surely can't put David's life in danger."

"No, of course not. But maybe there is still another possibility?"

Maynard shakes his head, "No Simon, I wouldn't know any." He sighs. "With this, the contract with Henderson Transatlantic New York is probably history."

"Why is that?" asks Simon, astonished.

"Don't be so thick-witted!" Maynard is visibly annoyed. "If these people, who have David in their power, get their hands on our plans, then we can't start building the ships within the agreed time. I won't even begin talking about completion and delivery." The senior director shakes his head in despair. "No, Simon, we can be happy if Henderson Transatlantic believes our story about the kidnapping and we get away without a penalty for breach of contract. Be that as it may: Now we have to put everything into getting David free."

"But how should we do that? Have you an idea?"

"Well, that's obvious – it is all written on the piece of paper. We wait until the kidnappers tell us where and when to hand over the plans." Maynard ruffles his hand through his hair. "Just who could do something like this? What sort of people can they be?"

"I can certainly think of someone …," says Simon pensively.

Maynard leans back in his office armchair, surprised. "Who do you mean?"

"One person is certainly obvious," explains Simon. "Who would have a motive for the kidnapping? Well? Alexander Rickleby, of course – he is the one who is harmed if we build the ships. And if Henderson Transatlantic has a good experience with us, perhaps they will even give us more orders."

This is sufficient to recapture Maynard's full attention. Tensely he bends forward in his armchair. "You are right. Why haven't I thought of that myself? Hm … But how can we find out for certain?"

"I've been thinking about this already. First we have to just try to keep calm and to treat the whole thing confidentially. I'll speak with Camilla. She should know that David is still alive."

236

"No, Simon," Maynard interrupts, "we'll invite Camilla here tomorrow morning and speak with her together. I think it is better if she sees that we all care about David. That will hopefully reassure her somewhat."

"Fine," Simon nods. "But I think we should keep our suspicion to ourselves for now."

"You don't even want to talk to the police about Alexander Rickleby?"

Simon shakes his head. "They are already investigating because of David's disappearance. I think we should first try to gather more evidence, otherwise the police can't do anything along these lines either. I will give Tyson the task of observing the milieu around Alexander Rickleby. He has proved himself in it and nobody will notice him. We should also not ignore the fact that Alexander Rickleby is extremely influential. Perhaps he even has spies in the police, who knows?"

"Do you distrust just about everyone, Simon? Even the police?"

"I am just careful. We most likely have a little time before the kidnappers get in contact again. They will definitely try to wear us down."

"And what will we do in the meantime?"

"Please take some time to recall if there are people with whom David has clashed recently or if anything else strange has come to your notice."

"Good, I'll do that," nods Maynard.

After their evening meal, Lindsay, Alastair and Simon sit in the drawing room talking about the day over a glass of wine. Simon does not find it easy to take part in the discussion; the whole time his thoughts revolve around David's kidnapping. But then it occurs to him that he wanted to visit John in Boston.

"Lindsay," he asks, "the tailor in Boston, at whose place we were once already ... who comes from France ... what was his name again?"

"Gilot ... Alexandre Gilot," answers Lindsay. "Why do you ask?"

"Ah, I need new trousers. One pair has already had it again. Besides I want to visit John and I can fit that in well. He did say during his last visit, that at present he was mostly home in the late afternoon, right?"

"Yes, that's correct," Lindsay confirms. "A good idea. How about tomorrow? I could keep you company and advise you on the choice of trousers." Enthusiastically, Lindsay turns to Alastair. "What do you think, darling? I could pick out a new hat. Then the journey would be worth it," she says, grinning mischievously.

Alastair has to laugh. "Women! Marvellous ... So that the journey is worth it, they buy a hat!"

"But Alastair!"

"It's fine, darling," the man of the house concedes. "I am delighted."

"Simon," asks Lindsay, "can you inform Mr. Snyder that Karol should harness tomorrow in the early afternoon?"

"A welcome opportunity to switch off," thinks Simon, rising from his armchair and explaining, "I'll stretch my legs for a few minutes. I can ask Karol myself while I'm at it."

Visibly in a good mood, Lindsay, followed by Simon, enters the shop of Alexandre Gilot the next afternoon. Simon's thoughts are still on this morning, as he and Maynard informed Camilla about David's kidnapping. Only with effort were they able to calm Camilla a little; the word 'kidnap' really sent her into a panic. Though Maynard's confidence of getting David back alive did finally have an effect.

Simon is torn out of his thoughts. A familiar face peeks around the corner and they are greeted cheerfully. "Bonjour, Madame Rowley, Bonjour, Monsieur … What was your name again?"

"Brown," answers Lindsay. "Bonjour, Pauline. How are you?"

"Excellent, Mrs. Rowley! The sun brings with it a love of life." In French Pauline adds, "Mon dieu, you are bringing this pretty young man to us again! That puts all sorts of thoughts into my mind …"

"Pauline, he speaks French." Lindsay immediately tries to rescue the situation. The tailor swallows her next words and says instead, "How can I be of service to you, Madame Rowley?"

"Well, Simon needs a pair of trousers and I would like to take a look at the hats."

"Wonderful, please come over here."

Pauline recommends material and patterns to Simon. While doing this she judges the hats that Lindsay is putting on and presenting in full. At the same time she keeps throwing stolen glances Simon's way. At last, Lindsay has decided on a hat and Simon has ordered his trousers.

"Would there be anything else?"

"No, Pauline, many thanks. As always you have advised us excellently, we feel very good at your place. Or what do you think, Simon?"

Simon speaks to the tailor in French, "Pauline, you are a specialist and very friendly, I like that."

"Monsieur Brown," Pauline raises her eyebrows in amazement, "where did you learn French so quickly?"

"It didn't seem so fast to me at all," says Simon, smiling. "From early childhood at home in Germany, I had a private tutor from Belgium, whose mother tongue was French."

Pauline goes pale. "Then you already knew French when you were here the last time?"

"Yes." Simon bites his lip.

"Mon dieu, you understood everything! How embarrassing!" Pauline stares at him with big eyes and her cheeks now take on the colour red for a change.

Lindsay presses a handkerchief in front of her mouth to hide her laughter. But Simon stays completely calm and charming. "Why embarrassing? You didn't utter anything negative – more a special type of compliment." Then he extends his hand out to Pauline. "That will remain our secret, I promise."

Pauline grabs his hand, waves fresh air in her face with her other hand and takes a deep breath.

"When Simon says it is just between ourselves, then that's the way it is," Lindsay reassures her. "Do not be worried, Pauline."

Pauline accompanies them both to the door and takes her leave in a friendly way. As Simon opens the shop door and allows Lindsay to go first, Pauline pulls him to her by the sleeve and whispers in his ear, "Au revoir, mon chérie, merci!"

Grinning widely, Simon takes his place beside Lindsay in the coach. She digs him playfully in the ribs. "What are you laughing about? What did she whisper in your ear?"

"She excused herself again."

"Excused … oh right!"

After a short journey through the city, Simon turns to the coachman. "Karol, please stop here; I think John must live in that house over there."

"You mean here, Simon?" asks Lindsay, somewhat piqued. "In this street? It does not make the greatest impression."

"What do you expect?" asks Simon. "It's not so bad here, just a lively residential and commercial street. Do you see there?" He points to a multi-storeyed brick house with a gold coloured lantern at the entrance that looks like a snail's shell. "That must be it. That's exactly how John described it."

"Yes, you are right," Lindsay agrees. "Karol, you wait here please. We will be back in about an hour."

Simon jumps out of the coach and holds Lindsay out his hand so that she can alight safely. Beside the entrance door there are many names, among them also John Parson, Architect. The stairwell is clean but narrow and dark. The creaking steps lead them to the fourth floor where John has his flat.

"Phew!" Lindsay stands still for a moment. "These stairs are absolutely endless! I wouldn't like to have to climb them every day. That is really tiring."

"We've made it," Simon observes. "It must be here." He knocks power-fully several times on the lightly coloured front door. A quick clearing of the throat, then the door swings open.

"Oh … it's you!" John Parson cries out, puzzled.

"Hello, John," Simon greets him cheerfully. "You did say we should come and visit you. Now we were just in Boston and thought we might just come around."

"Great!" John says happily, takes a step to the side and frees the way in to the room behind the door. "Good day, Mrs. Rowley, come in. Please seat yourselves … here maybe."

"Where else?" thinks Simon as he takes a look around. There is a table with two chairs, to which John now adds a desk armchair. The room seems to serve as both living room and study at the same time. In a corner there stands a writing desk onto which are piled files and books, beside it is a small bookcase. On the other side of the room, Simon discovers a cupboard, a small sideboard and a washstand. Beside the flat's front door there is another door which must lead to the bedroom. There are no pictures or other wall decorations.

"Small, but tidy," Simon notes.

"Small it is, there you are right," nods John. "But when I am just earning more …"

"You've laid the foundations for that with the job at MacShaw."

"Yes, and this shipyard is really an interesting project. Please do sit down," repeats John. "I'll make us some tea."

"That is a wonderful idea, Mr. Parson," says Lindsay delighted, as she stands at the window watching the street and its goings-on. "Boredom is not something that affects a resident of this street, or is it?"

"No, Mrs. Rowley," laughs John. "On this street there is always some-thing happening."

"Can you sleep at all during the night with the noise?"

"That varies very much. Sometimes they really party in the bar at the corner." The boiling kettle distracts John. After he has served the tea, Lind-say also joins the two gentlemen at the small round table.

"Where exactly will the new shipyard be developed?" Simon wants to know now. "Have you already got your eyes on a definite piece of land?"

"The land is even already the property of Rickleby & Smith. They bought the old Thornton's shipyard, which lies north of the North Battery. The old buildings are meant to be pulled down and replaced by new and much bigger ones."

"Then you have already looked at the site?"

"Yes, the property has already been measured, and I have the plans. I have drawn up three rough drafts, which I am to present at Rickleby & Smith next week. One is very traditional, the second very modern, and the third, well, it has something of the other two."

"That sounds exciting, Mr. Parson," Lindsay throws in. "Could you roughly describe your variations? And do you have a personal favourite?" She nips at her tea with pleasure.

"I would of course wish that the modern variation is decided for. I have developed lots of new ideas for it. Pity that I cannot show you the draft. It is in the office."

"And when is the new shipyard meant to be completed?" asks Lindsay.

"The first ships should be built there next spring."

"You have certainly taken on a big task there." Simon is astonished. "And the old buildings, when will they be pulled down?"

"That will already begin within the next few weeks."

"Is there nothing remaining in the old buildings?"

"No. As far as I know, we can begin the demolition at any time."

"Simon, why do the old buildings interest you more than the new ones?" Lindsay wonders.

"I would just like to know when John really starts with his work."

"But Simon, I have already," John objects. "Drawing up proposals and drafting building plans are an important part of an architect's work."

"Yes, that is true of course. Have you ever been in the old buildings?"

"Yes, why do you ask?"

"Is there a basement there or something similar?"

"Yes … more or less …" John too is amazed by now.

"The old buildings really seem to have awakened your interest more than the new ones," Lindsay observes and asks curiously, "What is the reason for this?"

"I'm asking myself the whole time if it wouldn't be easier to renovate the old buildings," Simon explains.

"No." John shakes his head energetically. "They are in a terrible condition and, on top of that, the ground plan is much too small. Speaking of condition: Can you already see the foundations in your tea cups?"

"Sorry?" Lindsay throws a glance into her cup, then at John.

"I just want to know how it is going with the tea," he explains grinning. "May I pour some more?"

Now Lindsay and Simon also have to laugh. "Thanks, John, you really cannot deny your profession, that much is certain."

With great enthusiasm, John begins to describe his modern draft for the biggest and more successful shipyard in the East Coast, and his guests listen to him with interest. In the end though they must say goodbye again.

"Very dim here," says Lindsay, as she climbs down the worn out steps of the dark stairwell.

"The lighting leaves a lot to be desired," Simon agrees. "And the house seems otherwise deserted. Are you frightened, Lindsay?"

"How could I be, with such a strong man at my side?" With these words, Lindsay grabs his left hand and pulls him to her. In the next instant her lips are already on his. For a few seconds, Simon holds her off instinctively – somebody could see them –, then he surrenders to the kiss. Finally Lindsay frees herself from him again and pulls her clothes back into shape.

"What was that?" asks Simon, astonished.

"Just so you don't forget me!" she says cheekily. "Like you've already said: almost deserted here." She pulls out a white lace cloth and wipes her lipstick off Simon's face. Suddenly a door opens on their floor; an old lady steps out and greets them as she passes, "Good evening."

Lindsay grabs Simon by the arm and places a finger on her lips. They try to leave the house as inconspicuously as possible and then climb back into the coach.

With the note from the kidnapper, we now had certainty: David had not been swallowed up by the earth, but even so, we did not know where he was. That made the situation hardly better, but I had at least an idea where I could start. After the visit to John Parson, I also had an idea in which place I could begin to search for David.

13. Cut and run!

The large drawings on the thick bright paper create a strong contrast to the dark hardwood floor on which they have been laid out in Simon's attic room. They are the construction plans for Ringfield & Lewis' new sailing ships – the coveted goal of the extortionists.

Deep into the night Simon sits highly concentrated at his writing desk and puts one black, millimetre-accurate line after the other onto more sheets of the heavy, cumbersome paper. With a lot of fantasy it can be surmised that the plans being created there could be the same as those that are already lying spread out on the hardwood floor. Simon goes about the work with such a light and quick hand that one could suppose he was a master ship builder. For many months he helped David to draw plans, and his friend did not hesitate to pass on his knowledge. Simon will still need one or two days for completion – a lucky chance that he could take the construction plans home with him so easily.

The night is not yet over, as Simon rides like the devil on his brown stallion to Boston. Yesterday already, he filled Karol in so that he would not be worried about the horse. By now Simon knows the brown one well, and so rider and horse appear like a unit as they gallop towards the day. This morning could be so beautiful – if Simon did not have the business with David breathing down his neck. Eventually he arrives at the premises of Ringfield & Lewis and gives the stallion into the hands of one of the few workers who is already there at this time of day. Without losing any time, Simon makes his way at a quick pace to the northern end of Boston. He has around two miles of walking before him, then he should arrive at the starting point of today's mission …

A sturdy high wooden fence is meant to prevent trespassers from gaining entry to the premises of the old Thornton's shipyard. From the opposite side of the street, Simon can make out individual buildings over the fence. Their derelict condition can hardly be overlooked. Only a few people are already on the street so early in the morning and none of them especially catches Simon's eye. After a few minutes, he crosses the street and walks along the fence for a while. Doing so, he registers every detail of the wooden fence. He does not have to go far before his eye catches three planks which have only been fastened at their top end. A quick look left and right, then he pushes them apart at the bottom and shoves himself through the gap. On the other side he remains crouched close to the ground, surrounded by nettles and undergrowth that stands more than a metre high. At first Simon tries to get a general view of the area. Two larger and two smaller buildings stand, it would appear at random, on the landscape; between them are piled mountains of scrap wood, tree trunks and rubbish. The whole area is more or less heavily overgrown. From here Simon cannot make out the water in the harbour at all. Is David being held prisoner here somewhere?

Slowly, in crouching position, Simon pushes the nettles away with his arms protected by his jacket, and cautiously makes towards the nearest building. It is one of the two smaller ones. On tiptoes Simon slinks underneath a window. Only a few big shards of glass sticking out of the frame are left of the window pane. Simon listens for a few minutes, but nothing happens, so he carefully pushes himself upwards against the building's wall and peeks through the window.

Shelves – the whole room is full of shelves: some are overturned, and lots of objects that have fallen out are lying around on the floor. A thick layer of dust has laid down over everything like a soft, fleecy carpet. After Simon has inspected the room as well as is possible from his position, he sneaks further around the building and reaches the entrance. A massive wooden door that is very worn along the edges blocks his way. He grabs the rusty door handle and slowly pushes it down. A smooth creak can be heard, then Simon jumps against the door which is under tension.

"Not locked after all!" flashes through Simon's mind. "Is that a good or a bad sign?" Slowly he pulls the door open and throws a cautious glance in the room with the shelves. Carefully he pushes himself through the door frame and pulls the door closed behind him again. Through the few windows comes only little light, so his eyes first have to get used to the dimness. But gradually the shelves, stacked on top of one another, or overturned, take on contours. Some are still filled with boxes and indefinable objects. On the floor lie tipped over boxes, loose nails, hooks and other material that is needed for ship building. The whole room looks like it has been thoroughly combed through. Slowly Simon goes between the shelves, climbing over boxes and other objects. Suddenly he freezes: something invisible is in front of his face; it pushes his hair back. Shocked, he ducks forward out of the way. But in the same second he is filled with relief, as it becomes clear that he has got tangled in a widely spun spider's web.

Cautiously he continues his way from shelf to shelf. At the opposite side of the room, Simon discovers two doors, one of which is standing open. Just as he steps through the door frame, something scurries quick as lightning over his foot, and from the corner of his eye he discerns a dark shadow. Simon's gaze follows the movement and he just about sees how two rats disappear under a plinth. He exhales and then looks in front of him again. Here his eyes must focus even more than before as the daylight only penetrates the windowless room through a few defective roofing shingles. Several worn out chairs, wooden benches and other worthless stuff lie around this room. Simon turns around and gives the second door his attention. It is closed, but as he twists the doorknob, it too turns on its hinges. Slowly Simon pulls the door open – and is disappointed for a second time. Of David, there is not the slightest trace.

Simon decides to leave the building. He goes back to the entrance, opens the door and observes how the bright daylight falls onto the heavily dusted floor. He turns around again and notices two sets of footprints in the room: one that leads in, and one that comes out. They are his own

244

footprints: proof that nobody apart from him has entered this building in a long time.

Outside Simon first allows his gaze wander again around the premises to make sure that he is still not being observed. Three hours later, he has also rummaged through the second small building and one of the larger ones. He has walked around every pile of wood and rubbish in the huge site – now he's standing in the second big building on the property. It is a type of hall, around 15 metres high, over 100 metres long, and at least 30 metres wide. Under the ceiling run two big pulleys on iron girders. Thick oak blocks and other objects are spread wildly around. Simon glances quickly here and there, capturing everything. In crouching position he sneaks to the end of the hall, while a rushing can be heard that keeps getting stronger. Eventually Simon is staring into the open harbour basin. At this place the new or repaired ships used to be let into the water.

Simon turns around again. In this hall he finds innumerable footprints; they are spread out everywhere, only of David there is absolutely no sign here either. Simon meticulously examines every corner, but cannot uncover anything unusual. Completely disappointed, he leaves this building behind him as well and starts to return to the spot with the loose boards in the fence. He placed such great hope in Alexander Rickleby and this site! He was so sure, he would have betted that the solution was to be found here. Now he has to start from zero again, and the worst thing is the fact that he has lost precious time.

Almost having reached the fence, Simon – hiding behind high under-growth – turns once again to the building that he last inspected. There he sees two figures who are engaged in conversation and appear to be moving purposefully towards the hall. Reflexively, Simon hunkers down and stretches his neck so that he can still observe the two men. He is hardly able to see over the tips of the nettles, when he makes out how the men disappear through a small side door in the hall. Simon thinks for a moment, then decides to turn around again. Carefully he slinks back to the hall. Should he slip in through the door that he has used once already today? Or had he better follow the way of the two men? In the end he opens, as quietly as possible, the side door. He is prepared for a squeaking and is surprised that the door can be noiselessly opened and closed. This door seems to be regularly used, which, besides the many footprints, confirms Simon's suspicion that in this hall something is going on – whatever that may be.

In the hall Simon hides skilfully behind a large pile of wooden blocks and listens. But everything is quiet ... no noise, no voices. What does this mean? Are the two chaps lying in wait, expecting him already? Or are they no longer there? Simon stays in his position for a few minutes, then he creeps onwards, using everything in any way suitable for cover. At the end of the hall he must acknowledge, baffled, that the two men appear to have been swallowed up by the earth. But suddenly there is a light sound, as if a door is squeaking, then voices can be heard as well. To be able to understand what is being said, Simon must get nearer to them. Besides, he also wants to know where the owners of the voices have come from so suddenly – after all just today he combed through the hall for the second time. Cautiously he moves closer to the entrance – and there: more or less covered by a tarpaulin, is an open trapdoor in the floor.

A cellar, there is a cellar here! That's something you have to find first. Simon springs over two heavy blocks of wood and now can see the two men in front of the trapdoor more precisely. The one with the worn out, dark brown coat seems to be calling the tune. "The day after tomorrow we'll get the plans. Place and time I'll tell you, then you'll drum up two or three men."

"Okay, boss," the other chap, a lanky blond, nods. "The day after tomorrow we have the plans – and when do we get the money?"

"Slow down, Marc. You'll get your dough, no worries. But one thing after the other … That we're agreed to, aren't we?"

"Yes, Mr. Howard …," the blond chap answers submissively. "Questions are allowed though, aren't they?"

"Be careful what you say and what you ask, you skinny fool!" threatens Mr. Howard.

"All right, all right. And how do we want to do the handover? This Lewis chap has seen us. He will recognise us again … And then we are sunk."

"Who tells you that he will enjoy his freedom at all?" Mr. Howard grins evilly.

"You want to do him in?"

"As soon as we have the plans."

"Hm – that would be the tidiest solution. We have the plans and he has his eternal rest. Sounds good. But how exactly do you imagine that?"

"The handover will take place here. The premises are big and confusing. When the Ringfield chap has given us the plans, we'll let him and Lewis go."

"What?!" The skinny fool looks confused. "I thought we were going to do him in? Now you want to let him go? So what do you mean?"

"Let me finish talking, Marc!" grumbles Howard. The two of them do not seem to get on very well. "So like I already said," continues Howard. "The site is big. We'll let them go, and when they are walking past the smaller building further in front, then we'll do them in."

246

"The two of them?!"

"Well, think for a moment: If Ringfield comes to the handover, he will see us as well. We can't meet him with cloths over our faces, then he'll immediately sniff out that we're up to mischief, and things will go wrong in the end. We don't do things by half. So that's enough, let's get away from here!" Howard turns around to the trapdoor and cries, "John, close the door – don't forget to bolt it! You have to hold out until the day after tomorrow."

"Yes, boss," is the brief answer from the cellar.

Only now does it hit Simon that the two men have to pass him almost directly if they leave the same way as they came. He had better hide a bit farther to the back of the building. Ducking, he creeps backwards, never letting the two men out of his sight. Step for step he gets more and more distance between himself and the two scoundrels. Suddenly he steps on an object – but he notices it too late: a small iron ball shoots out from under his shoe sole and hits a rusty iron girder a few metres away with a light metallic sound. Immediately Simon hunkers down.

"Marc, did you hear that? There was a noise!"

"Yes, Mr. Howard, it was back there."

"There is somebody! Let's go, we'll catch him, you left, me right!"

Simon freezes: away, he has to get away from here – but between him and the exit door are the two men. How can he get past them, just how can he do that? He hears the footsteps of his pursuers coming nearer.

"Marc, do you see anything? Surely another of these homeless chaps who hang out here."

"No, Mr. Howard, I can see nobody."

"Just don't let him get away. Doesn't matter who it is – we'll silence him."

Simon must think of something now, very quickly. Actually there is only one direction: backwards, because no way will get him past the two scoundrels. On the tips of his toes, Simon moves crouched down and as quietly as possible across the plastered floor, into the back area of the mighty hall. But he doesn't get far.

"There, Mr. Howard, to your left is the chap!"

"Yes, I see him. Let's go, now we'll catch him!"

From his hideout behind another block of wood, Simon sees the two men coming towards him. There is nothing else for it – now he has to act, and that means immediately. He leaves his cover behind him, jumps up and sprints towards the end of the hall.

"Mr. Howard, he's running there!"

"We'll grill him!" shouts Howard. "We have you now, boy!"

"There's nowhere he can go, boss," puffs the other man. "There is no exit there. Now he is trapped."

The two men run after Simon, who runs and runs and suddenly has the harbour basin in front of him. Without thinking he dives with a huge leap into the cold sea water and holds his breath. Even while plunging down, Simon dives to the right and tries to get out of the scoundrels' field of vision as fast as possible.

The two men stand at the harbour basin and stare, gasping for air, into the swashing water.

"Mr. Howard, who the hell was that?"

"No idea." Howard shrugs his shoulders. "A homeless chap looking for a place to shelter?"

"Black or white?"

"I think he was white. But I'm not sure."

"Did he hear anything?"

"About the kidnapping? No, I don't think so. Did you see the way he scarpered? He was really shitting it. It's good that he can now have a swim in the harbour water, so that he can wipe his behind, ha, ha, ha."

To take a big gulp of air, Simon emerges for a few seconds, then he disappears again and tries to get as far away from the hall as possible. Still in the shipyard, he climbs onto the shore and hides in high undergrowth. The water runs down him and he has to take several deep breaths of air. Hopefully nobody has recognised him ... For a few minutes Simon remains sitting motionlessly, then he gets up and leaps through the bushes towards the hall. Everything is quiet, not a soul to be seen. Simon makes his way through the thick undergrowth towards the fence. Eventually he finds the gap through which he came. Almost without a sound he pushes away the loose boards and is outside the site as quick as a flash.

Like a long-distance runner, Simon – totally wet through – makes the journey to the Ringfield & Lewis shipyard. One or two pedestrians on the street stare at him in confusion, but seconds later Simon is already past them. Completely exhausted, he stumbles into the office and allows himself fall into one of the armchairs. "I have him!"

"Simon! Who do you have? And just look at you. You are soaked to the skin!" Maynard Ringfield has jumped up in shock. Just now Simon notices that Ricky Eckstein is also in the office and engrossed in conversation with Maynard. On the senior director's desk, a drawing has been laid out.

"Excuse me," Simon is still fighting for air, "but I now know where they are keeping David hidden."

"Ricky, please get him a glass of water," Maynard commands. "He is hardly getting any air. One cannot understand a word that he is saying."

As Ricky returns to the office with a big glass of water, Maynard has already sat down beside Simon in one of the other armchairs. Simon drinks the glass in a single, greedy gulp. Then he says, already clearly calmer, "I have found David's hideout. I now know where they are keeping him prisoner."

Questioningly, they both look at him, then Maynard begins to speak. "Where have they hidden him? And how did you find him at all?"

"He is on the premises of the old Thornton shipyard, in a cellar. The new Rickleby & Smith Co. shipyard is meant to be built there. They have already bought the site."

"You know more than me again, Simon," throws in Maynard. "What in the name of God brought you to look for David on the premises of the Thornton shipyard?"

"A friend of mine is an architect and he …" Simon tells the background story and ends finally, "At any rate the handover is meant to happen the day after tomorrow."

"Then we should inform the police now."

"I don't think that is a good idea. At the moment we have the element of surprise on our side, and that will help us to get David out of there alive. The kidnappers have no idea that we know where they are keeping David hidden."

"You want to conclude this without the police?"

In this instant, the office door is pulled open and Tyson storms in. "Hello! Am I disturbing anything?" he calls cheerfully and then stops. "What has happened to you, Simon? Did somebody lower you into the rain barrel?"

"Good day, Tyson," Maynard greets. "You have come at a slightly inconvenient time. We are in an important meeting right now."

"That's fine … My information is not so important anyway … I'll wait outside."

"Stop, Tyson, wait!" Simon intervenes. "Maynard, let us allow Tyson to tell what he has found out. Perhaps there is something new."

Maynard assigns Tyson an armchair with a movement of his hand, then all four heads huddle together.

"Well," the boy begins his report. "I have observed Mr. Rickleby as well I could … of course very cautiously. But I could not have followed him everywhere; that would have been noticed. In the last few days he has met with quite a few people: with men and women, fine people with more or less expensive clothes. Only one person stood out."

"Now it's getting interesting," says Ricky. "Tell us, Tyson!"

"This man does not fit with the other people that Mr. Rickleby otherwise met. On top of that, they met in secret. It was already nearly dark outside and this man climbed into Mr. Rickleby's coach down a narrow alley."

"How did the man look like?" Simon probes again.

"I could not recognise much – he was scowling darkly and wore a shabby, dark brown coat."

"That could be him," Ricky blurts out.

"Indeed," Simon agrees. "Tyson, did you notice anything else about the man?"

"No … or, yes: As the chap climbed back out of the coach, Mr. Rickleby bent out of the open coach door again and said that he should deal with the matter once and for all. On top of that he said something like, 'Have you understood that, Mr. Howard?'"

"That is him!" Simon hits his knee with his fist. "I knew it. Alexander Rickleby is behind the kidnapping!"

"How do you come to this conclusion now?" Maynard Ringfield wants to know.

"One of the two men who chased me today at the Thornton shipyard was this Howard. He was wearing the same coat."

"This Rickleby fights with all available means." Maynard shakes his head. "We have to be extremely careful."

"This is the reason why I don't want any police," explains Simon. "If we are unlucky, Rickleby has a spy there, and then his people will be informed even before our appointment. We are not allowed to recklessly put David's life at risk."

"And how do you want to solve this business?" asks Ricky, excited. "You know there is no messing with Rickleby."

"Yes, I know. Listen …"

14. Free at last!

Simon, you can't just spend the whole night drawing."
Almost unnoticed, Lindsay has come into Simon's attic room. In her cream-coloured silk dressing gown, she sits on his unused made bed.

"You are getting too little sleep. That isn't healthy for you, especially not for your eyes."

"I'll be finished tomorrow," answers Simon, without looking up from his ship-building plans.

"I've seen that you've already been working on these drawings for a few days. Are you taking part in a competition? And why do you have to make several drawings of the same thing? Surely the ships are all completely the same."

Simon lays down his pencil, stands up from his desk and sits on the bed beside Lindsay. She strokes him tenderly on his stubbly cheek. "You should have a shave."

"Tomorrow."

"You haven't been to college in the last two days either, have you?"

"The last three days," corrects Simon and looks at Lindsay through tired eyes.

"You should really go to sleep now."

"Tomorrow."

"I keep hearing tomorrow, tomorrow, Simon. What's wrong? Alastair and I are worried about you."

"Today I really can't say anything, Lindsay, but tomorrow evening I'll tell you both everything. Is that all right?"

"My God, Simon, are you in difficulties?" asks Lindsay, shocked. "Can we somehow help you?"

"No. Don't worry. I'm not in any difficulties and you can't help me anyway. Please have patience until tomorrow evening." Simon throws Lindsay an insistent look. "Please trust me."

After a brief hesitation, Lindsay nods, pulls Simon to her and gives him a kiss on the forehead. Then she leaves the attic room just as quietly as she came in.

At about eight the next morning, Simon, Ricky and Maynard are sitting in the shipyard's office with a pot of tea and four cups in front of them.

"Great idea to copy the drawings," says Maynard approvingly. "Now we can exchange a few for David and still begin working on the ships on schedule. Why didn't I think of that myself?"

"The kidnappers were clever and put us under time pressure," says Simon. "First they left us in the dark. We didn't know that they were holding David, nor did we know that they were after the ship-building plans. When they eventually got in touch, I had very little time left for copying."

"And which are the original drawings now?" Maynard, still dumbfounded, wants to know.

Simon cannot hold back a proud grin. "Look at the ship's bow, then you will notice it," he says, giving the decisive clue.

Maynard stands up and bends deeply over the drawings on his desk. "You have to look very closely there. And why did you change it?"

Before Simon can answer, the door is opened and in walks a man who Simon has been well acquainted with from his first day at the shipyard: the bearish Spaniard, Diego is his name.

"Good morning, sirs," he greets, politely.

"Good morning, Diego, come and sit with us," answers Maynard, calling him to the table.

At exactly 11:50 am, a Landau carriage pulls up in front of the wooden fence at the premises of the old Thornton shipyard. In the carriage sit Simon and Maynard.

"Go through the entrance here and then between the buildings until the big hall back there," Simon gives the senior director final instructions.

"Good," nods Maynard attentively.

"On the left side you'll find a door. I think they will already be expecting you."

"It all seems like child's play," says Maynard, "but my heart is in my mouth anyway. I am too old for this type of excitement."

"I wouldn't be any different," Simon says, trying to encourage him.

"Oh you would! You are hard-nosed and as cunning as a fox, Simon. And at such a young age."

"It makes no difference – the extortionists want you to bring the plans, that was expressly stated and written in bold letters on their last note. Always remember: David needs you."

"Yes, then let's get to it!" Maynard takes another deep breath, climbs out of the Landau carriage and enters, without turning to look back, the premises of the Thornton shipyard. Simon asks the coachman to turn and follow the wooden fence to the end. There the Landau carriage stops briefly at the harbour basin before driving off again in a southerly direction.

The water is shallow enough here to wade through. Simon gets around the fence in this way and then moves cautiously through the high undergrowth towards one of the smaller buildings. As he gets closer, he makes out the heads of two people behind a window. They are obviously talking with one another, and they keep looking towards the big hall.

Simon creeps to the far end of the hall, where he puts his feet carefully into the water and from there peers around the corner into the hall. Nobody can be seen, but several voices can be heard. Slowly, step by step, Simon moves from the harbour basin up the ramp and seeks cover. He creeps onwards, exactly towards the spot where the hatch to the cellar is located. Suddenly, across several wooden blocks, he can see four heads, with one head facing them: Maynard Ringfield's.

"Mr. Ringfield, I see that you are taking this matter seriously," says Howard, seemingly amicably. But Simon can hear the arrogance in his voice. "You have the plans with you, very good. Give them here!"

"Mister … What was your name again?" Maynard tries to win time.

But Howard interrupts him and quickly loses his politeness. "My name is of no importance. Hand over the plans, now."

"Excuse me, please." Maynard is staying very calm on the surface. "But first I want to see David."

"Of course, you want to take Mr. Lewis home with you. But hopefully you won't bite off more than you can chew." Howard turns briefly to the trapdoor, places two fingers on his lips and gives a quick whistle. A few seconds later, David appears, supported by two men. He looks in a bad state. His clothes hang down from him like a wet sack, and despite the bushy beard on his pale face, there is no doubt that David is terribly emaciated. One of the men holding him up is of average height, wears a full beard and has a scar under the left eye. The other one is somewhat plump, much smaller, and his right thigh is set with two splints and some leather straps. As Simon looks into his face, he immediately recognizes again the man in the warehouse whose thigh he broke with an iron bar. He throws a look at the other men and also recognizes now the tall weedy one whose acquaintanceship he made as well.

"So, Mr. Ringfield, now you have your Mr. Lewis again," says Howard mockingly.

The two men holding David up just let go and join their accomplices. David collapses and groans with pain. Then he raises his right arm in front of his eyes in order to protect himself from the bright daylight.

"David, are you all right?" asks Maynard anxiously and wants to take a few steps towards his partner. But Howard snaps at him, "Stay where you are, Mr. Ringfield! First give me the plans."

Maynard obeys and then enquires, "Who guarantees us that we will get out of here alive?"

"Me! I guarantee you that you will leave this building alive." Howard grabs the document tube and laughs evilly. While he opens the tube and pulls out the ship-building plans, Maynard squats beside David and lays a hand on his shoulder. "David, will you manage? Soon you'll be free and we'll be going home."

Unfolding the plans, Howard jokes, "Going could be asking for too much, but he should certainly be able to crawl." The other men laugh maliciously, and Marc, who Simon already saw yesterday, asks, "Boss, are the plans real?"

Howard's gaze wanders to the bottom right hand corner of each sheet. Simon knows what he reads there: Henderson Transatlantic New York and David Lewis's signature. "Yes, they must be real."

Maynard Ringfield takes hold of David under his left arm, lays him across his shoulder and heaves his partner up with all his might, so that he can get to his feet. "So, David, now we're going home. The men have got what they want."

David must have gone for weeks without seeing any daylight, cooped up in a small, narrow room, with never enough water or food. Only slowly does he come around again and asks in a daze, "What do they have?"

"The plans for the new ships of Henderson Transatlantic New York," answers Maynard. David begins shaking over his whole body and pleads, "No, no, not the plans!"

"David, please calm down. I can't hold you otherwise." David is hanging off Maynard's shoulder, which must be increasingly exhausting.

"Really heavy, such a wet bag of flour, or what?" says Howard cheekily.

"Please, David, don't make it impossible for me to get you out of here." Maynard is still struggling.

"Not the plans … Please, not the plans … Our future …"

"Come on, David. Now we have to go home. Help me as much as you can." Maynard pulls David close to him and takes one slow step after the other.

While Howard rolls up the plans again and puts them into the document tube, the other men make fun of David and Maynard. They progress a few metres before the first one notices something. "Hey, everyone, they're going in the wrong direction! There is no door back there."

Without looking around, Maynard continues with David towards the back end of the hall.

"Oh, let them walk, they'll be back. That doesn't make any difference," Marc says, with a wave of his hand.

"They certainly won't be able to swim home, given Lewis's good condition," another one jokes.

The farther Maynard and David hobble, the more the scoundrels make fun of them. Suddenly though, Marc nudges his boss. "Mr. Howard, what if they just try to escape across the water now? Then they won't walk into the field of fire of our two gunmen out front on the premises."

It dawns on Howard as well. "Hey, you two! Come back! There is nothing back there for you," he roars in a loud voice.

254

"Keep going, David, don't look around," whispers Maynard and continues in the same direction.

Mr. Howard reaches into his coat and is suddenly holding a clumsy pistol in his hand. "Come back or I will shoot one of you dead!" he threatens and holds the muzzleloader visibly in the air. Now Maynard does turn around. Just at this moment, Simon leaps out of his hiding place on the other side of the hall and draws the attention to himself. "Let them go," he orders very calmly and sees through the corner of his eye how Maynard and David start hobbling again.

The little fat one with the splints on his legs starts with fright. "Boss, that is this Brown fellow; he is dangerous!"

"What, this chap?" laughs Howard. "He isn't even twenty years old."

"And there are six of us," continues the tall thin one. "Now he's going to get the beating he deserves."

Slowly the men move towards Simon in order to grill him. Simon forces himself to stay calm and to trust in the exact timetable that he has worked out. Almost twenty metres become ten, then seven; the scoundrels keep coming nearer to him, at the front, Mr. Howard. Maynard and David must by now be almost at the end of the hall – but it will be tight, very tight.

Suddenly two noises, with only a few seconds interval between them, can be heard. It is as if wood is being dragged over cobble-stones. Two big rowing boats, with more than twenty men in them, have landed at the end of the hall. The men – all of them workers at Ringfield & Lewis and armed with thick clubs – jump within seconds from the boats and storm into the hall. One group is led by Ricky Eckstein, the other by Diego, the Spaniard. Two men stay behind in order to help David and Maynard climb into one of the boats.

All that can be heard is the dull stamping of boots, and before the scoundrels know what is happening, superior numbers of strong, determined-looking men are facing them. Silently, Simon exhales with relief as the colour leaves his opponents' faces. "Hey, Simon," calls Ricky and throws him a club.

Howard is the first to regain control of himself and brings his muzzleloader to the ready. As quick as lightning, Simon grabs the club flying towards him and hits Howard with full force on the lower arm. A shot rings through the hall, and Ricky grips his lower arm in shock.

The kidnappers, armed with daggers, afford resistance only a few minutes. Then they oppose the harsh blows of the energetic shipbuilders no longer and surrender. With his left paw the bear-like Spaniard suppressed Howard against the wall, with the other he snatches the muzzleloader from his fingers. Simon gives the signal for retreat, and soon afterwards the men of Ringfield & Lewis are sitting in their boats and rowing back to the ship-yard. Ricky's injury turns out to be just a grazing wound, and Maynard's handkerchief has to substitute for the bandage.

In the afternoon of the same day, relative calm has returned to the ship-yard. The men go about their work as if nothing has happened. Maynard has promised them a decent helping of rum for the early evening.

Even the doctor who bandaged Ricky and looked after David has departed, and Camilla Lewis, overjoyed to have her David back in good health, has arrived with little George. The rescued man, after resting a little on the sofa in the office, is sitting, surrounded by Maynard, Ricky, Camilla with George and Simon, in front of a strong stew. Simon now relates how the extortionists already tried to get the plans out of him a while back and how the small, fat scoundrel ended up with the splints on his leg.

"But why did you not grab the plans when the chaps had forced you into a corner?" Maynard now wants to know.

"I don't understand that either," David chips in. His face is gradually regaining some colour.

Simon grins. "They wanted to get the plans into their possession come hell or high water. If we had retrieved them again, then they would be already thinking how to get them again; of that I am sure."

"That may be, but now they have the plans anyway. That means that Rickleby & Smith have all the new ideas that we developed over a long time," counters David.

"That cannot be changed," continues Maynard. "Our technical lead is lost."

"Not completely," grins Simon. "Our lead is concave, so to speak, not convex."

"What do you mean – convex?" asks Maynard, confused.

"Of course!" explodes Ricky Eckstein. "The bow of the ships! Simon spoke this morning about the bow of the ships, Maynard, when you asked how one could see the difference between the original drawings and the copy. Simon has turned the concave bug into a convex one."

Camilla looks at the gathering in confusion, then gathers the courage to interject, "Does one have to understand this?"

"Concave means curved inwards and convex means curved outwards; the bow of the ship is curved outwards," explains Ricky. "I was present when our two heroes here carried out the trials with the model ships."

David becomes curious. "How did you let the stem run?" He turns to his wife. "This is the end of the ship's hull at the front."

"Double curved," returns Simon. "Running out gently to the bowsprit and to the keel. Around the waterline, steeper, but not like with our model."

256

"You sly dog!" David cries. "You are certainly a cunning devil, Simon. I wouldn't ever like to have you as an enemy. No, that can't be …"

"David, what are you talking about?" asks Maynard impatiently and then looks at Simon. "Say something. What is up with the bow?"

But Simon just sits there and feels happy about David, who is getting visibly better by the second. Before he begins to speak again, he takes several deep breaths. "Right, I'll explain it to you … We developed the new bow for our ships during our model trials. During these trials, we discovered that a double-curved bow with a concave curve still cuts cleanly and quietly through the water at high speed. If the curve is turned outward into a convex form, then the bow begins to pitch, meaning it moves sharply up and down and gets slowed down as a result. The ship gathers pace because of the wind in the sails and is then slowed down again by the pitching of the bow."

"So then Rickleby & Smith will build two ships over six to eight months, and we already know that neither will actually function correctly?" asks Camilla, astounded.

"One cannot say that either," says David. "Here in America, from harbour to harbour, they can certainly be put to use. Just for overseas trade they are completely worthless."

"Put plainly, that means," continues Ricky Eckstein, "the two ships will be put on sale for a relatively low price."

"Exactly," nods David. "They'll only notice it though during the completion in six to eight months. The chances that we will continue doing business with Henderson Transatlantic New York aren't bad so."

Suddenly, all eyes in the gathering are focussed on Simon who has almost completely stayed out of the conversation up until now.

"Simon," Maynard says to him, "when did the thought occur to you to duplicate the ship construction plans? When I gave them to you to bring home?"

"No, a few days before that, but I couldn't get at them because they were locked in the safe."

"I am astounded how the individual parts of this plan are interlinked and how precisely you thought out David's liberation," Maynard has to admit. "And I say it again: You are as cunning as a fox, Simon Brown." With that he stands up and offers Simon his hand. Camilla leaps up as well and clasps Simon's hand tightly. "Thanks that you saved my David."

"Stop!" protests Simon. "That was a group effort."

"You are right, but I want to thank you as well." With effort David hauls himself up from the sofa.

For Simon though, the attention is too much. "If everything has been cleared up now, we can go to the wooden shed and drink a tumbler or two of rum with the men."

As Simon wants to take his place in the queue for the rum distribution, someone grabs him by the shirt collar and pulls him to the side. By the distinctly deep voice and the Spanish accent, he recognises immediately who has grabbed him. "Hey, Simon, you are all right."

Diego pushes a tumbler of rum into Simon's hand; they both place their tumblers to their lips and allow themselves a good mouthful. Then Simon says in Spanish, "Shut your mouth and get lost, otherwise we'll wring your neck!"

The two of them have to laugh and Diego asks, "Do you still remember my first words?"

"How could I forget them!"

When Simon comes home in the evening, Alastair and Lindsay are waiting for him in the salon. Alastair is sitting reading the daily newspaper with his legs crossed in an armchair, while Lindsay is leafing through several fashion magazines on the couch. Simon is incredibly tired, but nonetheless feels hugely relaxed.

"Hello, Simon." Alastair looks up from the newspaper. "We have seen little of one another in the last few days."

"Yes, that's true," answers Simon and makes himself comfortable in an armchair.

"Have you already had something for dinner?" Lindsay wants to know.

"No, but there is still a little time for it. I promised you that today I would tell you what I have been doing over the last few days." His hosts look at him attentively and with curiosity. "Well so, everything began when, a couple of weeks ago, two sinister figures accosted me down a narrow alleyway. They wanted to have ship-building plans from Ringfield & Lewis …"

Lilly Owens enters, but Lindsay waves her away before she can ask if the group would like anything else. For two and a half hours, Alastair and Lindsay hang on Simon's every word, and Lindsay's facial expression gets more and more frightened. As Simon describes today's events, he sees the tension leaving the two of them – almost like a mirror image of himself.

"Alastair," begins Lindsay finally, "we can no longer be friends with Alexander Rickleby. Not with all that we have heard – it's just terrible!"

"That has to be carefully considered," answers Alastair cautiously. "We should think about it, but it is not so easy either. You know that the social ties flow into economic ties."

"But you can't always just see the business side!" Lindsay cries, outraged.

"We don't have to reach a decision here and now, today," concludes her husband.

"Of course you are not capable of spontaneous decisions, typical! It is always just the same old game ..."

"Lindsay, please!"

Simon has to grin about them both, but then gets involved, "Lindsay, I don't want that either."

"What do you not want?"

"That you break off relations with the Ricklebys. There are concrete reasons for this, too. Alexander knows that I thwarted the first hand-over of the ship-building plans. But he can't know that I am also the main responsibility for the problems with the second hand-over. If you break off relations with him so suddenly then you will be giving him proof: this he shouldn't have. Besides, when he turns up here, I pick up something on his moods as well."

Lindsay cannot calm down. "That is just an unbelievable story! I would never have thought that someday we would get to see a side like this of Alexander Rickleby. I never even suspected that he had such a side in the first place."

"Alexander fights with all available means," concludes Alastair, "and I know well that he doesn't, let's say, have much of a conscience. But that he would go so far: I wouldn't have guessed that either."

Simon tries to mediate further. "It's understandable that you don't know this side of Alexander. You have never stood in his way."

"That's true," nods Alastair. "But you fell right across his road."

In my thoughts, I went over the sequence of the hand-over again and again and tried to incorporate every unpredictable event. In the end though, a lot of luck came into play as well. As I stood alone before these scoundrels, I certainly thought about whether there would be enough time. I think that David's kidnapping welded our men together very strongly.

As I told Lindsay and Alastair the whole story, I only noticed how much strain the secret had put me under and how good it was for me to review everything that had happened. I just didn't tell them that I had reconstructed the plans for the ships. In six to eight months it would be revealed if the ships would be built like that at all.

15. An alibi at the right time

A clear, raven-hued night: a sky like out of a picture book, onto which the stars have been razor-sharply deposited like large and small golden buttons on a noble black material. This sight compensates for the frosty, ice-cold winter hours. The Rowley's villa creates a lively contrast to this peaceful, picturesque image: brightly lit, it has received the guests of today's company. The celebration is, by now, in full swing. Harvey and Alice Barton, together with the Woods, were the first to arrive at around 7 o'clock. For them the first bottle of champagne, a Bouché Père et Fils, was immediately opened as well. To Simon's joyful surprise, Henrietta and Curtis Tremaine, who he has not seen since the crossing on the 'Whitecap', appeared in the company of the Thickstones and the Taylors. Curtis greeted him with a sturdy handshake and Henrietta could hardly contain herself for joy.

By now, almost thirty guests have gathered, among whom Simon also discovers a few new faces. Then the salon door opens again and Alexander Rickleby enters the room, followed by his wife, Ashley. While Ashley goes immediately to Lindsay, the lady of the house, Alexander takes a quick look at the gathering, then joins the circle around Alastair Rowley.

"Good evening, Alastair," he greets, as his eyes wander searchingly through the salon.

"Hello, Alexander," replies Alastair and states, "a cold night." At the same time he raises his glass and toasts Rickleby. Simon who finds himself in conversation with Henrietta Tremaine – or, more correctly follows Henrietta's lecture – observes how Rickleby's eyes comb the salon. Suddenly their gazes meet. Simon starts to smile amicably and lifts his glass in greeting, which Alexander Rickleby astonishingly reciprocates. Then the contact is broken off again. "What does that mean?" This goes through Simon's mind, but then Curtis Tremaine interrupts his thoughts. "Simon, have you heard anything already about the new mobile steam engines?"

"You mean the steam locomotives?"

"Yes, exactly. About two and half years ago, the railway line between Liverpool and Manchester in England was opened. At a race near Rainhill, they looked for the most suitable out of five participating steam locomotives. This race will go down in history in my opinion."

"And which locomotive won?"

"The 'Rocket' by Robert Stephenson. It reached a highest speed of almost thirty miles an hour. Just imagine the power that such an engine develops! But decisive at the end was its endurance; it was the only machine that survived the race without breaking down."

"'Rocket'," wonders Simon, "a strange name for a steam locomotive ..."

"That is not important," continues Curtis. "There is a reason why I'm telling you all that. On the 24th September 1831, the first railway line in the federal state of New York was opened, between Albany and Schenectady. Soon a network of railway lines will span across the whole of the United States. That will be a huge business. Simon, you are young and brave; you must invest in steam locomotives or railway lines!"

"Curtis," Henrietta interrupts now, "enough with your railways; you are completely besotted by these monsters!"

At dinner, Simon is directed to a seat between Harvey Barton and Isabella Wood and is relieved to get away from Henrietta Tremaine at least for the meal.

"How is it going in Harvard so, Mr. Brown?" asks Isabella, politely interested.

"Well, it's going well," Simon answers. "If it continues like this, I could have my finals in the bag in May already."

"Oh, then you've got through really quickly, haven't you?" she ascertains. "And how have your marks been up until now?"

"I think I won't get any higher than average."

Harvey Barton bends slightly forward to see Isabella past Simon. "It is not his only job after all, Isabella."

"I am aware of that, Harvey," the spoken to party replies, still amicably. "But tell us, Mr. Brown, how is the young Mr. Lewis doing after his kidnapping? I imagine something like that to be terrible. To have no idea what will happen to you or if you will even come out of there alive ..."

"Don't worry, Mrs. Wood; David is doing fine again. He has recovered again really quickly."

"Have they actually caught the kidnappers?" Harvey Barton wants to know now.

"No, not as far as I know. The police still don't have any clues as to who is behind the kidnapping."

"I imagine it must be twice as bad," interrupts Isabella once again, "to know that these criminals are still walking around in freedom."

"Of course you are right there, Mrs. Wood, but I think that David is coping very well. He has a wonderful, loving wife and a delightful son. Besides he has his hands full at the shipyard; that diverts him. Ringfield & Lewis are building two ships of a new type, which David was instrumental in designing. That is of course an extremely stimulating matter and takes up both his thoughts and his time."

This topic is of course especially interesting to Harvey Barton. "How far are you with the new ships, Mr. Brown?"

"Well on the way."

"Between you and me," Barton bends forward a little and sinks his voice, "I have heard that Rickleby & Smith are building two ships of a new type as well, which should be completed at the same time as your ones."

"That may be," Simon says, playing it down. "But I can't say anything about it. Rumours get spread quickly." He turns again to his plate with the main course and remarks, "The roast venison is a real delicacy, isn't it?"

"Yes, excellent, as always at Lindsay's," Isabella agrees.

Harvey gets involved in the new subject and takes a full gulp of red wine. "Mmm, that is good! What sort is it?"

"A red Burgundy," explains Simon, happy about the diversion, "a Clos de Vougeot, Grand Cru from the Côte de Nuits in northern Burgundy, dated 1815. It is a Pinot Noir and it complements the aroma of the roast venison with a trace of the animalistic very good."

Isabella now holds her goblet under her nose as well and sniffs with closed eyes. "Yes, now that you say it, I find again this animalistic fragrance."

After the meal, small individual groups come together again, to heatedly discuss important or trivial news from politics and society. Henrietta Tremaine is immediately standing in Simon's circle again and draws the conversation to herself. The hands of the grandfather clock in the salon move slowly but surely forwards. After they have covered several centimetres, Simon has been comprehensively informed about everything that has happened since the crossing to the present day.

Suddenly, at his back, a loud, aggressive voice raises itself above the general hubbub of conversation. As Simon turns around, like all the other guests, he sees how Alexander Rickleby is taking up position threateningly in front of an unfamiliar, middle-aged man. "Make that claim again!" Rickleby barks furiously.

The other man retreats in shock, so that the wine spills over the edge of his glass and leaves behind clear traces on his white shirt.

"Right so," Rickleby harangues his counterpart further. "Make the claim you've just said one more in public! Should it turn out that you are wrong then I must challenge you to a duel."

"Can we not sort this out like reasonable people, Mr. Rickleby?" the other man stammers.

"No less am I trying to do. We'll sort out this business the way men do. Now repeat that what you just said to me."

Alastair Rowley tries, as man of the house, to calm the situation. "Alexander, please, why are you confronting Mr. Timothy in such a coarse manner? Did he step too close to you?"

But Rickleby continues to stare his counterpart stubbornly and aggressively in the eyes. Silence has filled the room so that you could even hear a pin drop.

"Mr. Rickleby, your wife is having an affair."

A murmur goes through the salon. Lightning quick, Simon's gaze wanders to Ashley Rickleby who finds herself in a circle of her girlfriends. She stands like she is rooted there, with eyes wide open from fright and her breath held. With a jolt, her right hand in the soft white silk glove shoots up to the place on her breast where Simon supposes her heart to be. He has the impression that Ashley Rickleby is about to collapse. But it is Daisy Thickstone who, seconds later, collapses in a faint. Two strong men dash to her immediately and lay her carefully on one of the sofas in the salon. Dr. Taylor is also soon there and bends over her.

"Ashley!" a voice booms through the salon. Alexander Rickleby's gaze is also focussed on his wife now who is moving towards the two men like in a trance. Her husband grabs her by the arm roughly and stands her opposite Mr. Timothy. The tension among the guests is hardly bearable.

"What do you say to these accusations?" Rickleby asks curtly.

Ashley opens her mouth, but she does not get any sound out. Simon's mind is working rapidly. He fears the worst. Alexander Rickleby is very dangerous and the situation here is public – losing face is something that he will not allow. Which way out remains for Ashley? Is there one at all? How can she succeed in getting her head out of the noose? If she denies the affair and Alexander believes her, then it will come to a duel between the two men. There is no question in Simon's mind who would win then. This Mr. Timothy apparently has a big mouth, but it does not look like he would really be able to handle a weapon. If Ashley admits the truth, then she has no future.

Simon's thoughts are interrupted by Alexander Rickleby's voice. "So, Ashley, if you don't open your mouth, then we'll just put the cart before the horse." He takes a step towards Mr. Timothy and grabs him by the collar of his shirt. "Someone who would make such claims would also have some evidence, Mr. Timothy."

The man spoken to in this way tries to free himself from Rickleby's grip, but he does not succeed. An answer is unavoidable. "Yes, I have evidence."

Rickleby throws a quick look at his wife, "Do you want to say anything in your defence?"

But Ashley still does not utter a sound. On the contrary: She breathes rapidly, her gaze seems empty and her fine, pretty face is as pale as a corpse. "She doesn't even have the inkling of an idea towards a solution," thinks Simon.

"The evidence, if I may ask, Mr. Timothy."

"Well, hm …," Timothy hums and haws, "I saw your wife the Wednesday before last with a young man in the café of the Royal Boston Hotel. They seemed very familiar with one another."

"At what time was that?"

"At around half past four."

"A-ha … half past four … What do you say to that, Ashley?"

Ashley Rickleby is still standing there like a statue and gives the impression of being absent. Seconds seem like minutes. Simon looks at the gathering: every guest who is present is watching spellbound the drama playing out in front of their eyes. The scene seems frozen. Suddenly Simon has an idea and without hesitating pushes his way through to the adversaries.

"The Wednesday afternoon before last, in the Royal Boston Hotel? That was me." Consciously, he pushes between Alexander Rickleby and his wife and continues quickly, "Do you know, Mr. Rickleby, on this day I was going past the Royal Boston Hotel lost in thought and just missed walking into your wife by a hair's breath. At first we were both shocked, but then had to grin about the situation. Mrs. Rickleby asked me how I was and enquired about my studies. As a gesture to excuse myself for my carelessness, I then invited her for a cup of tea. We were in the café from about four until almost five o'clock. Even in my wildest dreams I would not have thought that someone could have construed an affair out of this."

"Ashley, finally open your mouth now and say something! Is that true, what Mr. Brown says?"

Hesitantly, a nod of agreement comes from Ashley. Simon immediately begins to speak again. "Mr. Rickleby, I would like to formally apologise that it has come to misunderstandings. But the fact is that I neither have a relationship with your wife, nor have I had one."

Slowly Alexander Rickleby releases his tight grip around the collar of Mr. Timothy's shirt, who breathes deeply several times. The tension eases from the other guests as well, and they turn again to the people they were originally conversing with.

"Mr. Rickleby," explains Mr. Timothy now, "it was not my intention to compromise or to vex you."

But Alexander Rickleby just throws him a piercing, contemptuous look and then steps back into the circle of Alastair Rowley and his friends. Simon looks for Henrietta and Curtis Tremaine in the crowd. For a fleeting moment he looks into the eyes of Ashley Rickleby, which exude relief and gratitude towards him. After a while, normality seems to have

264

returned to the gathering, but the mood remains like the night: frosty and cold.

A few days go by. Again Simon sits over his books deep into the night, after long exhausting lessons in Harvard. Beside him three candles struggle against the darkness and try to bring light onto the writing desk. As his eyes close over and over again, Simon decides to take a cold shower. The even rush of the water and the cool, fresh, tingling on his skin bring his life spirits back. Barefoot, only with a big towel wrapped around his hips, he sneaks through the stairwell back to his room. Just as the towel lands on the floor and Simon is reaching for his underwear, he notices a movement on his bed. The silhouette outlined there makes it clear to him that Lindsay is lying there and is now lifting the blanket in order to present herself completely naked to him. Beautiful and seductive to look at, she stretches herself on the sheet, conveying an invitation which Simon knows very well how to interpret. With a few steps he is at the bed; he lies beside her and presses himself against her soft, warm, body. What feels very pleasant for him after the cold shower, is for Lindsay the absolute cold shock. In order not to scream out loud, she bites into the blanket.

"Ahh …, Lindsay," Simon sighs pleasurably.

"What are you thinking of?!" The shaking in Lindsay's voice can not be missed, but she has to giggle again as well.

In the next instant, their lips meet and four hands feel everything that they can find in the semi-darkness. They do not have to be so extremely careful – Alastair already left for New York in the early morning. When silence has finally returned to Simon's room, Lindsay strokes through his hair. "Why did you give Ashley an alibi recently?"

Simon looks into her eyes, but does not say a word.

"Do you have something with her?"

"No," is the curt answer.

Lindsay is not satisfied with this. "I'm not stupid. Ashley is an attractive woman. And she can be really friendly, but then in the next second, quick-tempered, irascible and resentful. Then she talks negatively about anyone who she thinks of, finds fault with everyone. None of her friends and none of our husbands is spared … There is only one person she hardly speaks about, and if she does, then always in a friendly way. Can you imagine who I am talking about?"

"About me?"

"Yes, Simon Brown. Personally I think that stands out."

"Lindsay, I have and have had no relationship with her. Neither have I drunk tea with her in the Royal Boston Hotel. You are right: I did give her an alibi, but I want to ask you never to speak with anyone about it. I did it in order to protect her from Alexander. Besides, of course I didn't want that the two men had a duel."

"A smart solution, Simon. Alastair thought that as well, by the way."

Simon nods, but still feels obliged to give an explanation. "I somehow like Ashley, but actually I can't say exactly why I think she is nice. I think that something connects us."

"But that is obvious," Lindsay responds immediately. "Alexander Rickleby connects you." Again she kisses Simon, at first tenderly, then more overbearingly. Before he misunderstands, she sits on top of him, and it is clear where the journey is headed …

Why did I give Ashley an alibi? On the one hand, I was her confidant, because I knew that she did in fact have affairs. On the other hand: being married to someone like Alexander Rickleby – could a 'normal' woman bear that at all without affairs? Finally, Ashley Rickleby, in contrast to her husband, was always friendly and sincere towards me. On top of that, a very good friend of mine was also having an affair – with me.

16. On the run – to new shores

06.02.1832: Otto von Wittelsbach is meant to accede to the Greek throne as Otto I.
11.05.1832: To prevent the thefts of corpses, an anatomy law is passed in Great Britain.
28.08.1832: In the USA, with the capture of the chief Black Hawk the last Indian War east of the Mississippi River is ended.
24.11.1832: The customs laws of the United States of America from the years 1828 and 1832 are abolished by the Parliament of South Carolina for their state territory.
28.12.1832: John C. Calhoun, Vice President of the USA, retires from his office.

The sun shines curiously through the small windows that are glazed with colourful panes. It brings light and warmth into the solemn auditorium of Harvard College. The room is impressively high, powerful oak beams hold the heavy wooden ceiling in its place and glorious chandeliers hang on fine chain links over the heads of those present.

Here he is standing now, to receive his degree. Simon thinks briefly about the fellow students who have not made it. He is in the middle of the graduates of his year and is amazed at how they have spruced themselves up. In their fine suits with bow tie and white shirt, they now focus their expectant gazes on the professors who have gathered at the top end of the auditorium.

Who would have thought, that he, who as Simon Balthasar Braun set foot onto American soil on 24th June, 1829, today, on 21st May 1832, as Simon Brown, would be getting handed over his degree in Harvard? Simon is really delighted about his success, but he is also very conscious that other people have a large share in it. While, for most of his fellow students, the parents are naturally attending this solemn ceremony, Simon already decided weeks ago to invite the Rowleys to participate.

"Mr. Simon Brown," His Magnificence calls into the auditorium. Simon's neighbour nudges him lightly and drags him out of his thoughts. He goes forward and stands according to the instructions before the directors of the college.

"Mr. Brown, it is an honour for us to present to you, as a student of Harvard, the certificate for a successful completion of your degree. We wish you all the best for your future."

His Magnificence holds the certificate and simultaneously his right hand out to Simon. Simon first takes the hand respectfully, then accepts the certificate. Wordlessly, but with a smile on his lips, he allows himself to be congratulated by the other professors. Professor Hicks, the last in the row, grips his hand longer and asks amiably, "Well, Brown, are you going to join Ringfield & Lewis now as a partner? I have been observing the shipyard in recent years: it's developing really well. That would be something for you!"

"We'll see," answers Simon, somewhat embarrassed, without allowing himself to be drawn in to a clear commitment.

After the official part, a boisterous atmosphere miraculously develops within a few minutes in the previously somewhat stiff gathering. Canapés and champagne are served and suddenly Lindsay and Alastair are standing behind Simon.

"What an impressive ceremony!" cries Lindsay, beaming. "But now completely officially: my heartfelt congratulations on passing your degree, Simon."

"Thank you," answers the graduate, allows his gaze wander briefly over the crowds of people and adds a little nostalgically, "But now it means saying goodbye to the student life."

"Saying goodbye is always difficult," laughs Alastair. "But even so, the joy at passing the degree is at the forefront."

"Now show me the certificate!" asks Lindsay impatiently. "We are so proud of you, Simon." Fascinated, she reads the words on the document, written in accurate, fine handwriting, but Alastair is already taking the certificate from her hand.

"But the lion's share of my success is owed to you," replies Simon. "I will not forget what you have done for me the rest of my life."

Alastair studies the certificate very precisely, but only from the raised corner of his mouth can one see how delighted he is.

"That is wholly and absolutely your success, Simon," explains Lindsay. "You have worked very hard and ambitiously for it."

"Nonetheless," insists Simon. "As I set foot on the American continent, I could never have imagined in my wildest dreams that emigration would begin so successfully for me."

Lindsay wants to answer as Alastair gives Simon back the certificate and notes, "With the repayment you can still allow yourself a little time."

"But Alastair!" Lindsay bursts out, slightly piqued. "What do you mean by that?"

A grin widens over Simon's face. "Alastair is just coming back to his own words: 'The business will start off on its own.'"

"Exactly," nods Alastair smiling. "You can still remember."

"Of course I can. I will keep to our deal, too. I promise!"

"I have never presumed anything else."

"Now that's enough about business!" objects Lindsay and raises her champagne glass again.

After several more minutes of casual conversation, Alastair's facial expression suddenly becomes serious. He steps a little closer to Simon and whispers, "One more thing, Simon. I've heard rumours that Rickleby & Smith have completed two new ships in recent weeks, which they want to offer for sale to Henderson Transatlantic as products competing with your ships. Alexander Rickleby is not defeated so easily."

"We are taking that into account," nods Simon.

"Rickleby & Smith build many more ships than Ringfield & Lewis in a year, and they naturally want to maintain their business with Henderson Transatlantic, too. It is said that they will offer the two ships for twenty percent under your price."

"Yes, that is possible." Simon stays very calm, in Alastair's eyes much too calm.

"Do you already know about this situation with the competition, or are your contracts so water-tight that nothing can happen to you?" he asks, astonished.

"Henderson Transatlantic can exit the contract if price differences above fifteen percent arise during the construction time due to increases in material costs or offers from competitors."

"But then I can see some problems for you."

"Not me."

"But why, Simon? That is surely patently obvious." Even Lindsay seems concerned now. "What Alastair has said is not really so absurd. You know Alexander Rickleby very well by now, too."

"Henderson Transatlantic are buying two ships for oversees trade," Simon starts to explain. "The main factor in this situation is time, and this will become even more important in the future. Overseas trade connects countries and continents that are of great distance to one another. Bringing perishable, perhaps even fresh goods to the world markets, demands that the transport time is kept as short as possible. And how can transport times be decreased?"

"Either with shorter transport routes or with higher speed," answers Alastair, almost automatically.

"The transport routes have already been pretty much optimised. Maybe they can achieve something here and there by building canals. But Ringfield and Lewis see their possibilities in the development of faster ships."

"And regarding speed, do you have an advantage over Rickleby & Smith?" Alastair wants to know now, extremely interested.

"Yes," answers Simon concisely and conclusively. He simply doesn't want to give too much away yet. "By the way, I am very excited about the launching of our ships on Thursday."

"What date is that?" asks Alastair.

"24th May. The crews from Henderson Transatlantic take control of the ships then on Saturday. I am curious to see if everything will go smoothly."

"And then there is the coming Monday as well," says Lindsay mischievously.

"Of course it is there …," answers Alastair with an uncomprehending facial expression.

"Alastair, it is Simon's twentieth birthday! At the moment there is really an awful lot to celebrate."

"Oh God, I would have completely forgotten that." Alastair is visibly embarrassed about this.

"It's not really so important," Simon reassures him and lifts his glass in toast. "The ships are much more important to me."

The next few days are very busy at the shipyard. Maynard Ringfield and David Lewis want to hand over two ships that are as perfect as possible to Henderson Transatlantic. That is the best recommendation for more orders; they have kept emphasising this over the last few weeks.

On Thursday Simon is already at the shipyard in the early morning; together with several strong workers, he ensures that the whole premises make a clean, orderly impression at the official launch. At around nine o'clock, a worker approaches him and informs him that he should come to the office, because the gentleman from Henderson has arrived.

When Simon enters the office, Maynard Ringfield, David Lewis, Ricky Eckstein and a tall, thin man in a valuable brown Cashmere coat are already waiting. Simon estimates the visitor to be in his mid-forties.

"Good day, Mr. Henderson, my name is Simon Brown."

"Ah, so you are Mr. Brown," the guest greets him. "Clyde Henderson, delighted to meet you. To be honest, I imagined you to be somewhat older. May I ask how old you are exactly?"

"Of course," replies Simon amiably. "On Monday I will be twenty."

"Only twenty!" marvels Clyde Henderson. "And, as I have just learned, you received your degree from Harvard a few days ago. Heartfelt congratulations, Mr. Brown. Already a Harvard graduate at twenty – my greatest respect!"

"Hm, hm …" From Simon only vague sounds can be heard.

"On top of that, you seem to be one of the most important employees at Ringfield & Lewis."

Somewhat insecure, Simon asks, "Why do you think that?"

"When I drove onto the premises in my carriage, I was given a friendly greeting and heard one worker saying to the other that he should find you, because the visitor had arrived. In the office Mr. Ringfield in his turn, after greeting me, also immediately sent somebody to find you. It obviously seems very important for the shipyard that the two of us get acquainted."

Some time later, the invited guests have taken their places on a festively decorated tribune, from where they have a better view of the ships. Underneath them are friends of Maynard Ringfield and David Lewis, suppliers, existing and potential customers. In short: for Simon a large crowd of unknown, new people. In the confusion of all these faces, he discovers someone familiar: Harvey Barton. Maynard Ringfield is introducing him to Clyde Henderson.

Simon observes the glorious ships that seem to be already waiting, full of desire, to get water under the keel. Pride fills him – he too has a small share in these ships. Shortly before the official part begins, Simon springs with a few leaps from the tribune to the place that has been reserved for the shipyard's workers. There he exchanges with one or the other a few words.

What he does not know, is that Clyde Henderson is watching him from the tribune. The workers seem to treat this Simon Brown in a very familiar manner, without losing respect for him in any way. Clyde Henderson is impressed: Simon Brown seems to be able to move between the social classes effortlessly.

A moment later, Simon is back standing at the side of David Lewis on the tribune. David turns to his customer just at that moment. "Mr. Henderson, have the first destinations for the new ships already been decided?"

"First our crews are sailing the ships to New York. We hope to be able to test the ships extensively on the way there. In New York they will then be loaded and afterwards it is overseas. One ship will travel to Amsterdam in The Netherlands, the other journeys to Canton in China."

"Did you hear that, Simon?" marvels David. "To China, that is just insane – halfway around the world."

"Over thirteen thousand sea miles," adds Henderson.

"One should really take a trip like that some time, thirteen thousand sea miles of experience!" sighs David.

"What do you mean by that?" asks Simon.

"Well, that is patently obvious. If a ship-builder experiences for himself, how his ship reacts in extreme situations – and on such a long sea journey there will certainly be several – then he can incorporate these experiences into building new ships afterwards."

"An interesting way of looking at things, Mr. Lewis," notes Clyde Henderson. "Can I take it that you are accompanying the ship on the way to Canton and back?"

"No, I don't mean it so directly," replies David with a somewhat insecure smile. "I am engaged here in Boston. But Simon, you would be the right man for such a venture."

"How do you mean?"

"You have just completed your studies, have already gathered several years experience in building ships here and are well acquainted with technical drawing. Besides, during your studies you occupied yourself with navigation, sailing and all these things."

"That sounds good, Mr. Brown," Mr. Henderson thinks now as well. "In New York we'll surely need another three or four days to load the ship. If you have decided to accompany the ship by then, you are cordially invited."

"Thank you for the offer," answers Simon politely. "But this is of course very short notice." After a brief hesitation, he adds, "Mr. Henderson, may I ask you something else?"

"Yes, certainly."

"What actually is the situation with the ships from Rickleby & Smith?"

271

The New York ship-owner starts to grin. "They will be launched tomorrow, to set sail for New York on Saturday as the case may be. We will see who wins the race." Henderson's scrutinizing gaze is focussed on David. "As you know, Mr. Lewis, for us it is about the fastest and best ships at a good price. Those from Rickleby & Smith look very similar to yours by the way, gentlemen. One could almost get the impression that one of you copied from the other."

While Simon does not lose his smile, David's face shows a little insecurity.

"Mr. Lewis," says Henderson, still in good humour. "You no longer look so confident that you will win the race. Mr. Brown, on the other hand, appears very certain."

"We'll win," Simon says with emphasis.

"Really?" Henderson probes again.

"Certainly!"

At this moment Maynard Ringfield begins to speak, to perform the official part of the launch. Clyde Henderson baptises one ship with the name 'Chicago'; the other receives the name 'Norfolk'. Shortly afterwards, a blunt beating of metal against wood can be heard. Several shipyard workers are hitting away the support and brake blocks under the ships's hull so that the ships have free passage into the water. Slowly they inch towards the water, speeding up gradually and rushing under gigantic fountains into the previously so calm harbour basin. A couple of times they sway to and fro, then everything is peaceful again and the ships lie majestically in the water. Jubilation and applause break out.

Not until Tuesday is Simon back at the shipyard to find out how the past few days have gone.

"Simon, nice that you've come – sit with us," greets David euphorically.

Puzzled, Simon takes a seat in one of the comfortable armchairs in the seating area in the corner. "Well then, you are both beaming ..."

"No wonder," says Maynard, "Henderson is really a terribly agreeable fellow."

"That he is," David agrees with him. "By the way, on Friday I was at the launch of Rickleby & Smith's two ships."

"And – how was it?" Simon asks curiously.

"In the staging, two classes more impressive than with us. Henderson was in a good mood; I can't say anything more, because I stayed in the background. Early on Saturday afternoon, the four ships then set off from Boston harbour and sailed out of the bay in a southerly direction. I had

272

Maynard's large binoculars with me and my jaw almost dropped open. Our ships sailed close to the wind and cut through the waves in a straight line. Simon, I can tell you they let rip, simply unimaginable!"

"And the ships from Rickleby & Smith?" Simon wants to know in curiosity.

"They kept dipping deep with the bow again and again, as if they wanted to nod, and of course lost speed because of this. As far as I could follow with the binoculars, our ships just left the ones from Rickleby & Smith standing."

Maynard grins with satisfaction. "What did I say to you once, Simon? Cunning as a fox ... You are cunning as a fox, Simon Brown!"

"Yes," nods David too, "It was a wonderful idea of yours to redesign the bows of the two ships. Now they are no longer any competition to us. The ships are sold!"

"Let us wait and see," says Simon cautiously. "I think the people from Rickleby & Smith will also have been watching the ships' departure from the harbour very closely. They will solve the problem with the next ships and then our advantage is already lost."

"Hey, Simon," David nudges him playfully in the side. "This is your lucky month: first getting your degree, then your birthday, the successful launch and now the proof that our ships are faster than those of Rickleby & Smith."

But Simon remains cautious. "We'll see, there are still a few days left in May."

"Gosh, Simon, don't always be so sceptical!" Maynard intervenes. "It is only four more days precisely."

"So, friends," Simon ends the conversation decisively. "Please excuse me, I'm riding home now. We'll see each other on Thursday."

"You're not coming here tomorrow?" David wants to know.

"No," grins Simon, "I'm putting my feet up on the desk and doing absolutely nothing."

The heavy door to the stable is opened briefly to be immediately closed again. For just a moment Simon looks up, recognises Karol, who comes around the corner, and continues grooming his brown stallion.

"Hello Simon, how are things?"

"Fine. How are the horses?"

"They are doing really well," replies the coachman. "Your brown one as well, it would seem: he's standing there so relaxed. He enjoys the grooming. Have you seen it up at the villa yet?"

"What?" Simon asks amazed. "I rode directly to the stable and wanted to attend to the stallion first, before I went in the house."

"Mr. Rickleby's coach is standing in front of the villa."

"My God," thinks Simon. "Has he found out already? He certainly reacts quickly."

"Can you continue here please, Karol?" he says out loud. "I think it is a good idea to show my face in the house."

"Well then, go ahead, I'll do this here."

As Simon enters the villa, he has a queasy feeling in his stomach that abates though when he sees Lindsay and Ashley Rickleby sitting on the couch in the salon. Only at the second glimpse does he notice Ashley's tear-stained eyes and Lindsay's worried face. He has no time to think about it before Ashley springs up, comes to him and pulls him to her. "You are alive, Simon, my God, you are alive! I was already fearing the worst."

"But Ashley, I'm doing fine. Please sit back down. What is wrong?" Simon wants to know and throws Lindsay a questioning look. She just shrugs her shoulders. "Ashley didn't want to tell me anything. She absolutely wanted to speak with you personally, because it was a matter of life and death."

"Simon, you have to disappear from here, immediately!" Ashley announces, her voice trembling.

"Slowly, Ashley," Simon tries to calm her. "I don't understand anything."

Ashley takes a deep breath and collects herself. "A few hours ago, I overheard a conversation between Alexander and a man who – I believe – works for him. A Mr. Howard." A shiver runs down Simon's back. "I didn't completely understand the beginning. There was talk about ship-building plans. Then Alexander said that Rickleby & Smith had you to thank that the new ships were a flop. He was certain that only someone like you could think of redesigning ship-building plans. Alexander was terribly annoyed; he gave this Mr. Howard the command to grab a few 'boys' and to eliminate you, Simon, immediately." Ashley looks at him fearfully. "Alexander means it seriously. They will kill you; they are looking for you already. You have to go into hiding, at least for a few months."

Lindsay is as pale as a corpse by now. "Alexander wants to have Simon killed? But that is unbelievable!" Then she composes herself. "When does he have to go into hiding?"

"Now … tonight. It's best if he disappears today even. Simon, this Howard chap will waylay you with his men tomorrow at the latest. You know Alexander, he doesn't joke around."

Lindsay is still confused and wants to know, "Why are you helping Simon?"

274

Ashley looks back and forth between the two of them. "I like Simon," she answers then. "Besides he is a gentleman; he is reliable and, Lindsay, he gave me an alibi in the matter with my affair. I just don't want that something happens to him." She raises herself from the sofa. "Now I have to go back again. Alexander will surely already be wondering where I've been all this time."

After Lindsay and Simon said goodbye to Ashley, they sit silently for an unending five minutes in the salon. Finally Simon breaks the silence and says very quietly, "I will pack my things now and set off."

"Do we not want to speak about it with Alastair first?"

Lindsay argues. "You can't just disappear. Where do you want to go anyway? That has to be considered."

"Lindsay, I'll definitely come back again. But Alexander Rickleby is responsible for David's kidnapping, he manipulated Ricky Eckstein and is absolutely determined to have me killed – that is beyond question. I have made this Howard chap's acquaintance – he will try everything to carry out his contract."

"And where do you want to go?"

"Clyde Henderson made me the offer of travelling on the first voyage of the 'Norfolk' to China, so that I could observe the ship in the practice."

"To China! My God, that will take many months!" Lindsay looks increasingly shocked.

"Yes, it's meant to be nine to eleven months. After that Alexander will hopefully have calmed down again."

"That is almost a whole year!" Lindsay jumps up and briefly paces the salon, then hunkers down before Simon to look him in the eyes. "I want to keep you beside me, Simon, please!" she pleads to him.

Simon shakes his head. "There is no other possibility. To stay here unharmed, with you, that I cannot do." He jumps up from the sofa. "I still have to find out which is the quickest way for me to get from here to New York."

"With the horse," replies Lindsay who is slowly calming down. "At best you ride with Karol; he knows the way." She falters. "Simon, I am very worried. This long journey by ship is very dangerous; so much can happen there." Now tears are running down her cheeks.

Simon swallows, but he has to act now. While he packs his rucksack, Lindsay explains to Karol, that he must accompany Simon to New York. The three of them are already standing in front of the villa, where two freshly saddled horses await the journey.

"Simon, you must promise me that you will return," Lindsay demands tearfully.

Simon takes her in his arms and tries to reassure her. "I'll definitely come back. I've found a new home here with you and I still own Alastair a great deal."

"Come Simon, we have to go," urges Karol.

Simon nods, releases himself from Lindsay and swings into the saddle, his rucksack on his back.

"Lindsay, I'll come back to you as soon as the ship arrives in New York again, this you can rely on. I am an American now!"

Their journey leads through Cambridge, Worcester, Manchester and Meriden, eventually near to New Haven on the coast. From there, they follow the road through Bridgeport, Stamford and New Rochelle to the East River, until they finally arrive in the harbour of New York. There they enquire after Henderson Transatlantic and are soon standing in front of a huge building which bears the lettering 'Henderson Transatlantic New York'.

It has taken them two and a half days to cover more than 200 miles. They have swallowed a lot of dust and have got too little sleep. The exertion can be clearly seen on the two men and also on their horses.

"So, Simon we've made it!" Karol declares.

"Thank you for accompanying me, Karol; I appreciate it very much."

"It goes without saying," the coachman mumbles in embarrassment. "But there's one thing you have to promise me."

"What then?"

"That you come back. You must come back to Boston again."

Simon nods earnestly. "Promised!"

"Look," Karol points at the entrance to the shipping company. "You go in there now, and I'll find myself a stable and some accommodation for tonight."

Simon shakes his hand firmly. "Safe journey, Karol, and greetings to the others at home."

Shortly afterwards he is standing in the queue before one of the shipping company's counters, waiting his turn.

"Good day, sir, what can I do for you?" The man behind the counter hardly glances up.

"I would like to see Mr. Clyde Henderson."

The employee's head rises as quick as lightning. He takes Simon in from top to bottom. Then his face relaxes again and he starts to laugh. "So, you want to speak to Mr. Henderson?"

Amiably and patiently, Simon answers, "Exactly, Mr. Clyde Henderson." As he says this, he looks down at himself and is shocked at how dusty his clothes are.

"Do you have an appointment with Mr. Henderson?"

"Not exactly, but … yes, in fact."

"Which now? Do you have an appointment or not?"

"Just inform him please that Simon Brown is here to accompany the 'Norfolk' to China. I come from Ringfield & Lewis – that is the shipyard where the ship was built."

The man behind the counter just shrugs his shoulders. "The 'Norfolk' will set sail in about two hours, Mr. Brown. I cannot tell you where Mr. Henderson is and who could precisely help you now. The two hours may not be enough."

The other people waiting in the queue are getting impatient and the shipping company employee looks past Simon at the next in line. "Next please!" Turning to Simon he adds, "Would you please step to the side?"

"Excuse me," Simon will not be put off. "Do you have any little tip for me? What would you do in my place?"

"Go home," comes the laconic answer.

"That really won't work," thinks Simon and wants to answer something when the man behind the counter points at a corner of the ticket hall. "Try it with the officer back there, maybe he can help you further."

Simon turns around and sees a tall thin man in uniform who is speedy crossing the hall. He quickly approaches him and talks to him. "Excuse me, please – my name is Simon Brown and I come from Boston, from Ringfield & Lewis. Mr. Clyde Henderson offered that I could accompany the first journey of the 'Norfolk'. Could you help me maybe? Please excuse my dusty clothes; I have just arrived by horse from Boston."

"Mr. Brown?" marvels the man. "That is a coincidence! My name is Roger Harrison. I am the first officer on board of the 'Norfolk'." He grins. "So, we're getting an expert on board who will tell us what we are doing wrong?"

"No," Simon hurries to ensure him. "We at the shipyard merely hold the opinion that it would be of benefit to gain practical experience with one of our ships on such a long sea journey."

"That's all right, was only a little joke I made. Well, just come with me so I can introduce you to the captain. On the way you can speak with Mr. Henderson. Do you have any more luggage?"

"No," replies Simon briefly, shoulders his rucksack and follows Roger Harrison. They go through wide and deep passageways and corridors, up stairs and back down again. Eventually Harrison knocks on a door and a woman's voice answers, "Come in!"

They enter an outer office in which is sitting a middle-aged secretary. "Ah, Mr. Harrison, a last visit to the boss?"

"Hello, Miss Plogger. Can we see the Junior for a moment?"

"Just go right in. The Senior is there as well though."

Simon follows Harrison into the boss's adjoining office. The room is extraordinarily spacious and has a huge panorama window that opens to a glorious view of New York harbour. They must be on the second floor here. Countless masts rise up into the sky like spearheads. A flag has been attached to each end and the colourful flags of many nationalities blaze in competition. The office is covered in dark wood and Simon feels like he is in a captain's cabin, similar to the 'Whitecap's', only much bigger.

"Mr. Brown, this is a surprise!" Clyde Henderson has leaped up from his armchair and is coming towards Simon.

"Good day, Mr. Henderson, please excuse the disturbance."

"You are not disturbing at all." Clyde Henderson turns to an elderly gentleman who has also risen from his armchair by now. "Father, this is Mr. Simon Brown. I have told you about him." To Simon he says, "What's up? Has Ringfield & Lewis considered sending a man along to Canton after all?"

"That is exactly why I am here."

"Great, that's what I call spontaneous! By the way, your ships move excellently in the water; they are quick and decidedly manoeuvrable. The ships are bought!"

Clyde Henderson is obviously in a great mood and now says to his first officer, "Roger, take Mr. Brown on board with you and assign him a cabin."

"Aye-aye, Sir."

"And introduce Mr. Brown to the captain immediately, otherwise the old warhorse will feel by-passed."

For a few minutes the men speak about the journey ahead, then Clyde Henderson points to his waistcoat pocket watch. "So gentlemen, let's go. Break a leg!"

Now everything goes really quickly. Simon goes on board with Roger Harrison who leads him directly to Captain Leonhard Mac Brodie. Mac Brodie is smallish and plump and seems to be a grumpy old sea dog. After Simon hears his loud, dark, penetrative voice, he gets an idea how this sea dog gains respect. The captain does not seem enthusiastic about Simon's presence, but after a few explanations from Harrison, he accepts Henderson's instructions and summons the officer Callum Milton.

"Mr. Milton, this here is Mr. Simon Brown who will be accompanying us on the journey to Canton and back. He works for Ringfield & Lewis, the shipyard that built this ship, and he will occupy the second bed in your cabin. You are responsible for Mr. Brown learning how things are here and getting to know the crew."

"Aye-aye, Captain!" Milton salutes and waves Simon to follow him below deck. Shortly afterwards, Simon is standing on the quarterdeck, watching the sailors store away the remaining goods and provisions. Then the sails are raised, the gangway and the ropes hauled in, and the 'Norfolk' moves slowly away from the quay. Captain Mac Brodie allows the proud ship sail down the short stretch of the calm East River, then it sails directly into the Upper New York Bay and past Governors Island on the port side. On the right hand lie Ellis and Liberty Island, and a short time later they cross Low Bay into the Atlantic.

There I was standing now on the stern of the 'Norfolk'. It was the evening of 31st May, 1832, and I was on the way to China. I didn't have the slightest inkling what would await me, but I was able to presume that it would be adventures, some more, some less exciting.

Almost three years ago, I said goodbye to Marala and my relatives in London and set off for a new life in America. In these three years I finished my studies and got to know lots of new people. Some of them became my friends. I had lots of experiences and had become, to put it plainly, more grown up. In short: the step into the 'New World' had been worth it. Now a new one was waiting for me, the next phase had just begun, and somehow I had the feeling it would be worth it again.